THE SIN EATER

Also by David Penny

The Thomas Berrington Series
The Red Hill
Breaker of Bones
The Sin Eater

THE SIN EATER

DAVID PENNY

River Tree Print

River Tree Print

Publisher's Note: This is a work of fiction. Names, characters, places, and incidents are a product of the author's imagination. Locales and public names are sometimes used for atmospheric purposes. Any resemblance to actual people, living or dead, or to businesses, companies, events, institutions, or locales is completely coincidental.

The Sin Eater / David Penny -- 1st ed.
ISBN: 978-0993076145

CHAPTER 1

As he passed beneath the city gate into Gharnatah, Thomas Berrington's shoulders lost a tension he hadn't been fully aware of until that moment. Coming home was how it felt, and he knew he had been gone too long.

"Aixa will want us to report at once," said his companion, the eunuch Jorge. He sat on a cart, guiding the mule that drew it through crowds beginning to fill the streets.

Thomas glanced at the familiar buildings, at the palace looming over the city, and nodded. "I have something to do before we see her."

"She won't like it."

"Don't tell her we're back until I come to you," Thomas said.

"Word will spread. As soon as I enter the palace she'll know."

Thomas glanced across at his friend. If he hadn't spent over six months in his company, he would barely recognise him as the sleek palace eunuch that had left Gharnatah. Now Jorge's hair was long, dark in colour, which had come as a surprise. The whiskers on his chin matched.

"She'll expect you to clean up first," Thomas said. "That should give me at least an hour."

Jorge smiled. "At least."

Thomas swung off his mount, the movement familiar now, and tied the reins to the back of the cart.

"No more than an hour," said Jorge. "She'll want to know about Muhammed."

Thomas nodded. Politics again. It seemed impossible to escape them. Muhammed XII, the Sultan of Gharnatah, remained a guest of the Spanish after a foolish and badly planned raid.

As Thomas walked away he heard Jorge call after him: "Tell Lubna I missed her too!"

Thomas raised a hand and kept walking. The scent and sound of Gharnatah wrapped around him like an old, familiar robe. Even the street urchins were welcome. He tossed small coins at them, immediately regretting his generosity as others slithered from alleyways. He flung a last handful behind and turned into a narrow street that led to the foot of the Albayzin. When a voice hailed him he almost kept going, but he recognised Da'ud al-Baitar and turned.

His old friend approached, head cocked to one side. "I thought you were in Qurtuba."

Thomas held his arms out: *here I am*. "I'm on my way to see Lubna."

"Ah." Da'ud shuffled his feet. "I was on my way there myself, but seeing as you're back..." He let some unspoken question hang in the air.

"Barely," Thomas said.

Da'ud continued to stare at him.

"What?" Thomas finally said. The sooner whatever it was had been aired the sooner he could continue his journey.

"I've been called to a death, but I could do with a second pair of eyes."

"Why?"

"The house isn't far. You'll see for yourself when we get there."

Thomas glanced at the steps leading upward through the jumbled chaos of the Albayzin. He turned away. "Make it quick, then. I have to be at the palace inside the hour."

Vincenzo Alvarez lay in the centre of the bed. What showed of his body was paler than it had any right to be. The man was dead, despite any hope expressed by his wife as they had entered the house.

"When did she call you?" Thomas asked Da'ud.

"A little before noon."

Thomas pressed his fingers into the body's cold arm, into a thigh. He placed a hand beneath a knee and lifted. The leg bent. He turned to the head, pushing it to one side then the other. His fingers palpated the jaw and neck before he glanced at Da'ud.

"He's been dead a while, but not so long. Three hours, no more." Thomas turned his gaze to the man's wife, who stared at the scene with a distinct lack of emotion. Her skin was almost as pale as that of her husband, but not from shock. She was of northern Spanish descent, by her looks, and may once have been considered handsome. "At what time did you find him, madam?"

4 - DAVID PENNY

"When I came in from work for our midday meal. He's usually downstairs by then, waiting to eat. When I couldn't find him I tried here and…and found him this way. I went in search of the physician at once. I thought perhaps he had passed out." She continued to give no outward show of emotion.

"What time did you leave for work?" Thomas asked.

"A little before dawn."

Thomas turned back to Da'ud. "See, the rigor is only now beginning to show." Thomas lifted the man's eyelids and peered at the whites beneath, brushed back thinning hair to examine the scalp. He looked once more to the wife. "He was this way when you discovered him?"

"Exactly as you see him now."

Thomas lifted the cotton sheet to reveal the naked body beneath. He leaned closer, lifted the right hand. The end of the smallest finger had been removed. Thomas bent across the body and lifted the other hand. It showed an identical mutilation.

"You can see why I wanted you to come," said Da'ud.

"What is your employment?" Thomas asked the wife.

"I work on the hill." She straightened and her features changed, reflecting an inner pride. "I sew for the ladies of the court."

The harem, she means, Thomas thought.

"And where was your husband when you left the house?"

"In bed, as usual, complaining of a bad head."

Thomas glanced at Da'ud, who lifted a shoulder, no doubt considering the same thought as Thomas. A burst vessel in the brain?

"What kind of bad head?"

"The kind that comes from too much wine."

"He drank too much the night before?"

"And every other night."

"What time would you normally expect him to rise?"

It was the woman's turn to shrug. "He is always at the table when I return. For all I know he might dress only minutes before I arrive or have risen moments after I left."

"What is his profession, Madam Alvarez?"

"He sells wine and ales to the inns of the city."

Hence the constant drinking. No doubt it had begun as an essential part of his employment, gradually becoming something more. Thomas leaned close and sniffed at his lips. There was a slight taint of the coming putrefaction, but nothing more. No clue as to what might have caused the man's death. The loss of his fingertips would certainly have been irrelevant—to his demise, at least. As for the cause of it…

"He was good at his job?"

"He is. We enjoy a comfortable life."

"Where do you come from originally?" Thomas had no idea why he asked. It had nothing to do with the man's death, and he cursed his own inability to stop picking at things until he understood every part of them.

"Valladolid," said the woman.

"It's a long way to travel to al-Andalus. Not a journey most Spaniards would make."

"I am skilled, and Gharnatah is rich. Or was rich. I'm not so sure these days. But I can find work anywhere, and the wages here are more than in the north. The climate suits us both."

Thomas glanced around the room. It was large for a bedroom, no doubt reflecting the couple's status. Dark furniture stood against the walls, set with silver candlesticks. The floor was of heavy oak, stained dark, well laid and flat. A high-backed chair stood between the bed and the window.

"And this is exactly how you found him?"

The woman nodded. Her hands twisted together in front of her, restless.

"Naked, as he is now?"

Again the nod. "Of course. Why would I undress him?"

"And his clothes—you said you would expect him dressed on your return. Were his clothes nearby?"

This time the response was a shake of the head. "I didn't think to look. The shock, I expect. He was as you see him now."

"Would his clothes usually be close to the bed, for when he rose?"

"Yes…on the chair. He would have removed them when he came to bed. He never folded anything."

"Would you look downstairs for me?" Thomas said. He didn't think the clothing was significant, but it was an excuse to get the woman out of the bedroom. He wanted a chance to examine Don Alvarez more closely.

Donna Alvarez glanced once at the figure in the bed then turned away. Thomas listened as her footsteps descended the staircase, slow and steady, before he turned to Da'ud.

"I can see why you came looking for me." Thomas lifted the man's right hand again.

"I don't think I was wrong to be suspicious." The old physician came to stand beside Thomas. "I have seen men who bleed into their skulls do strange things, but never anything like this."

"If it was a bleed it might have affected his judgement."

"There is no sign of slackness on the face. And what man would remove his own fingertips?"

"And if he did they should still be here somewhere, and there would be more blood. Why did you come looking for me even though you believed me in Qurtuba?"

"I was going for Lubna," said Da'ud. "Of course I believed you were still in Qurtuba, but who better to ask in your stead than her?"

"You should have gone to the city guard."

"Since when have they ever taken an interest? And don't pretend you missed these, I know you better than that." Da'ud indicated a scattering of crumbs beside the body, more across the floor close to the bed.

"Pieces of bread?" Thomas smiled. "Perhaps he grew hungry waiting for his dinner."

Thomas turned his attention back to the corpse, nodded to Da'ud, and between them they rolled the body onto its side. "It's obviously murder. If not for the fingertips it might be mistaken for something else. So it seems strange to me to take those and make is so obvious." Thomas bent close to examine the man's back and thighs. He found nothing.

Was he tortured, do you think?" asked Da'ud. "Perhaps for something he knew. That might have caused his heart to give out."

Thomas grunted. He rolled the man onto his front

and ran his fingers across the cold skin, searching for any marks. There were faint scratches on his back and shoulders, but nothing that would kill him.

"He doesn't seem to have put up a fight," said Da'ud. "What man would allow someone to cut off his fingers without a struggle."

"He was already dead when they were taken," Thomas said, and then, when he saw the frown of Da'ud's face, "No blood. If he was alive when this was done there would have been blood. Quite a lot of it."

"Of course. I should have realised."

"You weren't looking. Besides, most of our patients are more obvious than this." Thomas referred to their work together on the battlefield. There was little subtly in what they undertook there. Thomas straightened and pushed his fingers back through his hair, clearing it from his face. "He died of something—unless it was simply his time. Except there are the fingertips. If you wanted to kill a man without trace, why take them?"

"There is no rationality to killing," said Da'ud.

Thomas glanced at him. "We both know better than that."

He bent to the body again. Alvarez's thinning hair hung long, parted at the back now as his face pressed into the mattress. Thomas lifted it to expose the base of his neck. Leaned closer.

"See this?"

Da'ud pressed against his shoulder, his eyes older than Thomas's. "That?" He placed a fingertip against a small mark.

"This is what killed him," Thomas said.

"Too insignificant," said Da'ud. "And again, no

blood."

Thomas stretched Alvarez's skin, opening the tiny wound at the base of his skull. He let his breath out. "Whoever did this is skilled."

"You really believe that tiny wound killed him?"

"Not the wound, no. The weapon that was used to make it." Thomas knelt on the edge of the bed, getting closer still. "Look–something narrow, sharp. Inserted here where the skull meets the spine. Rammed hard into the brain. Death would come instantly. Too fast for blood to escape."

"And then they took his fingers?"

"I doubt anyone else did."

"Why?"

Thomas smiled. "If we knew why we might know who, so that is what we need to discover."

"No, that is what you need to discover," said Da'ud. "All this is beyond my skill. I mend bodies and ease pain, nothing more. You're the one with the suspicious mind, Thomas."

"A mind that does not welcome this death."

"Then walk away from it. I'll inform the guard of a death and his wife will have him buried or burned or whatever they had planned. You don't have to take on the troubles of the entire world."

Thomas picked at the crumbs beside the body. Dried bread. He walked around to the other side of the bed and examined the pillow there. It showed an indentation, but that may simply have been from Donna Alvarez.

"What about his wife?" said Da'ud.

Thomas glanced at him. He said nothing, but

continued to examine the bed with care.

"Everyone knows nine times out of ten it's the wife or husband who's guilty," said Da'ud.

"Is that so."

"Do you dispute it?"

"No. But in this instance I believe the wife innocent. At least until I see any evidence of guilt. Her husband was a drunkard, but a functioning drunkard, and it is likely his job contributed to that state. She has a good living on the hill. Why put all that in jeopardy?"

"Perhaps she hopes to move into the palace without him holding her back."

"She's too intelligent to believe she could get away with killing him, don't you think?"

"I don't know her. Perhaps she believes herself too intelligent to get caught."

"This is doing us no good," Thomas said.

"So what do we do?"

"Go find a couple of strong men and have him carried to your house. Prepare him for burial. I'll ask the wife what arrangements she wants. I suspect they are Christian, but you can never tell these days. Send a message to the guard, they'll need to know of the death."

"And you?"

"I'll search the house, then I intend to finish my journey."

Da'ud stared at him.

"What?" Thomas snapped.

"You might want to go to your house in the Alkazaba first."

"Why would I do that?"

"To see Helena, of course. I believe she has news for

you."

Thomas suppressed a scowl. Surely Da'ud knew how bad things were between him and the ex-concubine who once shared his bed.

"No news I'm interested in."

Still Da'ud's eyes stared into his. "I believe this is news you will want to hear."

"God's teeth, man, if there's something I should know tell me, no more of this mystery. Coyness doesn't suit you."

"It's not my place." Da'ud turned away. "I'll go fetch some men. You do what you need to here."

Thomas found the man's wife sitting at the table in the single room downstairs. The sight of her dispelled any last suspicion he may have had. She was weeping, shoulders shaking, face wet. Caught in her hands was a man's nightdress that she pulled at over and over.

She startled at his presence, lifting the nightdress to wipe at her face.

"Have you finished?"

"Da'ud will have your husband taken away, madam. Do you have any preference for the manner of internment?"

"There is..." She pulled a shuddering breath into her lungs, started again. "There is a place outside the city where Christians are buried. He would want to lie there."

"Speak with Da'ud, but not yet. You might want to wait here until your husband is taken away and then go to his place to make arrangement. Da'ud will prepare him with all respect."

"It is why I went to him. He has been our physician since we came to the city."

"When was that?"

"Seven years now."

"So you know Da'ud well."

She shook her head. "We had little need to call on his services. Until today we went only for the occasional treatment. I needed herbs when..." Her voice trailed away. "When I reached a certain age."

Thomas understood and allowed her to keep her dignity.

"I would like you to stay here while I finish examining the house. Are there more rooms upstairs?"

"Yes–there is another bedroom. It is empty now. Our children have grown and have houses of their own."

"How many?"

"Children? Three that live. Two boys and a girl. Men and women now. Married with children of their own." She spoke without emotion, as though they meant nothing to her. Thomas put it down to the situation she found herself in.

"They live in Gharnatah?" He hoped the question sounded casual. True, he didn't suspect the wife, but Da'ud had been correct–nine times out of ten it was a family member that did the killing. And children could be as deadly as anyone. Particularly if there was money involved, and looking at the house, the woman, the bedroom, Thomas believed they were not poor.

The woman nodded in reply as she stood, still clutching the nightshirt in her hands. "Yes, still in Gharnatah, though for how much longer who can tell."

As she went to move past him, Thomas reached out and gripped the nightshirt. "If I could take this I will cover your husband's nakedness before anyone comes."

She looked down as if unaware of what she carried. "Of course." She released the garment and wandered through to the far end of the room where an open fire burned. Thomas made a mental note to ask Da'ud to mix her some poppy before he left. The shock of events were starting to sink in.

Once alone he lifted the nightshirt and examined it, but found no sign of blood. He sniffed at the fabric, but there was only the scent of a man who had slept in the garment several nights. Thomas climbed the stairs and examined the smaller bedroom, but it was sterile, unloved and empty. He returned to the bed where Alvarez's body lay and heaved him onto his back, manhandled him until the nightshirt covered him. He was about to turn away, to draw a line under the whole event and pick up his old life when he glimpsed something on the other side of the bed.

Thomas walked around and examined the pillow. His vision had not misled him. He reached out and picked at what rested there. It was a hair, long and dark. He held it against the small window to examine it more closely. It told him little other than it was likely from someone younger than thirty, and therefore did not belong to Donna Alvarez. Had her husband been enjoying an illicit liaison? Was this a falling out between lovers? Or a whore taking more than she was due? Without the evidence he had already seen that might be a natural conclusion. A man left alone while his wife climbs the hill to work. Who knew he wouldn't be disturbed until noon. But the manner of his death hinted at something more. Some men, Thomas knew, were slaves to what hung between their legs. He smiled, thinking of his companion of the last six months. Even Jorge suffered the same weakness, despite lacking some of the equipment.

Thomas heard voices downstairs, then rapid footsteps. He quickly wound the long hair around his hand and pushed it into the pocket of his robe. He didn't know who it belonged to, but better the wife knew nothing of it yet, not if there was no need. Whoever had been with her husband had been the last to see him alive–might be guilty of his murder.

Before he gave any more thought to where that guilt might lie there was something else he needed to do first. Something he would prefer to avoid even while knowing he could not.

CHAPTER 2

Thomas was in a foul mood as he stood on the narrow bridge over the Hadarro. He stared at the towering walls of the palace perched on the bluff of al-Hamra, the red hill, and wondered why he was here and not with Lubna. From his lowly position the palace dominated the city of Gharnatah, as it was meant to. The walls harboured beauty and opulence, a life of ease for those who resided within. Had he been less angry he might have acknowledged that the palace also spread wealth throughout the city and surrounding region. But he was angry, and as soon as he could work out who to direct his anger at he would allow its release. Too many people were making demands of him, and this new death felt like one demand too many.

The Spanish king and queen, Isabel and Fernando, had reminded him of his duty before he left Qurtuba. As if that wasn't enough, while he and Jorge rested at an inn at al-Khala, the final Spanish outpost before the newly drawn borders of al-Andalus, a knock had sounded at the door of their small room. When Thomas opened it he recognised Martin de Alarcón immediately, even though he had only met him on a few occasions. How could he forget the man who held Muhammed, the captured Sultan of Gharnatah, as his guest? Martin was tall, dark haired, with a fashionably pointed beard. Thomas knew him as a hard man, with a hard intelligence.

"I hadn't expected to see you again. Who's taking care of the Sultan?"

"Boabdil needs only a guard and food and women."

Thomas knew the Spanish refused to use Muhammed's title. They always referred to him by his common name, although incapable of pronouncing Abu Abdullah correctly.

"I take it your presence here is no coincidence," Thomas said. He remained blocking the door to the bed chamber.

"Is your friend with you?"

"He is." Thomas knew Jorge, stretched on the bed, would be listening. The tall eunuch also knew Martin, although what his opinion of him was he had kept to himself. An unusual enough occurrence in Jorge to be noticeable.

"I would speak with you both while I can." Martin took a step closer, pushing the bounds of civility.

Thomas saw no reason to play games any longer and stood aside. He checked the corridor, wondering whether Martin had brought soldiers with him, but if he had they remained downstairs.

He watched Martin glance around, and knew he would find their room wanting. So did he, but it was nothing more than a place to sleep before their final day's journey home.

"There is no need to remind us of our duty," Thomas said. "Fernando made it clear before we left Qurtuba." If Martin refused to afford Muhammed his proper title, Thomas could take some small pleasure in doing the same for the Spanish king.

"I am aware he did. But you are almost home now. It does no harm to reinforce the message."

"Money and the release of prisoners." Jorge finally joined the conversation.

Martin glanced at him. "Yes. Money and prisoners. And we would have the exchange made quickly. That man has already outstayed his welcome."

Thomas hid a smile. "I will ensure the Sultana is made aware of the urgency. But you must remember where my loyalties lie. There was no reason for you to make the journey—I will do what I can to ensure Muhammed's swift return."

Martin pulled a face. Thomas knew he didn't understand why an Englishman sided with the Moors. Sometimes he barely understood the reasons himself. Even less so of late. Too much politics. Too much internal fighting over a waning power. His time in Qurtuba, his friendship with the King and Queen, had shown him a different side to Spain. One which had not been present when last he travelled through that land.

Now Thomas remained on the bridge while others walked around him. The roadway here was busy, merchants carrying baskets of goods upward, others bringing themselves down into the city. Some climbed through the twisting alleys of the Albayzin where Thomas wished to go. Instead he found himself about to climb the familiar roadway and pass once more through the guarded gates. They would know him within the palace, perhaps even welcome him. Was it that which angered him—a return to an old familiarity that now felt stultifying? He shouldn't be here, shouldn't be going in this direction, and because he recognised this he forced his feet to begin the climb.

As Thomas had journeyed from Qurtuba to Gharnatah he carried a cloying fear—that when he walked into his house on the Albayzin he would no longer recognise Lubna. In his mind he tried to picture her face, her hair, her eyes and her slight figure. Each time the image that came was different to the last. He feared he had forgotten how she looked. He had been away a long time—not a year, but a good portion of one. And there had been another fear, bigger even than the first. That she would have forgotten him.

Now he was travelling away from her again, once more following the call of duty. The anger, he knew, was directed at himself—he acknowledged it even as it grew and sparked into flame in his chest, burning there. He had spent months serving a different mistress. He had hoped to put such demands aside on his return, but now he knew that was impossible. Damn Isabel and Fernando, damn Martin de Alarcón too. Most of all damn Muhammed who had been foolish enough to get himself captured in a pointless raid.

The death Da'ud al-Baitar had called him to investigate wasn't the duty that brought him to the hill, although that would have to be dealt with soon enough. Instead the duty was one he had abandoned in his haste to see Lubna. As soon as he allowed the thought to enter his mind the anger began to fade. It had been directed at himself—anger for abandoning his duty, anger at his own selfishness, anger at war and death and too many things to comprehend. Perhaps it wasn't too late to make amends for what he could. Thomas increased his pace, breath coming short as he climbed.

It was as if he had never been gone. The guards at the gate nodded at Thomas and moved aside to let him pass into the citadel. He wondered briefly if they held any curiosity over where he had been all these months, then realised he was giving them too much credit. Guards didn't think, not in the way of other men. He should be grateful they still recognised him, which meant he didn't have to prove who he was to enter the palace.

Thomas stopped a moment and turned back to the more senior of the two.

"Did Jorge come this way?"

"The eunuch? I thought it was him, except he looked different."

"He's been away."

"Like you."

So they did notice.

"Where did he go?"

"To the stables, I assume. He had a cart and a mule and two horses. Where has he been?"

"Qurtuba."

The guard laughed. "Spain? Well there's a first time for everything."

Thomas didn't bother mentioning Qurtuba was the city Jorge had been born in, or that while there they had managed to track down a brother, sister-in-law, nephews and nieces. Instead he nodded and continued into the outer grounds of the palace, the change immediate but not as great as if he had entered the inner sanctum itself. The roadway went from cobbles to fine stone. There were trees and bushes in abundance, flowering shrubs, although at this time of year most of the flowers had faded.

At the stables Thomas found no sign of Jorge, although the cart was there and a stable-hand was rubbing down the horses. The mule had been led from sight. The stable-hand had no idea where Jorge was, not even who had brought the cart in.

Thomas wondered if Jorge had gone to the Sultana Aixa already, as they were both meant to, but he didn't think so. Jorge would wait for his return so they could report to her together. Jorge was closer to the Sultana than Thomas, but she could be a formidable presence when she chose, likely even more so now her eldest son and new ruler in Gharnatah had been captured. She would be expecting the pair of them to report on Muhammed's health immediately on their return.

So if not there, where would Jorge be?

Thomas's feet led him toward another gate, an entrance to the second level where those who serviced the harem lived and worked. The guards stationed here took only a little longer to admit him. Thomas was one of the few outsiders privileged with access to every part of the palace, even if it was normally in his role as surgeon.

Inside the temperature rose and Thomas loosened his robe. He had been cold for weeks. The winter months didn't suit him, not even here in Spain, but at least they were usually warmer than his native land of England, whose snows and frosts were now a distant memory. One he was glad to keep at a distance.

As he entered an outer courtyard he called out to a young girl who was crossing, a pot balanced on her shoulder.

"Hey, have you seen Jorge?"

She turned, slowing only a little. "I think he's gone to bathe."

"Where?" Thomas knew the bathing places within the harem, but had always believed they were for the use of concubines and wives only.

The girl gave him a look to show how stupid she believed him. "Where the eunuchs bathe, of course."

"And that is?"

Finally, the girl stopped walking and turned to him. She was young, with barely sixteen years behind her. Her face was familiar, and Thomas realised with a jolt she was the friend of another girl, Prea. He still held himself responsible for Prea's death two years before, when she had helped him track a killer through the tunnels within the palace. He saw in this girl's eyes an accusation. There was disdain there, a hatred the passage of time had failed to erase.

"You don't know? I thought you were Jorge's friend." It was obvious she was having doubts. Thomas tried to remember the girl's name but it failed to come to him, even if he had ever known it.

"I truly don't know. Can you show me?"

He saw uncertainty on her face. She already had a task he had interrupted, but Thomas was an important servant of the palace. And then, of course, she hated him.

"Go toward the eastern gate until you find a wide corridor on your left. Follow that and you will smell the oils. You'll find Jorge there, unless he's already finished, but I doubt it. He was extremely dirty." The look she gave Thomas made it clear she considered him similarly tainted, and it occurred to him he might have grown too used to Spanish ways while they were in Qurtuba.

Before Thomas could thank her she turned and trotted away. He watched her go, an ache in his chest at her familiarity. She and Prea could have been sisters.

He found Jorge exactly where the girl had told him he would be, sitting on a stone bench while two girls applied soapy rags to his body. His hair and beard, which had grown long while they resided in Qurtuba, remained uncut, but Thomas doubted it would stay that way for long. Already a third girl stood close by with a glinting razor. Despite Jorge's profession, it would take a keen eye to guess at what had been done to him. When Thomas had operated on him many years before he had taken care to cut as little as possible, and the man still retained most of what made him a man, the only items missing those two nuggets that might cause a problem within a harem.

"Thomas!" Jorge lifted a hand in greeting and waved him across. "Come here. I'm sure you'd welcome a bath as much as me." Then he frowned. "I thought you were going to see Lubna." The frown turned to a grin. "Though I'm sure she'll welcome you being clean even more. Gods, I'd forgotten how much I stank until the dirt was washed from me. Come on, get in the water." He nodded toward a small, deep bath set into the floor.

"I'm only here because we haven't finished yet."

"Why do you think I came here first? Aixa won't want us going to her smelling like Spaniards. Get in the damn water and stop being so stubborn."

Thomas was about to object when he realised Jorge was right. The Sultana would refuse him entry if he turned up dressed as he was, in stained robes covering an even more stained body. He sighed and began to disrobe, allowing a new girl to help him when she came across.

"Won't your compatriots object to an outsider bathing here?"

Jorge laughed. "Probably, if they ever find out, but I don't plan on telling them and I'm sure the girls won't either. Will you?"

There was a shake of heads.

Thomas gripped the girl's wrist as her hand fumbled at the cloth wrapped between his legs. He removed it himself and stepped into the tub, relief flooding through him as he sank to his nose in the water. The girl tossed his soiled clothing aside and slipped in beside him, began soaping his face, running water across his hair. Thomas was uneasy, but he knew these girls were more used to dealing with those who were something less than full men. He wondered how she would react if he responded to her ministrations, but when he glanced across he saw that the others were already ignoring Jorge's partial arousal, as skilled at their own job as Thomas was at his.

The girl lathered his head then began to comb the wet hair. Her lips tightened as her comb worked something small free from his thick locks, but she ignored her distaste and dropped the flea into a pot of boiling water already waiting.

"I was covered with them," Jorge said, "but at least they're going to shave me. You should do the same, just this once. It'll rid your body of everything we brought back with us."

"She'll work them loose," Thomas said, his shoulders relaxing.

The girl's movements, repetitive and gentle, soothed him, and he felt himself drifting. The journey from Qurtuba had been long, arduous and cold. His time in the Spanish city had brought satisfaction, but also danger, and he recalled the time he thought his life was about to end until Jorge saved him. He turned to watch his friend, whose head was now half hair and half skin.

"You look pleased to be home," Thomas said.

"How was Lubna? *She'll* have been pleased you have come home at last."

"I didn't get that far."

"What have you been doing since you left me? You could have helped unload the cart."

"I saw the boy taking care of the horses. I've been with Da'ud al-Baitar, investigating a death."

Jorge stared at him a long moment before shaking his head. "You've been back barely an hour and already managed to involve yourself in some new mystery?"

"Not involved. I was consulting, is all." Thomas jerked as the girl moved her attentions from his head to his body. He began to reach for her wrist again then stopped. This was how things were done here, and he knew his own weaknesses too well.

Jorge made a sound. "Consulting." He lifted one arm

so the girl with the blade could shave beneath.

"Do we visit Aixa once we're finished here?"

"Have you anything else to wear?"

Thomas looked at the pile of discarded clothing he had removed and wrinkled his nose.

"Then I'll have something brought for you," said Jorge.

"As long as it's not silk pantaloons and shirt. And none of those silly slippers."

Jorge smiled, knowing Thomas was teasing. A few of the eunuchs continued to wear what was considered traditional dress, but Jorge had long since exchanged his silks for linen and cotton. Thomas knew it was partly because of the work they had done together the last two years. Jorge had changed greatly over that period, even managing to kill a man, although it had been in self-defence.

Thomas continued to observe his friend as his own servant cleaned him, while Jorge's removed every trace of hair from his head and body. It was interesting to watch the old Jorge emerge from the one he had become over the last months. Even when the girls had finished Jorge looked different to how he had before. Some of his softness had been eroded. His chest and belly were more delineated, legs slimmer, his face too. He didn't yet look dangerous, as Thomas had been told he sometimes could. Jorge would never look dangerous, but he didn't look like a pushover anymore.

The girl with the razor came across and knelt beside Thomas. He reached up and gripped her wrist. "I prefer to keep my hair."

"I will only shorten it. And shave your beard. Is that

all right?"

Thomas considered, nodded. The girl set to work, combing hair which had grown long and thick, using the razor to trim the excess length before starting on his face. Thomas drifted once more, the ministrations soothing, his concerns put aside while this girl took care of him.

"Have you seen anyone yet?" Thomas finally asked as he pulled himself from the bath, water cascading from him. He held his arms out, allowing two girls to pat him dry, thinking he could get used to this kind of treatment.

"Someone came and took the chests and papers away, but that's all." Jorge picked through a pile of clothing, selected linen pants and shirt of a fine weave, the shirt plain white other than for a fine gold thread woven at the neckline. He left his shaven head bare but pushed his feet into leather slippers lacking any ornamentation or fancy.

Thomas walked to the stack of fresh garments, unconcerned at his nakedness in front of Jorge or the girls, who now busied themselves with tidying away their oils and soaps and unguents. He searched through the clothing Jorge had discarded as not worthy and quickly found an outfit that was comfortable, if a little too fine for his tastes. The remaining pair of slippers were plain enough. Too large, but they would suffice for now. The girls had already taken his stained clothing away and he doubted he would ever see it again.

"So now we wait?" he asked.

"Aixa will send for us when she's ready. I'm hungry, shall we find something to eat?"

"You're always hungry. And it's the middle of the afternoon."

"Bazzu will find us something if I ask."

Thomas shook his head. "You, maybe. She still hasn't forgiven me."

"She will. She knows it wasn't you who killed Prea. But maybe you're right." Jorge stretched, yawning. "I could sleep though. In a real bed." He grinned. "Even alone if I must."

Thomas grunted. "I have things to do. Da'ud told me I need to visit Helena, even though she's not the first person I want to see."

Jorge cast Thomas a strange glance, but only said, "I'll come with you."

"To visit Helena? Are you feeling unwell?"

Jorge punched Thomas on the shoulder, harder than he meant, but Thomas took it without comment. "I'm curious."

"About what?"

"Nothing in particular. Just curious."

They got as far as the gate from the palace to the Alkazaba when they were caught by a messenger, who took a moment to catch his breath before informing them the Sultana Aixa was ready to see them.

CHAPTER 3

It was a lie, of course. Aixa wasn't waiting for them, but Thomas hadn't been expecting her to. She was bathing. Aixa was Sultana of Gharnatah, mother to the captured Muhammed and his younger brother Yusuf. Wife still to the deposed Sultan Abu al-Hasan Ali. She would want to appear to them as perfectly as her servants could make her, so Thomas and Jorge sat in silence in the ornate inner chamber and waited. Eventually voices reached them, then footsteps, and finally Aixa appeared in all her splendour.

She was no longer young, but to someone unfamiliar with the Sultana it would be difficult to tell. She had added a little weight over the years, but her skin remained flawless, her red-brown hair uncovered inside the harem, unconcerned at their presence. Jorge was of course familiar to her, they would have spoken and played together often. He would have amused her, played a lute and sung songs. Jorge was not the senior eunuch in the harem, that honour went to Samuli, a dark skinned Berber who had been almost unbearably handsome in his youth but was now an old man. Thomas suspected Jorge was Aixa's favourite for the streak of mischief that ran through him which echoed her own. As for himself, as her physician he had seen this woman as naked as the day she was born. But now Aixa had drawn on the mantle of Sultana, her face grave as she reclined on a pile of cushions which had been raised to ensure they had to look up at her.

An older woman beside her held a tray on which lay a stack of papers, one of which she handed to Aixa.

"Tell me, what is the meaning of this?" said Aixa, flapping the page.

"I don't know what it says," Thomas said.

Aixa scowled. "You pretend you are not party to this betrayal? I have my spies in the Spanish court and they tell me of your actions. All of your actions." Her dark eyes bored into Thomas's.

"Thomas did what you sent him to do," said Jorge, attempting to deflect Aixa's anger.

Thomas glanced at Jorge, who was living dangerously. He might believe himself Aixa's favourite, but she had seen neither of them for several months, and in the febrile atmosphere now gripping al-Andalus loyalties could change in a day.

"I sent him to cure a prince," snapped Aixa, "not to befriend a queen. Nor to chase down criminals in the company of the King of Castile. And certainly *not* to become involved in the capture of my son!"

"Muhammed's capture had nothing to do with either of us," said Jorge, still defending. "He chose to attack the Spanish even as we were helping them. On his and your orders."

"My orders?" said Aixa. She turned her attention

from Jorge to Thomas. "Why did you not petition for his immediate release?"

"I was acting as physician, Your Grace–" Thomas stopped himself, caught in the act of using an honorific he had grown used to in the Spanish court, but if Aixa noticed she showed no sign.

"You were acting as my ambassadors. Both of you." She glanced at Jorge but her attention returned immediately to Thomas. "I would expect you to protect my interests, my *son's* interests, at all times. And now I have this… this *demand*!" She waved the paper again.

"If I could see it, malika…" Thomas held out his hand. It appeared for a moment Aixa would refuse him, then she thrust the document at the woman, who brought it across.

It was written in Arabic, which Thomas was grateful for. He could read Spanish if he had to, but did so badly and slowly. He skimmed the single sheet of paper before looking at Aixa.

"It is an offer for his release," he said. "Isn't that what you want?"

"You see what they demand in exchange?"

Thomas raised a shoulder. "Money and a return of hostages. It is no more than you expected, I'm sure."

"But not the amount!"

"They are only putting a price on Muhammed equal to his worth to al-Andalus."

"He will be sent home," Aixa said, "but I am not paying what they ask. You will negotiate."

"*I* will negotiate?" Thomas had to suppress the laugh that wanted to escape him. "You have a vizier for such matters, malika, there are nobles and other learned men."

"None of whom are *familiar* with the Queen of Castile." Her eyes narrowed. "As I understand you are. Suspiciously familiar, my spies inform me."

"Then you need to replace them, malika."

"Is it not true? You did not spend many hours alone with the queen in her son's chamber?"

"I spent many hours with her son, some of which his mother was in attendance for, together with two nurses, often a priest, and occasionally another doctor." Thomas didn't know how much Aixa really knew, but hoped he might get away with a half-truth.

"Did you cure him?" Aixa leaned forward, her gaze sharp.

It seemed an odd question in light of her others, but Thomas answered. "Yes, I cured him. As well as anyone could."

"Not anyone," said Aixa. "I hear he barely limps when before he could not walk at all. Not just anyone could have done that."

Thomas chose to keep his silence. It was not his place to comment on his own abilities.

Aixa relaxed, reclining once more against the cushions. "And for this help you gave, this help I sent you to give, my gift to the Spanish, they owe me something in return. It is only just. Which is why you will negotiate. Remind them of what you did. Remind them of your friendship." She waved a hand. "Take the queen to your bed again if you must, but you will return my son to Gharnatah. No!" She held up her palm as Thomas began to object. "Of course I will send my vizier, my nobles, many others too, and they will talk with the

Spanish. But it will be you and Jorge who conduct the true negotiations. I demand this of you."

Thomas knew there was no possibility of argument. Aixa was determined. He wondered why she chose to trust him over those far closer to her, but perhaps she believed the rumours, all false, about him and Queen Isabel, and trusted him to deliver what she wanted. *And perhaps I can*, Thomas thought.

"Is she mad?" Jorge said as they passed through the exquisite corridors of the inner palace. "What does she expect us to do?"

"She expects me to fuck the Queen of Spain—who will then, of course, do anything I ask."

Jorge smiled. "I'm afraid she overestimates your abilities as a lover. Now if she had asked me…"

"You still miss her, don't you?" Thomas said. He referred to the Spanish Duquessa Jorge had fallen in love with while they resided within the palace in Qurtuba. The Duquessa Esperanza who was murdered by the Bonebreaker, the madman Thomas had sought.

Jorge slowed, stopped. They had reached the invisible barrier which marked the inner and outer palace. In the courtyard beyond a group of men were working, some filling in the tunnels Thomas had discovered a year and a half before, others making good, bricking up hidden entrances, applying fresh tile over the surface. Some mixed lime mortar, some chipped at blocks of stone, others wheeled barrows of rubble to pour into the now opened tunnel entrances.

"Am I not supposed to miss her?" Jorge said, also

watching the men, but Thomas knew his mind was elsewhere. "I will miss her forever."

"What will she say when we fail?" Thomas returned to Aixa's request, knowing Jorge would follow his drift.

"Are we going to fail? I have seen little evidence of you failing in anything you set your mind to, Thomas."

"But those were all things I knew how to do."

"Tracking down killers? Beating a trained soldier in armed combat?"

"Don't forget healing a prince," Thomas said with a smile.

"As if I'd be allowed to. When do we leave again? Damn—I haven't even slept in my own bed yet, let alone anyone else's."

Thomas knew Jorge was only half joking. His heart might have been stolen and then shattered, but he knew it wouldn't stop him bedding whoever he took a fancy to. Female or, Thomas sometimes suspected, male in equal measure.

"We won't be sent away yet. There will be many preparations to make, and you know these things take more time than seems reasonable."

"Talking of healing princes," said Jorge, "I have a favour to ask of you. Samuli has grown worse while I've been away. I'd like you to take a look at him."

"Of course. Do you want me to come now?"

"Do you have time?"

Thomas thought of the alternative, a meeting with Helena, and nodded. "Of course."

"Good." Jorge punched Thomas. For the second time that day. Thomas thought it was a habit he would have to discourage.

* * *

As soon as they entered the room Thomas smelled the perfume of death emanating from the man. He glanced at Jorge, but his friend appeared unaware, as were those in attendance. He knelt at the bedside to examine the chief eunuch anyway. He might as well find the cause of his illness and perhaps be able to offer some respite from his obvious pain.

"Have you seen another physician?" Thomas asked. He knew Samuli, but not well. He had always been an almost unapproachable presence at the head of the harem.

"The Sultana sent me her man while you were away. If you had been here I would have asked for you."

Thomas moved sideways as Samuli's breath washed across him, tried not to show his despair. Even had he been sent for earlier he knew there was nothing he could have done.

"When did the pain start?" He lifted the man's robe and examined him. His arms and legs and chest were stick-thin, but his belly was distended. When Thomas palpated it the presence of a hard mass was unmistakeable.

"A year ago. I thought it indigestion. Too much rich food."

"And now?"

"Some days it is more than I can bear. I cannot work, I cannot even walk. I have to ask others to take me to void my bowels, not that I need to do that much anymore."

Thomas leaned back. He had seen enough. Putting the man through more physical examination would be an unnecessary torture.

"I can make you some drafts to ease the pain, but they will need to be made stronger and stronger as time passes."

Samuli met Thomas's gaze, his own unflinching. "I have seen this in others. I know there is but one inevitable end. If your potions can help me pass in peace them make them as strong as you wish. My time here is at an end." He looked beyond Thomas. "I am glad Jorge has returned to take my place."

"Not while you still breathe, old friend," said Jorge.

"How long will that be, Thomas? The truth, please."

"I can't be sure. A week. A month. No more."

Samuli gave the faintest of nods. "It is as I thought. I will welcome an end to the pain."

"I can ease your pain now," Thomas promised.

"And will you end it all if I ask?" said Samuli.

Thomas stared at the old man, at his skeletal face, and nodded. "If you wish it I will help you. But make your peace with the world first."

Samuli smiled. "I did that long ago. I have lived through the best of times, and now I am glad to leave the world. This life I have led will soon be no more. Times change, and I am too old to change with them."

Thomas would have said something, but he wasn't sure he didn't believe the same thing. He made his way into the corridor and along to a courtyard. He needed to breathe clean air. It wasn't the smell of death that concerned him but the cloying sweetness of the palace. With a shock he realised he might even prefer the stench of the streets in Qurtuba.

The air was cold in the courtyard, but Thomas welcomed that too. On the far side workmen were coming and going and he saw they were filling in one of the tunnels Prea had shown him two years before. He turned as someone entered behind him, expecting Jorge, but instead discovered someone he hadn't seen in almost a year. Aixa's younger son, Yusuf, stood ten feet away. His face showed both excitement and fear, and Thomas saw a tremble in his limbs.

"Mother told me you were back," said Yusuf. He took a step closer, stopped once more.

Thomas nodded. He took pity on the boy and went to him, put his arms around shoulders broader than he remembered and pulled him to his chest. Yusuf returned the embrace, and Thomas felt the tension leave the boy's body. Quite why the youngster worshiped him as he did was a mystery. Perhaps it was because he received little attention from father, mother or brother—the curse of the younger son. Although not so young now, almost sixteen years of age and suddenly raised to a position that might bring him to power.

Thomas held him by the shoulders and looked into the boy's face. "You've grown."

"My beard is coming in. Look." Yusuf lifted his chin to show a dark wisp along his upper lip and cheeks. "The women of the harem say it makes me more handsome. Are you going to see Helena?"

"You too?" Thomas said. "What is so important I would want to see her?"

"Because she—" Yusuf stopped himself. Another first. Usually he could keep nothing a secret. "Because you should." His face brightened again. "Is Muhammed coming home? Mother says he is, but you truly know, don't you, Thomas?"

Beyond Yusuf, Thomas saw Jorge enter the courtyard. There was nothing stopping him from going to Helena now.

"Don't you want to be Sultan?"

Yusuf gave a shiver. "Mother says I am made of the wrong material to rule–and it's true, don't you think?"

Thomas smiled. "Any man can rule if they have the right people around them."

"I would make you vizier," said Yusuf.

Thomas tapped a knuckle on Yusuf's skull. "I said the *right* people." He released his hold on the boy's shoulder. "Now, I have things to do, and I expect so do you."

"Olaf wants me to practice with the sword. He says I must practice every day, but the men he sends to train me are too hard."

"Do as he says. You never know when a sword will be necessary. Even Jorge knows how to fight now."

Yusuf glanced at the waiting figure, his face showing doubt. "Olaf says it is one thing to fight, another to kill a man."

"Jorge knows that too."

The doubt on Yusuf's face changed to incredulity. Then he laughed and punched Thomas on the chest before turning and running away along the corridor.

CHAPTER 4

"What's wrong?"

"Nothing." Thomas kept walking, unwilling to discuss the thoughts that chased each other through his mind, but Jorge was, as ever, persistent.

"Then why have we taken the same corridor twice in succession, and—"Jorge's hand came out and gripped Thomas's shoulder, "—we will take it again unless you lift your eyes from your feet. Is it Samuli? I know he is dying, just not how soon."

Thomas stopped, looking around. They were back at the entrance to the courtyard, the masons still in place but now taking a break as they waited for some event only they were privy to.

"It's not him. I see such every day. I should be on my way to Lubna, but instead I'm going to see Helena, and I have no idea why."

"You need to talk to her."

Thomas glanced at Jorge. "You too, then. Am I the only one not to know why? Has she a new scar? Has her hair turned black? Has she lost an arm?"

Jorge raised a shoulder but offered no explanation.

"You said you were hungry," Thomas said, in an attempt to deflect attention from his reluctant task.

"And I am. But we can eat later."

"You go eat now. I'll visit her alone."

"No you won't. I don't want you disappearing. Or falling into her bed again."

"Again?"

Jorge rolled his eyes. "Isn't that what this is all about? Do you take me for a complete fool?"

"No," Thomas said. "Not a complete one."

"If you're going to insult me perhaps I will let you visit alone."

Thomas's sprits sank even lower as they approached the house he had not entered in months. It sat on the edge of the drop to the city below, with a magnificent view across the misted Vega surrounding the city. Distracted by his thoughts, Thomas had almost stopped walking when Jorge thumped him on the shoulder.

"Get it done, then you can visit the one you really want to see."

Thomas nodded, annoyed at himself, annoyed at his weakness. Helena meant nothing to him anymore, and he didn't understand this new reluctance. He started down the last of the slope to the side door and pushed it open. Inside was warmer than out. And scented with a familiar aroma.

Thomas started to call out then stopped. This was his house. There was no need to announce himself, even if he was returning from an absence of several months.

He passed by a kitchen he had never used and doubted Helena had either, stopped in an arched entrance to a large, open room with windows that offered a view across treetops to the plain. Helena sat with her back to him, her head inclined toward a second woman, a stranger with long, dark hair which obscured her profile. From the way she was clothed, the way she sat, Thomas knew she too was someone used to the luxuries of the harem. It was this woman who first became aware of his presence. She turned to reveal a pale face of exquisite beauty.

"You must be Thomas," she said, her voice showing no surprise. She switched her attention. "And you are Jorge—you can be no other from the way you've been described. Both of you."

Then Helena turned and Thomas felt a rush of memories surge through him, rich, dark and troubled.

Helena's expression puzzled him. He had expected disdain, dislike, even a welcome. You never knew what you might get from her. What he hadn't expected was the fear he saw in her eyes. Then she rose to her feet, her movements slow and laboured. She turned fully toward him to reveal the secret everyone had been too afraid to tell to him of.

Thomas stared. Helena's belly was swollen, enormous, her breasts similarly abundant. Her face too had filled out, the scar that had brought her to him as a gift now barely visible. Her features were as perfect as they had been at the height of her beauty.

He understood now why Da'ud al-Baitar had sent him, understood too why no-one had been willing to disclose the reason.

* * *

The dark haired woman reached out and rested her hand against Helena's belly. Thomas thought it a strange, almost proprietorial gesture.

"Who—when did you—how…" Thomas's voice trailed away.

"I think the how is obvious, don't you?" said Helena.

"How long?"

"Until it comes?"

Thomas nodded.

"Can't the great surgeon Thomas Berrington tell such a simple matter?"

"Not… not without examining you."

"A month, a little more. That's what the midwives tell me."

"Have you consulted Da'ud?"

"At the start. But he could do nothing for me. Neither could my sister. I don't need them now. Don't want them anywhere near me." Her eyes hardened. "Nor do I want you here." She placed her own hand over that of the woman's.

"I would like to examine you. To check the baby is well."

"Why?" She scowled. "It's not yours."

He stared at her for a moment, remembering all the times she had drawn him in only to turn affection to hate. "It could be. You know it could."

Helena waved her free hand. "A woman knows these things."

Thomas almost laughed, fought hard to suppress the welling up. "What do you know of pregnancy?"

"I have people who know." She glanced at the woman. "Eva knows about such things."

"Eva?" Thomas looked at the stranger, who stood now, back straight. She was a head shorter than Helena, who was tall, but carried a presence that belied her stature. She was dressed in a silk robe, an ornate broach catching it together at the shoulder. Another held one side of her hair in place so that on the right it fell long but was held up on the left. "I don't know you," he said.

"You don't need–"

Eva touched Helena on the wrist. "It's fine, my sweet, he has a right to know."

"He has no right–"

Once again Eva interrupted Helena, her gaze directed at Thomas. "Please forgive her, she suffers such mood swings now. The pregnancy, I expect. I arrived here at the right time, I believe. Perhaps it is fate that brought me."

"Who are you?" Thomas asked.

"I am a member of the harem of al-Zagal. And a compatriot of yours, of a kind, I believe. You are a friend to his brother, I understand."

Thomas didn't bother to explain that his friendship with the deposed Sultan, if it had indeed been such, was now shattered. "Al-Zagal is in the palace?"

"Politics hates a vacuum." Eva glanced at Jorge. "Your friend understands, perhaps better than you. Helena tells me you take little interest in such matters." The way Eva spoke made the words sound innocent enough, but Thomas could imagine exactly how Helena might have phrased it, and what venom there would have been in the telling.

"I need to–" Thomas stopped. He didn't know what he needed. And then he did. "I need to go. I have more important things to do."

Eva smiled. Helena's face remained the cool mask it had been since she revealed her current state to him.

Outside Thomas turned to Jorge, angry. "You could have said something before letting me walk in there."

"I didn't think it was any of my business."

"Well, it's not...but that's never stopped you in the past."

Jorge shook his head. "Go see Lubna. If al-Zagal has set himself up in the palace I have work to do here. Go see her and tell her how you feel and forget about the one in there."

"She is carrying my child," Thomas said.

"She claims not."

"It's mine. The timing is right."

Jorge smiled. They had come to where they would need to part if Thomas was indeed to return to his house on the Albayzin. "So you did weaken, then, that night before we left for Qurtuba."

"Don't make it sound like it's a sin. Not you."

"I don't blame you," said Jorge. "I would weaken for Helena myself, even though I know the darkness she harbours. But you know as well as I how other men lust over her, and she was never faithful to you for long."

"Thank you for the reminder."

"So what will you do?" Jorge looked as if he wanted to be somewhere else.

"Go see Lubna, as you suggest."

"I meant about the child."

"Oh. I don't know." Thomas washed a hand across his face. "I really don't know." He glanced at Jorge. "Will you do something for me?"

"No."

"You don't know what I'm going to ask."

"Yes, I do. If you want to know who else could be the father, then you'll have to find that out for yourself."

"But I don't have the same access to harem gossip as you."

"And I don't care. I will do almost anything for you, my friend, but this is something you need to work out for yourself." Jorge pointed. "Go back there and ask her. Demand the truth. After everything you've done for that woman the least she owes you is that."

After they parted Thomas found he couldn't descend the hill yet. He had almost started down, but instead stood on a paved platform which offered a view of the far hillside. He stared at the jumbled shacks and houses, the winding alleyways, the grand mosque sitting above it all, and he tried to make sense of his bruised thoughts. He knew Helena would not have been faithful. He had never expected her to be. He was more surprised she had allowed him back into her bed the night before he left for Qurtuba, for he knew he no longer held any claim over her, if he ever had. Still, it would be good to have confirmation of who the father might be, if not him. And it could still be him, Thomas knew, and with the knowing came a wave of self-disgust at his weakness. Helena wasn't who he wanted. Once, perhaps, her beauty and sensuality had enchanted him, but now the woman he wanted waited in the house across the valley, still ignorant of his return. He glanced to the west. The sun was almost touching the top of the Elvira hills. The days were growing short. Soon the year would turn. Another year in al-Andalus, a long way from his birthplace, but this was home now. For how much longer, he wondered. And then... what then...?

Thomas sighed and turned away from the path that would lead him home. He hadn't finished this day yet, but at least he might discover something from his next meeting. If the man was there. And if he would see him.

"Thomas! Come in, we are about to eat. You will take something?" It was Olaf Torvaldsson's wife, Fatima, who offered the welcome. She liked him well enough now, liked him almost as a son. When it had been Helena who shared his bed she hadn't been so sure. But of course she wasn't Helena's mother, who had died giving birth to her. Now Fatima, the Berber wife Olaf had taken when his loneliness grew too great, believed it was her own daughter who lay beside him.

"Is he in?" Thomas asked. The smell of baking and some kind of meat, kid he thought, filled the air.

"He'll be along soon. Giving orders, I expect. Come, take a seat. You've been away, haven't you? I thought you hadn't visited in a while. Where were you? What have you been doing?"

Olaf Torvaldsson's second wife stood behind the scarred table which her husband insisted on. He, like Thomas, was more used to a chair than a cushion when he ate.

Thomas knew the food would wait for Olaf's return, so he began to tell Fatima of his time in Qurtuba. Of meeting the King and Queen of Spain. But he neglected to tell of the incident he had become embroiled in that had almost cost his life. She was questioning him on the fine details of fashion at the Spanish court when the door opened and Olaf Torvaldsson entered. A tall man, closer to seven feet than six, with blonde hair caught in a pigtail that hung down his back.

"Thomas!" He greeted him with the same enthusiasm as his wife, came across and slapped his back, almost causing Thomas to plunge into the tabletop. "Has Fatima asked you to eat? Of course she has. When did you get back? Have you seen Lubna yet?"

Thomas waited until Fatima disappeared into the kitchen before replying.

"Not Lubna, no. But I have seen Helena."

"Ah…" Olaf pulled out a chair and sat, causing it to creak.

"I need to ask if you know who the father might be."

"How would I know? My daughter is as wilful as she is wicked, you know that as well as anyone."

Thomas stared at Olaf a moment. He could still hear Fatima in the kitchen, pots being scraped, her voice soft as she talked to herself. "You know, don't you."

Olaf lifted a shoulder. "She has her favourites. Or rather, she is a favourite of a few. Why do you ask? Surely this is none of your business anymore."

"Oh, but it is," Thomas said, and watched as something changed in Olaf's face. Despite the general's protestations he wasn't a stupid man. He would not have reached the position he held, and kept it, if he was. Sultans came and went, but Olaf remained. "I would never betray Lubna."

"Yet it seems if what you claim is true you already

have."

"Lubna and I share our work, but not a bed. I know you and Fatima believe we do, and I have never tried to change that opinion, but trust me on this—I would *never* betray her." Thomas punched the table top with a finger to emphasise the point.

Olaf shook his head. "I don't understand. You say you've laid with Helena again, but not her sister?" He frowned. "Why?"

Thomas let his breath go in a long sigh. "Your daughter is very beautiful."

"I always believed you a better man, Thomas Berrington. I don't understand."

"I'm a man, Olaf." He glanced over his shoulder, lowered his voice. "Are you telling me you've never taken comfort with a woman when you've been on the battlefield?"

"That's different. My men would consider me weak and a fool if I did not."

"Is this any different? Most men would consider me stupid if I didn't lie with Helena."

This time it was Olaf's turn to lean close and lower his voice. "I know what my daughter is, my other daughters too, the older ones. They are all the same. Except Helena is…different. Special, perhaps. But flawed. I *know* this. But you and Lubna are…" He sat back, shaking his head. "Why not, Thomas? I don't understand. The pair of you are so suited to each other everyone assumed you were—"

"Were what?" asked Fatima as she emerged carrying plates of pulses, sauces and meat. She arranged them on the table, their spiced richness filling the air, then took the far seat so Thomas and Olaf could continue talking. It was a sign, Thomas thought, of her trust in him she chose to eat at the same table. A trust he had betrayed.

"Nothing," said Olaf. "We were only talking about Lubna."

Fatima smiled. "She comes to see me every three or four days. She's a good girl." She glanced at Thomas, her eyes shy. "She misses you."

Which only made Thomas feel worse for not going to her immediately. This was not turning out to be anything like the day he had expected.

"I saw a dead man this morning," he said, addressing his words to Olaf.

"Good for you. I have seen many, but none today, I admit."

"Is this business talk?" asked Fatima. "Because if it is I will finish my meal next door."

Olaf glanced toward Thomas. "Is it business?"

"Perhaps."

Fatima picked a few items from the platters and took her plate through to the kitchen.

"I think she prefers to eat in there anyway," said Olaf. "I take it this body wasn't merely dead, or you wouldn't use it to distract me from conversation about my daughters."

"He was killed."

Olaf nodded. "How? Is it something I need to know about?"

"A blade was inserted into his brain. The act was skilful."

"And?"

"I wondered if you'd heard of any other deaths."

"Why would anyone come to me? Where did the man die?"

"In the city."

"If it wasn't on the hill it's none of my business."

"I know you better than that."

"You have to understand, these are difficult times," said Olaf. "The old Sultan and his brother have returned. Power is shifting."

"That must be awkward for you, after transferring your loyalty to his son."

"Muhammed's captured. He'll not be coming back, and Abu al-Hasan knows full well my loyalty is with whoever rules here."

"Would you make enquiries for me?" Thomas asked. "About any other deaths?"

"If you think it will do any good. Why don't you just let the matter lie. Is it any of your business?"

"I thought you knew me better than that," Thomas said.

CHAPTER 5

It was fully dark by the time Thomas finally dragged his tired body up the last flight of rough steps to the cobbled alley that led to his house. His real house, here on the Albayzin where he belonged. Not on the perfumed hill, not in the green fields of England, the land of his birth, but here among the teeming shacks and alleys of a town outside a town, protected by its own walls, protected by its own citizens.

It was cold. What little heat the December sun brought had departed swiftly with its setting. Thomas's breath plumed as he approached the door. A closed door, as he would expect. A nervousness rose in him and he pressed it down with a fierce will. Fatigue, nothing more. He had spent a week on horseback, a day chasing a phantom, and made more discoveries in the few hours since his arrival than any man should have to accommodate.

Thomas lifted the iron latch on the door and pushed. It gave, as he knew it would, but he had been away a long time and Lubna might have grown nervous in his absence. He smiled at the thought of Lubna growing nervous.

He closed the door softly, wanting to surprise her, to see her reaction at his return. He half expected her to be in the workshop, bent over a book or preparing some tincture, but as he entered the courtyard he saw the workshop was dark. Light spilled through the window of the single room on the ground floor that served as kitchen and living room, and he heard the scraping of pans being cleaned.

Thomas went to the door, also closed to keep out the night chill. He waited a moment until the sound of the pans reached a pinnacle before he lifted the latch. He still wanted to see her surprise.

"It took you long enough to get here," said Lubna as soon as he stepped into the room. "I hear you arrived this morning." She stood with her back to him, and Thomas recalled the fears that had plagued him as he travelled toward Gharnatah, that he would no longer recognise her, the memory of her fading the closer he came.

"Who told you?"

Lubna half turned, her face in profile, and Thomas discovered he had never forgotten how she looked. The force of the memory weakened his knees as he stumbled to the table and sat.

"Are you all right?" She turned fully, coming toward him.

"Tired, that's all. I'm fine."

Lubna stopped. She was close enough to reach, and Thomas smelled her essence, the scent that would always be her. He smiled at how that scent had never been in doubt, the senses always holding tight to their treasured memories.

"Da'ud came looking for you." Lubna cocked her head to one side, her dark lips curling into a smile. "He told me he'd caught you on your way here. Said too he asked you to look at a body. A suspicious death."

Thomas nodded.

"Again?" asked Lubna.

"It's not my fault."

"No? If it's not your fault why do these things always happen to you?" She pushed her fists into her waist, the movement emphasising how tiny she was, how much smaller than her sister. "How many murders did you solve while you were in Qurtuba?"

"Only one or two, no more."

Lubna laughed, her amusement fading when she saw Thomas was telling the truth. "Truly?" She shook her head.

"Like I said, it's not my fault."

"It's lucky you're back home then, isn't it." She turned away. "Do you want something to eat? There's probably a little left. If you'd sent word I could have prepared a feast more fitting for your return."

"I've already eaten. With your father."

Lubna stopped, her back to him once more, one hand touching a pot that was half cleaned, sand still clinging to its surface. The lamp flickered in a sudden draft and Lubna's shadow danced against the stone wall.

"You've been to the hill?" she said.

"Yes. And I've seen her."

Lubna turned to him, her face held stiffly, shoulders back as if she needed to show her courage. Show him she didn't care one way or the other.

"She came to me," she said, her voice so soft Thomas had to lean forward to hear. "As soon as she knew."

"When was that?"

"Toward the end of *Rabī*. She wanted my help to get rid of the baby." The expression on Lubna's face told Thomas all he needed to know about how she felt. He worked out the timings and knew it was possible.

"How far along was she?"

Lubna's face showed no expression at all. "Three or four months. She wasn't showing. But I wouldn't have helped even if she'd come to me in the first month." She came to the table and sat, reached out to pluck dried fruit from a bowl, nibbled at one edge of an apricot with small white teeth.

"What did she say when you turned her down?"

"What do you think? She went to someone else."

"Who also wouldn't help her, obviously."

"Would you have, Thomas?" Lubna's eyes captured his, her own a strange mix of violet and green. "Would you have killed her baby if she had asked?"

"You know what I'd have done."

"I like to think so."

"You do."

Lubna reached out and placed a hand over his where it rested on the table. Her fingers were sticky from the fruit, but her touch sent a shock through Thomas's body. These moment of soft affection had started before he went away. She would stroke his arm, touch his cheek. He in turn would brush her shoulder with his fingers, occasionally hold her hand inside his. Nothing more, but they both knew where, eventually, the touches would lead. So why hadn't he given in to this woman he loved instead of allowing himself to be seduced by the one he despised?

He turned his hand over so Lubna's rested inside it, curled his fingers around hers.

"This changes everything," she said, her eyes no longer meeting his.

"I know."

Lubna sighed. Said nothing.

"But not for ever."

"What will you do?"

"I don't know. Not yet."

"She told me it wasn't yours," said Lubna, and Thomas thought he heard a note of hope in her voice.

"She told me the same. But she knows different."

Lubna slid her hand from within his. She stood.

"I'll fetch my things and move them back into the workshop."

"You don't have to do that."

"No?"

"I'll sleep in the workshop tonight. We'll decide what to do tomorrow."

Lubna shook her head hard, dark hair flying so it obscured her features. "No. I'll move them now. You need a real bed tonight."

Thomas watched her go. He sat listening to her moving around upstairs. The knocking of objects together, the stamp of feet. He couldn't blame her. Couldn't blame her at all.

It was strange to be surrounded by familiar sounds and scents. The bark of the dog from the farm at the top of the hill. Voices as people passed in the alley below. Creaks and groans as timbers settled. The scuttling of a mouse through the space between bedroom and kitchen.

Thomas rolled over and punched the narrow pillow. Sleep eluded him despite the weariness in his bones and confusion of his mind. He could pretend it was his return to Gharnatah, but knew it wasn't that.

Lubna's scent clung to the bedclothes and pillow, and they were having an effect on him.

She had carried her clothes downstairs wrapped in a blanket, gone directly to the workshop and not returned. Thomas had searched for wine or ale or spirits and found none, because of course Lubna didn't drink alcohol, and this had been her house for the last six months. He had toyed with pulling on his robe and descending to al-Hattabin square. Despite the lateness of the hour he knew there would be people there, and wine to drink. It wasn't the lateness of the hour that dissuaded him so much as the thought of the climb back when drunk, so he had finally given in and made his way to bed. But not before first stepping into the courtyard to see a light still burning in the workshop.

He knew if he went and asked her to come to his bed she would do so. Not because she wanted to, but because he was master of this house, newly returned, and she considered herself his servant and would do whatever he asked.

Thomas knew he would never make that short journey. He could never force himself on her.

Except her scent! It enfolded him where it had seeped into the bedclothes, weaving a magic spell on his body.

Eventually he flung the covers aside and descended the staircase, but only as far as his robe. He plucked it from the hook beside the door and carried it into the kitchen, curled beneath it, the hard stone floor somehow comforting in its reminder of the hardships he had endured while he was away. In the morning he would change the bedclothes and get Lubna to wash the old ones. He knew he should have thought of it before. And despite the cold stone and hardness beneath him sleep came like a thunderclap, rolling over him with sudden darkness.

Thomas worked his way down and across the hill, some alleys taking him in the direction he wanted, others proving almost deliberately obstructive. Da'ud al-Baitar maintained his house and work rooms on the western edge of the Albayzin where the precipitous hill gave way to the flat valley floor. From there he was able to treat both rich merchants and the poorer inhabitants to the east. It was also the way Thomas lived, although he had to wonder how many of his regular patients had deserted him while he had been away. He should have asked Lubna the question last night instead of letting his weariness get the better of him. But he knew there would be enough of the rich kind still wanting his skills, if only because he was known as physician to al-Hamra. Or had been, at least. Perhaps sending him away to treat the Spanish prince would have more subtle repercussions than he had considered.

Da'ud was treating a patient when Thomas arrived. He sat to one side, watching the older man's gentleness and patience. It was a trait Thomas envied even as he knew it was not his way. He was aware of the name people called him—*qassab*, butcher—and why. He would rather be effective and called a butcher than allow people to die or suffer without need, even if they rarely thanked him afterward.

Da'ud's assistant, a young boy, ushered the patient out.

"Hold onto the next until I'm finished here," Da'ud said, and the boy nodded. Thomas had passed a small crowd gathered outside the house, walking straight past them despite the mutters of protest.

"Did she come to you?" Thomas had no time for subtlety, assuming Da'ud would know what he meant, because it was all that filled his own mind. And indeed Da'ud did know.

"She came to me after Lubna refused her."

"Did you offer help?"

Da'ud cast a glance that required no further comment.

"Who did she go to after you?"

"What good will it do now? Nobody would treat her. Nobody."

"She would have found somebody if she kept trying."

"You don't understand, do you."

"I understand Helena. Men have difficulty refusing her anything."

"Not when the alternative is you finding out they helped kill your child."

Thomas gave a harsh laugh. "*If* the child is mine."

"You doubt it?"

It was Thomas's turn to speak with a mere glance.

"I believe it is," said Da'ud, who Thomas knew was

always too willing to believe the best in any situation. "Which is why she wanted it taken away. Why nobody would help her."

"But she still tried, I wager."

"No doubt. There are other ways of killing a child in the womb, and I expect she tried whatever she could. Obviously none of them worked."

"Have you examined her since?"

"As if she would allow me, a friend of yours."

Thomas grunted. "Did the dead man get taken care of?"

"He was buried before sunset. His wife attended. I assume the children couldn't make the time."

"Did you attend as well?"

Da'ud shook his head. His fingers arranged the instruments of his trade on a small wooden table.

"Did you discover anything else when you prepared the body?" Thomas asked.

"I didn't look. Was I supposed to?"

"I would have lifted the skull to see what damage was done to the brain."

"But I'm not you."

"Whoever did this has skill," Thomas said. "Would you have been as precise? I'm not sure I could have done it so well, not to require a single thrust of the blade. A narrow blade at that. The heart must have stopped at once, which is why there was so little bleeding."

"I believe you could have achieved it," said Da'ud.

"Not me."

"Hmm." Thomas pushed himself away from the bench he had been perched against. "If you hear anything more, or something occurs to you, send for me. I might question the wife again. Perhaps find out where her children live and talk to them as well."

"If you must." Da'ud glanced toward the open doorway. "I don't suppose you could stay a while and help, could you? There must be a score or more out there."

Thomas followed Da'ud's gaze. He was minded to refuse, but then remembered what the man had done for him, the small kindnesses over many years, not the least of which was friendship.

"I can give you an hour."

Da'ud laughed. "By the gods, man, an hour of your time and they'll all be cured."

But that wasn't true. As the last of the patients left and Thomas prepared to make his own departure closer to two hours had passed. He embraced Da'ud and thanked him. The work had distracted his mind, reminding him of what his true profession was, and as he climbed the hill to the palace he believed he might be able to put aside thoughts of the murdered man after all. No doubt Da'ud was right, it was a mystery that would never be solved. Worrying about such things only distracted him from more pressing matters, and there were enough of those even though he had barely been in Gharnatah a day.

CHAPTER 6

The house lay empty, sterile, its simple beauty untouched by any human spirit. As Thomas stood in the large room looking across the Vega he wondered how the space would differ if it was he and Lubna lived here instead. There would be flowers in vases, small objects on shelves and tables. There would be books—many books—and the scent of cooking. The smell of herbs from the space at the rear he had already marked out as suitable for a workshop and consulting room. In place of that the house was tainted by sparsity. The only personal note was Helena's scent, sultry, redolent of female sensuality. Thomas wondered what would have happened had he been detained in Qurtuba another month or two. The child, he was sure, would have been born and spirited away. He would have known nothing of it.

Thomas straightened his shoulders. Even if the child Helena carried was not his he felt a sense of duty, merely because it *could* be.

He turned and strode out along the wide roadway, nodding to the guards, who returned the gesture. As he passed through an inner courtyard he saw once again the masons and plasterers working and made a mental note to seek one out later, if he could find the time.

Jorge was absent from all the places he might normally be found and Thomas steeled himself and entered the redolent kitchen, alive with bustle and smells. Bazzu saw him in the doorway and sat back, crossing her arms across her ample bosom. She said nothing, waiting for him to speak first.

"I'm looking for Jorge. Or Helena."

"I doubt you'll find them together."

"One of them would be a start." Thomas's reply was sharper than he intended, but he was growing tired of tiptoeing around the woman. He had been fond of Prea too, and it wasn't as if it had been him who struck the blow that killed her.

"Helena will be easier. I understand Aixa sent for Jorge."

"Without me? Why?"

Bazzu offered a smile that lacked warmth. "Because it is his job to go to her whenever she asks. I expect she requires amusement of one form or another, and clever as everyone tells me you are, Thomas Berrington, you lack those particular skills she requires at this moment."

"Helena then. Do you know where she is?"

"With her new friend, I expect."

"Eve."

"Eva." Bazzu studied Thomas for a moment, her silence stretching on while behind him pots clashed, water splashed, and washes of heat touched him as ovens were opened and closed. "They are inseparable since she came to the palace. Perhaps Helena sees something of you in her."

"Something of me?"

"Is the child yours?" asked Bazzu, a genuine curiosity in her eyes—or perhaps it was merely disbelief.

"I believe it is."

"You *believe* it is? You're not sure, not certain, but you believe?"

"You know what Helena's like."

"They're in the courtyard of lions." Bazzu dismissed him, turning her gaze to the papers spread on the wide table before her.

There were real lions somewhere close to the palace, prowling iron-barred cages. They had been carried across the narrow sea from Africa together with other exotic creatures, but the lions that prowled the courtyard were fashioned of marble, their almost amused expressions facing outward from a round, water-filled bowl supported on their backs. The sun cutting across the midline of the courtyard offered only a little warmth, but enough to bring people out. On the far side sat a number of women, ladies of the harem, their servants, and others from beyond in the Alkazaba, like Helena, although she too had once been a valued member of the court.

Thomas slowed, hidden by shadows, his eyes scanning the group until he found them. Helena's blonde hair was unmistakeable, Eva almost the opposite. He started across toward where the pair sat on a bench, cushions softening the stone. The last time Thomas was in the courtyard the air had been filled with the squealing cries of swallows and martins, but they had all flown south now and the air above his head was a sharp, clear blue.

It was Helena who caught sight of him first. She rose as quickly as she could and bustled through to an inner chamber where she knew Thomas couldn't follow. Eva remained on the bench. As he approached she patted the vacated cushion beside her.

"She will soften as her time gets closer." As it had when Thomas first met her, something about her accent nagged at a memory. "She knows she might need you."

Thomas considered remaining on his feet, then relented. It appeared this woman was now closer to Helena than anyone, and he might have need of her help.

"She won't call for me. Birthing is the work of midwives, and the best and most experienced reside within the palace walls."

"I hear you saved a Sultan's son with your skill."

Thomas studied Eva's face, the stark beauty, her dark eyes bright with intelligence. She sat upright, her chin raised so her gaze fell against his. Beneath her robe he was aware of masked curves. She was of the harem, so of course she possessed beauty beyond beauty.

"I can't imagine you heard that from Helena."

Eva smiled. "She mentions you hardly at all. In fact, until you came into her house yesterday I had no idea you and she had once lived together as man and wife."

"Hardly man and wife. But if Helena has said nothing, how do you know of me?"

"You are famous in the harem, Thomas. Best friend to Jorge, the favoured eunuch of Aixa and many others.

And you *are* the man who saved the Sultan's son, aren't you?"

"Why would you even want to ask about me?"

Eva laughed in delight, clapping her hands together. "Do you not hear it when I speak to you, Thomas Berrington?"

He shook his head. "I hear something, but you're not from England."

"But close, so very close."

He stared at her. Black hair. Pale skin. Dark eyes. The lilt buried deep in her voice, masked by the Arabic they spoke but, as in his own voice, never completely obscured. And the brooches that decorated her shoulder and hair, fashioned of gold, fashioned also in a form he now saw more clearly as he studied them.

"Irish, Scots or Welsh," he said.

Once again Eva clapped her hands, leaning forward now as if they had become co-conspirators.

"But which, Thomas? Which of those races am I?"

"Say something in your native tongue." He knew the conversation was meaningless, a distraction from the reason he came to the hill, but her presence cheered him, distracted a mind in sore need of distraction.

"If I do that you will know at once."

This time Thomas laughed. "You overestimate my ability with tongues, let alone my memory."

"*Yna yr wyf yn blentyn o cymru*, Thomas."

And he laughed even harder because, although the sense of the words was beyond him, their cadence was not.

"Where in Wales?"

"I am of Brycheiniog." And now, when she spoke

in English, her accent was stronger. "Not so far from where you were born."

Thomas sat up, aware he had been leaning toward her, aware her scent had coiled itself around him. The curve of her pale neck, revealed where her hair was raised on one side, was exquisite. "You know far too much of me, and I hardly anything of you."

"Countrymen must stick together, is that not right?" Her hand reached out, hesitated, then her fingertips touched his wrist and remained there.

"Wales and England were at war when I left," Thomas said.

Eva laughed. "Wales and England are always at war, but at least we worship the same God. Is that what brought you to this heathen land, a crusade, like the one that brought me?"

Thomas shook his head. "Not a crusade, but war, certainly." And even as he spoke he wondered why he was telling this woman anything at all. Unless it was because she was close to Helena, and a friend with that degree of access might prove useful. Even as the thought came to him he knew he had to take care. Eva had already shown far too much interest in him. Was starting to show a different kind of interest. Thomas knew in comparison to Jorge he was ignorant of women, but even he could see the way Eva was trying to entice him. Why was another matter.

"We must sit and talk about our shared past," said Eva. "I would enjoy that very much, if you can make the time for a mere woman of the harem."

"I have much that keeps me busy," Thomas said, and watched as Eva gave a perfect moue of teasing disappointment. "But I would be grateful if you kept a watch on Helena, and come to me if she shows any sign of illness. I would like to examine her but know she won't allow that."

Once again Eva's fingers touched his wrist. "I will talk with her. She can be stubborn, I know, but she isn't stupid. I will see if I can persuade her to allow it."

"Thank you." Thomas knew it was his chance to move away, but instead he stayed where he was, half-mesmerised by this woman. He might have remained so, drawn into her web until she had fully captured him, if Jorge had not at that moment stridden into the courtyard.

Samuli's pain had worsened overnight. Thomas mixed a stronger draught than he had planned, lifted the old man's head and raised the cup to blue lips.

Samuli's eyes sought Thomas's. "I pray this is the tincture that will send me to heaven."

"Not yet, my friend. What this will do is make you stop wishing for such."

Samuli pulled a face and sipped. Thomas raised the cup until it was empty. He reached back, not looking, knowing someone would take it from him. He wiped Samuli's lips and laid his head against the pile of pillows.

"You will feel the pain ease soon. I won't leave until I know you are comfortable."

"At least I will die with a Sultan resident in the palace once more. It is right for it to be so."

Thomas saw Samuli's eyes lose focus as the opium began to take effect. He would sleep soon.

"I'll come again tonight."

Samuli closed his eyes. "When you are ready, Thomas, then so am I. The Sultan came to see me, did Jorge tell you?"

"He didn't."

"He thanked me for my service." Samuli's lips thinned in a brief smile. "I told him there was no need. Service has been my life, and I have done it for love, not duty." His words grew fainter the longer he spoke. His head twitched once, became still.

Thomas reached for his wrist and felt the pulse. Slow and steady. He rose and stretched.

"He's asleep?"

Thomas turned to find Jorge almost touching him. "Yes." And then, seeing Jorge's expression, added, "Only asleep."

"But you will end his life if he asks. I know you."

Thomas couldn't decide if there was criticism in Jorge's words or not. "Even if he doesn't ask. He may not be able to at the end, and I won't see him suffer."

"Nor me. But…" Jorge turned away. Thomas saw his shoulders stiffen.

"Who came to see him? The old Sultan?"

"Abu al-Hasan. His brother too. Both together."

"So who claims to be Sultan now?"

"The brother. Maybe for the best. Abu al-Hasan's too old and frail."

A young man came to Jorge and whispered a question to him. His eyes shifted toward Thomas, stayed on him as he finished his request.

"Tell them I'll come as soon as I'm done here."

The youth looked as if he wanted to say more, then saw the expression on Jorge's face and moved away.

"Decisions," said Jorge. "All they want of me are decisions. No wonder Samuli is worn out."

"He's not worn out, he's sick."

"Overwork can make a man sick."

"I hope not," Thomas said. "So where do they stay in the palace? Does Aixa accept al-Zagal as Sultan or not?"

"Of course not. They set up their own quarters in the buildings on the far side of the bridge. That concubine who has befriended Helena is one of al-Zagal's." Jorge scratched at his head. "The old Sultan was asking after you when he was here." He started to move away and Thomas fell into step as they negotiated the wide corridors.

"Do you think he wants revenge?"

"I doubt you feature that much in his thoughts."

"So why the interest?" They entered the courtyard to find the masons packing up their tools even though there were several hours of daylight remaining.

"He's unwell. I believe he would like you to examine him. He asked Samuli about you."

"He never took my advice when he was Sultan. I can't imagine why he would do so now."

"Because he fears the coming darkness."

Thomas glanced at Jorge, surprised at the tone in his voice. Perhaps he too was feeling his own mortality. Taking another man's life, as Jorge had done during their pursuit of Abbot Mandana, could sometimes do that, turning the focus back on your own mortality.

"I'm sure there are other physicians who would flatter him better than I."

"Exactly. No doubt that's why he was asking after you."

"Did Aixa say any more about Muhammed when you were with her?"

"She didn't want me for my commentary on politics."

"So what did she want you for?"

Jorge laughed. "I never took you as someone interested in the workings of the harem."

"I'm not, I was only asking."

"Perhaps I'll come for dinner soon and regale you and Lubna with tales of debauchery and sin, would you enjoy that?"

"Don't be stupid." An irritation sparked within Thomas. Somehow Jorge always seemed able to pick at his sensitivities.

"I would still like to come for dinner. I miss Lubna."

"That's not such a bad idea. I don't think she's too keen on my company at the moment."

"Oh Thomas, you've only been back a day. How do you manage it? One sister with child, the other after your blood, and a dead body too. It could only be you, couldn't it."

"I wished for none of these things."

"Not even when you laid with Helena? And you did lie with her, didn't you. Surely the best physician in Gharnatah knows the result of such actions."

"I laid with Helena many times when she lived in my house without any consequence. I assumed she couldn't conceive."

Jorge shook his head and laughed as they made their way into an inner courtyard where both men stopped dead. Sitting on a stone bench on the far side was the expelled Sultan, Abu al-Hasan Ali, his brother al-Zagal standing beside him resplendent in silk robes.

CHAPTER 7

"Is it him?" Abu al-Hasan Ali's voice was soft, the sound barely carrying even though the courtyard was quiet, the water running in a rill through its centre almost silent. High walls protected them from the outside world, as if the bustling city beyond didn't exist.

"There are two of them," said al-Zagal. "I've never met the men, but one is a eunuch, the other poorly dressed, so it's likely them."

Abu al-Hasan raised a hand, beckoning. "Come to me, Thomas."

Thomas remained where he was, trying to work out the consequences if he turned and fled. The last time he had seen this man they had stood on a baked hillside, and he had almost ended Thomas's life.

Running would do no good. These two had returned to fill the void in the heart of the city. They were the power now, although which one ruled was not clear. So Thomas walked slowly across the exquisite tiled floor until he stood in front of the pair. Al-Zagal, he noted, was taller than him by an inch, unusual in this country. The man's dark eyes were like those of a hawk, seeing everything, measuring its prey. His thin-lipped mouth held the trace of a sneer behind a dark beard, the ends elegantly plaited and oiled.

"Say something then, Thomas, so I know it's you."

Abu al-Hasan Ali's eyes were clouded with cataracts. He appeared to have aged more than ten years in the two since he had ruled the palace. His hair was streaked with grey, his skin sallow. The man was ill, perhaps even dying. Being usurped by a son, as Muhammed had done to him, had aged him beyond his years. Thomas didn't have to be a physician to see that. Abu al-Hasan turned his head to one side, the other, sniffing the air like a hound.

"I smell the perfumed fool, too, so don't pretend he's not with you." He patted the stone beside him. His hand shook, a faint tremor running through his entire body. "Sit, Thomas, speak with me. I will send the others away if you wish."

"Brother—"

"Thomas will do me no harm."

Life, it seemed, was already doing enough harm to the man.

"You know I will not," Thomas said, and Abu al-Hasan smiled.

"Then sit with me. You—" Abu al-Hasan turned his head toward where he guessed Jorge was standing. "Go fetch coffee and some of those sweet cakes your fat lover makes so well."

Jorge made a noise, but he turned away to do Abu al-Hasan's bidding. Thomas glanced at al-Zagal, who remained unmoving, his body relaxed but ready. He was younger than his brother—only by a few years, but to look at them now you might mistake one for the father, the other the son.

Abu al-Hasan reached out a shaking hand, searching until it grasped his brother's sleeve. "You can leave as well, I need no protection from Thomas."

"I prefer to stay," said al-Zagal.

"You make me nervous hovering around like that." For a moment the old Sultan resurfaced, his voice sharper, commanding. He patted the stone again and Thomas could think of no way to refuse the invitation.

"Do you see anything at all?" Thomas watched as al-Zagal walked across the courtyard to disappear through an arched doorway. Perhaps the man was obeying his brother after all.

"I see light and dark and shape."

"I can fix your eyes, if you will let me. The palsy has no cure I know of."

Abu al-Hasan patted Thomas's leg. He left his hand there afterward, an uncomfortable familiarity. "You see much, don't you. It is why I wanted to talk with you. But I will not risk what little sight I retain. I thank you for the offer, but no."

Thomas knew Abu al-Hasan would see barely anything. The cataracts had developed quickly, clouding both eyes almost white. "It's a simple procedure. One I've performed a hundred times."

"Then you have no need to practice on me." The voice was sharper, and Thomas knew the mind beneath the body's infirmity remained as vigorous as when this man ruled the city. He caught movement from the edge of his vision and turned to see al-Zagal return. He set a stool down in front of them, perched on it and arranged his robes so they draped elegantly. As Thomas watched he sensed a vanity in the man he hadn't guessed at. Abu al-Hasan turned his head blindly toward his brother. "He wants to cut me."

Al-Zagal's hand went to his waist where a dagger waited, and hearing the move Abu al-Hasan laughed softly.

"He doesn't have to suffer from this blindness," Thomas said.

"It is only my eyes that are blind, old friend." Finally, he took his hand from Thomas's thigh, but it was a slow move redolent of a sensuality that brought a sense of unease. "Now tell me of my son. I understand you have seen him."

He might have been asking after Yusuf, but Thomas knew better. "Only briefly… Malik." Thomas hesitated before using the honorific normally due a Sultan. Had the old man usurped Muhammed's position yet? Did he even wish to? Whatever his plans he made no correction. "He was accommodated outside Qurtuba for most of the time I was there."

"Healing a prince, I hear. Why did you do that—help one of them?"

"I was asked."

"By my son, I know. Who then undertook a foolhardy raid and managed to get himself captured." Thomas tried to tease some emotion from beneath the flat words, knowing there was little love lost between father and son.

Thomas glanced at al-Zagal. He leaned forward, listening, keeping his own counsel for now. At least he had removed his hand from the dagger. Did he want to be Sultan himself, Thomas wondered. And if he did, would the city accept him? Would Aixa? Al-Zagal had ruled in Ronda for a decade and was known as a strong leader, a good general. Perhaps Gharnatah would welcome one such as him in place of Muhammed, who was not loved. And as for his military skills...getting himself captured seemed all the measure needed.

"I understand you have spoken with my wife," said Abu al-Hasan.

"I saw Aixa, if that's who you mean. You are a fortunate man and have many wives, Malik."

This elicited a chuckle. "I hear you have two yourself now."

Thomas shook his head, then realised Abu al-Hasan couldn't see him. He chose to offer no correction. Nobody believed him whatever he said.

Soft voices sounded from a corridor and a moment later three women appeared. Between them they carried a tray of ornate glasses encased in silver cages, a pot of steaming coffee and a smaller tray of tiny cakes. Of Jorge there was no sign. Thomas made a note to have a word with him about his cowardice later on. The women found a low table and proceeded to lay out the treats, ignoring the attentions of al-Zagal, who fondled the buttocks of one. Her stoic acceptance told Thomas more of the new hierarchy within the palace than any words so far spoken. He was growing tired of skirting around a subject each of them was well aware of. Two of the women left, the third poured coffee into three glasses and went to stand against the wall, eyes downcast.

Abu al-Hasan leaned forward and breathed in the sharp aroma. Al-Zagal picked up a cake, reached across and turned his brother's hand over before placing the sweet treat on his palm.

"Help yourself, Thomas," Abu al-Hasan said.

"What is it you want of me? I hear you have been looking for me since my return."

"How do you know it is not merely for the pleasure of your company?"

Thomas didn't bother with a reply, instead lifting one of the glasses and sipping at the dark liquid. It burned his mouth both with its heat and strength, and almost immediately he felt a kick as caffeine entered his bloodstream.

"We should get on with it." They were the first words spoken by al-Zagal. His voice was rough, dry as the desert sands beyond the sea which it was claimed were his preferred location, even though he had been born in the palace they sat in.

"My brother lacks the niceties of court, Thomas. Please forgive him."

"Your brother spends his life at war," said al-Zagal.

"As do I, at your side and on my own behalf." Abu al-Hasan finally popped the cake into his mouth, smiling at the sweetness of it. He reached out a trembling hand, waiting for a second, and after a moment his brother obliged. A small show of status, meant as a demonstration. "Is Muhammed to be released soon? This year or not?"

"I'm not privy to the negotiations," Thomas said.

Abu al-Hasan smiled. "That is not what I heard. My spies tell me you grew close to the Spanish king and queen. The queen especially. Some might say too close. Is she a beauty, then?"

"She is the Queen of Spain," Thomas said. "And yes, we grew close while I tended her son, but it was a friendship, nothing more. She was a concerned mother and I his physician."

Abu al-Hasan smiled. "Still the same Thomas, I see. Unable to let loose the ties of morality. Perhaps it is because you are not of this place. Is it true you have planted a seed inside Helena?"

"I do appear to have done so."

"Then my gift of her to you has borne fruit." He lifted his hand and popped the second tiny cake into his mouth. For a moment his expression showed pleasure, eyes closing, then his face changed as though someone had pulled tight all the muscles from within. "My wife has spoken with you and wishes her son returned. I believe she has asked you to help in the matter." Abu al-Hasan leaned closer, the scent of lavender and honey on his breath when next he spoke. "I do not wish those negotiations to succeed. I believe you would also prefer Muhammed to remain a guest of the Spanish. I am an old man now and cannot rule here again in anything other than name, but my brother is strong, a hard man, and between us we will bring Gharnatah back from the brink of defeat. You understand this, I am sure."

"I do not involve myself in politics," Thomas said.

"But politics always seems to involve itself with you, does it not. And you are neck deep in this matter, because you are the means of communication between both sides."

"Others will conduct the negotiations."

Abu al-Hasan barked a laugh, animated now, energised by the return of intrigue and the play of power.

"So they believe. What I believe is the matter will be settled among friends."

"Then you know more than I do."

"Which is as it should be." Abu al-Hasan once more reached out, his hand fumbling, catching Thomas's cloak before finding his wrist. The fingers that curled around were surprisingly strong. "Do not think you can play some game with me. There is time still to save what has been built here, but only if people do as they are told, only if people *obey*. Do not question me. Do not doubt me. I intend to save Gharnatah, and will sacrifice whatever and whoever I must to achieve this."

"Even your son?"

"Particularly my son."

Helena saw Thomas as he left the courtyard and held back.

"Are you unwell?" Eva's hand rested against the small of her back. A comfort and possible promise.

"I don't want him to see me." Helena felt Eva's breast against her side. "I don't want him to ever see me again."

"Why do you hate him so?"

"Because he made me the way I am. No man wants me in this state." Helena watched Thomas disappear. He walked tall, his steps long and easy, as if he hadn't a care in the world. Unlike her. She waited a moment longer until she was sure he was gone before starting across to the Alkazaba and home.

Once inside she went immediately to the stack of cushions in the main room and lay down. She rested her hand on her belly and pulled a face as the baby inside moved. It moved often now, and the sense of another life living within her disgusted Helena.

"Do your legs ache?" Eva knelt at her feet and put her hands around Helena's ankles. She began to knead them, the attention soothing.

"He's kicking again."

Eva raised her eyes to stare at Helena's belly. "It won't be long now."

"It can't come soon enough for me." She broke off, grunting as the baby kicked harder. Eva raised her hands and rested them on the shape that showed clearly through the silk of Helena's robe, as if her touch might soothe the hidden infant.

"Is Thomas the father?"

"More than likely."

"But possibly not?"

"There were others. Muhammed for one, a week after Thomas left. But it is probably Thomas's. Only he would put me through this." She watched Eva's hands on her belly. The child within had stilled, but Eva's touch offered continued comfort. She made no move to withdraw and Helena did not want her to.

"What will you do when the baby comes?" asked Eva. "Babies are so perfect, so innocent."

"Have you ever birthed one?" Helena was curious. She had seen Eva naked and her figure was so sublime she couldn't imagine her ever going through what she now suffered.

"I believe I cannot conceive. I have heard it can happen when a woman is taken too young and too harshly."

Helena sat up a little. "Who did that to you?"

Eva laughed, moved to sit beside Helena, returned

her hand to her belly and began to stroke it. "How did you enter the harem? Was it by force or willingly?"

"It was all I ever wanted. I was made to serve this place, these people."

"And I was not."

"Tell me," said Helena.

"Why? It was a long time ago and I have since learned to love what I do, as have you."

"Tell me because I love you. Tell me because I wish to know it. I wish to know everything there is to know about you."

Eva smiled, her hand continuing to soothe. "My father was a surgeon, too, I never told you that."

"Like Thomas's?" Helena shifted away so Eva's hand no longer touched her. "Why did you not say so before?"

"He wasn't anything like Thomas. My father was a butcher–"

"They call Thomas that, too."

"I have heard. But not in the same way. My father was a poor excuse for a doctor. He brought me with him to this land as a nurse, even though I was barely fourteen years of age."

"What brought him here?"

"A crusade. He had been to Jerusalem when young. I believe he developed a blood-lust that would not allow him to rest. He came to Spain seeking to expel the infidel Moor…" Eva laughed, the sound bright. "And made me a gift to those he fought after they killed him."

"Where?"

Eva shook her head. The movement dislodged the brooch holding her hair in place and she snatched out to catch it as it fell, her hair falling too. "It doesn't matter. Besides, I don't know where. Al-Zagal found me cowering among the dead. I think he planned to kill me too, then he saw I was a girl. He had me washed and brought to him."

"He broke you?" Helena asked.

"I wasn't a virgin, not even then. I liked soldiers. Liked the feel of them between my legs. But sometimes they had a different kind of lust on them." Eva sucked at her fingers. She held it out and smiled. "A blood lust." The pin on her brooch had broken the skin. She gathered her dark hair and twisted it around on one side, caught it with the brooch and expertly clipped it together.

"Does it hurt?"

"No, of course not."

"Did it hurt? Did men hurt you?"

"Have you never been hurt? You know what they are like. All of them."

"I was going to be hurt once, but–" Helena broke off. She was unwilling to tell Eva it was Thomas who had saved her on that occasion. "But no, I have never been hurt. Like you I like sex."

"Women are better than men," said Eva, and Helena nodded. "Once the baby comes and you are recovered, we can share a bed again like we used to."

"I want you to do something for me," said Helena. "When the baby comes."

"If I can, of course."

"I want you to take it away and kill it. Throw it from the palace walls. Drown it in the Hadarro. Whatever it takes. I don't want a child and I don't want Thomas to have one either."

CHAPTER 8

Thomas found himself descending the hill in the company of one of the masons, a short bow-legged man who carried his tools in a sac hanging from a shoulder. The tools inside jingled together as he walked.

"You finished early today," Thomas said, trying to distract his own mind from the conversation he had endured with Abu al-Hasan Ali.

"I know you, you're Thomas Berrington," said the man.

Not again, Thomas thought. *Is there no-one in this city who doesn't know who I am, and what I've done?*

"You have the advantage of me."

The man glanced across, dark eyes set above dense curly black hair. "I doubt that. But my name is Britto. And I've no work for a few days because they're filling in a fresh run of tunnels." His eyes remained locked on Thomas. "I believe you know all about the tunnels."

And because there was no point in pretence, Thomas said, "You know I do."

The man nodded. "You did well."

"I did what I had to."

"I hear you attended Vincenzo Alvarez yesterday."

"Does the entire city know my business?"

"Not the entire city," said Britto. "But Alvarez was…" He hesitated, once more glancing at Thomas. "How did he die?"

"Why the interest? Was he a friend of yours?"

"He was friend to no decent man." Britto sucked in his cheeks then spat into the dirt.

"How do you know him then?"

"Worked for him once. Never again."

Thomas found his steps slowing. Britto matched his stride until they came to a halt beneath a ragged pine tree. Its cones covered the ground beneath their feet, the scent of sap rising sharp in the air.

"Why do you speak as you do—what do you know of the man?"

Britto sighed and swung his pack from his shoulder, dropped it to the earth with a clang of metal on metal. He pushed fingers through his hair but it made no difference.

"I know it's not good to speak ill of the dead, but Alvarez… Well, the things he did were beyond humanity."

"Tell me what he did."

"So he was killed?" said Britto. "Good. I hope whoever did it is never caught. Could've been his wife, I suppose, but I always thought she knew and did nothing, which is almost as bad as the deed itself."

"Tell me what he did," Thomas said again.

Britto turned his gaze across the city's tiled roofs. "I'm thirsty. I could do with a cup of wine. Maybe more than one. Wine loosens tongues, you know."

"Yes, I do know. Al-Hattabin square?"

Britto shook his head. "Too civilised for one such as me. But I know a place if you don't mind drinking with commoners."

"What makes you think I'm not one myself?"

Britto laughed and picked up his pack.

Light had drained from the sky by the time Thomas arrived home. Lubna was out, so he walked into the workshop. It was the first chance to immerse himself in its familiarity since his return. He breathed deep, the smell of poppy and hashish and alcohol thick in the air. Except the alcohol might be coming from him. At least Britto had drunk almost twice as much, and despite his promises Thomas doubted he would see the man much before noon tomorrow.

He turned slowly, taking in the shelves containing jars and bottles and packets of seeds, roots, flowers, others stacked with papers. A thick book sat open on the table in the centre of the room. He imagined Lubna bent over it, her face a mask of concentration. He closed it around his finger and checked the title. It was al-Muntakhab's tome on the eye, and he wondered if Lubna knew of someone with cataracts, or was reading for the sake of it. He doubted she did anything just for the sake of it.

He laid it back and let it open where it had been before, walked out the far door into the small garden where he grew essential herbs. The cultivated land sloped, terraced down the hillside. Thomas glanced up at the back wall of the workshop, sideways to where the wall merged into that of the courtyard.

He would have to sacrifice something of each, he reckoned, but Britto would be better able to judge such matters.

When he went inside Lubna had returned. There was meat on the table and she stood with her back to him, preparing vegetables. She turned and smiled, the simple gesture softening something inside he hadn't known was hard.

"Have you eaten?" asked Lubna. "I can smell you've been drinking, but shall I cook something for you?"

"If you can remember how to cook for two."

She grinned, white teeth against dark lips. "How do you know I haven't been cooking for two all the time you've been away?"

Thomas pulled out a chair and sat. "Then both my women have given up on me. My own fault, I suppose."

"Except I'm not your woman." Lubna spoke without turning, her hands peeling and cutting. A pan sat above the fire waiting for the meat.

"I've a man coming tomorrow to see about enlarging the house."

Now she did stop, turning to face him fully, wiping her hands on a cloth tucked at her waist. "Why?"

"Because I don't want you sleeping on the cot in the workshop whenever I'm here."

"I don't mind. I'm small, and it's not too uncomfortable."

"Let me do this," Thomas said. "Please."

Lubna offered a brief nod. "If you wish. Just know it's not for me you do it. But if it makes you feel better then go ahead. What man?"

"One whose parents lacked in originality. A Breton by the name of Britto." Thomas smiled.

"We're all immigrants in this land, aren't we?" said Lubna.

"Not all. You were born in the city."

"But my father comes from the far north. My mother from the south." Lubna crossed her ankles and leaned against the bench. "Did you see Helena today?"

"Briefly. I would like to examine her but she won't let me. Perhaps you should offer."

Lubna snorted a laugh. "She refuses to believe I have any skill. She won't let me touch her. Does she look well?"

"Well enough, but I'd rather be sure." He didn't need to say more. They were both aware Helena's mother had died giving birth to her, hence Olaf taking a wife from across the water, who had borne him only a single child, the woman who stood across from Thomas now.

"She'll have her own physician somewhere. I'll make enquiries, see if I can find out who it is. Whether it's someone you trust." She smiled. "If you trust anyone."

"I trust Da'ud, and I trust you. The rest..." Thomas spread his hands. "I see you've been studying."

"I was looking in the al-Muntakhab because a patient called. I'd like you to examine him."

"Cataracts?"

"He can barely see the hand in front of his face. If you hadn't returned I was going to send him to Da'ud, but he's not so good with eyes."

"You could perform the procedure yourself, it's not difficult."

"As if he'd trust a woman."

"Do we still have some of the liquor we devised?"

"A little. I can make more if you need. You could have someone else make it if you'd write down how to do so." She cocked her head to one side. "How did it work on the prince? Was it effective?"

"Better than I could have dreamed. I think we might have created something that will allow us to operate without killing half our patients from the pain."

"Then write it up, so the secret's not lost." Lubna shook her head, and Thomas could see her frustration.

"I will once my head stops spinning."

"I'm sorry, you're right." Lubna started to turn away before a wicked grin crossed her face. "Although perhaps your head spins from the wine you've been drinking."

Thomas went to wash and change out of his sweat-stained robes. When he came downstairs Lubna was putting food on the table.

"Britto told me something else, too."

"About this house?"

Thomas cut a slice of meat with his knife, speared it and chewed. It was tough, but edible, and Lubna had done what she could to tenderise it.

"About the man who died yesterday. About his secrets."

"Secrets that might have killed him? I take it his death wasn't natural, otherwise you wouldn't still be talking about him."

"I came home drunk because it required a large quantity of wine to loosen Britto's tongue so I could prise the full tale from him. It's not a pretty story." Thomas pushed his plate away, no longer hungry. "The man liked children. Boys or girls. The younger the better."

Lubna pulled a face and put her own knife down.

"Sorry," Thomas said.

"Did his wife know?"

"I don't see how she couldn't. Britto..." Thomas stopped, shook his head as if the depths people could sink to were beyond him. "Britto said his own children too. They have two girls and a boy. Grown now, with their own families."

"Do you think they might have killed him?" said Lubna.

"I don't know. Perhaps. Perhaps not."

"But you say his wife knew about him."

"How could she not, something like that?"

"A man can buy anything in this city. In any city. Whatever he might want there is always someone willing to turn a profit. And you know as well as I, boys and girls sell themselves so they can eat, put a roof over their head."

"Not as young as this Alvarez man liked them," Thomas said.

Lubna pulled a face, picked up her knife and speared a slice of artichoke. After a moment Thomas drew his plate toward him and continued to eat. Neither of them spoke again until they were finished. Lubna rose and leaned across for Thomas's plate.

He reached out and gripped her wrist, not sure why he did so.

"I should have taken you with me," he said. "I missed you."

"I missed you as well." Lubna smiled. "The house was too quiet, and nothing at all dangerous happened."

"Do I have any patients left?" His hand still circled

Lubna's wrist, but loosely, allowing her to pull away if she wished.

"You'll be pleased to hear I haven't killed a single one. But most of them weren't keen on a woman treating them and went elsewhere. Word must have gotten around you're back because there were ten people waiting this morning. I had to disappoint them."

"Including the man with the bad eyes?"

"Yes, including him. I told them to come back tomorrow."

"Tomorrow they will be praying. As will you."

"They'll be praying you can help them. And I won't pray all day, I promise." Still she remained where she was, captured by his touch, and Thomas stared at where his hand circled the copper skin of her arm. He wanted to tighten his grip and pull her toward him, and because it was what he wanted, he opened his fingers and let her loose.

CHAPTER 9

Thomas woke from nothing to fear, scrabbling across the bed in search of a weapon as a deep dread exploded within. It was dark, the middle of the night, and someone was breaking the door down. Except none of it was true. When he opened his eyes sunlight streamed through the small window and Lubna was leaning over him, an expression of amusement on her face.

"What–" Thomas washed a hand across his face, blinked several times. His mouth was dry and his head ached.

"That mason is downstairs."

"What time is it?"

"An hour since dawn."

"Why did he come so early?"

"When did he say he was coming?"

Thomas sat up, then remembered he was naked beneath the sheet and pulled it back around himself. "He didn't."

"So he hasn't come early or late, has he. I'll let you get dressed." Lubna reached the door, turned back with a grin. "Although there's nothing I haven't seen before."

Thomas didn't know what she meant. Then it came to him, of how Lubna had nursed him back to health after he was injured in the fight with the palace killer almost two years before.

When he came downstairs Britto was standing in the courtyard surveying the arched wall, beyond which the bulwark of the palace could be seen. He turned at the sound of Thomas's boots on stone slabs.

"You have a nice house."

"I'm hoping you can make it nicer still."

"Depends. What do you want doing?"

"Through here." Thomas led the way into the workshop, watched Britto's expression as he surveyed the ranks of bottles and phials, the herbs hanging from hooks to dry, the instruments fashioned for him by expert glass-blowers, other items, some of which resembled instruments of torture more than healing. The air within was fragranced with a hundred different scents.

"I need at least another bedroom fashioned in some way. Two if it can be done."

Britto looked up into the rafters. "Not enough room here, unless you're willing to lose some of the space below."

Thomas shook his head. "There's a piece of land outside." He crossed to a small door and opened it. "I wondered if I could sacrifice some of this—a little of the courtyard too if necessary."

"Shame to spoil the courtyard, it's one of the best features. Is that woman your wife or servant?"

"She's my assistant."

Britto nodded. "Is the extra room for her?"

It was Thomas's turn to nod.

"You must think a lot of her to spend this amount of money."

"Will it be a lot of money?"

Britto smiled. "Having a change of mind?"

"No. But it would be useful to know how much."

"Don't know yet." Britto surveyed the garden. "Who built these terraces? You?"

"Are they bad?"

"They're not good."

"But they do the job."

"For now. I'll rebuild them for you, then they'll last forever."

"Forever's a long time."

"Until this city falls then."

Thomas laughed. He saw from the expression on Britto's face the man had been joking, and said, "The ones I built will last that long."

"True." Britto put his fists into his back and stared up at the side of the house, the roofline. "We'll take the roof off, raise the walls, add two more rooms up there. What about downstairs? Do you want more space there as well?"

"Downstairs is fine."

"A man of your stature should have an impressive house."

"I already have an impressive house."

"Yes, I heard that. So why do you live here? Take your woman onto the hill and set yourselves up there."

"Someone already lives there."

"The courtesan. I hear she's carrying your baby." Britto looked Thomas up and down as if he failed to understand how someone such as him could be so fortunate as to have two households and two women as beautiful as Helena and Lubna. "Sisters, too."

"Two more rooms will be fine," Thomas said.

Britto shrugged, happy for the work.

"When can you start? And how much?"

Britto pursed his lips. "I'll need to look inside, but we might be able to start in two or three weeks. They want us to fill in more tunnels soon, and that's going to take time. If they call me back after we start I'll have to go, you understand, but I can do a lot here before they need me again. Will you be moving out?"

"Do we have to?"

"It'll be easier if the house is empty. The workshop, too."

Thomas experienced a sinking feeling. He hadn't considered he would need to move anything. "That's not possible. You'll have to work around us, and the workshop, there's too much in there to move."

"It'll take longer, cost more."

"I expected it would."

"Let me take a look around upstairs. I can give you an idea of how much before I leave."

Thomas let him go ahead, stood for a moment in the cold December sunshine. He stared beyond al-Hamra to where snow that had crept even lower down the slopes of the distant Sholayr. Took a deep breath, let it go, tried to force the tension from his shoulders.

"Patients are starting to arrive."

Thomas turned at Lubna's words. "How many?"

"Ten, twelve."

"Including the man with cataracts?"

She nodded. A breeze came up, caught at her cotton

robe and wrapped it around her slim body, accentuating curves he had only imagined, a reminder she was Helena's sister and shared some of her attributes.

"Keep him until last, I'll deal with the others first."

"I can treat some of them. They will have aches and pains and little more."

"Do it, then. I'll deal with the ones you pass on." He started up the slope of the garden, negotiating steps he had laid himself many years before. The stones moved beneath his feet, and he knew he would let Britto rebuild them too.

"Are you going to use that man?" Lubna asked when he reached her.

"I am. He'll make a bedroom for you, another if he can fit one in."

"I told you I'm happy where I am."

"There'll be disruption while the work is carried out, it might be difficult."

Lubna smiled. "That's all right. I'm used to difficult."

CHAPTER 10

Thomas heard Britto upstairs, muttering to himself and banging on walls, as the first patient entered the workshop. It was a young woman who leaned close to Lubna, talking quietly. After a moment Lubna glanced across and nodded to indicate this was something she would deal with. Thomas rose and looked out through the door. Lubna's estimate of ten or twelve had grown to fifteen. Thomas called the closest forward and sat him on a stool.

"Tell me," he said, staring at the man.

"My throat is bad. Like I have sand trapped there which I cannot shift."

Thomas leaned close, grabbing the man as he leaned back. "Open your mouth."

As the man obliged Thomas used a wooden splint to depress his tongue. He took the man's chin and turned his head into a shaft of sunlight falling through the courtyard door.

"Make a noise."

The man gargled some sound.

"Again."

Once more he obliged.

"Does it hurt when you do that?"

"A little."

"Hmm." Thomas had seen little other than inflammation to cause the discomfort, and no particular reason for that. "Wait here," he said, and went to his workbench. He took down a bottle of mulberry syrup, the same of walnut. He poured twice as much of one as the other into a bowl and then flooded it with rose water. He put his hand over the top and shook the bowl briskly before pouring the mixture into a fresh bottle which he stoppered. He took the bottle back to the man.

"Take this. You must shake the bottle well before each use. Put six spoonfuls into a glass and heat it until it's too hot to bear, then allow it to cool. As soon as you can, take it in your mouth, gargle and spit it out. Do this first thing after you rise and last thing before you retire until it is all gone. If you see no improvement come back, but I don't expect to see you again. Can you remember all of that or do I need to write it down?"

"I don't read, but I'll remember. How much do I owe?"

Thomas had already judged the man's appearance and wealth. "Four marvedis," he said.

"For a tiny bottle like this?"

"The bottle costs nothing. The four marvels is for my skill in diagnosis and the years I spent learning how best to treat you." Thomas reached out and took the bottle from the man. "Or you can try to find less expensive treatment elsewhere if you wish."

The man snatched the bottle back. "No, it only seemed expensive for such a brief examination."

"I told you, it's not the examination you're paying for, it's my experience. Now are you going to pay or not, because I have others waiting who will."

The man continued to grumble, but searched in his leather purse and took out small coins. Thomas judged them almost sufficient and let him off with the rest. Had there not been so many outside he might have demanded payment in full.

There followed a trail of men and women. Some Thomas charged, others he treated for free, each weighed and judged according to their degree of need and his estimate of their wealth. The group thinned until only five remained.

There was a rapping at the door and Thomas turned to see Britto outside in the courtyard. He indicated for him to come in but the mason shook his head, perhaps afraid to enter the workshop in case he contracted some sickness from one of the patients.

Thomas sighed and rose from his stool, walked into the courtyard, which was growing a little warmer as the sun rose toward noon.

"So, can you do it?"

"I can."

"And can I afford it?"

"I hear you're a rich man, Thomas Berrington, but I won't hold that against you. I'll charge a fair price and I won't try to trick you like many in my profession would."

"How much?" Thomas asked.

"Four zahene."

Almost fifteen hundred marvedis. Thomas had no idea if the price was fair or not, but something about

Britto made him trust the man. Not that it would stop him making enquiries elsewhere to check.

"When can you start?"

"As I said, two or three weeks. To be safe let's call it three. You need to clear as much upstairs as possible, and in there too, but I'll work around things if I have to."

"And what will you do for these four zahene?"

"Two new rooms upstairs as well as an extension to your workshop. You'll lose some of the roof space, but only half of it, and I'll put a gallery across so you can access the house from the new part. Having the workshop so high is a waste of space."

"How long?"

Britto shrugged. "No less than ten days, no more than fifteen. But I told you the palace might call me back, so I can't promise to finish in that time."

"Agreed. When do you want paying?"

Britto gave him an amused glance. "I think I can trust you. Pay me when I'm done. Although an advance of two hundred marvedis will let me buy the supplies I need."

"You saw the chest in the bedroom?" Thomas said.

"Of course. I had to shift it to check the floor. I didn't think it was going to move."

"Take your advance from inside it."

Britto grunted. "You trust me that far?"

"Should I not?"

"No, you can trust me, but then I'm not like most men."

"Nor am I."

"Yes, I heard that."

Thomas watched Britto cross the courtyard and disappear inside, swaying from side to side on bowed legs. He would check later, although he knew he wouldn't be able to tell if the man had cheated him or not. He had no idea how much the chest contained, only that it was almost full. He would have to store it with his others soon and buy a new one.

The next patient was a merchant complaining of a pain in his temple and a sweet taste on his tongue. Thomas could find nothing wrong other than a flush to the man's cheeks, but he suspected a surfeit of blood and opened a vein in the man's arm, letting the blood drip into a bowl. The sight brought to mind the death of Alvarez, and Thomas promised himself he would revisit the man's wife and question her, but he wanted Jorge with him when he did so.

It was almost noon before they finished with the patients. Only the man with bad eyes remained. Thomas sat him on a stool where light came through the doorway and pressed the man's head backward.

"Here." He called Lubna across. "Not cataracts as you thought. This is *sabal*. Can you see the growth coming from the side of his eye? Cataracts are different, they make the lens milky."

"I didn't know. All I have ever done is read about them in books."

"Then I need to show you." Thomas went to the bench and rummaged through a drawer until he found what he wanted, returned with a glass lens mounted in a wooden frame. He used it to see the growth more clearly.

"Does it give you any pain?" he asked.

"Not pain. More a dull ache when I am tired."

"What work do you do?"

"I'm a scribe." The man lifted his right hand and Thomas saw the fingers stained from years of using ink. "It's beginning to get difficult to read small letters."

"You're lucky you can read at all." Thomas turned his attention to the other eye, which looked normal. "I can remove the growth, but it might come back."

"How long?"

"Half a year, perhaps as long as two years, possibly never."

"I'll take two years," said the man.

From across the city a single voice sounded, clear and commanding, calling the faithful to prayer. After a moment a second came from another mosque, and soon a dozen voices competed, their cries crossing each other.

Thomas straightened and looked at Lubna. "You need to go. We can deal with this man when you return."

"I will make it up later," said Lubna, "once we are finished here."

"You can't do that. Go, it's your soul. This man will need to pray as well."

"I'm a Jew," said the man. "I pray tomorrow."

Thomas turned to the man. "You can wait, can't you?"

"What choice do I have? Can't you treat me on your own?"

"I need Lubna. The procedure is tricky without an assistant."

"How tricky? Will my sight be improved or not?"

"More likely improved, but any cutting involves risk."

"You're cutting my eye?" The man began to rise. Thomas gripped his robe and pulled him down onto the stool.

"How do you expect me to help otherwise?"

"But my work–I can't risk losing my sight."

"Which is what will happen if you don't let me treat you."

The man pulled away again. "I'll find someone else."

Thomas released his hold, allowing the man to rise. "Go then. At least Lubna can attend prayers if you do. But tell me, why did you come to me first and not someone else?"

The man looked uncomfortable, his gaze refusing to meet Thomas's.

"All right, I'll tell you why," Thomas said. "Because you asked and everyone you spoke to told you the same thing. If you want to be cured go to Thomas Berrington. They'll also have told you what they call me, didn't they–the butcher." Thomas waited until the man nodded. "But that name isn't because of my savagery but my skill." He waved a hand. "Go if you want, but don't complain when you lose the sight in the eye altogether."

The man hesitated, then retook his place on the stool. "Explain what you're going to do."

Thomas didn't have the patience. "I'm going to cure you."

Prayers were long finished. The afternoon had grown warm despite it being almost the end of the year, and the man lay comatose, stupefied by a mixture of herbs, alcohol, opium and hashish. Thomas had decided not to risk his new anesthetic liquor but to save it for a more needy patient.

Lubna had brought a complex metal apparatus that resembled nothing less than someone's fevered nightmare image of a spider, and used it to pull back the eyelids of the man. Beneath, the eye was inflamed, a sign damage had already been done by the growth, and Thomas hoped he was right and the man's sight could be restored.

A tray sat beside him with the tools he needed–small blades, hooks, cotton swabs. He glanced at Lubna, who leaned close, her hair tied back, an expression of concentration on her face.

"Ready?"

"I should be asking you."

"If he starts to come around we might need the liquor."

"It's on the side if you do," she said.

Thomas nodded. He knew at this point other surgeons would have hesitated, going over once again, if not twice, the procedure they were about to undertake. But he knew exactly what he intended, and had learned long ago that the faster he worked the less damage would be done and the less risk of infection. It was his speed, he knew, that had given him the name people called him. That and his indifference to their pain–but most of that reputation came from his work on the battlefield.

He used a sharp blade and cut at the inner fold of the eye, easing loose the milky growth that extended half way across the orb. He slipped a hook beneath the flap and drew the growth away from the cornea beneath. He shifted position, looking through the spectacles he had fashioned for himself, thick round lenses magnifying his vision. He sliced a little deeper, careful not to go too far, lifting the growth as it came away. Beneath him the man stirred and muttered, but the drugs kept him oblivious for now.

Lubna leaned closer, keen to see exactly what he was doing, and when their foreheads touched he made no move away and neither did she, both of them concentrating hard. Thomas eased the blade beneath the flap of growth, working his way inward until with a final slice it came free. He tossed it into a pot beside him, used rose water mixed with lavender to sluice the eye. One or two small areas of growth remained and he carefully removed these before applying more liquid.

He returned the instruments to the tray and sat back, pushing his fists into the base of his spine. *Age*, he thought, *I'm getting older and my body protests like it never did before.*

Thomas walked to the doorway and stepped into the courtyard, turning his face up to capture what little heat the sun offered. From behind he heard Lubna clearing the instruments away, dropping each into boiling water. Then her footsteps, dainty and soft, bare feet on solid stone as she came to stand beside him. Her shoulder touched his arm. She loosened her hair, shook her head so dark waves fell across her shoulders.

"Was that difficult?" she asked.

"Not if you know what you're doing."

"You told him there was no-one else in Gharnatah who could do it as well as you."

"Should I have lied?"

Lubna gave a short laugh. "It's good to see your stay in Qurtuba hasn't changed you, Thomas. Go inside and rest. I'll call you when he starts to wake."

"I'll sit with him."

"You don't need to. Go rest."

Thomas sighed, lethargy flooding through him. The idea was tempting, but he knew he had more to do before his day ended.

"I'll rest tonight. I want to visit the dead man's wife. Britto told me something that might help in identifying who killed him."

"Then go now. I know what to do. When he wakes I'll tell him to bathe the eye three times a day, morning, noon and night. Apply the salve you prepared. He must come back in two days' time, again in a week. And he's to return immediately if there's any abnormal pain."

Thomas smiled. "And don't forget the willow bark liquor for his discomfort."

"I won't. Although what he'll think when he wakes and finds a mere woman looking after him I don't know."

"No mere woman," Thomas muttered as he moved away, unsure if Lubna heard his words or not.

CHAPTER 11

"You come to the palace and expect me to drop whatever I'm doing and respond to your every whim," said Jorge. They had passed through the outer walls protecting the palace and now descended through pines toward the bridge over the Hadarro. Alvarez's house was on the low lying ground to the west of the twin hills of al-Hamra and Albayzin, but still inside the city walls which had been extended outward several times over the centuries.

"I'm sorry," Thomas said. "Exactly what did I interrupt?"

"Nothing. But I could have been busy. I have additional duties now Samuli is fading. And you'd still have expected me to come."

"When we get to the house I'll make an excuse to look in the man's rooms again. I want you to talk to the wife. You're better with women than me."

"That wouldn't be difficult. What is it you want me to talk about? The weather? How the war is going? The price of figs?"

They reached the bridge and crossed, ignoring the

outstretched hands of a clutch of begging children. Thomas turned left, the cobbles awkward beneath his feet.

"Britto told me something the other evening."

"Who's Britto? You have *another* friend?"

"I expect you know him, he's a mason who works at the palace. He's going to extend my house on the Albayzin. He told me–"

"I don't understand why you don't simply throw Helena out and bring Lubna to the hill. Then you wouldn't need to spend money on a mason and you'd have all the room you could wish for."

Thomas continued as if Jorge hadn't interrupted. "He told me the dead man–"

"Alvarez."

Thomas stopped and looked at Jorge. "Do you want me to tell you or not?"

Jorge shrugged as if unconcerned.

Thomas started walking again. "Alvarez had a weakness for young girls. Boys, too. It might be why he was killed. Even his own children, according to Britto."

"I take it you mean a sexual interest rather than some other kind."

"Don't pretend to be stupid."

"Then explain clearly to me what you want."

"I want you to question the wife to see what she knows. Whether she was aware of his predilections. Whether she was complicit in them."

"Do you believe such a thing likely?"

"I don't know. Hence my asking you to find out."

"She might not want to talk about the subject."

"Almost certainly not. So you need to work around

the question without stating it openly. You're good at that kind of thing. I trust you to find out what you can."

"Oh, thank you. And what will you be doing? Hiding upstairs until I've finished?"

"I'll be searching his private rooms. There might be something there to incriminate him. If I'm lucky I'll find something to link him to others. Someone who might have killed to keep him quiet."

"If he was as despicable as you say, his wife might have thrown his things out by now. And whoever killed him is likely long gone. I see no point in pursuing this."

Thomas shook his head. He wasn't sure either, aware of a reluctance to get involved in murder again so soon after his return. "You know I can't simply leave it."

"Why not? Nobody cares."

"I care even if nobody else does. His wife might care. I'm sure the killer cares not to get caught."

"From what you told me it doesn't sound like a crime of passion. Didn't you say he was killed swiftly and with great skill?"

"Why should that mean there was no passion?" Thomas said.

"Another man would have smashed his brains out, not stuck him neatly. Do you suspect the wife? Didn't you say she was a seamstress? They have some vicious looking tools to work with that might be turned to murder."

Thomas slowed. "I don't know. We're almost there. What do you think–might she be guilty?"

"I don't know anything about the woman. All I know is what you've told me, and that's not much. You forget I've never been to the house before."

"I don't want you to pre-judge anything. You need to make your own mind up."

Jorge offered a glance as they turned into a wide road that led to a distant gate through the wall. "When have I ever done anything else?"

Around them the street bustled. Men and women crowded the roadway which was lined with stalls. Behind them stores dotted here and there sold meat, fruit, vegetables, cotton and silks and spices. Anything that could be grown or carried to what remained the greatest city of al-Andalus, weakened but not yet bowed. Thomas wondered how many of these citizens were aware of events on the hill, of Muhammed's capture and the return of his father and uncle. Even if they knew, did they care? The life of those on al-Hamra was so distant from the people they governed they might as well exist in a different country.

"We're there," Thomas said, stopping outside a tall door fashioned of dark oak, ornate brass decoration marking the surface. He rapped on the door with the heel of his hand and waited.

"Is she beautiful, the wife?" asked Jorge.

"Not particularly."

"Handsome then?"

"Nor that."

Jorge sighed. "Pity. It would have made the afternoon pass more easily."

Thomas banged a second time, but long minutes passed and nobody appeared.

"Did you let her know you were coming?"

"Of course not. I wanted to surprise her. We'll be more likely to tease out the truth if she isn't prepared."

"Then no doubt she's gone out. Didn't you say her children lived in the city?"

"It's the middle of the afternoon. Most people are resting."

Jorge looked around at the crowds in the street. "Like all these are resting? It's not summer, the heat doesn't drive people indoors at this time of year."

Thomas hammered on the door again with his fist.

"Is there another way in?" Jorge looked left and right, but there were only more houses and stores. "Nobody's answering, Thomas, we should go. We're starting to draw attention."

Thomas turned from the door. "As would anyone else coming to the house. It means nothing here."

"If we have drawn attention, then someone might have seen something."

It was a good idea. "You go that way, I'll take this. Find out if anyone saw something suspicious. Go only to the end of the street then work the other side. We'll meet up back here." Thomas began to turn away and stopped. "And ask if they saw any children coming or going. Poor children, beggars like those we saw on the bridge."

"They infest the city, how could anyone tell?"

"Ask anyway," Thomas said, turning away.

It was an hour before they met up again, both weary, neither with any answers. Some of the regular traders knew of Alvarez and his wife. They shopped in their establishments, were a common sight in the street, but nobody had seen anything suspicious. Nor had they seen children, no more than usual, and none entering the house.

"It might be worth coming back after dark," said Jorge. "There are eating places and inns that aren't open yet."

Thomas glanced at the sky, a pale blue between the roofs, a line of dark cloud to the south promising a change in the weather. "You might as well return to the palace. I'll come back and ask on my own."

"Did you notice anything at the end of the street?" asked Jorge.

"Only another street running hard against the city wall."

"I did, this way." Jorge turned and after a moment Thomas followed. Jorge led him to where the street crossed another, narrower, which ran away north to south. The northern side led into a maze of alleys, but forty paces in a small track led behind the shops and houses. It was rough dirt, wedged tight between the rear walls of properties and yards, barely wide enough to walk down without having to turn sideways.

"You saw this from back there?" Thomas asked.

"I came looking for it. It seemed strange there wouldn't be another entrance to these places."

Thomas stopped and gripped the top of a wall, boosted himself up until he could see over. A narrow strip of garden grew only weeds. A rough wooden door at the rear of the building offered access, but there was no door into the alley which might allow someone to come and go without being seen. What there was, however, were small gates leading from one plot to the next, some with no barrier at all between the rear of several houses. He looked to the right, trying to gauge where Alvarez's house lay. When he dropped down he found Jorge had moved on and was examining a narrow door set into the wall.

"There are one or two of these at intervals," said Jorge.

"You wouldn't be able to deliver much along this alley," Thomas said.

"That's not its purpose though, is it."

"No. It's an escape route in case someone attacks the front. And a means of entrance and exit without being seen. If Alvarez wanted to bring children in they could come through those alleys and they'd never be seen. Does that door lead to his house?"

"If not his then one close enough to give access. But it's locked."

Thomas grinned. "And it's weak." He put his shoulder against it and banged hard, felt the wood give. It was old, brittle, rotting along the hinges, and when Jorge added his weight it gave way with a suddenness that sent them stumbling into a narrow courtyard shaded by the two stories of a house. To the right sat a low wall, nothing more than a boundary giving onto the next yard. Beyond, a solid wall had been built to a height of eight feet.

"That's Alvarez's house at the end," said Jorge, and Thomas nodded.

"Yes, I think it is." He stepped over the low wall and jumped, arms outstretched. He caught the lip of the wall and cursed, dropping back. His fingers were lacerated, blood dripping onto the ground. "The top's lined with glass or flint, something sharp."

Jorge squatted and offered his hands linked together. "Try again, see what you can."

This time Thomas kept his hands away from the top of the wall. With Jorge supporting his weight he was able to see what had cut him. Nails were embedded in the mortar, their sharp ends pointing skyward. Beyond lay a small courtyard, a single stunted orange tree getting too little sun in the north facing space to bear fruit. On the other side of the courtyard was a second wall of the same height, but in that one was set a narrow door, barely four feet in height.

Thomas dropped down. "We can get in from the other side. There will be another door into the alley." He led the way out and moved along until they found a sturdier door, but fortunately this one stood half open. Thomas peered beyond it into a paved courtyard swept clean. There was no-one in sight and he stepped through, Jorge close behind. There was a line of sad bushes, their clipped tops and sides belying their poor condition. They separated the yard from the next, where lay the door Thomas had seen. He stepped across the hedge, but when he pushed against the door it stood firm. A sturdy metal plate showed where the lock lay. Thomas took a step back and kicked at the door, but it stood firm.

"You always carry a few instruments with you, don't you?" said Jorge.

"A few, why?"

"Let me see them."

"Are you going to cut your way through?" But Thomas reached into an inner pocket of his robe and pulled out a leather pouch. He unwrapped it to display several blades, other instruments, some notched, some hooked.

"This one and..." Jorge's hand hovered over the offered tools. "Perhaps this. Can I?"

"If you think they'll be of any use."

Jorge took the metal tools and knelt at the gate. He inserted one, feeling around inside the lock, twisting, turning. He shook his head and withdrew it, tried the second which had a wider blade with two notches along its length. It was used for holding small wounds open before suturing, but it was obvious Jorge had discovered its true purpose because with a turn and a grunt of satisfaction the lock clicked and the door swung inward.

"After all the time I've known you, you can still utterly surprise me," Thomas said.

"You forget I was a ruffian, just like those kids on the bridge."

"You at least had a family."

"Which I'd have been better off without."

Thomas knew it wasn't the whole truth. Jorge had rediscovered his brother while they were in Qurtuba curing the Spanish prince, had gained an entire new family, nephews and nieces he had spent many days with while they waited for the prince to fully heal and the queen to allow them to leave.

"Where did you learn to pick a lock like that?"

"Better you don't know. Are you coming?" Jorge ducked and went through. Thomas smiled and followed.

They found Donna Alvarez in a small bedroom at the rear of the house, arms folded across her chest. She was dressed in a white nightdress, her face peaceful. Thomas drew back the covers, rolled her onto her side and examined the base of her skull. There was no sign of a wound.

He dug his fingers into her jaw. "There's no rigor yet. She's been dead only a few hours."

"Was she killed?" asked Jorge. He stood just beyond the door, unwilling to enter the room, still uneasy in the presence of death.

Thomas opened Donna Alvarez's mouth and sniffed. The scent of almonds greeted him. He knelt and swept his hand under the bed, cursing when a splinter caught an already damaged finger, but he found a wineglass and drew it out. The same unmistakeable scent clung to it.

"Killed by her own hand, I believe," Thomas said. "What I don't understand is why she looks so peaceful. Poison isn't the kindest way to end your life."

"It might be if the alternative is disgrace. She knew about her husband, I take it."

"Of course she knew." Thomas rose from beside the bed and looked around. "We need to search the house, see if we can find anything incriminating."

"Can't we just leave her with her dignity?"

"Not if it means a killer going free."

"We need to report her death, arrange for burial. Was she a Muslim?"

"Her husband was Christian."

"We should contact her children so they can make arrangements. Tell them she died of natural causes, spare them the shame."

Thomas glanced at Jorge and shook his head. "You're

too soft."

"I'd rather be too soft than the alternative."

Thomas knew it was a criticism of sorts but chose to ignore it. Softness solved nothing. Jorge would learn that lesson eventually.

"Go see if you can track down the children. I'll stay and see if I can find anything. And yes, I'll lie and say she died of a weak heart if it pleases you."

CHAPTER 12

"Jorge!" Lubna squealed and threw herself at him the moment he came through the doorway. Jorge caught her, lifting her slim body so she could kiss his cheek, a grin on his face.

"And I missed you, too, my sweet."

Thomas sat at the table and watched the pair, recalling the less enthusiastic welcome he had received on his own return.

Lubna pulled a face when Jorge finally let her down. "Why did it take you until today to visit me?"

"Because I was afraid I would be unable to control myself, of course."

Lubna pulled his face down for another kiss, then turned and continued with what she had been doing, preparing a stew for the evening meal.

"I need to speak with Thomas," said Jorge, "but if there's enough for me I'd like to stay."

"I'll make it enough. Take a seat."

"We'll talk in the courtyard," Thomas said, ignoring the look Lubna gave him. He walked out into a night sharp with frost. The moon hung almost full behind the dark bulk of al-Hamra palace. Beyond the peaks of the Sholayr glimmered white with snow. Pale light spilled across the walled courtyard as Thomas paced to the corner, pulling his robe tighter. When he turned Jorge was still inside the house. Thomas felt a flash of anger mixed with jealousy but pushed it down. It was only Jorge being Jorge, as always, and Thomas knew he ought to be used to the man's ways by now.

When Jorge finally appeared his face had lost its good humour. Thomas watched him cross the courtyard, his steps slow, and even before he spoke he could guess the news.

"The wife knew," said Jorge. "All the children were abused by their father, boys and girls alike, over many years."

"You told them she died naturally?"

"They didn't care. All I saw was relief that both are dead. Now they can get on with their lives."

"How old are they?"

"Old enough to have children of their own. A little less than twenty for the youngest girl, perhaps thirty for the eldest. Why, does it matter?"

Thomas shook his head. "No, I don't suppose so. I was thinking it might be too late for them to forget. They're going to carry what was inflicted on them their entire lives." He looked away, out over the dark city. Sparks of light from candles and lamps pricked the gloom. Torches burned along the major streets, above them tiled roofs grey in the moonlight. "And their own children?" When he turned back he saw Jorge understood the question.

"I don't think so. I sensed they made sure to fight any

urges they might have inherited. If they had any."

"It happens," Thomas said.

"I know!" Jorge was uncharacteristically short. He wiped a hand across his face. "I'm sorry, Thomas, breaking the news to them was hard. Teasing the truth out even harder."

"You said they weren't upset."

"It was still awful. And..." Jorge gave a shake of his head, shaved smooth once more. "I'm sick from the stink of corruption the man carried with him. Did you find anything?"

"Nothing. There was a desk but it was locked, and without your skills I couldn't open it."

"He'd be a fool to keep a record of his perversions."

"I believe both of them guilty of the crimes against their children."

"But I don't believe it was they who killed either of them," said Jorge.

"Are you sure? People can be expert at hiding the truth."

"Which is why I'm tired and annoyed with you. They hid their shame from me, but nothing else. I need good food, good wine, and some easier conversation."

"Soon," Thomas said. "You can regale Lubna with tales of your family in Qurtuba, she'll enjoy hearing about them. But if it wasn't one or more of his children, who?"

"How am I meant to know that? Why not ask your new friend, Britto? See if he has any more gossip to impart."

"I might. He doesn't start work here for a while, but I know where to find him."

Jorge shook his head. "Why are you spending good money on extending this house? Take Lubna to your bed and be done with it and then there'll be no need for building anything. You know you're meant for each other. I have no idea why you fight it."

"Because…" But Thomas never did get to explain why, even if he could, for at that moment Lubna came to the door and called them inside. When they entered the kitchen it was to find she had put out the good glass goblets and a jug of wine sat on the table. Thomas let go of the thoughts that tumbled through his head and tried to relax, to follow Jorge's lead and enjoy the food, the wine, and the company.

It was Lubna's fault for the evaporation of Thomas's momentary lift in mood, but he could hardly blame her because she was only doing what he had taught her since she came to live in his house. It had started innocently enough.

"So do you plan to drop it now?" asked Lubna. "You've done all you can, surely."

"Have you ever known Thomas drop anything?" Jorge tore off a hunk of bread and wiped it through the sauce remaining on his plate. "Besides, we haven't reached a dead end yet." Jorge glanced toward Thomas. "Have we?"

"We're getting no closer. The wife is dead. You say the children are innocent. It's one more unexplained death. Perhaps we should give up. A thousand more deaths will occur and we can't care about them all." Thomas saw the look Lubna gave him and it caused him pain. Jorge was right—it wasn't like him to give up, but he couldn't think of anything else to do.

"So you'll let a killer walk away," said Lubna. She stood and began to clear the plates. "Nuts and fruit?"

"Figs if you have them," said Jorge as he reached for the jug of wine and topped his glass.

"And almonds," Thomas said. "Sweet roasted almonds."

"Is that what killed her?" asked Lubna as she stacked the plates on the stone slab beside the sink. "Did she mistake bitter almonds for sweet?"

"It might be as simple as that," Thomas said. "But I believe she knew exactly what she was doing."

Lubna turned, leaning against the bench. She wrapped her arms across herself. "Are you really going to leave it?"

"Unless someone comes up with a new line of investigation. There's more than enough going on elsewhere for me to waste my time on a pointless hunt."

"Helena," said Lubna.

"Yes, but also the old Sultan and his brother. I've been back three days and have barely returned to my profession, let alone visited friends."

Jorge laughed. "You don't have friends. Other than me and Lubna."

"Then people I would like to see," Thomas said. "I want to find out how Yusuf is taking the capture of his brother. Do you think he's aware he might be the next Sultan?"

"He's barely sixteen."

"Old enough, with the right help. And he has a claim."

"Yusuf's too soft. Muhammed was never that."

Thomas glanced at Lubna, who remained beside the sink, her face showing a hint of amusement.

"Have you seen him since you returned?" Thomas asked Jorge.

"Several times."

"And?"

"He's the same as always. He prefers music and girls to swordplay, hunting or politics. If someone tries to put him on the throne he'll make a poor Sultan."

"But a good pawn."

"His father or his uncle?"

"Abu al-Hasan's too sick. But the uncle is hungry."

"So there's plenty to think about besides who killed Alvarez."

Thomas saw Lubna move away from the sink, watched as she padded through to the pantry. When his gaze returned to Jorge his friend was smiling.

"But it does nag at me," Thomas said.

Jorge laughed. "So you won't let it drop."

"I don't know." As Lubna returned Thomas reached out and took a handful of almonds before she had time to put the bowl on the table. She gave him a glance which was totally wasted. Thomas popped two of the nuts into his mouth and chewed, absorbed in the texture and taste, their sweetness, the hint of charring from where they had rested over charcoal. "Could someone be mistaken—eat bitter almonds instead of sweet?"

"Not enough to kill them," said Lubna, taking her seat and selecting a handful of nuts for herself. "The taste alone would warn her. And she'd need to eat a score or more to cause death."

"I thought you had already decided it was deliberate," said Jorge, juice from the sweet fig smearing his chin. "She poisoned herself."

"I expect she did." Thomas chewed on more almonds.

"Then let it drop." Jorge leaned back. "I need to return to the palace before everyone goes to bed. Someone will need me, no doubt."

"I'm still not exactly sure what it is your duties are," said Lubna. She reached down and found a cloth she had secreted somewhere and handed it to Jorge to wipe his face with.

"What do you think I do?"

"I don't know. That's why I'm asking."

"Then what do you *imagine* I do?"

"If it's so secretive I'm not sure I care enough to press."

Thomas smiled.

Jorge looked disappointed, the chance to shock with tales of the palace stolen from him. He stood, wiped his hands in the cloth and tossed it onto the table. "Well, at the moment there's little fun in what I do. I'm worried everyone expects me to take over from Samuli, and the work doesn't suit me."

"Will you be safe walking home alone?" asked Lubna, and Jorge scowled at her, but when she rose he enfolded her inside his arms and kissed the top of her head.

"I'll be safe. Thomas and Olaf have finally turned me into a soldier."

Lubna only laughed.

Thomas walked with Jorge as far as the first flight of steps which led down to the river, stayed there while his friend descended, his figure growing less substantial until it merged with the darkness. Thomas remained where he was for a time, staring across at the palace, listening to the sounds of al-Andalus's primary city, which was never silent. He had grown used to the noise, to the bustle and urgency. He compared it with Qurtuba where he had spent half the year. They were not so different. Too many people, too much warfare. He knew now that Spain enjoyed the benefit of strong rulers while Gharnatah threatened to descend into civil war. If that came about it would trigger the swift end of Moorish rule in this land.

He turned away and walked slowly back to the house, bolted the outer gate and went through to his workshop and lit a lamp. He examined the contents of one shelf, reached up and took down a dark bottle. The stopper was old, a crust dried around where it entered the neck, and Thomas turned it gently to work it loose. He placed the stopper on the bench, tipped the bottle and allowed a single drop to fall onto his fingertip. He lifted it to his nose and sniffed, the sharp scent of almonds coming to him.

"What are you doing?"

He turned, unsurprised. He had, after all, tried to teach her to be curious.

"Come and smell this."

Lubna's mouth twitched, but she came across as he held his finger out.

"Do I really want to?" she asked.

"I want to know what you smell."

She leaned forward.

"Almonds."

"Only some people can smell it once it's been

processed down to a liquid like this."

"Does that mean I'm special?" said Lubna, the smile fully forming on her mouth, then fading. "Would it have been a painful death?"

"It depends how much she took. If she ate the nuts, then likely so. If she had access to something like this, it would have affected her more quickly. But there would have been some pain in either case."

"She was desperate."

"Nobody should ever be that desperate," Thomas said.

"For some people escape from life may be the most merciful option."

Thomas stoppered the bottle and replaced it, wiped his finger on his robe, thinking of Samuli. Lubna was right.

Lubna plucked at the shoulder of his robe. "Now I'm going to have to wash that before you accidentally poison yourself."

"It wasn't much."

"Enough for a bellyache, I expect."

"Yes, probably enough for that." Without knowing how it had happened Thomas grew aware of how close he and Lubna were standing. They often brushed together when they worked, or when Lubna leaned close to observe some intricate procedure, but he had always taken care not to touch her without need.

"Then I need to wash it." She touched his arm again, as if to remove his robe, but instead she simply rested her hand against him. "Why do you fight it so, Thomas?"

"Fight what?"

Lubna shook her head. "Don't pretend to be stupid.

You are many things but you are not that. You know you only have to ask. And it would save you considerable expense if we shared the same bed."

"Is that reason enough?"

Lubna laughed, and suddenly her hip was against him, a small breast pressed into his side. "For most it would be more than reason enough. But I have many other reasons I would like to explain to you. Don't over-think things so, Thomas."

"I have told you, you are an equal in this house, not a servant who has to do as I will."

"What about my will? Doesn't my will count for anything?"

"Of course it does."

Now her arms were around his waist, her face turned up to his, more than half a foot below his own, and without being aware of how it had happened his hands rested in the curve at the base of her spine and her body was moulded against his own. She would, he knew, be fully aware of the reaction she was having on him.

"Then my will is you take me to your bed. Take me tonight. I have wanted you to do so since coming to this house but was too afraid to ask. And I know you want me." She smiled and moved slowly from side to side. "Want me a great deal, it seems. I know I'm not beautiful like my sister but–"

There were no more words as Thomas's mouth covered hers.

And soon, in the familiarity of his bedroom, the silk of her skin slid against his as she guided him inside her, gasping at the initial penetration, and at the time, if he noticed it at all, Thomas assumed the gasp was one of pleasure.

CHAPTER 13

Thomas slept like a dead man. He had been doing so more of late. In the three weeks since Lubna first lay beside him something had worked loose inside. Something he hadn't even been aware of until its grip loosened. He had barely stirred when Lubna slipped from bed, merely rolling over as the sound of her preparing breakfast drifted from the kitchen below. His investigation of the death of Alvarez had finally been brought to a standstill from too little information, and slowly he had allowed it to seep from his mind. It became just another one of those things he could do nothing about. Instead he had sunk himself into work. Treating patients, reading, experimenting, all made easier by the presence of the woman at his side. Helena continued to refuse to see him, and she too had started to fade into the background.

He might have slept until noon if a hammering on the door hadn't woken him to bright sunlight filling the room. At first he thought the noise was part of a dream, but then it came again, as well as a voice calling out. Thomas rolled naked from bed and grabbed his discarded robe from the floor. When he unbolted the courtyard door it was to find Britto standing in the street.

"Did you forget I was coming?"

"I was asleep. Besides, you said you didn't know when you could start. Two weeks. Three weeks. You weren't sure."

"Well now I am sure. We start today." Britto pushed past. "I've got men arriving within the hour and I need to take another look at what's to be done."

"I've been thinking about that," Thomas said.

Britto stopped and turned back. "Oh?"

"What—can't I change my mind?"

"Not once we start. What have you been thinking?"

"When you were here last I wanted a separate set of rooms with their own entrance, but I've changed my mind. I'd like them linked so it's possible to walk into them from both ground and upper floors."

Britto nodded, but whether it was a nod of acceptance or something else Thomas was unable to tell. He wondered where Lubna had gone, but as he led the way into the workshop he discovered her sitting over a book he hadn't seen before.

"You do know you'll have to empty this room if you want the two sides linked," said Britto, staring around at the towering shelves holding their array of bottles and boxes and phials, at the rows of papers and books. He pointed upward. "We can come through the roof there and build a gallery linking both sides. I told you that before but I expect you've forgotten. Be cheaper if it's not enclosed, but it's you that's paying."

"It would have to be safe." Thomas leaned over, trying

to see what Lubna was reading, but she closed the book and pushed it to one side before rising.

"I'll get your breakfast." She turned to Britto. "Would you like something?"

"I ate hours ago," said Britto. "But if there's something going spare I won't say no. Of course it'll be safe." This last to Thomas as Lubna left.

"Then that's what I want."

"Of course. You're paying. When can you clear all this junk out of here?"

Thomas bit back his first reply. "When do you need it cleared?"

Britto scratched at his beard and looked around. "If we start outside, a week or more at least. You could move this into the new rooms once they're ready, while we knock through from the other side and take the roof off."

Thomas wondered what he had gotten himself into.

"Is there going to be much disruption?"

"No more than need be, but some. You can always call it off."

"No—we need the space. I'll make sure everything is cleared out in time." He had no idea where to start. Some of the bottles hadn't been moved in years. It might be a good thing to throw a lot away. It would offer him the chance to cull anything no longer useable. He wondered if there were any books he might also clear out, but was less confident, never sure when the information they contained might prove useful.

"I've put food on the table in the courtyard," Lubna said. "I'll go and make the bed then start washing your clothes." She glanced at Thomas with a sudden shy look, a secret smile meant to be shared between them.

"I heard you lived as man and servant," said Britto.

"We–" Thomas started to make an excuse, stopped. He had no need to explain anything, but something made him say, "Whoever told you that was right when they said it. Not now."

Britto grinned and slapped Thomas on the back, almost sending him stumbling as they made their way into the sun-filled courtyard, just as workmen appeared and descended on the food laid out on the table. Thomas watched for a moment, then returned to the workshop to make a start. He picked up the book Lubna had been studying and frowned. It was one he knew had no part in his collection–he would never own anything as unscientific.

He sat and began to leaf through, a scowl forming on his face. Each page listed the so-called medicinal uses of various herbs and plants. Which was all well and good–Thomas used many herbs in his own preparations, but here the common uses were tainted by myth and scattered with tales of old crones.

There was a page marked with a torn strip of cloth, and as Thomas opened the book and read the words his scowl grew. It listed pennyroyal, mugwort, angelica and cotton root, together with a menu of ways to mix them for different uses. One of which was to abort the foetus from a mother's womb.

Thomas snapped the book shut and stood, angry at Lubna, their new found closeness shattered. She had lied to him. Again. Although that first time hadn't been a lie, rather an omission. He thought back to the morning after she first shared his bed. He had come upstairs to find her in the bedroom stripping the sheets. On the side where she had lain was a smear of blood, another at the point she had mounted him.

She had glanced at him over her shoulder, her face expressionless.

"Why didn't you tell me?" Thomas said.

"Would it have made a difference? I have wanted you too much and for too long to let your conscience spoil anything."

"My conscience? I would have been more gentle."

"I didn't want you to be gentle. And it was only a moment of pain—the rest was pleasure." She stood upright and came to him, rested her palm against his chest, her other going beneath his robe where he remained naked. Lubna smiled. "Besides, it was funny, the great surgeon Thomas Berrington not even knowing he had taken my virginity. Such a sweet joke."

Three weeks had passed since that night, and each night since had proved as magical as the first. But now when he climbed the stairs once more in search of her Thomas was angry at what he had caught her reading.

Lubna was changing the sheets again, as she had back then. This time there was no smear of blood, only a reminder of what they did in this bed. Thomas almost bit back the words he had been about to say.

Lubna looked over her shoulder at him, her soft beauty once more taking his breath away, and he steeled himself. "I found the book you were reading. You told me you sent Helena away, but you didn't, did you. What happened, did you get the mixture wrong?"

Lubna's dropped the bedding and straightened. "I told you the truth—I sent her away. How can you not believe me? How can you not believe after what we do here, in this bed?" Lubna's face stiffened and she turned away from him.

"What we do here has nothing to do with it."

Lubna launched herself at him, fists striking his chest, his face, his arms. "Nothing to do with it! How can you say such a thing? Do you not trust me at all? I thought we understood each other. I thought we shared more than this bed–I thought we shared a bond."

"It was there as plain as daylight on the bench, the page marked. A potion to rid a woman of an unborn child."

"And I didn't use it! I know you don't believe me, but it's the truth. I bought the book for another reason and found that page after Helena came to me. But you're too full of your own importance to allow room for belief in anyone else. Make your own bed, Thomas." Lubna hit him again before storming from the room.

Thomas stared down at the rumpled sheets, wondering what else he had just broken.

When he went downstairs, sheets bundled together, Lubna was nowhere to be seen. Thomas filled a metal tub with hot water, added lye and left them to soak. He had done his own laundry before Lubna came and he could do it again. When Helena had lived under this roof she had certainly not sullied her hands with such mundane tasks.

The racket of men working filled the courtyard. Stone tumbled, voices called out, all of it an unfamiliar chaos. Thomas stared across at the palace, wondering when he would see Lubna again–or if he would see her again. Had she gone to her mother? To Olaf? Was she even now settling back into life on the hill? Thomas felt an unwelcome storm of emotion.

Work. He would lose himself in work. There was much to do.

He turned and began the apparently impossible task of clearing the workshop. The book of herbs Lubna had been reading remained on the bench. Thomas picked it up and threw it across the room in a flurry of paper. Afterward he felt no better.

He used what boxes he had, knowing he would need more. He packed what he could, marking each box with a sheet of paper tucked in around the contents to list what lay inside. Slowly the work distracted him. He lost himself in the steady rhythm of taking down bottles and phials and cartons, of checking each one, storing those that were still viable, discarding others which were not. The morning passed and he worked on in shirt and trousers, his feet bare and cold. Some kind of penance.

When he was finished with the lower shelves he dragged a wooden ladder across and used it to reach the higher ones. Then he looked around. No more boxes. He needed more boxes.

Thomas walked into the street and along his neighbours' houses until he found a youth who was willing, in exchange for a small coin, to go into the town and find what he needed. Thomas watched the boy run away along the cobbled alley and disappear down the steps at the end. He pushed his fists into his aching back and studied the sky. Cloud had gathered while he worked, and outside the air carried an unfamiliar chill.

More snow had fallen on the hills overnight, coating the tops of those close to the city. Thomas hated the cold. One of the reasons he remained in Gharnatah was the temperature rarely fell low enough to freeze water. This winter was different, and an irrational part of him wondered if it was a portent for the death of this land he loved. He shook his head, angry at his own superstitious weakness. As he turned to return to the work inside, a scarf-covered head appeared slowly, rising up the steps. Lubna returning.

She saw him and started forward, running.

The tension Thomas had been carrying locked inside melted away and he stepped forward, ready to embrace her, but she stopped three paces short.

"You have to come. There's been another death."

CHAPTER 14

Like Alvarez the man lay naked in bed, but in this case he was so grossly overweight rolls of fat spilled over one edge. Lubna had led Thomas to a substantial house close to the western gate, set back from the main thoroughfare. They had entered through the accommodation's own gate set in a wall that rose eight feet all around, reminding Thomas of the wall bounding the rear of Alvarez's house, and he wondered did this man indulge in the same depravity as the first. It sickened him to think of such a thing, sickened him to imagine this leviathan of a body pressed down on young flesh.

"You might want to wait outside," Thomas said to Lubna.

"I have assisted you in far worse."

"Who told you of this?" They had walked through the town in silence, Thomas unwilling to risk reigniting their argument. Lubna, he assumed, was still angry with him.

"Da'ud, of course. He was called by the man's servant. She found him this way when she arrived first thing."

"Did she consider the death suspicious?"

"You'd have to ask her. But Da'ud said it's like the first one."

"If that was the first. Do you have a name?"

"Javier. Fransisco Javier. He's a merchant."

Thomas nodded, only half listening as he examined the man. He lifted a hand first. The tip of a finger was missing. The man was too huge to reach across but Thomas assumed the other was the same. He moved on to look for an incision. It was difficult. Rolls of flesh gathered at the base of his neck making it impossible to see clearly. Thick, dark hair covered the man's back, merging into that on his head. Thomas buried his fingers, parting, peering.

"Let me help," said Lubna, coming closer. "What are you trying to do?"

"I'm looking for a small incision at the base of his skull. That was how Alvarez died."

Lubna stood close, using her own hands to lift a flap of flesh. "Gods, he's gross. How much does he weigh?"

"More than ten normal men. Too much, anyway. If someone hadn't killed him he was killing himself."

"There's food beneath him," said Lubna, indicating a line of crumbs which might once have been bread. "Did he just lie down on top of a meal and… I don't know what. Is this the same as the other one?"

"I think so… except I can't find the incision." Thomas grunted as he tried to manipulate the flesh of the man's neck. There was still a stiffness to the muscle, but the interior of the room was cold and would have been colder still overnight. "Here—see if you can hold this out of the way for me." He pushed a roll of fat obscuring the man's spine to one side and Lubna grasped it, the sinews in her arms standing out as she dug her fingers into the cold flesh.

Even as he leaned in and probed the dead skin, Thomas was aware of how Lubna had involved herself. No foolish qualms, their argument put aside for the moment. This was work, and she was a professional. He knew he would have to make things right between them because he needed her in more ways than he could express.

He grunted and stood back. There was nothing.

"What are you looking for?" asked Lubna.

"The other victim had a thin blade pushed into his brain."

"Is such a thing possible?"

Thomas glanced at her, but Lubna's gaze was on the man in the bed. "Possible, but not easy. The blade would have to be extremely narrow and inserted in exactly the tight place."

Lubna pulled at Javier's flesh. "It wouldn't have bled much?"

"If the strike was accurate death would come in an instant. The heart would stop, as would all flow of blood."

Lubna grunted. "Well if there's something here I can't see it."

"Do you think we can turn him over?"

Lubna looked at the body and shook her head, but not in negation. "If you pull from that side I'll try to push from here."

Thomas considered. He knew it made sense. Lubna was too slight to pull the man, but he didn't want her on the bed either.

"We should send for Jorge. Or look outside for a few

strong men."

"No, we can do this." Without waiting Lubna lifted her robe and climbed onto the bed. She stepped across the body and knelt, burrowing one shoulder beneath. Her face showed the strain.

Thomas leaned over, his head touching hers, and gripped the body. He pulled, lifting a little and Lubna burrowed deeper beneath the man.

"Careful, he will crush you if my grip slips."

"Then don't let it," said Lubna. She worked herself further under, setting her back against Javier's rolls of fat. "If we rock him it might be easier."

As Lubna strained Thomas pulled. The bed was soft, the mattress stuffed with feathers, but Javier's bulk had compressed it. Each time Lubna heaved, Thomas pulled.

"Now!" Lubna's voice was muffled from the effort and her position.

Thomas dug his fingers hard into cold flesh and heaved. Javier came over onto his side. Thomas stopped pulling and Lubna straightened. Her hair had come loose and hung across her face, but she was grinning. "I'm glad you're not as big as him, Thomas."

"Can you see anything? I don't want to roll him any further or he'll crash to the floor."

"Would it matter?"

Lubna pushed the man's head to one side, pulled it back. Thick wattles hung from his chin, compressing as she moved him.

"There's blood in the folds of flesh on his neck, here," said Lubna, pointing.

Thomas leaned over the body. He had to dig his

fingers in and pull the flesh apart where it creased before he found it. A tiny puncture wound. When he
squeezed hard a bloody liquid oozed free.

"I see it," he said as he straightened, putting his hands
beneath Lubna's and taking the slab of flesh she was
holding. "Take a look." He waited until she had examined the incision and stepped back before releasing his
hold. As he did so Javier's body began to roll. Thomas
grabbed wildly, pulling at the body, but this time he was
unable to stop it. Javier teetered, then crashed heavily to
the floor. His skull cracked on the wooden boards and
he lay on his back, still.

"He must have been eating before he died," said
Lubna, running a finger through some scraps of bread
that remained on the bed. "I don't understand. Did he
meekly accept his fate? Wouldn't a man fight? Or was
he held down?"

"Someone his size?" Thomas said. "It would take
three or four men to do so, and there would be marks,
bruises on his arms. It's as if he was complicit in his
own murder."

"Do you think his sins were the same as the other
victim? He might have welcomed death as an escape
from his own depravity. And what is the bread about—
some ritual?"

Something in Lubna's questions nagged at the back
of Thomas's mind, but when he turned inward to chase
it, the thought fled like an animal in the night.

"We don't know his sins were the same."

"It's too much of a coincidence, isn't it? Two men
killed in a similar way. It has to be someone punishing
them. One of their victims?"

"Don't jump to conclusions." Thomas looked around the room. It was well appointed, expensive furniture set against the walls, a rug from Africa gracing the floor. There was even glass in all the windows which it was possible to see out through it. "I would like Jorge to see this, he was at the first scene as well."

"As was Da'ud."

"Only briefly, and his mind works differently."

"Do you want me to go find Jorge?"

Thomas stopped his survey of the room. There would be time enough for that when he was alone. "Would you?"

"Of course." She touched his arm briefly, and he wondered if it was a sign or only habit.

After Lubna had gone, Thomas continued to survey the room. Well appointed, yes, but in a way that hinted at show over substance or comfort. He checked in drawers but knew it unlikely there would be anything to find there. If the man shared Alvarez's transgressions any evidence would be well hidden. More likely anything incriminating would be found below in the cellar.

Thomas moved out onto the gallery and looked down into the wide hallway where they had entered the house. It too was decorated with expensive furnishings. Along the landing a second door stood ajar. When he pushed it fully open Thomas found a sumptuously appointed office. It was set with a desk and chairs, but one corner had been arranged with cushions and a low table for entertaining Moorish visitors. After he had finished his search, finding nothing, one last look convinced him Javier was more likely a Spaniard. It was almost impossible to tell the lineage of people these days. Moor,

Arab, African and Spaniard had intermixed to such an extent over the centuries it was only religion and geography that offered differentiation. At least a third of the population of Gharnatah were Christian, that proportion seeming to rise year on year, as though they were preparing for the day when the city finally fell, making a position for themselves. Judging by the lavish furnishings, Javier had already made a good position for himself.

Thomas returned to the bedroom. He ignored the body and climbed onto the bed. It was wide enough to accommodate six. He examined the pillows and sheets, looking for similar evidence to that he found in Alvarez's bed. There were dark hairs, but they showed a curl to them and most likely all belonged to Javier.

He wondered who came in to make the bed, who to cook for the man, who to clean. There would be someone, likely the same person who discovered the body. Thomas made a note to himself to find out and question the woman, because a woman it would almost certainly be.

He stripped the bed but found nothing more.

Next he opened doors and drawers, pulled out silken clothes, fine linens and cotton, all in the Spanish style, all generously cut. Each garment was clean and neatly pressed. The room smelled of musk and cloves. An arrangement of flowers on the window sill was barely a day old. The flowers would have been expensive at this time of year.

Thomas walked the room in a grid, going slowly, looking for loose floorboards but finding nothing until he came to one corner and heard a creak. He went to one knee and examined the boards. There was a wider gap around one and when he used his fingertips it rocked, but he couldn't prise it loose. He descended the stairs and searched in the kitchen until he found a heavy blade that might be suitable.

Returning to the bedroom he worked on the board until it came free and sweat had gathered beneath his robe. He eased the board away and leaned it against the wall, peered into the opening revealed. There was dust, cobwebs, mouse droppings, but nothing that deserved to be hidden and Thomas sat back on his heels, disappointed.

This house didn't feel the same as Alvarez's. Thomas had no sense dark sins had been committed here. He was normally rational, allowing no room for what others called intuition and he called superstition. But even he had noted the darkness in the other house. Here the aura was of money and self-indulgence.

He straightened, realising there was something he *hadn't* seen in the house which should be there. He pulled himself to his feet as the sound of voices came from downstairs. Lubna had returned with Jorge.

Thomas went to the gallery and looked down on them, unobserved for a moment, jealous of the expression of pleasure Lubna showed as Jorge leaned close to whisper something in her ear. Then she glanced up, saw him, and the pleasure drained from her face.

"Was he rich?" Thomas asked.

"Who, Javier?" It was Jorge who responded. "I didn't know the man, but judging by this house and..." He glanced around. "From what I see here, yes, he was extremely rich. Why?"

Thomas started down the stairs. The cellar still remained to be searched.

"I have found a great deal of expensive furniture and fine clothes, but I've seen no chests. No gold or silver."

"Some men don't trust to keep it in their houses."

"Few men," Thomas said. He glanced at Lubna, who was idly circling the hallway. "But the richer a man the more likely he is to keep his riches close." He waved a hand. "Come up here, tell me what you think of the body."

Jorge pulled a face. "I've seen more dead bodies lately than I care to." But he crossed the hallway and ascended the stairs. He followed Thomas into the bedroom and knelt to peer at Javier's bulk. He glanced at Thomas. "Same method?"

Thomas nodded. "More or less. His neck rather than the back of the skull, but the fingertips were taken, the same as Alvarez."

"He'd been eating just before, I'd say," said Jorge, picking at some crumbs stuck to Javier's chest.

Lubna had come in to watch proceedings, and she laughed. "Looks to me like he never stopped eating."

"You're right," said Jorge.

"The rest of the house is pristine," Thomas said. "He must have someone, likely more than one someone, who comes in to clean for him. To prepare his meals. It would be good to know who."

"Da'ud said it was a servant who came to him," said Lubna. "She told him she'd found her master's body."

"Did he know who she was?"

"I didn't ask. Shall I see if I can find him?"

"If you could." Thomas watched her turn and leave

once more. He tried to work out if the atmosphere between them had thawed, but such a feat of empathy seemed beyond him.

"She's afraid," said Jorge.

"Who, Lubna? Afraid of what? These deaths?"

Jorge rose to his feet, shaking his head. "She told me."

"Told you what?"

Jorge sighed. "It is not possible you are as dense as you sometimes pretend, Thomas. About you and she. These last weeks. About your bed." Jorge grinned. "She told me more than she should, no doubt, but she considers me a safe pair of ears as well as a safe body."

"Little does she know."

"You know she is safe with me."

"I expect."

"Is it good, the sex?"

"That's between us."

"Lubna said it was. Good, that is."

"How would she know, she was a virgin when–" Thomas broke off, annoyed Jorge had managed to draw him into conversation after all.

"Ha! Now she didn't tell me that. "Jorge laughed. "But it does explain why she thinks the sex is good."

Thomas chose to ignore the remark and return to the task at hand. "He'll have money hidden somewhere. There's a cellar I haven't looked in yet."

"Then let's go look."

CHAPTER 15

Thomas began to wonder if he had been wrong and a cellar didn't exist after all. In most houses with a separate kitchen there was a doorway which led down. It allowed the cook to keep food cool below ground level. But there was nothing in the kitchen or the room next to it. They entered the hallway, Jorge circling one way, Thomas the other, tapping on walls.

Jorge found something and called Thomas over, but it turned out to be no more than a bad patch of lime plaster over wooden lattice. It was Thomas who found it, but not where he expected. They had been looking for a doorway. Instead there was a hatch flush with the floor. It was set hard against the wall beneath one side of the staircase, covered by an ornate Moroccan rug. With the hatch exposed it was plain it saw frequent use. Unfortunately, it also revealed a heavy padlock. Well oiled, free of rust, connected to substantial metal rings. One was embedded in the wall, a second bolted from below to the hatch.

"I suppose we could find an axe and hack our way in."

"Do you have your bag?" asked Jorge.

"Upstairs, next to the body. Not that I had need of it."

"You already knew he was dead," said Jorge when he returned. "Why bring it?"

"Aren't you glad I did? Are you going to work your magic once more?"

Jorge smiled. "I could teach you how, but it would take too long."

"I'm not sure I want to learn."

Jorge picked through the contents of Thomas's leather satchel, taking out various instruments, judging each before seeking another. "Ah, this is perfect."

Jorge extracted a blade ridged along one side. Thomas knew it was used to remove cysts from beneath the skin after an opening had been made with a sharper blade.

Jorge inserted one end into the eye of the padlock, turned it, scowled and drew it out, tried again.

Thomas sat on his heels to watch. "You appear to have lost none of the skill."

Jorge's face was an unfamiliar mask of concentration. He made no effort to reply. There was a sudden snap and the padlock shot open on well-oiled hinges. Jorge grinned. "See, I still have the old me inside."

"You must have been practicing, that was easier than at Alvarez's house."

Jorge raised a shoulder. "Sometimes there are places in the palace I might wish to visit without having to ask." He bent, grasped the edge of the hatch and lifted. "Shall we?"

There were rough steps descending into darkness, but as Thomas followed them he found a lamp set in a recess, a flint beside it. He struck the flint and the lamp caught, flared, smoky at first but soon settling. Holding the lamp high Thomas continued on.

The cellar when it came into view ran beneath the entire house and, Thomas judged, perhaps out beneath the yard at the rear as well. The earth floor was swept clean, as were the steps. Shelves lined three of the walls. Heavy trunks rested on the earth. When Thomas bent to examine one he found it, too, was locked.

"I need you again."

Jorge sauntered across. "I knew if I waited long enough you'd find a use for me."

"Don't press your luck."

Jorge smiled, knelt and began to work on the lock.

"Give me more light," he said, and Thomas moved the lamp closer.

While he waited his eyes scanned the shelves where the backwash of light showed an array of objects, all of them valuable. He saw dark ebony carvings, and for a moment excitement sparked when he caught sight of one representing a naked Nubian girl. Then beside it he saw a representation of an elephant, and further along an inlaid box. There was glass, stone, bronze, iron. Weapons and trinkets, oddities large and small. Each one no doubt valuable.

"Done." Jorge sat back. When he lifted the lid Thomas gasped.

The contents of the trunk caught the lamplight and reflected it back, multiplying it ten fold. Gold cups, plates and coins filled the trunk to the brim.

Thomas looked around, estimating how many other trunks lay scattered in the cellar. Over thirty, perhaps more than forty. If they all held the same treasure Javier might prove the wealthiest man in Gharnatah. For what good it was going to do him now. Thomas wondered if he had he ever been married, whether there were there children, other family who might lay claim over what lay buried here.

"This is pretty," said Jorge, lifting a necklace which twisted and turned in his grasp. "You should make a gift of it to Lubna."

"She doesn't care for jewels."

"She might pretend so, but she's a woman." Jorge reached into the trunk again. "I've a mind to take this ring for myself. It's very fine, is it not?"

"You would steal from a dead man?"

"Well it's true, he is dead, so I don't suppose he cares any longer."

Thomas shook his head, knowing he should be used to Jorge by now, but never quite sure whether the man was serious or not. He was about to ask him to open a few of the other trunks when footsteps sounded above.

"That'll be Lubna back with Da'ud," Thomas rose and returned to the steps.

As he appeared into the hallway it was to find Lubna had not brought the physician. Instead she stood next to a woman in her late twenties, with sleek dark hair, a buxom figure and calculating gaze.

"You shouldn't be down there," she said. "Master doesn't allow it. He only lets me down to clean, and only when he's present."

"And you are?" Thomas asked.

"Katerina," she said.

"You worked for Don Javier?"

"For the last six years. He's a good employer. Always wants the best, and has to have what he wants when he wants it, but he's willing to pay well for a job done right."

"Are there any other staff?"

"A cook comes in the morning to prepare his meals, then returns in the evening for dinner."

"Do you live in the house?"

"Do I look like I live here? I'm married, have a house on the Albayzin. Not far from yours."

"You know me?"

"You treated my husband once when he crushed his foot."

"Did I help him?"

"He can walk now, and work, so I suppose you did. If we ever need a physician again it's you we'll come to. They say you're a cold fish, but good."

"Was it you who found the body?"

"No, that was Pilar. She's the cook."

"Did she go to Da'ud al-Baitar?"

"She came for me then she left. I haven't seen her since. It was me who went to Da'ud."

"Why him?"

"Everyone knows if someone dies in this city you go to Da'ud."

"I didn't know that."

"No," said Katarina, as if that was answer enough.

"Were neither of you suspicious?"

"Why should we be? We both knew master Fransisco would keel over one day or another. A man doesn't get to the size he is and live long."

"What about the fact he was naked in bed with food beneath him?"

"He has some funny ways about him."

"How?"

"Sometimes…" Katarina glanced at Lubna, at Jorge. "It's not my place to say."

"None of us here are going to repeat anything you tell us."

"He is a good master."

"I'm sure he was."

"And generous."

"Indeed." *As he could afford to be*, Thomas thought.

"Well…" Once more the hesitation, and Thomas waited, knowing if he pushed she would keep what she knew to herself. "Like I said, he has some funny ways. It wasn't unusual to discover him naked. I think the size he is, he often found clothes uncomfortable."

"It was cold last night," Thomas said.

"He doesn't feel the cold like other men."

Thomas understood why. "So do you think he might have gone naked to bed and eaten some food?"

"Why all the questions? Did he die or did someone kill him? Is that why you were downstairs. Have his trunks been ransacked?"

"They're safe, for now. I'm not sure they will remain so once the city guard arrive. Which of you was last to leave here yesterday?"

"It would be me. Pilar had cleaned his dinner away, left him a flagon of wine and some treats for the night, as she always does. I washed the plates and brushed the floor, then went upstairs to his study to see if he wanted anything else before I left."

"And did he?" Thomas cast a glance at Jorge, who was apparently ignoring the conversation, but Thomas knew better.

"Not last night. He said he had someone coming, a visitor. I asked did he want me to stay to let them in, offer wine or something else. Sometimes master likes a little opium. Never much, you understand, but I think his body aches. It would, being the size he is, wouldn't it? Someone like you would know that."

"Did he say who the visitor was?"

"No."

"Man or woman?"

"I told you, he didn't say. But…"

Thomas waited for her to go on. When she didn't he prompted her, impatient. "Did he have female visitors?" Thomas knew he didn't need to spell out what kind. A rich man in this city, living alone, even at the size he was Javier would be able to pay for company.

"Not that I know of. But I'm not here all the time. I have my own home to go to. And a husband."

"Naturally. So you have no idea who it was."

"None. But it wasn't the first time he had a visitor lately. Three times in the last two weeks he has asked me to leave early."

Thomas glanced at Jorge. "We should ask the neighbours if they saw anyone arriving last night."

"We should," said Jorge, uninterested.

"Thank you," Thomas said to Katarina. "You have been most useful."

"Do you think I can come back later?" she asked. "I have a few things in the kitchen, and upstairs. I suppose I'll have to clear them out now."

Thomas nodded, suppressing a smile. "But not today, likely not even tomorrow. Lubna knows where you live. I'll send her to tell you when you can come back."

Katarina gave a curtsy, all politeness stripped from the gesture by its curtness.

"She was doing more than cleaning for him," said Jorge when only the three of them remained.

"Of course she was. You were listening, then."

"I know how to act when you're that way. Pretend to be doing something else but take everything in. I thought it was what made us a good team."

"And she wants some of his riches," Thomas said. He turned to Lubna. "What was her house like?"

"Small, neat. She's not poor, but not well-off either."

"Did you see the husband?"

Lubna shook her head. "But I wouldn't expect to this time of day. He'll be at work."

"I wonder what he does," Thomas said, but he was only thinking to himself and expected no answer.

"He's a metal worker. Has a shop at the foot of the Albayzin. Not a smith but a metal worker. She was insistent on that, as if it conferred some measure of status."

"Perhaps it does. Smiths are known to be a rough lot." Thomas glanced at Jorge, who pulled a face at him, knowing he was making a joke about his brother, who was a smith in Qurtuba. He looked toward Lubna. "I would like to talk to the cook, this Pilar. Did Katarina say where she lived?"

"The same as everyone else who works."

"Did she say exactly where?"

"We called there on our way here. I thought you would want to speak with both of them, but she wasn't home."

"Does she have family?"

"Katarina says Pilar lives alone."

"Do you think she offered the same services as Katarina."

Lubna raised a shoulder. "The man had little to attract a woman, but who knows with a servant."

Thomas thought it a strangely cynical comment from Lubna, but at the same time felt a thrill run through him at her keenness to be involved. There was a camaraderie between the three of them that brought a sense of satisfaction even through the horror of the man's death.

"What's likely to happen to all those riches down there?" Jorge asked, nodding at the raised hatch.

"It'll be confiscated, of course. What lies down there is enough gold to finance a small war, if not two. Da'ud will inform the city guard soon. Once he does men will come and spirit the gold away."

"I'll go find a hand cart, then," said Jorge, and Thomas stared at him a long while before finally offering a nod.

"We don't need the gold," said Lubna when they were alone.

"Would you rather it go to the palace? Or worse still, one of the nobles like Faris al-Rashid? Besides, we're only going to take one trunk, two at most. We should talk to the neighbours before Jorge returns. And then you can tell Katarina she can come and pick up her things." He saw no reason for the woman not to be rewarded in some way. There was certainly enough to go around.

"Are you really going to steal from a dead man?" Lubna's face showed no emotion.

Thomas sighed. "Have you ever known me steal anything, Lubna? Ever?"

"So why now? Has Qurtuba changed you so much? Or did you change before you left?"

It had been a long day. Long weeks since his return. And now there was another dead man to deal with as well as everything else. He tried to think when his life had grown so complicated, but couldn't pinpoint the exact moment. It seemed to have been a slow accretion of events and responsibilities. He needed to let something go, to get back to what truly mattered.

"I've already explained," he said, knowing his voice was sharper than intended. "By morning the cellar will be stripped bare. Its riches will be added to the palace's hoard, or that of someone else. Whoever manages to move the fastest. Do you think people don't know of the man's wealth? Word of his death is going to spread. They will descend like vultures on this place. If we spirit two trunks away, we can put the gold to better use."

"Two trunks now?"

"Or do you think we should leave it all here? Would you rather see his gold spent on adding yet more luxury to the palace? Or see Rashid buy himself another hundred mercenaries? This city is destroying itself from within. A little gold might make the difference between chaos and escape."

Lubna stared at him, her face set, eyes hard. Thomas knew he had driven one more splinter into their relationship. He wondered how many more it would take to destroy it completely.

He turned away. His own problems would have to wait. There were people he needed to talk to.

CHAPTER 16

In the end it took them over an hour to drag the cart, carrying three of the trunks, to Thomas's house on the Albayzin. Unable to manhandle them up the myriad steps, they had been forced to take a circuitous route that wound back and forth around the hillside until they could finally descend toward home. They were fortunate the light had faded by the time they'd left Javier's house, and that no-one had been curious about what might lie beneath the covering blankets. If anyone had asked, Thomas was going to tell them it was Javier's body, knowing nobody would want him to reveal it.

"Did you discover anything when you talked to the neighbours?" Jorge asked. He and Thomas knelt side by side in the small cellar beneath his kitchen. Their heads almost touched the bottom of the floor above. An oil lamp sat on a stone shelf to cast a wavering light across the riches in the chests. They had already examined the contents of the first. The second held the same mix of silver and gold, but it was the third they stared at. It was filled to the brim with gold coin. Small, large, a myriad of honeyed metal, even the smallest worth a month's wages to most men. More riches than either dreamt could be contained in the world.

"Perhaps." Thomas reached out and pushed his fingers through the coins. They felt warm to the touch, as if alive. "Most of the houses were empty. It's a wealthy neighbourhood and people work. We spoke with one woman, but she had seen nothing and didn't even know Javier's name. Around there they keep to themselves."

"So—nothing at all?" Jorge repeated Thomas's action, burying his hand in the gold. There was something about the wealth that demanded to be touched, cradled and stroked.

"Something, possibly. Two of the servants said there had been a new visitor recently. One had only glimpsed them from behind, but the other almost ran into them when she was leaving one evening."

"Late? After Javier's own servants had left for the night?"

"Most likely. The servant said she had been kept later than usual, which was why she was hurrying. She ran into the figure as they came down the roadway. Almost knocked her over."

"Man or woman?" asked Jorge, finally withdrawing his hand. He stared at his fingers as if expecting some of the golden glow to have transferred to them.

"Woman. She was certain. Said she can tell a breast when it's placed in her hand."

Jorge smiled but said nothing.

"But she didn't see her face. The woman wore a dark robe, the hood pulled low."

"Height?" asked Jorge.

"Shorter than her, she said, and she was about the

size of Lubna."

"So short."

"Yes, short."

"Anything else?"

"She heard the woman speak, but only to curse her, and she couldn't tell anything from it, whether she was Spanish or Moor."

"Could she have been the killer?"

Thomas stared at the gold, half mesmerised. "I don't know." He dragged his gaze from the trunk to look at Jorge. In the confines of the cellar their shoulders touched, their faces close together. "A man the size of Javier—a woman couldn't move him if he didn't want to move."

"Neither could most men," said Jorge.

"Alvarez was the same. It's as if they were complicit in their own death."

"Or complicit in something," said Jorge. "Both were naked. Both in bed. Even you, Thomas, are not so innocent to misunderstand why that might be."

"Suppose it was so, it would explain being naked, but not the food. That is plain strange. I should have checked to see if they had ejaculated recently."

"They may not have been given the chance," said Jorge. "How could it have been done? Would they know what was about to happen or not?" Jorge glanced at the gold before his gaze returned to meet Thomas's. "You said the killing thrust was quick. Could someone do that while riding a man, without them knowing it was coming?"

"Of course. Death appears to have been near instantaneous in both cases."

"Why was Javier killed? Not for his riches, because nothing was taken."

"Nothing we know of," Thomas said. "As no-one will miss what we have taken."

Jorge smiled. "You hope." He looked around at the cramped space. Shelves against one wall held bottles of wine, root vegetables, some old papers curled almost black. "Who knows you have this cellar?"

"All houses have a cellar. But why would anyone come here?"

"To search for missing gold."

Thomas shook his head. "No-one's going to look here. We need to speak with those who knew Alvarez. To find out if there's a link between the two men." Thomas twisted himself away from Jorge. He reached out to grasp a beam, pulled himself crouched over toward the narrow stairs.

"It's a pity Alvarez's wife is dead," said Jorge, from behind.

"You spoke with the children before. Can you go back to them tomorrow and see if you can find anything else out?"

"While you will be doing what?"

"Going back to his house to search for whatever might lie there."

They were able to stand at last in the hallway below the stairs. Thomas heard Lubna stirring something. The smell of food reminded him of his hunger. He started to move away but Jorge grasped his wrist.

"What have you done to upset Lubna?"

"I accused her of something to do with Helena."

"She already knew about Helena."

"She wasn't sharing my bed then." Thomas pulled away from Jorge's grip. "Or now."

"What are you doing here?" said Britto.

Thomas opened eyes that were gummed shut and groaned at the pain in his back. He might have slept on the cot in his workshop before, but not for a long time. After dinner the previous evening, after Jorge had embraced Lubna and left for the palace, she had cleared the plates, washed them and then, glancing at Thomas without expression, climbed the stairs to the bedroom. He had sat in the kitchen for an hour before coming to the workshop. He still didn't know why. Perhaps because he knew Lubna hadn't truly forgiven him. She had gone to his bed as a gesture, not a forgiveness. And that didn't feel enough. He wanted her to come to him out of love and passion, not a sense of duty or apology.

"I was sleeping," Thomas said.

"Poorly, by the look of it. Why?"

Thomas shook his head as he rolled from the cot, used the table to pull himself upright. He looked around at the almost empty shelves, at the hole in one wall where stone had been removed.

"You're early," he said to Britto.

"You want the job finished quickly, don't you?" It was his turn to examine the room. "You're going too slowly in here. I'll get my men to empty the place. Where can we put everything?"

"Pile it in the courtyard and cover it with a waterproof sheet. Lubna will help." Thomas twisted from side to side, easing the kinks from his back. His plan to empty the workshop himself had barely survived into the second week, the enormity of the task beyond him.

"She offered me breakfast when I came in. You look like you need something too." Britto turned away and Thomas, feeling foolish, followed.

"Good morning." Lubna greeted him no differently than usual, if anything with a little more warmth. "Sit, both of you, there's hot broth and coffee. I take it your men won't need feeding as well, will they?"

"They'll be another hour yet. I came early. I wanted a word with Thomas."

"As I want a word with you."

Britto looked up, a spoonful of broth half way between bowl and mouth. "You haven't changed your mind again, have you?"

"It's nothing to do with the work. I was foolish to believe I knew more than you. Do what you know is right. Whatever it is will be better than my ideas. No, I want the benefit of your knowledge of the city again."

"I've told you all I know of Alvarez." Britto raised the spoon to his mouth, blew on it before savouring the taste.

"It's another man I ask about now."

Britto looked across the table at him. Lubna passed behind, her own bowl in one hand. Her fingers trailed across Thomas's shoulder before she took her seat.

"I heard someone else had died."

"A man called Javier. Fransisco Javier. Do you know him?"

Britto scowled. "Unfortunately. The man's a rogue and a thief. I worked for him and he never paid me. Told me the work wasn't of good enough quality. *My* work! Said I'd have to take the matter to the palace if I wanted justice."

"They know you in the palace. Why didn't you appeal to the Sultan? It's the right of every citizen."

Britto uttered a harsh laugh. "If I knew which Sultan, maybe I would have. But there's no leadership anymore, only pretenders. The old certainties have been cast to the winds. You've been away too long. Much has changed since you left."

"It's true," said Lubna. "Even my father says so, and you know how loyal he is."

"Your father?" said Britto. "Who is your father? Is he employed in the palace?"

Thomas laughed. "You don't know who Lubna's father is?"

Britto looked from one to the other. "Should I? Is he someone I ought to know? I apologise, Lubna, if you are someone I should have recognised."

"You wouldn't know me," Lubna said. "But you will know my father. He is Olaf Torvaldsson, the Sultan's general."

Thomas laughed at the expression on Britto's face. The spoon went slack in the mason's fingers and dropped into his bowl, splashing broth on the table.

"Truly, you are his daughter? You don't look like the others."

"I know I don't."

"Gods, if I had known you a year ago I would have gone to Olaf for justice. Even Javier wouldn't be able to get out of that, despite his friends."

"He had friends on the hill?" Thomas asked.

"Money attracts money, you know that. And Javier

had money. Most of it ill-gotten. I don't think he ever struck a deal he didn't cheat someone on."

"If he was such a rogue why did people continue to trade with him?"

"Because he had influence. He knew something about everyone of importance." He glanced at Lubna. "He probably knows some secret of your father's."

"I doubt that. My father has no secrets."

"Everyone has secrets," said Britto, reminding Thomas of the trunks nestled below their feet.

"What were Javier's secrets?" Thomas asked, sure Britto had knowledge about many people in this city. A tradesman was as good as invisible. He came and went, he did his work, and people talked, failing to hide what should be hid. "Were they the same as Alvarez's? Did he like children?"

Britto shook his head and picked his spoon from the bowl. "Not that I ever heard. Women, yes, but they were all of an age, not even that young. He liked them mature. Not old, understand, between twenty and forty. And experienced." He began to eat his broth once more. "And he was willing to pay for the right skills."

"His cook is missing," Thomas said, wondering if that was still true or not.

"Dark haired woman? Can't remember her name. Pretty enough. Old enough too, certainly."

"Pilar," Thomas said.

"If you say so. I'm not sure I ever did know her name. There was another one as well, Katherine?"

"Katarina."

Britto nodded. "She was close to him, like the cook. They may even–" He stopped and glanced at Lubna.

"Don't hold back because of me. Remember, my sisters are concubines. I'm beyond being shocked at anything. You think he shared them, don't you."

"Probably. He wouldn't be the first master to do so."

"But they wouldn't have killed him because of it."

Thomas sat back, content to let Lubna pose the questions. She was doing a good enough job at the moment.

"Why would they want to? He was their meal ticket. And a good one, I expect. He might have been tight with his money, but inside that house things may well have been different." He scraped his spoon to extract the last trace of broth. "Did you go into the house?"

Lubna nodded. "With Thomas and Jorge."

"Did you search it?"

Lubna laughed. "What, you want the money he didn't pay you?"

"There were rumours of gold and jewels."

"There always are when a man appears wealthy."

Britto stared at Lubna for a long time. Thomas watched her hold his gaze, her face expressionless, aware he had underestimated her abilities. He knew she was brave and headstrong, but this sureness and subtlety was a new side to her, one he hadn't seen before.

It was Britto who broke the stare first. "Ah well, I expect I'll hear soon enough. News of money travels fast in this city." He turned to Thomas. "Was there anything else?"

"Can you think of some connection between the two men?"

"Nothing that comes to mind. I'll think on it while I work and come back to you if anything occurs to me, but they moved in different circles. And I can do the work as I see best?"

Thomas nodded. "You can."

After Britto had gone Lubna rose and came to stand behind Thomas. Her arms came around him, crossed over his chest. Her small breasts pressed against his shoulders.

"You didn't come to bed last night," she whispered into his ear.

"I had things to think about."

"What things? There is nothing to think about. All you have to know is I want you."

"Even after I insulted you?"

She laughed softly. "That was hardly an insult."

"Even after I betrayed you with Helena?" Tension knotted his neck and Lubna dug her fingers into the muscle there.

"You slept with her when I was your servant. You owed me nothing then."

"You've never been my servant, you know that."

"I was a patient servant. Now, are you going to come upstairs with me or not?" She kissed his earlobe and her hand snaked down his belly. "I can tell you want to."

"The workmen will be arriving soon. And Britto is out there right now."

Lubna giggled. "I have no intention of inviting them as well, if that's what you're worried about."

CHAPTER 17

"You look pleased with yourself this morning," said Jorge as he strode through the busy street beside Thomas. The weather had turned overnight, the temperature rising from close to freezing to something almost comfortable, and it had brought the citizens out as well as traders. The stalls held little in the way of fresh produce, but there was meat and salt fish as well as spices from across the sea.

"It's the weather," Thomas said, but caught the smile that crossed Jorge's lips and knew he was a bad liar. "It's going to rain before nightfall."

Jorge shook his head and laughed. "You always see the worst in every situation."

"Usually with reason. As in our task today. I doubt we'll learn anything useful."

"We won't if we don't try. You're convinced there's a link between the men?"

Thomas was forced sideways by a trio of boys racing down the street, trying to trip each other with sticks. When he fell into step beside Jorge again he said, "They're both dead, aren't they? And killed in the same way."

"There was no link between the women we saw killed in Qurtuba, other than bad luck. It could be the same here. There doesn't have to be reason behind murder."

"Of course there does–for the killer at least. It might not make sense to you or I, but to him it will be perfectly logical. All we have to do is put ourselves in his mind and find that reason."

"I'd rather not put myself in the mind of a killer, thank you. I leave that kind of thing to you. Just let me know when you have a revelation."

They came to the street where Alvarez's house lay. Thomas reached into his robe, pulled out a key and unlocked the door. A sense of abandonment had invaded the space. The essence of those who had lived here, their resonance seeping into the walls, had faded to leave nothing.

"There was a desk in the room at the back," Thomas said. "I'll search that. You look around the rest of the house."

"What are we looking for?"

"If I knew that we wouldn't need to be here. Anything out of place, anything unusual, anything suspicious. And anything, obviously, that might link him with Javier. You spoke to the children again, didn't you?"

"Of course."

"And?"

"Other than giving me the key–reluctantly–they claim to know of no relationship between the men. They knew of Javier, he was an important man in the city, but they could see no reason for their father to have dealings with him. They're selling the house, by the way, so this is likely our last chance to search it."

"It's a fine house," Thomas said, glancing around. "Not like Javier's, but fine all the same. Don't any of them want to live here?"

"Too many memories." Jorge turned away. "I'll start upstairs. Bedrooms are where secrets are kept."

Thomas watched him climb the stairs, grateful for his presence. He wondered if Jorge was being missed in the harem. For all his talk of having to take over Samuli's workload he still had enough time to spare for this. Thomas turned and entered what had obviously been Alvarez's study. A fine leaded window looked into the small back yard. Set in front of it was a solid oak desk stained almost black with age. Each of the drawers held a lock, and each of them resisted opening. Thomas had expected as much and came prepared.

He dropped the leather satchel he always carried, opened it and withdrew a long steel rod and hammer. He had borrowed both from Britto that morning before leaving home. He wedged the pointed end of the bar into the first drawer, tapped it twice to drive it home, then levered his weight down until the wood cracked and splintered. Using the tail end of the hammer he worked the drawer until he could pull it out. There were papers inside together with two bound journals. Thomas emptied the contents onto the desktop before working on the remaining drawers.

Once he was finished he pulled a chair up to the desk and began to sort through the pile of documents. He worked quickly, scanning only the first line or two of each. He tossed those without interest to the floor. Most were written in Arabic, as he would expect, but a few were in Spanish, one or two in Latin, others in French, Italian, one even in English. Thomas stared at it for a moment, the letters unfamiliar to him, his lips moving as he translated them. It was nothing of interest, no more than a letter of introduction from one friend on behalf of another. Thomas discarded it even as he wondered where Alvarez had acquired an English friend from. It was not unusual, he supposed. There were many Englishmen in Spain, drawn to the crusade against the infidel Moors. Fewer like himself who had chosen to live among them, but he had met others now and again. Perhaps Alvarez's friend was one such as him.

Occasionally he heard Jorge moving about upstairs. At one point there came a loud crash that startled him, and Jorge's voice called out an apology. Thomas continued to sift and sort, working fast, falling into the rhythm of discarding the meaningless chatter of trade. Before long he had a manageable pile remaining on the desk, while the floor was littered with papers.

The journals remained. It was they that interested him because they were also locked. The leather binding was closed by metal strips set with finely tooled latches. Finely tooled they might be, but the hammer soon released them.

Thomas opened the first journal and leaned close. Within two minutes he pushed it away, his mouth turned down in a grimace. Alvarez had recorded each of his perversions in graphic detail, often including sketches of pornographic clarity. Thomas breathed deep, washing his hands together as if the words had tainted his skin. He stared at the open journal, then leaned close once more, steeling himself. He turned rapidly through the pages, looking for something else, anything else, but the first book was the same throughout. A bible of depravity. He tossed it to the floor, broke the seal of the next, scanned and discarded. Three more remained, each identical to the others. Thomas was reluctant to immerse himself any further in the mire of Alvarez's mind. He recalled his conversation with Jorge on their way to the house, regretting his words now. He didn't want to put himself in the mind of the killer, even less in the mind of his victims. But he knew he must, or abandon the quest.

He snapped the third lock, angry. His mouth set in a tight line as he tried not to read the words, looking only for a change of pattern. Alvarez had been a skilled draftsman. The illustrations burned against the back of Thomas's eyes, so hot he feared they would never fade. Still he continued, ignoring a second even louder crash from above.

He found what he was looking for at the end of the last journal. In retrospect he realised he should have started at the end, not the beginning, for the end was where Alvarez's death lay.

The first note of interest occurred a score of pages from the last entry. A third of the journal was still untainted by the man's spidered scrawl. Thomas wondered what new depravities had been prevented by his death. He found it hard to think of Alvarez as a victim. When he did track down his killer he might congratulate rather than punish them. And when he thought of Javier the world seemed a better place without him too.

Thomas took a deep breath and started to read.

She is more than I could have imagined, more than a man might ever wish for, and I will be eternally grateful to Martinson for the introduction. She came early, eager to start, fetching with her two children of less than ten years. A boy and girl. Innocents both, and I knew at once what pleasure we would enjoy together. One grows weary of street urchins who are too knowing for true pleasure. But the pair she brought were different.

At first I thought she had procured them for me, nothing more, and then she revealed her true nature. And what a nature it is.

We began by–

Thomas spun away from the desk and ran for the back door. It was locked. His chest heaved as he fought to hold his breakfast down. Words scrawled themselves across his vision. He closed his eyes, pushing fists against them until bright sparks exploded, but still the words came.

"Thomas–what's wrong?"

Sharp footsteps and then a hand on his arm. He shook it off but it came back, Jorge as always unable to leave him alone. Thomas leaned against the wall and opened his eyes.

"That man," he said, his voice barely a whisper.

Jorge met his gaze and nodded. "I found evidence upstairs. What about you?"

"Journals. He documented every single act he undertook. I–" Thomas clutched a hand to his mouth as his stomach heaved again. Then as Jorge drifted toward the desk he moved fast, intercepting him before he could taint himself with what he had already suffered. He slapped the journal shut, picked it up and flung it against the wall. The spine broke and three pages fluttered free. "There's a letter in that pile somewhere, a letter of introduction. It's written in English. I need to find it."

"Then you'd better do that, I wouldn't recognise it. What can I do?"

"Break the lock on that door. Take those books outside and burn them. Burn the rest too, once I've found the letter."

"I saw wine in the kitchen. You look like you need something."

"No—nothing from this house. Nothing of this man."

"Then I'll go to the inn at the end of the street and fetch wine. You find your letter. Then I'll break the lock and we can both burn his evil."

Thomas nodded, waiting until Jorge had gone before stooping to retrieve the journal he had thrown against the wall. He needed to finish despite knowing what it contained, because the record of those last days might offer a clue to who had killed Alvarez. He knew the who could be almost anyone. Thomas wondered whether he might not have killed the man himself had he known what he had done, and believed it possible. He had killed men before, and often for far less.

Thomas knelt and searched through the pile of papers until he found the letter of introduction. Then, steeling himself, he returned to the journal, opened it to the final pages and began to read. When he was done he tore the last two sheets out and folded them into his pocket. But not until he had stared at the drawing etched in ink on the lower third of one page. It was of a woman, naked, kneeling on all fours. Her face was turned away, unrecognisable, but her body was clear enough. And, above the drawing, the last lines.

She comes again today, with a promise of more than we have yet indulged ourselves in. What it can be I barely comprehend, because what she has already brought me is more than I could ever dream of. Now I sit here at my desk, pretending to work. My heart beats fast in my chest, but it is another part of my body that reflects most the excitement I feel. I will be ready for her when she calls, willing to immerse myself in whatever she demands.

Thomas didn't wait for Jorge. He took the metal spike and hammer and broke the lock on the door. Then he carried the papers out and piled them in the yard. They were already starting to turn brown and curl, flame creeping through them, by the time Jorge returned with two mugs of sharp red wine. Thomas drained his in a single gulp and turned away, dragging his friend with him into the street. He needed more wine. He needed oblivion.

CHAPTER 18

"Harder," Thomas commanded. Hot water sluiced over his head and ran from his body as the youth complied. But however hard the boy applied the cloth, Thomas continued to feel tainted. It was a stain he feared might never be removed, one that came from within rather than without.

Across from him Jorge sat unashamedly naked, his own ablutions complete. His hairless body glowed pink in the heated steam of Aamir's bathhouse.

"What was the name again–Mallinson?"

"Martinson," Thomas said. "It sounds familiar. I may even have met the man."

Jorge laughed. "May? Wouldn't you be sure if you'd met with one of your countrymen?"

"I try not to seek them out. There must be a score in the city, but I know the names of barely any of them."

"Except you think this Martinson might be familiar–how?"

The youth shut off the water spout and handed Thomas a towel. "Do you want me to send a woman?" He glanced at Jorge, unsure. "Perhaps two?"

"No women. You will find coin in my robe. Take what is due." Thomas dried his face, waited until the youth had taken payment and left.

Jorge laughed. "Did you see how he looked at us? He thinks you're going to fuck me." Then when he saw the expression on Thomas's face he laughed even harder. "What—is it so strange? I am exceedingly handsome, after all. An ugly brute like you should be grateful he even considers you worthy of me."

Thomas threw his wet towel at Jorge, who let it slap against his chest and fall to the stone floor. "The boy knows well who we are."

"Perhaps people talk. We do spend more time together than is seemly for a surgeon and a eunuch."

Thomas had nothing left to throw. Instead he made an effort to return the conversation to something more meaningful. "I met him once, this Martinson. He has a house close to the eastern walls below the palace."

"What was he like?" Jorge leaned forward, rested his arms across his knees. Sweat dripped from his chin to the stone floor.

"Self-important, as I recall. But it was several years ago and my memory might be playing tricks."

"I doubt that. What does he do?"

"I don't believe he did anything. He was a middle-man, a trader of information. One of those people who know everyone but remains an enigma himself."

"A good man to go to if you want to know about someone," said Jorge. "A good man to broker an introduction."

"But why?"

"I don't understand—why what?"

"Why would the killer use him to choose a victim?"

"I assume he's well known. Suppose the killer has only recently come to Gharnatah. They would need a man like Martinson."

Thomas sat up. "Or someone who mixed in different circles. Someone like Javier's cook."

Jorge laughed. "That's a leap of logic." He held a hand up as Thomas started to protest. "I'm not saying you're wrong. But why would she kill her own employer *after* Alvarez? Doesn't killing him draw attention directly to her?"

"If she has a rational reason. We both know rationality often has nothing to do with killing. We need to find this Pilar and question her. The more I think on it the more I'm convinced she's involved."

"Could a woman have done what we've seen? Wouldn't she need help? There aren't many men would be able to manhandle Javier, let alone a woman. And from that sketch of her she doesn't look strong. Beautiful, but not strong."

"I don't want to think of the drawing. Or the words." But it was impossible to erase the images seared on his mind. Not just the dark haired woman, also drawings of the children she had brought Alvarez.

"What I don't understand," said Jorge, "is how Alvarez could have read that letter if it was written in English."

"Perhaps the woman brought it, an introduction, and read it to him."

"Then he must be more trusting than I'd give him credit for."

"You said yourself she is more than likely beautiful.

And she was offering him something he craved." Thomas stood and pulled on his shirt. It stuck to his damp skin, but he would soon dry.

"Can you remember where he lives?"

Thomas shook his head. "No, but Hasdai ibn-Shaprut will." Thomas had used the Jew and his staff of scribes many times in the past. Both for drawing up documents for him, also for tracking those he sought.

"In exchange for gold," said Jorge.

Thomas smiled. "We have a surfeit of that, don't we? We'll go to Hasdai later. I want to search Javier's house before I do anything else. There may be another letter of introduction."

"From the same woman?" Jorge stood and pushed his hands down his flat belly, sluicing it clear of water. He shook his legs before reaching for a towel. "If it is this Pilar, she would need no introduction."

"The neighbour said she saw a woman coming to the house after the servants left. Would she have recognised Pilar returning if she was cloaked?"

"She'd have to be blatant." Jorge began to dress, slipping his shirt on and tying it up the front.

Thomas laughed. "As blatant as you, it seems."

Jorge glanced down. "You've seen me enough times before. You even cut me all those years ago. Besides, you know me, I have no sense of shame."

"Yes, she's blatant," Thomas said. "Hopefully blatant enough to make a mistake, blatant enough to leave a clue to incriminate herself." He grinned, his mood lifting as he reached for his own clothes. "With luck we'll catch her before she kills again."

Jorge stopped dressing and stared at Thomas. "You

think she will keep on killing, then?"

Thomas halted with only one trouser leg on. He looked at Jorge. "I believe she's killed before. It hadn't occurred to me until recently, but if she has there'll be a trail. We need to find out if there have been other deaths while we were in Qurtuba."

"Unless she's new to the city, as a letter of introduction might indicate."

"Then we'll do what we can."

There was nothing for them at Javier's house. Nothing for anyone. The entire building had been ransacked, wood-paneling torn from walls, floorboards ripped out. Upstairs Thomas waded through a sea of grey feathers where the mattresses and pillows had been slashed open. They found a lone man upstairs with a metal bar similar to the one Thomas carried in his bag. The man was working wood panels loose to explore behind each. He turned casually, unconcerned as they approached.

"You're too late, everything's gone. Who are you with?"

"We're investigating Javier's death."

The man laughed. "Good luck with that." He eased another panel loose and made a sound, reached in and pulled out a small leather sack. When he shook it coins tumbled together inside with the soft noise only gold can make. He opened it and withdrew a coin, tossed it toward Thomas. "For your trouble."

It hit Thomas's chest and clattered to the floor. The man stared at it, frowning. The act of his tossing the coin told Thomas all he needed to know about how much wealth had been hidden inside the house.

"Were there documents anywhere? Journals, letters?"

"There was something in a desk. It's all out back."

"On whose command are you here?"

The man stared at Thomas a long time. Eventually he seemed to decide it was easier to answer than not. "Who's asking?"

"I am Thomas Berrington. My companion is Jorge al-Andalus. We work for the palace." It wasn't strictly true, not in Thomas's case at least, but it was easier if the man believed they had influence.

"As do I," he said. "Although I don't recognise you. The other one is familiar. I've seen him around, but not dressed like that."

"How much has been found?"

The man shook his head, laughing. "Oh—more than enough to wage war for another year at least, likely more." He reached into the leather sac again, tossed a coin into the air. It rose through a shaft of light falling through the window, glinting shards of reflection. As it fell the man reached out and caught it. "So much, there is a little for everyone. Do you not want that?" He nodded toward the coin at Thomas's feet.

Thomas knelt and picked it up. He examined the coin. Small, fashioned of smooth gold, worth enough to feed a man for weeks.

"I thank you, I will take it."

"Welcome." The man winked. "I'll not mention it when I take my spoils to add to the rest. Not if you don't tell of my presence here."

"Are you the last?" Thomas asked.

"I am." The man looked around. "This was a fine

house once, wasn't it?"

Downstairs Thomas and Jorge found the pile of papers, as promised. The only problem was they had been piled into a bonfire and now only dark embers remained.

Hasdai ibn-Shaprut welcomed Thomas like an old friend.

"I heard you were away from the city."

"Now I'm back, and looking for information."

"Some things never change." Hasdai stared off beyond Thomas's shoulder.

"What do you know of an Englishman by the name of Martinson? Have you ever had dealings with him?"

"Hmmm…" Hasdai continued to find the wall fascinating until Thomas withdrew the gold coin the man had tossed at him and held it out. Hasdai took it, turned it over, over again. "You must want to find him very badly."

"And urgently," Thomas said.

Hasdai pocketed the coin then snapped his fingers. "Habib, here." He waited until the clerk stood before him. "Martinson, does the name mean anything to you?"

"An Englishman?"

"I believe so."

The clerk glanced at Thomas, at Jorge, returned his gaze to his master, who nodded his permission.

"Where does he live?" Thomas asked.

"South of the palace."

"Can you draw me a map?"

Once more the clerk glanced at Hasdai, who nodded

in turn. The coin Thomas had passed him would pay for a great deal of information.

"It will take me a moment." The clerk returned to his desk and drew a fresh sheet of paper from a small pile. He dipped his pen and stared into space for a moment, visualising the tangle of alleyways and roads that made up the lower section of the city.

When he handed the finished drawing to Thomas all the complexity had been ignored. One circle said *city*, another *palace* and a third line was labeled *wall*. The major roadways were shown in enough detail to guide them.

"You are sure this is the place?"

"Of course. He comes occasionally to have contracts prepared."

Thomas looked at the map—if it even deserved such a name—and decided it would have to do. The house shouldn't be hard to find, not that close to the city wall.

"If there is anything else," said Hasdai as they left, "you have credit remaining."

"Do you suppose this Englishman is an accomplice of the woman—or the killer himself? Why are the English so treacherous, Thomas. Is that why you left your land?"

"I had no choice in my leaving. And what makes you think the English are treacherous? Do you believe that of me?"

"No, but neither do I think of you as English. That man Lawrence in Qurtuba betrayed us, didn't he?"

"He did." Thomas wondered, not for the first time—nor likely the last—what had become of Lawrence after he showed his true nature as they pursued Abbot Mandana through the Spanish wilderness. Had the wolves killed him, as they had his master, or had he escaped? "But we're not all the same."

Jorge fell silent. A blessed relief Thomas was sure would not last long. He stared ahead to where a single-storey stone house sat hard against the city wall. It was not familiar. It had been long ago, but he was sure Martinson used to live in something bigger. This looked little more than a hovel.

"Do you think Martinson is involved with the woman?" Thomas said. "It makes sense for there to be two. One to overpower the subject, to hold them down while the other strikes the killing blow."

"Why kill them at all?" Jorge said.

"If we knew that we'd know who. It is always easy after the event, less so before. What turned Mandana and Lawrence into the killers they were? Or that soldier, Qasim, the year before? There are too many fascinated by death. More and more, it seems to me."

"We live in violent times," said Jorge. "Do you expect this Englishman to be home?"

They were within a hundred paces of the house. Alongside them the bleached city walls of Gharnatah loomed. Thomas glanced at the sky. As they had walked to this unfamiliar part of the city the wind had gusted erratically, changing direction at whim. Dark clouds gathered to the south. The air had grown warmer once again, and in the distance a grey veil stretched across the horizon where rain fell. Thomas hoped they could talk to the man and return before they were soaked, but he suspected they would not.

They stopped outside the door to Martinson's house. It stood half open, and Thomas knocked against it. They waited a minute, two, then he knocked again, but already he was expecting no reply. The air drifting through the doorway was contaminated by an odour he had smelled far too often.

"Stay here," he said, before shouldering his way in. He entered a single room that ran the width and depth of the house. A second door at the back, also open, showed hard packed dirt beyond. There was a stove against one wall with a rudimentary chimney. A bed. Pots and pans and chairs. And a table. It was a far cry from the opulence Thomas remembered.

Martinson lay on the table. His death had been more violent than that of Alvarez or Javier. His throat was so deeply cut his head seemed to be barely attached. He was also fully clothed, his shirt soaked dark brown from congealed blood that had sheeted across the floor and table and man.

Behind Thomas, Jorge uttered a curse in Spanish—it was odd how a man always reverted to his native tongue to curse in. Thomas knew he did the same.

"I told you to stay outside."

"And you expected me to? How long has he been dead?"

Thomas approached the table, the stench of decay growing stronger. He pulled the sleeve of his robe across his nose and mouth. Sated flies rose buzzing in a cloud as he waved his other hand. He leaned over, trying not to breathe.

There was no need to touch the body. It was clear how the man had died, and from the maggots that squirmed within the wound it hadn't been recently.

"He's been dead a week, possibly even two."

"When did Alvarez receive the letter?"

"It wasn't dated, but going by other entries in the journal I'd say three or four weeks ago at least."

Thomas stepped away from the table, looking around at the collection of meagre belongings. There were no books, no papers, nothing but the bare essentials of existence. As he moved away Jorge came closer. Thomas watched his reaction unobserved, interested to see how much harder he was now than when they had first worked together. Whether that was a good thing or not he couldn't decide.

"If what you say is true," said Jorge, "it's a strange coincidence for him to be killed so soon after Alvarez."

"You don't believe it a coincidence, do you?"

"Did he know too much?"

"He couldn't be allowed to live."

"Not a co-conspirator then. Just another victim."

"He was used," Thomas said. "By whoever's behind the killing. By this woman."

"You're so sure it's a woman doing the killing?"

Thomas looked around the room again, a weariness filling him so suddenly and completely his knees almost gave way. He reached out and grasped the back of a chair, its wood creaking in protest.

"The deaths have a... I don't know, a kind of gentleness to them, don't you think? The strike that killed Alvarez and Javier was finely judged, almost delicate. This, on the other hand... this is butchery."

"A different person?"

"It doesn't make sense for there to be more than one.

Not when Martinson knew Alvarez and introduced the woman to him. Look at his hands. She was here, no doubt. But unlike the others she cut deep into his throat. There was anger here. Retribution. Even so she remembered to take his fingers." Thomas walked to the door. "Why does she do that?"

"It's no good asking me. She's been careful so far. The only clue we have is Alvarez's drawing, and all that tells us is she has a great arse and even better tits."

Thomas grimaced at Jorge's crudity, but he couldn't dispute the truth of what he said. If, that is, the drawing was in any way accurate and not merely the fantasy of a depraved mind.

CHAPTER 19

It began to rain before they reached the the foot of al-Hamra. Thomas drew his hood over his head and trudged on, face turned down. The wind grew in strength, tugging at his clothes, and together with the rain made conversation impossible.

They stopped beneath an arched entrance to al-Hattabin square and Thomas wiped a hand across his face. "Are you going to the palace? I can't come with you, not after this."

"I have to," Jorge said. "There are things I must do. People have begun to notice my absences."

"I have one more favour to ask. Look in on Helena for me, if you can. I would go myself, but there are things I must do first. Tell her I'll visit later if possible."

"Come find me when you do," said Jorge. "You can take at look at Samuli, as repayment for my favour. But if I don't see you I'll assume there's no news."

Thomas smiled and placed a hand on Jorge's shoulder, feeling a strength there that had once been lacking. "Be careful, you sound almost as if you care."

Jorge shrugged Thomas's hand off. He turned, pulled

his hood over his head and strode out into the rain. Thomas watched him go, his stride long, and recognised how much he had changed from the effete harem eunuch he had known a few years before. The hours of practice with Olaf Torvaldsson had helped, but more than that it was life that had changed him. Whether for better or worse Thomas wasn't sure. He had seen too much of the dark side of life to believe it came with any benefit other than knowing how to survive. And what a man sometimes had to do in order to achieve that made him wonder if the price was worth paying.

Jorge turned a corner and was gone from sight. Two young girls ran laughing from a doorway, their bare feet splashing water in a spray behind them, and Thomas smiled. There was good as well as evil in the world. Better to hold the good close while you could.

He was about to turn away when another figure emerged and made him pause. It was a dark-robed woman. She had been standing beneath an overhang and he hadn't noticed her until she moved. She turned her head, but he couldn't make out her face as she scanned the street, then she strode out in the same direction Jorge had gone. Thomas watched until she disappeared from sight. An instinct urged him to follow, to catch her and turn her around so he could see her face. Then he shivered and told himself not to be superstitious. He was reading too much significance into everything he saw. The woman was no doubt doing nothing more than hurrying to get out of the rain, the same as everyone else.

* * *

It was mid afternoon when Thomas returned to his house, but Britto's men had stopped work and left already. There were gaping holes in the workshop walls and the courtyard was half filled by a pile of new stone.

"They said it was no use working in the rain," said Lubna, as Thomas stood in the kitchen towelling his hair dry.

"Then I hope it stops soon."

"Britto said they could make the time up."

"You've been talking to Britto, have you?"

"Should I not? I took the men water and a little food at noon. They were grateful."

"I'm sure they were. I'll ask Britto to take the cost off his bill."

Lubna turned sharply, then saw the expression on Thomas's face and came to him. Her arms snaked around his waist and her face turned against his chest. "You tease me. You've never teased me before."

"You've never shared my bed before." He kissed the top of her head, inhaling the scent of her hair.

She hugged him tighter. "I like sharing your bed. You were stupid last night not to join me. Don't ever do that again. I know we're going to fall out, lovers do, but you must promise never to sleep apart from me when you are beneath this roof."

"I promise."

Thomas wanted nothing more than to lead her upstairs, but there were things he needed to do before he could give in to his instincts. He unwrapped his arms from around Lubna and took her shoulders, peeling her reluctant body away from his. She pouted, but the expression was so out of character he could only laugh.

"Javier's cook, Pilar, you said you visited her house with Katarina."

Lubna nodded. "It's not far from here. Why?"

"I want to talk to her." Thomas wasn't yet ready to air his suspicions, but he considered Pilar worth questioning. If not as a suspect, then for whatever she might know. He recalled Lubna saying she lived alone. A woman alone would have no-one to watch her comings and goings. The more he thought it through the more logical it was Pilar had to know more.

"Now?" said Lubna, trying to embrace him again, and Thomas laughed.

"As soon as the rain eases."

Lubna looked past him through the window. "That will be hours yet."

"Yes," Thomas said, "I expect it will."

The light was draining from the sky as they left the house. The unseasonal warmth that had presaged the rain was gone, replaced by a harsh cold. The southerly wind had turned north-east and the rain, which still fell, contained icy motes of sleet. It was not unusual for it to snow in Gharnatah, but it didn't happen every year, and rarely lasted more than a day. For some reason Thomas felt this time might be different. It reminded him of the start of a winter storm in England, when the snow could hold the land fast in its grip for a month on end.

They walked swiftly, huddled in their cloaks, nodding a greeting to the few they passed. Most people remained indoors, and chimney stacks showed more smoke than the usual cooking fires supplied.

Pilar's house was at the crest of the hill and the air grew even colder as they climbed. The house was set near the outer wall that ran along the ridge, and had the air been clearer would have afforded a fine view across to the palace on the other side of the Hadarro. Thomas wondered briefly what Jorge was doing, what duties had called him back.

"It's here," said Lubna, stopping.

Thomas rapped on the door, a solid barrier fashioned of elmwood, with a fine brass handle and hinges. He wondered whether Javier's servants might not have helped themselves to some of their master's riches. There had been so much gold Thomas doubted the man would be able to tell if a little had gone missing. Although his experience with men of wealth told him they generally knew to the smallest coin how much they possessed.

"Try again," said Lubna. "It's too cold to stand out here long."

Thomas knocked harder, the sound echoing inside the house. He stepped sideways to peer through a narrow window set with bars. There was no glow of a lamp from inside.

"Do you think there's a way around the back?" He looked left and right. The doorways and frontages formed a solid barrier. Most of the houses were single storey, with only the occasional upper floor breaking the symmetry. There was no-one in sight, but as he walked along the alley he saw the glow of a lamp or candle in half the windows. He continued on, Lubna falling into step beside him. At the top of the alley they turned into another which dipped away downhill, and Thomas knew there was no access to the rear of the houses. They would be built on the same pattern as his own, with rear courtyards set above the next row on the slope. It was the corner position of his own house that allowed for more than one entrance. That only possible because he had bought the two adjoining properties years before to build his workshop and small garden. Now he was giving up some of each, and it occurred to him that the initial need for the work had passed. He would let Britto continue, because he had an idea in the back of his mind for a use of the extra space.

"We should try a neighbour," said Lubna as they walked back to Pilar's door.

Thomas slowed, knocked on the closest door that showed light beyond. Footsteps sounded on a stone floor and an old woman peered out at them, a shawl wrapped around her shoulders.

"We're looking for Pilar." Thomas allowed Lubna to ask the questions, a woman less threatening than a man.

"Not seen her in a day or two," said the woman. "That's not unusual. She comes and goes at odd hours."

Thomas had specific questions and took a step forward, but before he could speak, Lubna, as if reading his mind, posed the first for him.

"Does she have many visitors?"

"Visitors? She lives alone."

"But she must have friends. Men friends, perhaps."

The old woman laughed, showing a mouth devoid of teeth. "Pilar's not that way. I never saw her with a man, not once."

"Women then?" asked Lubna.

The old woman's eyes tracked from Thomas to Lubna, came back. "Who're you to be asking? Are you friends of Pilar?"

Once more Lubna knew exactly what to say. "We are concerned for her. Her master was killed a few days ago. We are worried she may have been targeted by the same person."

"A killer, up here?" The woman began to close the door. "Pilar's brought a killer up here?"

This time Thomas was forced to intervene. He pushed his foot into the narrowing gap to prevent the door closing. "There's no killer coming," he said, trying to soften the impatience he felt, "but Pilar may know something to help find one."

"I don't know anything. You'll have to speak to her if you want to know more." The woman opened the door then shut it harder. Thomas yelped, his foot caught between door and post. When the woman went to repeat the movement he pulled it clear, allowing the door to slam shut.

"We should try the other side," said Lubna, smiling as Thomas lifted his foot and rubbed it.

"With the same result, no doubt."

Lubna turned and walked to the house two doors down from Pilar's, the first one that showed light behind the window. She knocked, waited, the door opening before Thomas reached her.

This time the owner was a younger woman, blonde-haired with an infant resting on her hip. A streak of flour dusted her cheek and her bright eyes were more welcoming.

Thomas missed the first part of the conversation, but

was pleased with Lubna when the woman said, "Well, if you want you can come through to my courtyard. There's no direct access, but I'm sure a tall man like him can scale the wall between."

"What about next door?" asked Lubna. "Won't they mind us climbing into their courtyard?"

"He works at an inn and won't be home until midnight." Her tone told Thomas she didn't much like her immediate neighbour. "Come on, both of you, don't let the cold in." The woman stepped back. Thomas allowed Lubna to enter first before he ducked through the low doorway. They entered directly into a room that ran the depth of the house. A burning fire warmed the space. The smell of baking bread and a spiced stew bubbling above the fire filled the air with homely fragrance. The woman plopped the baby onto the floor and walked into a narrow hallway. It offered a single door to one side, another at the far end.

"It's not locked." She pointed to the far door. "I'll not come with you, my husband will be home soon and he'll want to eat."

"Thank you," Thomas said, and the woman smiled at him, brushing hair from her face with the back of her hand.

"You're welcome. I like Pilar. I hope nothing's happened. She's not seemed herself the past month."

Thomas hesitated, stepping back into the kitchen behind the woman. "Did you know her well?"

She looked at him, unconcerned as she crossed to the pot and stirred what it contained. "Not well, no, but we'd say hello when we passed, and she came around once or twice and showed me how to make a few meals.

She's a cook, you know."

"Yes, I do know. Did she ever talk about her employer?"

"In this city? She did say it was a good job and wanted to keep it."

"She didn't say who he was? Anything about him?"

"Like I said, you don't tell tales." Something in the way she said it made Thomas believe Pilar *had* told tales, but he also knew this pretty woman wasn't going to pass any information on. He knew he could return if he must, but was reluctant to apply pressure unless he had to.

He nodded and went to join Lubna, who had already opened the back door. It gave into a small courtyard containing an olive bush in a pot, a narrow raised bed filled with soil and dormant flowers. Lubna went to the brick wall and tried to pull herself up, but wiry as her arms were she wasn't strong enough.

Thomas put his hands on the top of the wall and heaved himself up until he was sitting astride it. He looked down on Lubna. "Are you going to stay here or come?"

"Can you lift me?"

He smiled and reached down, wrapped his hand around her wrist and lifted her from her feet. Lubna gave a yelp as he raised her high before setting her onto the wall beside him. She gripped the bricks, staring at him, a strange expression on her face.

Thomas turned and dropped down the far side, then held his hands up. Lubna swung her legs from one side of the wall to the other and fell, trusting him completely to catch her. Thomas remembered her courage. A sudden vision filled him, of her in his own courtyard.

Lubna had attacked a soldier who was threatened them. Things might have turned bad for them then, but the chaos of events had overtaken the danger they were in.

He repeated the process on the next wall and they found themselves in the courtyard behind Pilar's house. There was no olive bush here, no flowers, nothing other than plain tiles and bare brick. The long wall was lower than the rest to afford a view across the city and houses below. They staggered down the hillside as if descending giant steps, one tumbled on the other, lime washed walls grey in the gloom.

"It's not locked." Lubna's voice pulled Thomas from the view.

"Why would it be— nobody would expect someone to invade this space. Can you see anything?"

"Only you."

Thomas pulled a face and brushed past her. It was dark inside and he reached out for the wall. His hand fumbled until it discovered a nook and then, within, a candle and flint. Left there so Pilar, coming in from the courtyard, would be able to find it easily. Thomas struck the flint onto a waiting scrap of wool, blew and used the flame to light the candle. He held it up and looked around.

They were standing in a small room set out for washing. A metal bath rested in the centre of the floor, jugs of water sitting on a stone shelf. There was space enough for someone to enter, to bathe, and to leave. There was nowhere to hide anything, and nothing out of place.

A narrow door opened directly into a larger room which filled the entire residue of the house. An open hearth with hooks above for pots. A table, its top scarred from sharp knives. Shelves held pots and pans, herbs and spices, a haunch of lamb, a scattered trio of pomegranates, some apples, oranges and apricots. Empty hooks on one wall showed where the tools of Pilar's trade had been removed. Thomas went to a narrow table beneath the hooks and pulled open a drawer. Reached inside. Held up what he had found.

"What is it?" asked Lubna.

"You tell me."

She came closer, took the implement from him. "A meat skewer. Used to test if a haunch is hot in the centre." She handed it back. Ten inches long, with a slight twist at one end, a ring at the other.

"This could do what I saw," Thomas said. He gripped the spine in his fist and thrust it upward in a stabbing motion.

Lubna laughed. "Every kitchen in the city has one of those."

Thomas scowled and tossed the skewer back in the drawer. He sniffed, testing the air like a hound on the scent of a hare. There was a faint aroma of cooking, nothing more. Not the thing he had half-expected.

Pilar obviously lived and slept in the single room. A narrow bed lay pushed hard against one wall. Clothing hung from a wooden rail set into an alcove. A narrow dresser with a stool in front offered a surface for small earthenware pots containing kohl and rouge.

The house felt deserted.

"What did you expect—to find her body?" asked Lubna, her hand resting on Thomas's arm.

"Do I look so disappointed?"

"Puzzled, I'd say. You believed her dead, didn't you."

"Like Martinson? I'm not sure. She's one of two things. Either an accomplice, or the killer herself. Of the two I thought she was the first."

"And now?"

Thomas looked around. Thought about the meat skewer. Lubna might have dismissed it as a common implement, but that didn't mean it wasn't the murder weapon, hidden in plain sight by its ordinariness. "I wish I knew what she looked like. Was she beautiful, I wonder? It's a pity the sketch didn't show her face."

"What sketch?"

"I was thinking aloud." Thomas didn't want to show the drawing to Lubna. He knelt and reached beneath the bed. Nothing. Next he opened the drawers of the dresser. They were empty. There was a clouded mirror on top, a hair brush. Thomas picked it up, holding it close to the lamp. One or two hairs were caught among the bristles and he teased one loose.

"What is it?" Lubna came to stand close.

"I have another hair I can compare this to." Thomas held it against the light. The hair was dark, like the other had been, the one taken from Alvarez's pillow. Then it came to him. He had coiled the hair into the pocket of his robe. The robe he had worn from Qurtuba. The robe the servants at the palace had taken and burned while he bathed.

"Do you think it's the same?"

"It looks similar, but we'll never know now. I forgot, I don't have the other anymore." Thomas looked around, a sense of frustration filling him. "Lubna—look at the clothes on the hanger. Do there appear to be enough for a woman, or are some missing."

Lubna stepped across, moving the garments from side to side. She shook her head. "There may be enough, but these... these are all old. See, this one has a tear that's been repaired, and this is stained at the hem." She looked at Thomas. "You want to know if she's fled, don't you."

"If she's the killer then it would make sense, if she knows we're on her trail."

"How would she know?"

"We've not been secret about our movements, and..." Thomas's voice trailed away as he stared into space, not seeing the room.

"What?" Lubna tugged at his sleeve.

"There was a woman today, as we came back from Martinson's house. I noticed her because she fitted the description of the one we are seeking. She was dark haired. Had a good figure, from what I could judge beneath her robe. But I dismissed the sighting, perhaps too quickly. I thought I was seeing ghosts everywhere."

"Where did she go?"

Thomas turned to stare at Lubna and she put a hand to her mouth when she saw his expression.

"She followed Jorge," he said.

CHAPTER 20

"I must stop seeing danger everywhere," Thomas said. "It's clouding my mind, preventing me from thinking straight."

"Don't stop," said Lubna. "It's kept you alive in the past and will do so again. Better to see a false danger that not see the real thing when it comes."

They stood in an outer chamber, beyond the palace, waiting for Jorge. They had sent a message with a servant, but a quarter hour had passed and still he hadn't come. Beyond the open archway the sleet had turned to heavy snow, flakes tumbling through the light of torches, settling on the floor of the courtyard.

"Are you going to visit Helena?" asked Lubna. "If so I'll stay here and wait. I can come and fetch you when Jorge comes."

"Jorge won't keep us waiting much longer. We can visit her together later, if you'd like to."

"How is she?" The question was casual. Thomas tried to find some undertone in Lubna's voice and failed.

"Uncomfortable, but she's close to her time now."

"Do you know when?"

"Soon." Lubna could work the numbers as well as he. He knew she was aware of the night he had spent with Helena before he left for Qurtuba. Knew of the moment of weakness that was now being repaid.

"There's no point us both freezing out here. If you insist on staying I'm going to visit my parents. Come find me afterward. I would like to see Helena."

Thomas nodded and pulled Lubna briefly against him, kissed her soft mouth and watched her pull her cloak around herself as she stepped into the swirling snow. Her slim figure disappeared almost immediately. Even as Thomas stared at where she had been, footsteps sounded behind him and he turned to see a different servant returning than the one he had sent a message with.

"Jorge says he can see you now, if you're going to be quick." The young man turned without waiting for a reply and Thomas walked fast to catch up.

They passed through a doorway into the inner palace. The air immediately warmed, growing warmer still the deeper they went. The youth turned and turned again, causing Thomas to lose his bearings, which might have been the purpose. The palace preferred its secret places maintained as such. Through an occasional doorway Thomas glimpsed others going about their business, but he caught no sight of members of the harem or those who ruled al-Andalus. He had come here often in the past, welcomed then for his skill. Now he was being treated as an intruder, and the change sat uneasily with him. The ornate luxury all around only served to reinforce his unease. He wondered what his neighbours would think of the riches here. Or those who slept

curled together under bridges and in doorways, the dis-
possessed who had flocked to the city as the Spanish
grew stronger and took more and more land. Then he
felt a wash of disgust at himself. He could hardly judge.
He had money and owned two houses. He led a life
regarded with envy by many.

Which is why, when he saw Jorge dressed in his fin-
ery, he scowled.

"Who stuck a knife up your backside?"

"Nobody."

Jorge stared at him a moment, then seemed to dis-
miss his truculence as nothing new. "Any news?"

"I can't find the cook, Pilar."

"You think she's dead too?"

Thomas shook his head. "I think she's fled. But
whether from fear of the real killer, because she's afraid
someone might come looking for Javier's riches, or because she's the killer herself I don't know."

"You think that's it? She killed them both?"

"She certainly had access to Javier. She might have
known Alvarez too. She's a cook, and cooks move about
from master to master. It would be easy to slip something into their food to make them senseless. Then she
could do as she wished."

"Did she killed him to steal his money?" asked Jorge.

"Javier's? Possibly. But I was wondering if she might
have been one of Alvarez's victims when she was a girl.
A thing like that can fester a long time before coming
out."

"I hear there are two score new wooden trunks in the
treasury tonight that weren't there before."

"Good. If they have two score they won't be looking

for any more. When you left me I saw a woman following you. I'm wondering if it was her."

"Did you see her face?"

"I wouldn't recognise her even if I had. But no, I didn't. It was raining, remember, and she had her hood raised. Likely as not it wasn't her and she wasn't following you. How is your friend?"

"Samuli? Fading fast–but you know that better than me. Would you look at him again?"

"Where is he?"

"In his room." Jorge started away and Thomas followed. The quarters they moved through, housing the eunuchs, were less-well appointed than the rest of the palace. The rooms were small. Most lacked windows, but they were warm, and a faint moisture softened the air. Thomas presumed they must be close to where the water was heated and fed to the bathing chambers. It made for comfort on a night like this, but would be almost unbearable in the summer.

They entered a narrow corridor with openings to both sides. When Thomas glanced into one he saw a man reclining on a bed, a book open on his chest. The man looked up and nodded a greeting before returning to his reading. They passed seven other such chambers. Thomas knew one would be where Jorge lived. The rooms were sparse, reminding him of the monks' chambers in the monasteries he had visited.

Jorge turned into a chamber at the far end. This one had the luxury of a door, but it stood open. Samuli lay on his bed, propped on a pile of pillows. His chest rose and fell in shallow gasps. His skin was sallow, lips tinged with blue. But his eyes were bright, showing a keen intelligence. Thomas knew the man was fully aware of his condition and its inevitable result. He had visited him every few days, left draughts to ease the pain.

"Have you come to send me on my way, Thomas? I feel death close to me now–like a welcome friend."

Thomas felt for the pulse in Samuli's throat. It ran fast then slow, irregular, failing. He pressed an ear to his chest and listened, but the heartbeat was too faint to hear.

"Do you have pain?"

"The same as ever. But new now, across here." Samuli ran a finger across his chest, up toward his left shoulder.

"Does it ease or is it there all the time?"

"There is no easing, but sometimes it grows worse."

"How is it now?"

"Bad." Samuli stared into Thomas's eyes then glanced beyond him. "Jorge, would you fetch me some wine? Warmed, if possible." He waited until only the two of them remained. "I know I am beyond healing, Thomas Berrington. I'm no fool. I also know you have a reputation for being honest. I would like you to help me."

Thomas saw no point in offering false comfort, he never did. It was a trait that caused some to avoid his services. Others to seek him out for the truth he spoke. "You know what you are asking."

"I do."

Samuli watched as Thomas opened his leather satchel and drew out two small glass phials. They had been there for weeks, waiting for this moment. Now he turned and placed them on a stone shelf set beside the bed.

"I can ease your pain tonight, but I'm not sure what

the morning might bring."

Samuli tried to laugh. It turned into a cough that wheezed from his lungs. "I have no time, Thomas, we both know that. Give me the dose tonight. I'm tired of the pain. My life has been good, but I am tired now and ready to meet my God."

Thomas returned the old eunuch's unflinching gaze. "I can do what you ask. But you must be sure."

"Stop everything for me. I know you have helped others the same way." Samuli's gaze shifted as Jorge returned with a goblet of wine. He knelt beside Thomas and helped Samuli sit upright, but the old man pushed him away. "Thomas is going to prepare something to help me sleep. He will mix it with the wine to improve the flavour. I know these physicians and their remedies."

Thomas took the wine, the goblet warm in his hand. He carried it, together with the two phials, across the corridor into an empty room. He unstoppered both bottles and allowed the contents to drain into the wine.

"What are you doing?"

Thomas turned to see Jorge in the doorway.

"This will ease his pain."

"He's dying."

Thomas nodded and turned back to his task. It was simple enough—it wasn't as if he needed to measure the dose, only to empty the bottles.

"You're going to help him pass, aren't you."

Thomas didn't believe a response was necessary. He stoppered the empty phials and stood, swirling the wine to mix the contents. He saw Jorge staring at the goblet, his face set hard.

"Knock it from my hand if you want, but if you do

he will die in agony. Either tonight or tomorrow. The growth has spread and his heart is failing."

"Do you feel nothing?"

A flash of anger surfaced in Thomas. "Of course I feel! I thought you knew me well enough to know I feel. It's because I feel Samuli's pain I am helping him."

"But you're so cold about it. This is the ending of a man's life."

"It's because I care I do it. And don't forget—you have ended a life, too." Thomas reminded Jorge of his fight in the woodland beyond Qurtuba.

"In the heat of battle. Not this…" He waved a hand, "…this rationality."

"Would you have me irrational? For Samuli to suffer?"

"Of course not, but…he is my friend. My mentor. And I love him like a son loves a father. He's more father to me than my own ever was."

"Then be glad he will pass without pain."

Jorge's hand came out and Thomas took a pace back, protecting the goblet, but Jorge wasn't trying to knock it from his hand.

"Here—I want to give it to him. You can go."

"I should stay."

Jorge's gaze burned into Thomas's. "Then stay here. If I need you I'll call out."

"Don't let him drain it all at once. He needs to sip it slowly. Only when he begins to grow drowsy allow him to drain the goblet. Come for me when he's asleep."

Thomas watched Jorge turn and cross the corridor, then he sat on the bed and waited. He didn't have to wait long.

"It's done." Jorge stood in the doorway.

Thomas crossed the corridor. Samuli lay on his back, face peaceful. Thomas sat on the edge of the bed and felt for a pulse. It was there, faint, drifting away, returning each time a little slower than before. Thomas waited, an unfamiliar emotion rising inside as he felt the life draining away from a man he barely knew. A life Thomas had deliberately taken.

And then he rose.

"Is he…"

"He's gone. There is no more pain."

"I'll call some girls to wash and prepare him. He will be buried in the morning. There's a place already set aside for him in the palace graveyard."

Thomas smiled. "Do they have a place for you as well?"

"Of course. We all have our places, even down to the youngest serving girl."

"It must be a comfort."

Jorge raised a shoulder. "I think it was for Samuli." He walked into the corridor. Thomas checked his satchel, making sure the empty phials were there. He didn't want someone finding them and misinterpreting what had gone on here tonight.

He found Jorge talking with another eunuch in his twenties, someone he hadn't seen before. There were many in the palace he had never met. The man was crying, tears streaming down his face to drip from his chin. Jorge put a hand on his shoulder and pulled him against his chest. He glanced at Thomas but his expression showed nothing. Thomas waited, unwilling to interrupt, and eventually the young man wiped his face and straightened. Jorge put his hands on the man's face and kissed him on the mouth before pushing him away.

"That's all of them told now."

"Will you take his place?" Thomas asked.

"More than likely."

"You're not the oldest, though."

"No. But I still expect to be asked."

"Will you accept?"

Jorge smiled. "What I want has little to do with it. You forget I'm not a free man, however much I sometimes act as if I am. I belong to the palace. They own me heart and soul and body, to do with as they will. So if I'm asked I will accept." He pulled a face. "God knows how I'll manage. Samuli loved the administration, the making of lists, the pushing of pieces around a chessboard."

"He was old—perhaps it was all he had left."

"Perhaps. But it still needs doing."

"Then get someone to help you."

"None of the others have the skill."

"I don't mean another eunuch. Someone else. Go talk to Bazzu. She knows everything that goes on in this place, she'll have someone who can help you."

"Perhaps I will. And you're right, I don't have to do everything myself." Jorge clapped Thomas on the shoulder. "Look, here they come for him now."

Except the man who scurried down the corridor was nothing to do with Samuli. He had a message from Aixa. They were to attend her immediately. Both of them.

The messenger disappeared, trusting Jorge to know the way to Aixa's chambers. Thomas trailed along, weary of being ordered about, of the seemingly endless demands being made of him. He wondered what random request Aixa had of them now.

They passed servants, one or two harem concubines who smiled at Jorge and ignored Thomas. They had come to a familiar part of the palace when a harsh voice stopped them in their tracks.

"Where are the pair of you sneaking off to?"

Thomas turned to see the tall, bearded al-Zagal standing in a doorway, as if he had been waiting for them. Behind him, seated, his elder brother Abu al-Hasan Ali drew smoke from a hookah into his lungs, the air sweet with the scent of burning opium.

CHAPTER 21

"My brother wants to see you," said al-Zagal. He pointed at Jorge. "You–get on with whatever you were doing."

Thomas slowed, stopped and turned. First Aixa, now these two. He knew he couldn't refuse the request, and no doubt Aixa would keep them waiting again. He could almost visualise golden threads of authority twisting through the palace, tangling people in their bright embrace.

"Jorge was coming with me to see Helena. Your brother knows him. Surely he can enter too."

Al-Zagal shook his head and placed a hand on Jorge's chest. Thomas noticed Jorge leaning forward, applying his own strength. Al-Zagal's shoulder bunched from the pressure of resisting. It was a small token, no more, but one Jorge would not have dared until recently. It told Thomas a great deal about the shifting tides of power within the palace. He turned away and entered the room, allowing the pair to play out their childish game.

Abu al-Hasan Ali reclined on a stack of silk cushions. The mouthpiece of a hookah lay close at hand.

The old Sultan reached for it, his trembling hand searching. Thomas knelt but made no offer of help, knowing pride would reject it. Finally, Abu al-Hasan found what he sought, lifted his hand to his mouth. As he drew a crumbling block of resin glowed. The gift of smoke passed through cooling water and into the old man's lungs.

"You have pain?" Thomas asked.

"The pipe eases it."

"It won't do your eyes any good."

"I have others who see for me. I always have had even when my eyes worked. And now they tell me you are involved in some new investigation. Why, Thomas? Does it affect the palace?"

"Other than enriching your coffers, there is no connection I know of."

"So why pursue it?" The words were slurred, but Thomas knew it would be foolish to underestimate the man's mind, which was as sharp as ever.

"Because someone has to, and no-one else will."

Abu al-Hasan smiled and drew deeply on the pipe again. When next he spoke his words emerged wreathed in grey smoke. "You cannot fix the entire world, Thomas, however hard you try. You should move to the hill while you still can."

"I don't understand."

The old man closed his eyes. "These are the end of days, Thomas. The end of days. Difficult times. You need to think of yourself, think of your women, too. Come here, to safety."

"I'll remember your words." It was difficult not to offer the man the honorific he had grown used to uttering.

"Was that all you wanted? To know what I am up to, and offer an invitation?"

"And to warn you."

Thomas waited.

Abu al-Hasan drew on the pipe, over and over, the only sound the bubbling of water and his soft exhalations. Thomas continued to wait. He wondered if Abu al-Hasan had drifted away into his own thoughts until he spoke again. "I bear you no ill will, despite your part in my downfall. You must know that things are changing here on the hill. Power shifts to those who can wield it most effectively. Those who can clasp it tight." He drew on the pipe, held the smoke in his lungs before releasing it. He waved a hand. "Not me, no, certainly not me, but... well, I don't have to spell it out, do I? You are an intelligent man. Sometimes too intelligent." Abu al-Hasan chuckled. "Except where that woman is concerned."

He fell into silence, his eyes closing.

A minute passed, then another. Thomas rose and returned to the door. Jorge had stopped leaning and al-Zagal had lowered his hand, but the two of them continued to stare at each other in some childish show of one-upmanship.

"What did he want?" Jorge asked, as they continued their interrupted journey.

"I'm not entirely sure." They had left the smoke-filled room behind. Left the brothers to their plotting. "Either a warning or a promise, I can't decide which."

"There are changes going on," said Jorge. "Whispers in corridors. People taking sides."

"What sides?"

"Don't be stupid."

Aixa's chambers weren't cold, but she stood at the glazed window with a shawl around her shoulders, covering her lustrous hair. Thomas knew she heard them enter but remained staring out. The snow continued to fall, waves of it drifting past the window. Beyond, where normally the lights of the city and Albayzin would be strung across the darkness, there was nothing. The palace could be set a hundred miles from its nearest neighbour for all the clues the window offered.

"Will it stop or last?" Aixa said, still not turning.

Thomas glanced at Jorge, who remained tight lipped.

Finally, Aixa half turned. "I was expecting an answer. More likely from you, Thomas. I don't suppose Jorge knows much of snow, but I hear you have a surfeit of it in England."

"I left that place long ago, Malika."

"But you know about snow, surely. It's a thing young boys welcome, isn't it?"

"I know about English snow. Less of the Spanish kind."

"We are not in Spain!" Aixa snapped, her eyes latching onto his.

"I apologise, I wasn't thinking."

"Obviously not."

Her odd moment of stillness had passed, Thomas had seen to that. Aixa moved from the window and walked to a pile of waiting cushions. A servant held a hand out and she took it as she knelt, then reclined, arranging the shawl around herself so when it fell loose it revealed silk beneath.

She waved a hand. "Come closer. What we have to talk of should not be overheard."

Thomas glanced around as he moved to stand in front of Aixa. There were only the servants, and in normal times they would never utter a word. But these were not normal times.

"Sit," she said. "I don't like the pair of you looming over me like that. Fetch cushions for Thomas and Jorge."

Two of the servants ran off. When they returned they scattered cushions on the floor and Thomas and Jorge sat cross legged. Aixa sent the servants away again, this time to fetch coffee and food.

"Something small and sweet," she instructed, before turning back to the two men. "I hear Samuli has passed away at last."

"News travels fast, Malika," Jorge said.

"It had no great distance to travel." Her eyes tracked Jorge. "You will take his place, of course."

"If that is your wish."

"It is."

"Then I will take his place."

"And get someone to help you. I told Samuli the same, but he never would. He had lost interest in the affairs of the harem, and administration proved a useful distraction. I wouldn't wish to see you waste your undoubted skills in the same way."

Jorge inclined his head. "Thomas was only telling me the same thing, Malika. I will do as you say."

Aixa turned her attention from Jorge to Thomas. It was as if a sleek predator had fixed him in its gaze.

Whichever Sultan ruled in al-Andalus, Thomas suspected it was this woman's fingers would always tease at the strings of power.

"I have heard from your friend the King of Spain," she said.

Thomas's lips tightened to hold back a retort.

Aixa's lips in turn curled into a smile, as if content she had scored a point.

"We have been in communication since your return, and they have agreed to release my son. There are one or two conditions I do not agree with, but that is what final negotiations are for. Only one thing confuses me. They have asked for you to be present."

"Me, Malika?"

"Both of you. Jorge too." She glanced across but Jorge, as usual, was casually appearing not to listen to a word.

A servant arrived with a steaming glass jug of dark coffee and a plate of sweet delicacies. A second arranged glass cups and small plates edged in silver. When they were done Aixa waved them away. A third person had accompanied the servants and Aixa did not wave him away. She patted the cushions beside her. But instead of going to his mother, Yusuf came and sat beside Thomas, resting his head against his shoulder.

"You need to know of politics," Aixa said, "so you should stay."

Yusuf nodded but remained silent. He looked tired, his eyes heavy-lidded.

Jorge reached out, poured coffee into the first cup and placed it where Aixa could reach it easily. He placed two of the sugared fruits on a plate and set them beside the coffee.

Aixa nodded at the food. "Please help yourselves."

"I don't understand why the Spanish want us," Thomas said. "We aren't negotiators. I don't even know what a negotiator does."

"I agree," said Aixa. "It makes little sense to me either. But your presence is a condition of the talks. Without you there will be no agreement, so you will go, both of you."

"Can I go with Thomas, Mother?" Yusuf took one of the cakes and nibbled at the edge, before adding, "Go where?"

Aixa cocked her head to one side and studied her son. She turned her attention to Thomas. "Is he old enough, do you think?"

"The negotiations will be extremely boring." Thomas said it more to Yusuf than Aixa.

Aixa leaned forward. "But that is an important lesson he needs to learn. Ruling is not about battles or bravery or intrigue. Being able to sit through long, boring talks is equally as important–sometimes more so. But Thomas is right, Yusuf, you would be bored. Stay here and help me."

"I want to go with Thomas."

"And I said you cannot." Aixa ignored Yusuf and lifted her gaze to meet Thomas's. "I want you to keep your eyes and ears open. You won't be involved in the discussions, but you know these people better than anyone. I want to know if there are things being left unsaid."

Thomas knew there was little use in pointing out he wouldn't hear anything if it was left unsaid.

"And I'm sure I don't need to say that no word of this can reach my husband or his brother." Aixa leaned forward. She picked up one of the small delicacies and popped it into her mouth. Nothing more needed to be said. "Leave us now, Yusuf."

For a moment the boy clung to Thomas's side.

His mother glanced toward one side. Raised a hand. From somewhere a guard appeared. He must have been there all the time, sunk back into the shadows. "My son is tired. Please take him to his chambers." She looked toward Jorge. "Can you send him someone tonight?"

Jorge nodded and made to stand.

"No—send a message. I want you to stay here."

It was obvious the interview was at an end, but not an expectation of their presence. As the guard came to stand next to him Yusuf released his hold on Thomas's arm and stood.

"Goodnight, Mother." He went to her, knelt and kissed her cheek.

"Goodnight, my sweet. Sleep well."

As soon as the sound of Yusuf's feet faded, Aixa allowed the shawl to slide from her shoulders and tossed her head to settle her hair. She reclined against the stack of cushions. As if released by her shawl the air was suddenly filled with the scent of the perfumes and oils which anointed her body. Thomas knew Jorge had been used by this woman, but this was a side of her he had never witnessed himself, and a deep unease filled him. Despite examining her intimately as her doctor, he had never before experienced the sensual charge now filling the room. He wanted to turn and escape, but knew that was impossible until they were dismissed.

He glanced at Jorge to find him smiling, leaning in toward Aixa. Of course, Thomas thought, this is what he does. This is the side of the man I never see. The sensuality, the obedience, the skills only the finest eunuchs possess. Outside the harem most people considered them less than men. Inside, to those who knew, their role was immensely different to common preconception. Jorge had regaled both he and Lubna with tales intended to shock. Now Thomas feared those words had been no exaggeration, were perhaps not even the whole truth.

Aixa stretched, still lithe as a cat. Thomas knew she must be his age, forty-three or even older, yet her skin remained perfect, her face unlined, her hair as dark as it had always been. Some of that would be the attention given to maintaining her beauty, but she had also been blessed at birth, one of those who hold on to their youth long after others become crones.

Thomas saw Jorge take her hand and turn it over. His finger traced the lines of her palm and she smiled, eyes half-lidded. She turned her other hand palm up and placed it on her thigh–an invitation. Thomas's unease grew. He didn't belong in this place. He didn't belong in this situation. He coughed and shifted away from the unfolding scene. Did they expect him to stay and witness whatever was about to occur? Or did they expect him to be an active participant? Thomas was aware the proximity of death sometimes acted as an aphrodisiac, as if people needed to confirm life in its presence. Was that all this was, or something else, something more calculated? The tension in him was almost painful. He fought the urge to flee, knowing he could not move without Aixa's dismissal. He wondered what he would do if the scene unfolded as he feared.

And then, in an instant, everything changed.

A door crashed open and running feet sounded.

Aixa sat up sharply, all softness leaving her face. "What is the meaning of this? Did I not give orders I was not to be–"

Eva ignored Aixa and ran to Thomas. "You have to come now. It's Helena–she's dying."

CHAPTER 22

Thomas had forgotten about the snow. He ran so hard into the courtyard his feet skidded from beneath him. He fell hard, his head cracking against the wall. For a moment the world drew away and he felt an immense peace settle onto him like the still swirling storm. Then pain came crashing through and he cried out, rolling onto his knees. His head hung down, drool running from his open mouth. He thought he was about to throw up, but the moment passed and he grabbed Jorge's hand and pulled himself to his feet.

"Take it easy. You're no good to her with your head smashed open."

Thomas lifted a hand, found a lump the size of an egg above his eye. His fingers came away sticky.

"Help me a moment, please."

Jorge took his weight on one side, Eva on the other. They started across the courtyard once more, staying close to the wall which afforded a little shelter.

"What happened?" Thomas said to Eva, his head still swimming, and he closed his eyes a moment, trusting the pair to guide him.

"She complained of a pain in her belly. I asked did she want me to send for you but she said no, she'd had the pain before and it always passed."

"I know nothing of any pain. She should have told me."

"Perhaps she should, but you know how stubborn she can be. I was making herb tea with honey when she screamed. When I came back in she was on her knees and... and there was blood between her legs."

"You came straight for me?" Thomas opened his eyes again, the intense pain finally beginning to ease. They had left the confines of the palace and were now on the narrow roadway which led deeper into the Alkazaba where his new house lay.

"I sent for the midwives and then I came for you."

"You should have come directly. They'll interfere."

"It is their job. Helena didn't want me to come for you at all."

"Let's hope it's not too late and they haven't dosed her with some home-made remedy."

But it was too late. A servant girl Thomas had never seen before was in the kitchen heating water. Helena had been taken into the bedroom, the door locked.

Thomas hammered at it, demanding entry, but the only response he got was a piercing scream from within.

"I have to get inside. Fetch that girl."

Jorge went, dragging her back by the arm.

"What's the sign?" Thomas said, gripping her shoulders.

"Sign? What sign?"

"When the water's ready, how do they know to unlock the door?"

"There is no sign. I am to call out, that is all."

Thomas dragged her to the door. "Then do it now, call out."

She shook her head, afraid, and Thomas shook her hard.

"Do it!"

"They'll know it's too soon. The water is barely warm."

"Do it," he said again, his fingers digging into her arm, and she did cry out, but in pain.

"Leave her." Jorge pushed between them, peeling Thomas's fingers from around the girl's arm. They had left deep marks which would bruise. Jorge drew her to one side, talking softly, while Thomas hammered on the door again, shouting at the top of his voice to be allowed entry. When someone touched his shoulder he spun around, his fist raised until he saw it was Eva. She stumbled backward, an arm raised, and the rage drained from Thomas. He lowered his fist and went to Eva, touched her wrist, feeling the bone beneath her skin and a tremble deep inside.

"I care, too," she said, her head down, long black hair obscuring one side of her face. "I care as much as do you. I can never carry a child. It is as if she carries this one for me."

"It's *my* child," Thomas said, not yet able to let go of his anger.

"These women do this job day in, day out. She is in the best hands."

"There was blood. You said there was blood."

"They will have dealt with that as well." She reached out to him, hesitated, then touched his hand. "Come sit with me, tell me things about Helena while we wait. She will be all right."

Thomas looked around, aware his neck was stiffening up. He could only turn his head to one side by ducking at the same time. Jorge had taken the serving girl into the kitchen. He heard them talking but couldn't make out the words. Eva sat on a couch and patted the seat beside her. Thomas went, docile now, grateful to be told what to do. Eva took his hand and placed it in her lap. Thomas rested his head on the silk cushions and closed his eyes.

There were no more screams from the bedroom. He hoped it was a good sign but feared it was not.

Jorge emerged from the kitchen and crossed the room, disappeared.

The servant girl came through with a heavy wooden bowl of hot water. She placed it on the floor beside the door before knocking. Three sharp raps.

Thomas watched the door open. A sturdy woman he recognised knelt to pick up the water. She stared at Thomas without expression, then pushed the door shut with her hip. While it stood open he had managed to see the edge of Helena's bed, two other women standing beside it. The white sheets were stained with blood. Such a lot of blood, but he knew they would tell him nothing until it was over.

"You said you couldn't carry a child," Thomas said, as much to distract himself as from curiosity. "Why not? It can't be difficult. Even I seem to have sparked one into life."

"I'm damaged," said Eva. "Things were done to me when I was captured. At least, I assume I am damaged.

I have never conceived."

"Neither had Helena until now."

"Then it was meant to be. At this time. In this place. With friends around her."

Thomas started to laugh, stopped when it shot shards of pain through his head. "At least she has one friend."

Eva was silent for a while. Her hand was warm and dry against Thomas's. Then she said, "She talks of you sometimes. I think–"

"She hates me," Thomas said. "I don't blame her. I didn't ask for her to be sent to me."

"You repaired her face. She told me no-one else could have done that. And it's not true, she doesn't hate you."

"She certainly doesn't love me."

"How can you be so sure? Helena is a complicated woman. I'm not sure she knows what her own emotions are." Eva's free hand touched Thomas's chest. "She told me of the scars you carry. She tells me of your past."

"She knows nothing of my past."

"If that is what you want to believe."

Thomas noticed Eva was leaning against him. Her thigh along his. Her breast pressed to his side. Her scent enfolded him, rich and heady. He felt weak, not fully in control.

Jorge returned accompanied by Lubna. She sat on his other side. Took his free hand and placed it in her lap so he sat like a child cosseted between two beautiful women. Jorge went into the kitchen. The sound of pots and glassware drifted through. Thomas drifted. His head pulsed, his vision dark in one corner.

And then the door crashed back and the midwife came out.

"We need you."

In an instant Thomas's lethargy shattered into a thousand shards and he rose at once, ignoring the pain, ignoring the dizziness and nausea as he strode into the bedroom.

"Tell me," he said.

"The bleeding has stopped, but the child won't come. Helena grows weak." The midwife looked up at Thomas. "She can't make the decision. It's up to you."

He knew exactly what the midwife was asking. Which should be saved: mother or child.

"No." Thomas stared at the bedsheets, at Helena lying pale. She was conscious, her eyes tracking the ceiling as if an answer to her pain might lie somewhere there.

"I can't save both," said the midwife. "*I* can't save either. Only you have the skill to save one or the other—and you have to decide which."

"No," Thomas repeated. He turned. "Lubna, in here, now."

She came running, skidding to a halt when she saw the scene of carnage.

"Your hands are small. See if you can find the baby. It may be in the wrong position."

Lubna stared at him for what seemed an age before nodding, and Thomas felt a surge of hope despite the desperate situation.

"Have you given her anything for the pain?" he asked the senior midwife.

"Of course not. Pain is a part of birthing, it makes the baby strong."

"Not in this case. Go to the other room, you'll find a

leather satchel. There should be opium inside." When the midwife only stared at him he stood directly in front of her. "Do it now!"

She turned away, bustling, letting him see her disapproval.

Helena groaned as Lubna knelt on the bed and began to examine her.

"She's fully open, Thomas. I see the baby's head. I also see…" She leaned closer, her face set, not seeing the blood and worse staining the sheets. "I can see the cord. It's wrapped around its neck."

"Can you get your hand in and free it?" Thomas felt helpless but knew there was nothing he could do, only direct Lubna.

"I don't know. Not without hurting her."

"She's already hurt. Try."

Lubna set her lips and pushed her slim fingers in alongside the baby's head. Thomas leaned close behind, saw what she had seen. The top of the infant's head was dark blue, a coil of birthing tube hanging free on one side. Lubna pressed on, ignoring her sister when she screamed.

"I think I have it. It's tiny."

"Can you free the cord?" Thomas believed it was already too late, but they had to try.

"I don't think so. It's knotted around something."

"What about the baby, will it come free if you encourage it?"

Lubna totally ignored Helena as she moaned, her head rocking from side to side.

"I don't know. There's no room in here, I don't think I can–" Lubna broke off as a fresh gush of blood streaked

Helena's thighs, and in one movement both her hand and the baby slid free. Thomas reached in, cradling the child's head, working his fingers beneath the cord wrapped around its neck. As yet there was no sense the baby was his. His mind was cold, professional.

He waved a hand behind him. "A blade, a knife–give me *something!*."

A moment later he felt a sharpness against his palm and glanced back to see Eva standing there, her face even paler than usual. The bedroom was growing crowded. Even more so when the midwife returned with warm wine. She pushed in on the other side of the bed.

"Slow with that," Thomas said. "A little at a time until she starts to get relief." He turned back to the chaos of the birth, feeling for a point he could slip the blade into. He found one and stretched the cord.

"No, stop!" Lubna cried. "It's not… it's not the baby's cord."

"What? It must be."

"No–look, this one is the baby's." Lubna lifted a wrinkled blue cord and Thomas traced it with his eyes, one end attached to the baby's belly, the other snaking away inside Helena.

He frowned, switched the blade from one cord to another and cut, worked to loosen the first cord from around its neck.

"It won't come." He grunted.

Lubna pushed him aside and slid her smaller fingers into the slippery space. She worked, straining, and slowly Thomas saw the cord loosen. Lubna drew it to one side, unknotted where it had become tied, and all at once the child was free. Thomas passed it back to the midwife. It was dead, he was sure, but they would do all they could to revive it if possible. He had another child to deliver yet, and that one might still live.

CHAPTER 23

"Have you got a name yet?" asked Jorge.

"When have I had time to think on names? Besides, I need to be sure I have a right to give them names."

"Them? Only the boy, surely."

"They will both have names," Thomas said. He stood beside Jorge in the kitchen, using the last of the hot water to wash the mess from their hands. Lubna had already cleaned herself and sent a message to her father to tell him he was now a grandfather. Thomas wasn't sure how Olaf would take the news.

"Then give them a name now, before someone else lays claim." Jorge moved away, wiping his hands dry in a cloth. Eva sat at the kitchen table, her head resting on her hands. She had removed the brooch that normally held her hair in place. It rested on the table top, a soft shimmer of gold, a spark of gemstones. She looked up when Jorge sat beside her and smiled. "It's lucky you were here," he said, and his words brought tears to her eyes. Jorge pulled her against his side, his arm around her shoulder.

"I thought she would die. Even after I came for

Thomas I was sure she would die."

Thomas moved from the sink, drying his own hands. "I did nothing. It was Lubna who saved Helena and the boy. Nobody could have saved the girl. She'd been dead a day at least. That's why Helena started to bleed. Her body knew and wanted to eject it."

"Will she recover?"

"I don't know." Thomas pulled out a chair and sat on the opposite side of the table. "She's strong, but she needs to want to live."

"She does want to," said Eva. "I'm sure she does."

"Her life has changed a great deal," Thomas said. "I think she has trouble coming to terms with what it now is."

"She told me everything," said Eva. "About the attack on her, coming to live with you, the downfall of the Sultan. And you're right, her life has changed beyond recognition. But there is talk of her returning to the harem. After the baby was born, of course."

Thomas wondered what Helena had told Eva. How much was true, how much based on her own skewed version of the truth. He supposed he was past caring where Helena was concerned. He didn't want her to die, would have been ecstatic had both children lived, but his concern for their mother was now purely professional.

"Eleanor," he said, surprising himself as much as anyone else. "And William. Eleanor for the girl. William for the boy."

Jorge smiled. "I think it would be better the other way around."

Thomas swatted at him. As he did so his fingers left a trail of sparks in the air that faded only slowly. His head pounded with each heartbeat. The dark stain in his vision had spread. Now the adrenaline had left him all his aches and pains were returning.

"Wasn't Eleanor the name of that girl in France you told me about?"

Thomas nodded. "It was."

"What girl is this?" Eva leaned forward, her interest obvious.

"It was a long time ago, and a long way away," Thomas said.

"And who is William?" asked Jorge. "Or did you pluck that from the air?"

"He was my brother. Not father's favourite, and one who died too young. He was such a sweet natured thing. That was no doubt the reason father didn't like him." He looked up at Jorge, who shimmered with a light that emanated from his body. "It's a good name, is it not? A strong name."

"An English name," said Jorge. "There are some who might not like that."

"Then they can go fuck themselves." Thomas glanced at Eva. "I apologise, but they can."

"Yes," said Eva. "They *can* go fuck themselves." The words sounded stiff on her tongue.

Thomas stared into her eyes. When he blinked he couldn't remember how long the stare had lasted. "Helena is lucky to have you as a friend." He reached across and patted her pale hand. "Thank you."

"I am lucky to have her as my friend," said Eva.

There was a commotion at the door. Thomas looked up to see Olaf Torvaldsson enter the room.

"Where is he?" asked Olaf. "Where is my grandson?"

"In there." Thomas pushed himself to his feet. He led the way to the second bedroom.

The midwife looked up as they entered. She had been tending to the boy child. To William, Thomas thought, and smiled. The girl had already been washed, wrapped in linen and taken away. She would be buried before sunrise. A Moorish burial. Thomas believed in no God, but a Moorish burial felt right, for she was of this land.

Olaf leaned across the cot, his bulk out of place. "Is he strong? He looks strong. I can teach him how to fight." He straightened and slapped Thomas on the back. The blow raised more sparks in his vision and his head pounded. "Like I trained you to fight."

Thomas made no mention he already knew how to fight before he met Olaf. Long before. Instead he said, "Yes, he's strong. Small, but that's because he's a twin."

"I heard about the girl," said Olaf. "It's a shame. Fatima would have loved a baby girl on her knee. But at least it proves the Torvaldsson name can birth boys and not just girls. When can I take him to see her?"

"Not yet. I want someone with him all the time for the first few days." Thomas reasoned he might have to stay on the hill instead of returning to the Albayzin. He would ask Lubna to stay as well. Helena could make no objection.

"Can I bring her here? To see... does he have a name yet?" Olaf looked expectantly at Thomas.

"His name is William. William Berrington. And of course Fatima can come."

"William..." Olaf rolled the name on his tongue. A line between his brows indicated uncertainty. "Is that an English name?"

"And French. Spanish too, I'm sure. And they have a version in Italy. Do they not use it in Sweden as well?"

"Yes, they do. William." Olaf stared at Thomas. "I expect it is your right to name him. Yes… Will… a good name. A strong name." The man seemed to be coming around to the idea.

Lubna entered with a bowl and washcloth, strips of torn bedding draped over her arm. She saw her father and smiled, put down her burdens and went to him, hugging him tight. Her arms could not reach all the way around, and the top of her head did not come to his chin. He hugged her back, trying to be gentle but still pushing the air from her lungs.

"You next, perhaps," he said to her as he untangled himself. He cast a glance at Thomas, a look between men to indicate he had no objection. They didn't live in Sweden anymore, nor England. In al-Andalus it was perfectly acceptable for a man to have several wives if he wished, and could afford to keep them.

Lubna, too, cast a glance, but it was of a different sort, more secret.

"We should allow him to rest," Thomas said. "I can wash him, but he will need milk soon. I'm not sure Helena is up to the task. Lubna, will you ask and see if someone can find a wet nurse for him? Only for a day or two, I hope. Until Helena is recovered enough to feed him herself."

She nodded. Olaf loomed over the crib once more, his great fist hesitant. It was obvious he wanted to touch the child but afraid he might cause harm.

"He won't break," Thomas said. He leaned over from the other side and lifted William, protecting his head in his palm. "Do you want to hold him?"

"Me? I don't think…"

Thomas held William out and waited. Olaf stared at the infant. William's eyes were open. They appeared to be looking from one to the other. Thomas believed there was no meaning in it, that the baby saw nothing, not yet. Olaf reached out and Thomas transferred the tiny bundle. He fitted into one of Olaf's hands.

"He weighs nothing," Olaf whispered. He brought William up to his face, which had gained a softness he had never shown those under his command. "A boy, Thomas. You have a son."

Thomas nodded, saying nothing.

Olaf lifted William again and planted a gentle kiss on his brow, then handed him back. "I have to go. It's not a good time to be away from my post. But you'll keep me informed."

"Of course." Thomas accepted William, laid him on a wooden table top and began to unwrap the cloth from around him. The midwives had cleaned him but he wanted to do so again. He was aware of Olaf leaving the room, aware that for the first time since the birth he was alone with his son.

He wetted a cloth and wiped at the boy's feet, working his way up the chubby, bowed legs, careful around the junction of his thighs. A frown clouded his face when he recalled how close William had come to being circumcised. The midwife already had a blade in her hand, the child's foreskin gripped between two fingers when Thomas walked into the room and shouted. There had been an argument, but Thomas was insistent. It was one of the reasons Thomas now washed him, because the midwife had taken umbrage at not being allowed to do as she saw fit. But this child was no Moor, and Thomas was determined not to raise him as such. As least, he hoped he was no Moor.

As he washed the boy he studied his skin. It wasn't pale, but neither was it dark. The trauma of birth would take a day or two to fade before he could make a judgement on the true skin colour. William's eyes were pale blue, but Thomas knew that meant little. They would change as the months passed. His hair was light brown, the same as Thomas's. But that, too, would change.

He wiped at the last traces of blood in the folds of the soft skin, unable to decide if the child was his or not.

He could be. Of course he could be his. He had lain with Helena before he and Jorge left for Qurtuba. Had planted his seed inside her. The timing fitted. What he had indulged in was right for the making of a child, even if he could no longer recall exactly why he had weakened.

But he also knew Helena had shared her favours with others. Muhammed being among them. How many others? He supposed only she knew. If indeed she did know. What had come over him? He should have been beyond her seductions by now, but knew he was only a man, and Helena was nothing if not skilled in her chosen profession.

There was no putting off the inevitable moment and Thomas steeled himself. He wrapped William in fresh cloths and lifted him. He hadn't cried yet, not really, a moment of bawling when he greeted the cold world, but he had soon quietened. Since then he had slept or, as now, been calmly alert.

"Do you want to see your mother?" Thomas whispered, inhaling the wondrous scent of him. He walked through into the large main room, glancing at those who sat around the table. Jorge, Lubna, Eva, Olaf still there, each unwilling to break the thread that bound them to the child.

"Did you find someone?" Thomas asked, standing between the two doorways.

"Jorge sent a message to Bazzu," said Lubna.

Thomas nodded. Of course. The palace cook knew everything and everyone. He turned and entered the other, larger bedroom. Helena lay on her back, eyes closed, but he didn't think she slept. Despite the opium the midwife had administered she would still be in pain, would remain so for days yet.

"I have brought him to see you." He leaned across, offering the infant, hoping against hope she would accept him and put him to her breast.

Helena only closed her eyes tighter and shook her head. "Take it away."

"Him. His name is William."

"Take *him* away. I want nothing to do with him. Nothing at all."

"He is your child as well as mine."

Helena laughed, the sound filled with scorn. "What makes you think he's yours?"

"You know as well as I he could be."

"Don't flatter yourself, Thomas."

"He could be." Thomas's voice was insistent. "Even you know how children are started. That thing between your legs is for more than just giving men pleasure."

Helena's eyes snapped open, blazing blue fire. "Yes, he could be yours, but he is not mine! Take him away. Never bring him near me again. He must be yours—only you would put me through all those months of pain and discomfort. I hope you're pleased with yourself, Thomas Berrington, for what you have done to me." The entire time her gaze didn't leave his. Never once did it waver to look at her son.

"You're not rational at the moment," Thomas said, and Helena laughed, a bitter sound that carried not a trace of humour.

"Oh, I'm more than rational. Now leave me. Take it away. I'm sure my sister will be more than happy to look after it. And don't come here anymore. Ever. If I need a physician I'll ask for one I trust."

Thomas hesitated, sure there must be some way to reach her. But when her hand came out, fast and hard, aimed at the cloth wrapped bundle in his arms he jerked away and cried out.

Helena grinned, her eyes slowly closing. Thomas left her to whatever dreams she might conjure. In the main room Lubna came to him, her arms out, and he transferred William to her. At least one of Olaf's children possessed a maternal instinct.

"I really should leave," said Olaf, but he remained seated at the table.

"I'll go to Helena," said Eva, rising. "She needs a friend at this time." She glanced at Lubna, at William cradled in her arms, but there was no expression on her face as she passed.

"Can I hold him?" asked Jorge, turning on his chair, his eyes on Thomas, not Lubna.

"Of course. Do you remember how?"

Jorge shook his head, a smile touching his lips, and Lubna moved across and placed William in his arms. Jorge drew him to his chest, wrapping a long hand around the tiny body. He looked completely happy, and Thomas wondered how it must feel to hold a child and know you could never father one yourself. He turned away and went to the window. He looked out across the wide courtyard, now ankle deep in snow, more falling steadily, and thought of other snows and other places. He thought of Eleanor, the girl he had once loved and abandoned when she was with child. Their child. Did that child still live? Had it been a boy or girl? And Eleanor–what had become of her? She had been taken by the Count d'Arreau in a fight that had almost ended Thomas's life. Was she a countess now? Was she happy, or did she sometimes stand at a window and recall the young man she had lost all those years ago?

Thomas saw Lubna coming toward him, reflected in the glass, and he held an arm out so she could duck beneath it, then drew her against his side. Her slim arms wrapped tight around his waist.

"He can live with us," she said.

"Of course he can."

"We'll raise him as our child."

Thomas nodded. "And you? Do you want a child of your own?"

Lubna made a noise, a snuffle through her nose. "Well, we have been doing all the right things. And I do nothing afterward to prevent your seed catching inside me, so I expect one day something will happen."

"Is it what you want?"

She drew against him. "I want you. And if you want children I want that too. But yes, I would like a child, Thomas. I would like your child."

This time he snuffled a laugh. "I'll see what I can do."

He felt the flat of her hand slap his buttock.

Behind them William cried out, and Jorge said, "I didn't do anything."

"He's hungry," Thomas said, addressing the reflection in the glass.

"Should I give him back and go chase Bazzu?"

"She'll find someone as soon as she can. Chasing her won't help." There was a sound from the corridor and Thomas turned. "Ah, I expect this is her now."

Except the figure that entered the room was an armed guard, followed soon after by Aixa and two others. She glanced around at the gathering, her gaze taking in Olaf's presence. The general had risen as soon as the first armed man entered, coming around the table to put himself between them and William. Then he stopped as the Sultana appeared, conflict clear on his face.

"Is this the child?" said Aixa.

"William," Thomas said, moving to stand beside Olaf, setting his shoulders, trying to ignore the pounding that crashed through his skull. "His name is William Berrington."

Aixa laughed. "You should have known better than to name him." She nodded to the leading guard. "Take him, but be gentle. I will hold you responsible for any harm that comes to him."

Thomas moved, standing in front of Jorge. "Take him into the bedroom," he said, not bothering to turn, knowing Jorge would obey. When the guard moved to intercept, Thomas blocked him once more.

The guard's hand went to the hilt of his sword.

"There's no need for this to become a battle, Malika," said Olaf. "The child is Thomas's. He is my grandson."

Aixa glanced at him. "Your grandson, certainly, there is no doubt of that. But the child is Muhammed's." She pointed to where Jorge had stopped in the doorway, unwilling to leave the room. "That child might one day be the Sultan of Gharnatah, and I am taking him to the palace." She nodded to the guards, who gathered in a line and started toward Jorge.

Thomas moved again, but a hand reached out and stopped him.

"You can't fight them all," said Olaf. "Let them take him for now, until they realise their mistake."

"There is no mistake," said Aixa. "This is my son's child. He leaves with me. Now."

Thomas tried to pull away again, but Olaf's grip was stronger than iron, and his head pounded so hard his vision pulsed. He watched as Jorge turned his back, but the guards merely spun him around and pried the infant from his arms. It was a matter of seconds, no more, before Aixa swept from the room. As she did so William burst into a wailing cry, as if he too knew what was happening.

Thomas jerked inside the vice of Olaf's arms but it was like being encased in rock, and besides the strength was draining from him fast, the room dimming, and when Olaf finally released him Thomas slumped to the floor, clutching at his head where a thunderstorm raged.

CHAPTER 24

When Thomas opened his eyes it was to find a dark haired vision leaning over him. For a moment he thought it was Lubna and began to reach out. Then his senses fully returned and he saw the skin was too pale, the body too slight.

"What are–" His throat hurt when he spoke so he stopped.

Eva dipped a cloth into a bowl of water, wrung it out and wiped his forehead and face.

"You've been talking in your sleep. I thought you would wake soon."

"William?"

"Still with Aixa. She allowed me and Jorge and your new woman to visit but we stayed less than a minute before we were ushered out. He was sleeping, but he's been fed, and I'm sure he was smiling."

Thomas shook his head, immediately regretting it. "Has anyone checked my wound?"

"Your woman did before she went out. She says you'll live."

"Lubna. Her name's Lubna. What about Helena?"

"She sleeps peacefully. Will she recover?"

"She lost some blood, but it wasn't as bad as it looked. Has the girl been taken care of?"

"She was laid to rest at dawn. Jorge and I attended."

Thomas rose on an elbow. He pushed a leg clear before realising he was naked beneath the thin linen sheet and pulled it back.

"Rise, Thomas, it was your–Lubna and me who undressed you and put you to bed. You have nothing I have not already seen."

"Fetch me a robe," he said. "I was unconscious then, and now I am not."

Eva smiled and rose, padded through to the other room on bare feet. Thomas watched her go. Despite himself her sensual beauty drew his gaze. There were many such as Eva in the harem, but there was something different about her. Perhaps because she came from a land close to his own, perhaps something else. Thomas knew men in power sought out the different, the special ones, and drew them close. For himself he failed to understand the attraction. He had been gifted a special one, and Helena had turned out to be nothing but spite and viciousness and trouble. Beauty could only mask so much. But he doubted Sultans spent much time with their concubines outside of the brief moments of passion.

When Eva returned Thomas waited for her to leave once more before standing and slipping into the robe. The rough linen rubbed against his skin, but it would do until he could send for more clothing.

The main room was empty. Beyond the window the snow had stopped falling but remained on the ground a foot deep, pristine and beautiful. It brought back memories of winters in Leominster, of waking to a dawn dusted anew. It wouldn't last beyond noon, it never did in Gharnatah, but for now he took in the calming scene. He heard voices and went into the larger bedroom to find Eva sitting beside Helena.

"How are you?"

"She is well," said Eva, replying for Helena, who turned her gaze away from Thomas.

"I want to examine you," Thomas said, coming closer, unwilling to accept Helena's spite.

"Isn't that what got me into this condition in the first place?" Helena's voice was emotionless.

"You've been through a difficult birth. I need to make sure there's nothing going to stop your recovery."

"Call another doctor."

"I am the best doctor in the city, you know that."

"Not for me."

All the while Eva stroked Helena's hand, staring up at Thomas, her face expressionless and perfect.

"Will you allow Lubna to examine you?"

"She's not a doctor," said Helena.

"But she is better than most you might call. I suppose you won't allow Da'ud to examine you either, will you?"

"He's a fixer of bones and prescriber of herbs, nothing more."

"That didn't stop you going to him when you knew you were with child."

Helena finally turned to meet his gaze, her own eyes chips of blue ice. The colour of William's eyes. Thomas knew he was examining everything about her, everything about himself, trying to decode the truth.

But if he did, and it turned out not to be the truth he sought, would it make any difference? He liked to think not.

Helena pointed at her face. "Look at me, Thomas. Thanks to you I am beautiful again. The scar is barely visible anymore and getting better all the time. There is talk of allowing me back into the harem. But a concubine carrying a baby is no use to anyone. Did you expect me to carry it to full term as I have done? I wanted it destroyed, but nobody would do as I asked. Because they are all scared of you. Is that what you want, to strike fear into everyone in the city? Because that's what you do."

Thomas shook his head, once again regretting the movement, although it didn't raise a trail of sparks across his vision anymore.

"You didn't say if Lubna could examine you."

"Send her to me if you must. Better her than you." Helena's face took on a sly expression. "Is she good between the sheets, like me? Does she allow you to do the things I did?" She laughed. "I can't see that happening."

Thomas turned away before his anger got the better of him.

He heard Eva's soft voice calming Helena as he left the room, wondered what she saw in her he never had. What did the two of them share in common that might ignite such friendship? Thomas had never seen anything attractive in Helena other than the obvious physical beauty, but he knew he too was not to everyone's taste. Perhaps they had simply been too unlike each other for their relationship to be anything other than a disaster.

He had managed to forget Helena while he was away in Qurtuba. He had almost forgotten how he had weakened the night before leaving. Now William's birth would be a constant reminder of what they had done together. Whether he, or she, wanted it or not, they were linked once more.

Thomas walked into the kitchen to pick through the remnants of food from the night before. He chewed on stale bread wrapped around a hunk of lamb sweetened with cinnamon and dates. The outer door opened, a gust of cold air bringing Lubna through as she removed her outer robe. She caught sight of him and smiled. She looking tired, and Thomas wondered how long she had sat with him before going out on her errand.

She pointed to a chair and said, "Sit."

Thomas obeyed, glad to do so. She came to him, her fingers touching the lump on his forehead, parting his long hair in search of other damage and finding none. Thomas laid the food he had been eating on the table and put his arms around her waist, pulling her against him. He rested his head between her breasts, breathing deep of the scent of her. Tears welled in his eyes and for a moment he closed them, content to be in the presence of this woman he loved as much as anyone he ever had in his life. The recognition lifted a weight from him he hadn't been aware of until it was gone. He felt her kiss the top of his head, and then she was untangling his arms. He tried to wrap them around her once more, to pull her onto his lap. Lubna laughed and slapped his hands aside.

"It's good to see you're feeling better."

Thomas gave in and picked up the dry bread and

lamb. "I hear you went to see William. How is he?"

"Sleeping peacefully."

"I want him back."

"I know."

"And do you know what that would mean? To you–to us."

"He will live with us on the Albayzin. I want that too, Thomas."

He nodded, finally discarding the remains of his breakfast as inedible.

"I'd like you to examine Helena."

"Will she allow me?"

"She says so. And you know almost as much as I do now. More about some things such as herbs and potions. I shouldn't have said what I did about that book you were studying. You're right–there's no such thing as wasted knowledge. Perhaps I'm getting old, stuck in my ways."

Lubna smiled. "Yes–a grumpy old man with a lump on his head."

"Has Jorge gone back to the palace?"

"He said he has new responsibilities." Lubna smiled. "He didn't look too pleased at the idea."

"He'll manage, he always does. I want to see your father and thank him for last night. It couldn't have been easy for him, but he tried to protect both William and me, and for that I'm grateful."

"I'll come with you," said Lubna. "I'm sure my mother will have something better for you than stale bread. And then I'll come back and examine my sister." Lubna glanced at the closed bedroom door. "Is that woman still with her?"

"Eva? Don't you like her?"

"I don't know her. But it seems odd they are such close friends all of a sudden."

Thomas sighed. "Helena probably wants something from her. And you know when she does she can be extremely persuasive. Where did you go when you went out?"

"Oh, I should have told you as soon as I came in. I went to Hasdai ibn-Shaprut. Jorge and I were talking while you slept, and he said it was he who told you where Pilar lived, and something occurred to me. If you want to know anything about anyone in the city where do you go?"

"To Hasdai, of course. But he holds his knowledge close."

"You have credit with him, Jorge told me."

"I have credit, yes, but he doesn't know you."

Lubna smiled. "Hasdai knows everyone."

Thomas said nothing, staring outside. Fat flakes of snow were starting to fall once more, drifting through air thick with anticipation. Perhaps the snow would not be gone by noon after all.

"He was happy to talk, and I flattered him a little."

"Hasdai?"

"Men are easy to flatter. It doesn't take much."

Thomas couldn't see Lubna using her wiles on a man in the way she described, but he supposed it was possible. He knew he must get to know her as a woman as well as companion. He looked forward to the discovery.

"So did he have any information?"

"Only a little, but it was interesting. He told me where Pilar came from, where her home was before she came to Gharnatah. Where she still owns a house. There is a place her parents lived before they died. The papers ended up coming to Hasdai and he handled the transaction."

"Will the knowledge do us any good?"

Lubna stroked Thomas's brow above the lump. "I think you must have bruised your brain. She has fled her house. Is that not admission enough of her guilt? And if she owns another house, don't you think that's where she will have scuttled away to?"

"You're right, I'm not thinking straight. Is it close?"

"The house is in al-Khala. I had Hasdai show me where it is on a map."

"I know where it is," Thomas said. "It was taken by the Spanish earlier in the year. After they captured Muhammed they grew bold and continued to advance. It's less than a day from Gharnatah."

"That's what Hasdai said. I think it's where she went. She'll believe herself even safer now if the town is in Spanish hands."

"Moors come and go all the time. We could follow."

"We could."

"Jorge and I could," Thomas said. "You need to stay and look after William, to look out for your sister. Not to mention those men tearing my house apart."

"It's unlikely they'll let Jorge leave. You'd be better taking me. A man and woman travelling together are less threat than two big men. We can ask questions when we get there, before we confront Pilar."

"And if she is the killer? What then?"

"We take her into custody and bring her back. Pay soldiers if we must." Lubna smiled. "You have plenty of gold now."

"It's a good plan," Thomas said, but he had no intention of taking Lubna with him to a town so recently captured by Spain. He had seen too many such places, existing in the borderland between two cultures. They were more often than not lawless and wild. Which was exactly the kind of place someone like Pilar would run to if she wanted to avoid capture. An excitement sparked within Thomas. They were closing in, he was sure. He would go to al-Khala alone and track the woman down. As soon as his head stopped pounding. As soon as he was sure William was safe. Perhaps for now the harem was the best place for him. He stood, stretching the ache from his back and shoulders.

"Hasdai told me something else of interest," said Lubna.

"Yes? What was that?"

"He showed me a document."

"Ah."

"Why did you do it? Why did you sign over the entire house to me before you went to Qurtuba? And why didn't you tell me?"

"Because you would have acted exactly like you are now. I wanted you secure if anything happened to me."

Lubna laughed. "What could happen to you? You're too stupid to get killed–God knows enough people have tried."

CHAPTER 25

Thomas sat in a chair in Olaf Torvaldsson's house, his head leaning back against the wall. He allowed his eyes to close as he listened to the soothing murmur of Lubna and Fatima talking in the kitchen. The scent of cooking filled the air. Olaf was out but expected home for the noon meal. The walk from the house on the Alkazaba to Olaf's quarters on the edge of the training ground had been a strange, silent progress through an unfamiliar world.

When the door crashed open Thomas jerked, unsure if he had fallen asleep or not.

"Well, you look better than you did last night. That's an impressive black eye, though." Olaf grinned. "How is my grandson?"

"Jorge and Lubna were allowed to see him. I expect he's being well cared for."

Olaf pulled a face as he shrugged out of his heavy coat. He unbuckled his belt and hung it on a hook on the wall so the short sword he favoured swung down. He sat beside Thomas and pulled off his boots.

"I can't remember being this cold since I left Sweden."

"Me, neither," Thomas said.

"You've been to Sweden?"

Thomas smiled and glanced at the open doorway, but the two women were still busy preparing food. They would have heard Olaf arrive—probably half the palace had—and know he was ready to eat.

"I came to thank you for last night. It can't have been an easy thing to do, standing up to Aixa."

"She was threatening my grandson," said Olaf. "Threatening you and Lubna."

"You still have my thanks. Who is going to win this power struggle?"

"Nothing to do with me—not until it's decided."

"You're not as uninterested as you pretend," Thomas said. "Lubna told me there are soldiers throughout the city, more than there have ever been. Are you expecting trouble?"

"I send men where I am asked."

Thomas sighed. "And who is doing the asking?"

Olaf shrugged, washing his hands across his face. "The usual culprits. Until things are settled I take orders from anyone above me. Wouldn't do to antagonise whoever ends up in charge."

"Who asked you to send men to the city? Is trouble expected?"

"Abu al-Hasan, but his brother's behind it, no doubt. And no trouble, not that I know of. Not yet anyway."

"Is something coming?" Thomas asked.

Olaf glanced at him. "Not for me to say, already told you that." He stood, twisting the kinks from his back, rocking his head from side to side until his neck made a snapping sound. He called out, "Hey—any chance of food in here?"

Lubna came out and kissed his cheek after he bent down to allow it.

"A few more minutes. You and Thomas carry on talking." She looked toward Thomas. "Have you asked him?"

"Asked me what?" Olaf sat at the head of the table, his scarred forearms resting on the surface.

"I need to visit al-Khala. As soon as possible."

Olaf looked at him a long while. "Is that wise? You're a father now. You have responsibilities."

"Now is a good time, as William has been taken from me. He's going to be safer inside the palace than anywhere else."

Olaf leaned forward. "It might not be my place to ask, but I need to know. Is he yours or not?"

Thomas smiled at Olaf's question. The man was as blunt as ever.

"He is mine."

"There is no doubt?"

Thomas raised a shoulder, and Olaf nodded. "I thought so."

"He's still mine, even if he's not," Thomas said.

Olaf nodded again. "Good enough for me. I almost took a boy child in once, you know. His father was a friend, killed in some pointless skirmish. His wife was carrying the boy at the time, and when he was born I offered. I would have liked a son." He glanced at the kitchen, lowered his voice. "I love my daughters, but a son—a son is different, isn't he? Did you have brothers, or were you the only boy?"

"I had an older brother," Thomas said. "A younger

one who died. And a sister."

"Of course, your brother's name was William, you said last night."

"It was, but he was the brother who died. My older brother was named John, the same as our father."

"If I'd had a son I would have wanted to call him Olaf. But I couldn't have done it, not in this land. Why didn't you call your son Thomas?"

"Because I called him William."

"After the brother who died. You're not superstitious, then? Do they still live, your other brother and sister?"

"Not the brother. The sister… I don't know. She'll be thirty-five years of age if she does."

"What happened to your brother? Was it war?"

Thomas shook his head. "He died of the sweating sickness. It was rife in England then and might still be for all I know. It's what took the younger one too, but that was earlier. I caught it but recovered. My brother didn't. Nor my mother."

"And your sister?"

"She never caught it. But my father couldn't manage her, not a girl of five years. I tried, but I was only twelve myself. I think father was going to hand her over to the church, so one night I stole away with her. There was an aunt in Ludlow and I took her there. I'm not sure the aunt was too pleased when I turned up on her doorstep, but she took her in all the same. Blood, you see."

Olaf nodded his understanding. "What was her name? Eleanor?"

"No… that was someone else."

Olaf grinned. "A lover?"

"Something like that."

Olaf's grin grew wider. "You're a strange one, Thomas. Something like that. You amuse me, you know."

"I'm glad I have my uses."

Olaf's expression turned serious, but a sparkle remained in his eyes. "Look after her, won't you." He didn't need to say who. "When are you planning on leaving for al-Khala?"

"As soon as possible." Thomas glanced at the window. "But I'd like to see this snow gone before I do."

"You forget, don't you," said Olaf.

"Forget what?"

"How to deal with it. When I was young we wore woven birch on our feet to keep us on the surface. We could travel ten or fifteen miles a day. And now we have one night's storm and the city grinds to a halt. I expect my troops are the only people on the streets."

"What are their orders?"

"To look out for trouble, nothing more. As far as I know there's nothing sinister behind their presence."

"Does al-Zagal have his own men here?"

Olaf's eyes watched Thomas carefully, his nod barely perceptible. He appeared ready to say something more, but then Lubna and her mother came into the room carrying platters of food, filling the air with conversation, and the moment passed, if it had ever been there to begin with.

Thomas found Jorge pink faced, surrounded by chaos. He hesitated in the doorway, reluctant to add to the man's troubles, but as soon as Jorge saw him he waved him over.

"Save me from this hell," he whispered. "Everyone wants a decision from me, and I've run dry."

Thomas grinned. "I thought you were getting help."

"I am. Bazzu said she'd send me half a dozen, but none have arrived yet."

"I expect they'll have to finish preparing the evening meal first."

Jorge shook his head. "Oh, don't."

A young man approached and asked who was meant to be with the old Sultan that night, if anyone.

"It's on the rota," snapped Jorge.

"And where is the rota? Samuli always pinned it to the wall beside the concubine bathhouse, but it's not there."

"Because it's in my room," said Jorge. "Go with…" He scanned those around him. "Ahmad," he called, "go with this man and hand him the rota for today so he can pin it to the wall."

Thomas watched the two hurry away.

"Why not just send them all away?"

"Because the palace must continue to operate." He looked around once more, but at that moment nobody was seeking his advice. People appeared to be moving with more purpose. Jorge wiped a hand across his perspiring face. "And they've lit fires in the braziers underground so now it's too hot in here." He stepped back, leaned against the wall. "Peace at last." He glanced at Thomas. "Unless you bring me news of more chaos. I called in to see your son again, by the way. He looks peaceful enough, but I don't have enough experience with children to know whether that's normal or not. Most of them seem to do nothing but cry when I'm around, so likely it's not."

Thomas smiled, remembering how Jorge had handled his new-born nephew in Qurtuba after his sister-in-law gave birth while they were there.

"I'm leaving the city for a day or two. Lubna's found an address for Pilar, so I'm going to look for her."

"Do you think she's the killer?" Jorge waved as a woman approached and she stopped, not moving away, simply waiting, her hands folded in front of her.

"Everything points to it. She had the opportunity, and Javier's wealth was certainly motive enough. I'd like to link her to Alvarez, and if I talk to her I may be able to. I suspect she was one of his victims."

"You know I can't come with you, not with all of..." Jorge waved a hand, "...all of this. No!" He snapped at the woman, who had started to approach again, believing his wave had been at her. "Oh, all right then, what do you want?"

Thomas stepped back as Jorge tried to manage events he didn't understand. Once the woman trotted away he came back.

"I didn't expect you to come," Thomas said. "I'll go on my own. Stay here and get yourself organised. Use Bazzu as much as you can. I'll come find you when I return and see if you can find time to help then. Otherwise there's Lubna. She's surprised me with her willingness and ability."

"I don't know why you're so surprised. I always believed she was smart. I think all you saw was what suited you."

It was an atypical comment from Jorge, who usually saw the best in everyone, but Thomas considered it fair.

He knew he tended to judge people through the filter of his own expectations.

"I'm going to try and see William," Thomas said. "I don't know if they'll let me, but I have to try."

Jorge nodded, his eyes darting from person to person, and Thomas didn't believe he had heard what had been said. He stepped away, waited a moment, but Jorge had already moved on, issuing instructions to a woman who listened intently before dashing off on an errand.

Thomas turned and made his way through the palace corridors. He passed servants and guards but nobody tried to stop him, nobody questioned his presence. He was a familiar sight, and even with the tension the old Sultan's return had brought, Thomas was considered safe and allowed to pass. Until he came to the boundary of the harem. He had entered before, but only when summoned, and it was here he was stopped. Two guards moved to block his way. He didn't recognise them, but that wasn't unusual. The allocation of soldiers to the harem was changed frequently to prevent any one becoming too familiar with those who resided within.

There was much ignorance amongst the general population regarding those who inhabited these inner chambers. Thomas knew, for the most part, the women who resided within spent a great deal of time trying to avoid boredom. They played instruments and sang, they practiced calligraphy, read from the extensive palace library, and cared for their bodies, their hair, their nails, every part of them fashioned to be as exquisite as possible. And they teased.

Women entered the harem for two reasons. There were those such as Aixa whose marriage was for political purposes. Then there were the concubines whose sole purpose was pleasure. It was these the guards feared most. They were chosen because of their love of a sensual life, and a single Sultan, not even a score of Sultans, was enough to satisfy the natural instincts of these women. Thomas knew their mischief and their power, had treated many of the residents and found it difficult to keep his mind on the practice of medicine when in their presence.

All of this was on his mind as he approached the guards. "I am here to see the child."

"We know nothing of a child."

"But you know me. I wouldn't be here without cause."

"We are usually told when you're coming."

"An oversight, I'm sure. There was a birth last night and I have been called. Now let me pass." Thomas saw uncertainty on their faces, but a sullen sense of duty as well, and knew this way was barred to him. He shook his head and turned away, picturing the passages around him in his mind, trying to think of an alternative way inside and coming up short. He considered returning to enlist Jorge's help, torn between the man's obvious panic and his own need to see his son. He ached with the missing of him, as if it had been he who had given birth, not Helena.

Turning a corner, Thomas saw three figures ahead of him crossing the passageway and he darted back from sight, praying they had not seen him. The old Sultan and his brother continued to haunt the palace, signs all around of their growing confidence and power. The third had been Yusuf. It was not unusual he should spend time with his father, Abu al-Hasan Ali, but his presence hinted at more. At the tugging of those strands of power and influence. Al-Zagal's guards were already edging out Aixa's, his concubines infiltrating the harem. And as the thought came to him Thomas wondered if there was some significance he had missed in Eva's seemingly constant presence beside Helena. Had one of these men placed her there? And if so, why? Because of her closeness to him?

Thomas shook his head. They would have no interest in him. He could only worry about so much, and William was his first priority, even above the search for the killer of Alvarez and Javier.

Thomas peered around the corner to find the corridor empty. He stepped out, head down. There was a courtyard on the right, and if he crossed it he might gain access to a way inside. There had been a hidden passage there he had become familiar with two years before, when the servant girl Prea had laughingly led him through the twisting tunnels. Britto had been helping seal them up since, but there were many passageways and this one might yet remain intact. If not there would be another way.

He was half way to the doorway which would offer access when movement ahead brought his gaze up, afraid it might be the old Sultan again. Who he saw was even worse.

Aixa stood facing him, her feet spread as if she was trying to block his way. Thomas considered turning and running, even as he knew it would be an enormous insult to the Sultana. Still, he glanced behind, only to discover the two guards he had seen before blocking his escape.

"Did you think we'd simply let to wander around?" said one of them.

"With me," said Aixa. She looked past Thomas. "Fetch the other."

Aixa turned away, expecting obedience. Thomas glanced behind again. Only one of the guards had gone on whatever errand Aixa had sent him on. Thomas knew he could disarm the remaining man, but did he even want to consider the repercussions of such an action?

He followed Aixa, catching her before she could reach her chambers, and fell into step alongside. Aixa slowed as they approached a corridor leading away to the right. She waved the remaining guard ahead, waiting until he had checked it was clear before calling her on.

"I want to see my son."

"Forget him, Thomas. You don't have a son. And I need you. Things are moving rapidly now."

CHAPTER 26

"I won't go," Thomas said.

He saw Aixa's fingers curl into her palms, tendons standing out in her arms.

"You have no choice."

"Of course I have a choice, every man does. And I choose not to go." Thomas risked a brief glance at Jorge, who had also been brought to Aixa's inner chamber. Here the air was sweet with perfume and warmed by hidden pipes running beneath the floor. The windows continued to show swirling snow, but with the light fading the air beyond the glass had turned the colour of slate.

Aixa reached for a parchment and waved it in Thomas's face. "They demand your presence, you and Jorge. It is *not* conditional, it is a *demand*. You must both attend or there will be no discussions, there will be no release of my son. So you will go." Her face was white with rage, but a rage she was unable to release because she needed him.

Thomas knew this was his only opportunity. He had deliberately brought Aixa to this state. It was a dangerous play, but he was desperate.

"The Spanish have someone you want. You have someone I want."

Aixa's dark eyes bored into his.

"You would blackmail me?"

"We are negotiating," Thomas said. "As I will negotiate with the Spanish once you release William into my care."

"You will be in al-Khala. How will you look after an infant?"

"I have a house and a woman who will care for him." Thomas had forgotten about the location of the negotiations. It made it even more difficult for him to attempt this strategy, knowing it was where Pilar had fled, but restoring William to him overrode everything else.

"You have a house here in the Alkazaba. I might be willing to release him there, with someone I know to care for him. I understand Helena has a friend who spends a great deal of time with her. Perhaps she would agree to help."

"Helena doesn't want him. I do. He is released to my care or I don't go to al-Khala."

Thomas watched Aixa's fingers crush the document she held.

"By all the gods, you're a dangerous man to know," said Jorge. They had returned to his quarters to await William. Aixa had sent orders for him to be brought, and in turn Thomas had sent a messenger to find Lubna.

"This might be the last time I'm allowed into the palace," Thomas said. "Do you think Bazzu could send for some food for us? I'm starving."

Jorge shook his head, laughing. "I'll ask, but I'm not sure I want to distract her right now." His mood had lightened considerably despite the tension of their meeting with Aixa. The change was brought about by the ample presence of Bazzu, who had arrived to organise his life. From the look of busy contentment on her face as she handed out orders, it was a role she was more than happy to take on. Thomas only hoped Jorge was aware of the price he would have to pay for her help. Jorge raised a hand and waved a girl over, the same one Thomas had seen in the kitchens and around the palace. She came, eyeing Thomas coldly. Jorge gave her instructions to bring enough food for everyone and she trotted away.

"She still blames me for what happened to Prea," Thomas said. "She'll likely spit in my food."

"She knows it wasn't you who killed her, and she knows you punished the man who did. So does Bazzu. They'll come around, but you might be right. I'd check what she brings, if I were you."

"Where is he?" Thomas said. "It's been a half hour since we left Aixa. How long does it take to carry one child through a few corridors? She'd better not renege on her promise now."

"You have the upper hand and she knows it." Jorge leaned against his cushions.

Thomas wriggled, unable to find a comfortable position. "What I don't understand is why the Spanish are so insistent on you and I being there for the negotiation. They must know we are ignorant of politics."

"The Queen likes you," said Jorge. "It may be no

more than she wants a trusted friend there."

"This is a transaction, nothing more. Trust has little to do with it. They will settle a price and Aixa will pay whatever it is and Muhammed will be returned."

"Al-Zagal won't allow him back in the palace. You've seen how his influence is spreading through every part of the city. He might restore his brother as Sultan, but it is he who will rule."

"He'll have to return to Ronda soon," Thomas said. "Without his presence the Spanish will consider it an easy target."

"They'll never take Ronda," said Jorge. "You've been there, haven't you?"

Thomas shook his head. "Malaka and the towns along the coast, but never that far west. Why?"

"It's impregnable. Set at the top of sheer cliffs two hundred feet high, there's no way in from the west, and in all other directions it's protected by mountains. It's al-Zagal's stronghold—and will be the last place in al-Andalus to fall."

"I hear he's a strong ruler of men," Thomas said. "It would be a mistake to allow Muhammed to return."

"Which is why al-Zagal and his brother are here."

Thomas shook his head in confusion. "So much deceit being played out within the walls of this place. I'm glad I'm a simple physician. I believe—" But Thomas was interrupted by the sound of running feet, then a woman appeared clutching a cotton wrapped bundle.

Thomas darted to his feet, reaching out, afraid the woman was going to spill his son to the floor.

"Go," she said, handing William across. "Go quickly. The old Sultan has sent men to take him."

Thomas glanced at Jorge, who remained on the cushions, and knew his friend couldn't accompany him.

"I'll stall them," said Jorge. "Do as she says. Now."

"If Lubna comes you know where I've gone."

Thomas walked fast, refusing to run but moving at speed along the shortest route to the outside. On two occasions he had to stop and hide in an alcove as guards crossed his path. He didn't know if they were looking for him or not, but it was safer to assume they were and be wrong than be caught.

Thomas wondered if he should be concerned about William. The child was too quiet. Little more than a day old. Torn from his mother. Moved from place to place. And through it all he remained passive. The birth had been difficult and Thomas had seen other babies whose development was stunted from such trauma.

As he approached the last gate from the palace he saw five soldiers stationed there—three more than usual—and knew they were waiting for him. He pressed himself into the shadows and watched, but each was alert, eyes tracking toward the palace, and Thomas knew the way was blocked.

He slid along the wall, ducked from sight and tried to work out where he and William would be safe. He discarded the idea of returning to the Alkazaba, they would look there first. And then it came to him. William's grandfather. Smiling, Thomas began to climb back toward the barracks as the snow continued to fall around him.

Thomas followed a single set of footprints left when a guard had come on duty. The edge of the training square was sheltered by an overhang, the ground safer beneath. As he approached the far side the snow became more churned. At one point he had to stop and flatten himself against the wall as a group of men crossed the open space, but none glanced in his direction. On the far side Thomas could see Olaf's quarters. He glanced left and right, but saw no-one.

He stepped out, moving fast before skidding to a halt. From the right eight men appeared from inside the palace. They came in two ranks, looking straight ahead as if on a mission of some kind. Thomas sank back into the shadows as they passed, their weapons jingling.

The amount of activity indicated something was happening. Events were coming to a head. Thomas tried to still his breathing, feeling William squirm against his chest, praying he wouldn't wake, although he knew the child was growing hungry again.

He knew he couldn't stay where he was and strode across the roadway, head high, shoulders back, confident he should be here. He glanced toward the palace, glimpsed two men inside the entrance, but they were looking the other way

He reached Olaf's door and it opened to his touch. As he stepped through warmth engulfed him. A pair of thick candles burned on the table where a sheaf of papers rested. One was a hand drawn map.

Thomas reached beneath his robe, extracting William, holding him up to check on his condition. William squirmed, eyes coming open at being separated from comfort, and cried out.

"Who's there!" Olaf appeared in the kitchen doorway, a steaming cup in one hand, the other on a knife at his waist.

"Why do they want you to go?" Thomas asked.

"I could ask you the same thing. But I hear the Spanish favour you." Olaf's face showed no expression, not now William had been taken from the room by Lubna, who had appeared soon after Thomas. The wet nurse had come a quarter hour later and she too had left the men alone.

Now Thomas sat across the table from Olaf, both of them leaning forward. There was a tension between them reflecting that which gripped the city. And perhaps for the same reason. Thomas considered himself of the Albayzin. Olaf was the Sultan's man. The palace on one hill, the seething populace on the other. At one time a strong hand had maintained order, but now it was no longer clear who ruled.

"I asked first." Thomas expected the hint of a smile but none came.

"Two reasons," said Olaf, holding up his fingers. He curled one into his palm. "The Spanish need to see we take the negotiations seriously. How better than sending the Sultan's general?" He folded the second finger. "And there are those here want me out of the way. They're not sure they can trust me."

"Who asked you to go? Abu al-Hasan or Aixa?"

"Neither."

Thomas nodded, not needing to be told who. Al-Zagal was digging his grip tighter into the body of the city. Lubna had told him of troops on the streets, clashes at the base of the Albayzin.

"Does he believe you are his man?"

"I told you—he's not sure."

Thomas stared at Olaf, wondering how far he could push him. "And are you? His man?"

"When events have played out, only then can I decide."

"When that happens will I be in danger?"

Olaf returned Thomas's stare. "I like you well enough, Thomas Berrington, but I am a soldier. I follow orders. If my master asks me to kill you I will. You know that."

"You can try."

"No—I will kill you. Don't think our play fighting means anything. You're good with a sword, and fast, I give you that, but you know I can kill you whenever I want."

Thomas didn't bother disputing Olaf's opinion. "You supported me two years ago when Abu al-Hasan ordered you to kill me."

"He was in the wrong, and I could already see which way the wind was blowing. Muhammed would become Sultan, and for whatever reason he wanted you alive."

"So friendship had nothing to do with it."

"I've already told you, I do as I am asked. I follow orders."

"Al-Zagal's orders."

"Is that so bad? He might be the last hope for this land. Muhammed can't save us, and Abu al-Hassan's too old. Zagal's the only one who can fight the Spanish."

"You respect him."

"Of course. He's a general too. A good one."

"So what time do we leave tomorrow?"

Olaf glanced at the window. "As soon as it grows

light enough to see."

"With the snow and the moonlight it'll be like day out there."

"We wait for the sun. You should go and prepare yourself."

"I'm ready now. I could do with a change of clothes but I'm sure Jorge will have something I can wear."

"Get some sleep then. There's a bedroom you and Lubna can use."

"I'd like it if she and William could stay here until we return," Thomas said. "I'll feel happier if they are somewhere safe."

Olaf nodded. "Of course. Although I doubt anywhere is safe anymore. Things are coming to a head. Next year will see the war won or lost, I'm sure of it."

Thomas said nothing. Olaf's words hinted at despair, and it frightened him to think this rock of a man saw only defeat on the horizon. Olaf would die before he surrendered, and there was no stopping the Spanish tide. Thomas felt ill at ease, cast adrift between worlds. He had given up his old life–England no longer meant anything to him. Now he believed himself a Moor, adopted to be sure, but Moor all the same. Except he had experienced a deep empathy with the Spanish queen that confused him. Thomas believed in rationality, and she had struck him as a rational woman. Despite Spain winning the war it was also bankrupting their country. There had been talk in Qurtuba about finance, and he knew money was the biggest worry for Isabel and Fernando. The rational approach would be to broker a peace deal that would allow the Moors to rule in al-Andalus, but when had rationality ever had a place in conflict. Even as the thoughts tumbled through his mind Thomas knew they were a vain ambition. Peace was impossible. There was always going to be someone who broke it, on one side or the other. Always men who thrived on conflict. Too many of them. Thomas shook his head, trying to dash his worries clear.

"You know why I'm being sent, don't you," he said, his voice quiet.

"To negotiate Muhammed's freedom."

"Are you being sent to stop that?"

"I am being sent to protect our negotiators. You know Faris al-Rashid is in the party, don't you?"

"No, I didn't. Why him?"

"He's a friend of Muhammed. They're cut of the same cloth, full of thick headed privilege and the arrogance of young men."

"If Muhammed returns there'll be civil war," Thomas said.

"There may be, yes." Olaf stared at Thomas, waiting.

It took a moment before he saw the way it was, and he let his breath go. "That's what the Spanish want, isn't it. They know al-Zagal has returned, and they know releasing Muhammed is just the spark that's needed. Why fight us when we can destroy ourselves." Thomas spoke looking at the table top. From the other room William cried and stilled. Thomas raised his eyes. "Which is why you side with al-Zagal."

Olaf rose and turned away. "I've fought for this land too long to give it up now. I'm going to bed. I suggest you do the same."

Thomas watched the big general move from the room, light on his feet despite his size. Olaf hadn't needed to spell it out. The message was clear. Thomas's presence was a concession to Aixa's vanity, nothing more. And if it came to it Olaf would kill Thomas rather than allow Muhammed to return to Gharnatah.

CHAPTER 27

There was something illicit about their lovemaking. Dim grey light crept into the room, casting no shadows, the sun still an hour away. Both of them heard movement beyond the door, but they could no more hold back their passion than they could still their breathing. Lubna bit her palm to stifle her cries and Thomas clenched his jaw tight. The strain made the pleasure only the greater. At the end a cry escaped Lubna as she quivered atop him, then she slumped, her body slick with sweat. Thomas held her fast, knowing he would not hold her again for weeks. A knock sounded on the door and he pulled the covers over their nakedness. Fatima entered, as if she had been waiting for them to finish.

"I've made coffee. Olaf has left already." She glanced at them, then at William lying in a crib made of pillows. "He's such a good baby."

"He is."

It was lucky only Thomas could see the grin on Lubna's face. Even so he knew Fatima was no fool. The scent of their joining hung thick in the air of the small room.

Once she was gone Thomas slapped Lubna, raising a tiny squeal, then climbed from the tumble of cushions and blankets that had formed their bed. He lifted his clothes and sniffed at them, pulled a face. He would need to find something fresher before he talked with the Spanish, unless he wanted to deliberately antagonise them.

"I wish you didn't have to go." Lubna stretched, naked among the covers, her perfect skin both hidden and revealed in turn.

"So do I. Particularly when you do that."

Lubna smiled and stretched again. "We should have done this long, long ago."

"We should have. But we didn't. And now is good too. Better than next year."

She grinned and rose in a single lithe movement. "It is. You are so clever, Thomas."

"Don't press your luck." He pulled on the sour robes then picked up William, who was finally beginning to stir. Fatima had found him some sheep's milk during the night and he had gulped it all down, burping with contentment afterward, but he was growing hungry again now. "I need to visit home before I leave. Will the wet nurse come here, do you think?"

"I asked her to come at first light," said Lubna, also sorting through her clothes and dressing.

"I'd like it if you and William stayed here until I get back," Thomas said.

Lubna stopped, her hair still uncovered. "I belong on the Albayzin."

"You're safer here."

"I'm safe there. And your patients will expect some-one. Besides, Britto and his men are still working." She padded across to him and slapped him softly on the cheek. "Don't worry about me, Thomas, or William. Go meet your precious queen—I'll still be here when you come back."

"I don't expect either king or queen to be there."

Lubna laughed. "Good. I don't need to be jealous then."

"Last night Olaf said the palace is no longer looking for me, or William, so I expect you could return home." He glanced at the window, which glowed with a rising sun. "But if you sense any danger, anything at all—"

"Go now, before I drag you back into bed." Lubna held her hands out for William.

Thomas turned, stopped at the door. "Do nothing about the deaths. Leave it until I am back."

"I should be safe enough now Pilar's in al-Khala."

"If Pilar *is* the killer."

"You believe she is, don't you?"

"I think the likelihood is it's her, yes. But take care anyway, and do nothing that might draw attention."

Lubna shook her head and turned away, dismissing his pointless fears.

In the bedroom of his house on the Albayzin, Thomas opened a leather bag and laid clothing inside, choosing items for their practicality and warmth. A sudden switch in wind direction had brought a thaw. All over the land snow was melting fast, swelling streams and rivers, but he was aware it could just as quickly turn again.

Thomas knelt and drew a long wooden box from beneath the bed. No dust discoloured its surface despite it having been resident where it lay for over a decade. He wasn't entirely sure why he had pulled it out now, other than he was still uneasy after his conversation with Olaf the night before.

He unbuckled the leather strap holding the box shut and raised the lid. Inside a velvet robe lay wrapped around some objects. Thomas loosened it, drew out a leather scabbard. The sword within was a little over three feet long, sharp and well cared for. It had been his father's. Thomas had taken it from the man's dead hand on a battle field in France almost thirty years before. At the time he hadn't known why. The sword was almost two thirds as long as he was then, impossible for a thirteen-year-old boy to wield, but he had taken it anyway. It hadn't been through sentiment. Thomas had never loved his father. Had not even liked him. Mutual hate would have been a better emotion to describe their relationship. Hate when indifference wasn't enough. But the sword felt like a talisman of some kind. And as he grew older, grew stronger, he found he could use the weapon. With difficulty at first, then with growing skill. At seventeen years of age he had been almost as tall as he was now, even stronger because he had spent four years living off his wits and the land. Four years of running wild like the feral dogs of southern France, where he constantly moved from place to place with a band of ragged companions. Thomas had been the youngest, the strongest, the wildest fighter, afraid of nothing. Or rather, unafraid of death. Until he met Eleanor.

Thomas laid the sword on the bed. It would need no cleaning or sharpening. He took it out once a month to oil the surface and run a stone along its length.

He lifted out the other contents of the box. A mail vest, a pair of leather boots capped with steel. A long, narrow shield, his family crest still faintly showing on the scarred surface. He had discarded it once, before returning for it a year later. He considered each item before returning all but the sword and boots to the box and pushing it back into place. The sword and boots were enough. More than enough.

Thomas caught sight of the negotiating party an hour after passing through the western gate of Gharnatah. The roadway—now little more than a track—climbed a low hill, and from the crest he saw them ahead. It was a larger group than he expected. Still too far to count accurately, but he estimated forty horses and men, as well as carts. He urged his horse forward, a spirited Arabian. The soldier who had led it from the barrack stables made no attempt to hide his amusement when he saw Thomas's expression.

"The general said you rode well, so to make sure you had a worthy mount," the man said.

Thomas only grunted, putting a foot in a stirrup and pulling himself up. The horse skittered, bucked, and Thomas pressed his knees tight and jerked the reins hard, letting it know who was in command.

Now they were coming to some kind of accommodation and Thomas was starting to enjoy himself. The pure physicality of controlling the beast left him little time to dwell on his thoughts.

The party ahead disappeared as they crossed the rise. When Thomas reached the ridge he had closed more than half the distance and could make out individuals. He saw Olaf on the right flank, his head constantly moving as he scanned the land to either side and ahead. Beside him rode Jorge. Thomas was sure he could make him out talking, which was no surprise.

Thomas waited a moment, the stallion's flanks pressing against his thighs as it breathed. Ahead the ground rose to north and south. A narrow valley wound between low hills. He had studied the map on Olaf's table the night before, and knew al-Khala sat on a wide break between higher ground. At one time it had been considered impregnable, with mountains to the west offering protection. That had been before the Spanish encroached ever deeper into al-Andalus. The town had fallen earlier in the year in a counter attack after Muhammed was captured. Thomas and Jorge had spent a night there on their return from Qurtuba. Thomas urged his mount forward, keeping it in tight check as the descent steepened. A little snow remained on the ridge, but as he descended it disappeared. The ground was wet, churned by those who had already passed.

He came to within half a mile before urging the horse into a trot. It wanted to gallop but he fought it, his confidence growing. Thomas passed the slow tail of the group. He was about to veer right, intending to join Olaf and Jorge, when a woman's voice called his name. He reined in the horse and turned in the saddle.

Eva waved, her silk robe falling back to reveal a pale arm.

Thomas turned and trotted to the cart. Eva sat on the flat bed, but had found a wooden trunk to perch on. The driver glanced at Thomas then turned away, uninterested.

"What are you doing here?" Thomas asked. "Who's with Helena?"

"I'm not her nurse," said Eva, "I'm a friend. She's moved into the harem infirmary. Don't worry, she's being well looked after."

Thomas grunted. "How was she when you left?"

Eva smiled. "I thought you didn't care."

"Is that what she told you?"

"That and much else besides."

"No doubt. You still haven't told me why you're here. Did al-Zagal send you for some reason?"

Eva glanced quickly at the man steering the two mules pulling the cart and gave a shake of her head. "We can talk over dinner this evening."

"What do we have to talk of?" Eva made Thomas uneasy. Her sharp sensuousness reminded him of Helena, except he knew he shouldn't judge her simply because of that. There were few women like Helena in the world, which was a blessing.

"I will exchange my company for information." She waved a hand in dismissal before he could turn away. It was a small victory, but one he was sure had been deliberate. "Join your friends. I will find you when I want you."

Thomas veered aside. When he glanced back Eva was still watching him, a look of amusement on her face.

Olaf glanced at Thomas's horse, back up to him. He smiled. Thomas met his gaze, jerking the reins so the horse skittered in objection until his knees brought it under control. *Small victories*, he thought, *we are all capable of pettiness.*

"What kept you?" Jorge asked. His face was placid and Thomas believed he was glad to be away from the harem and his new responsibilities.

"Some of us have things to do."

"What have you done with William?"

"He's with Lubna. I wanted them to stay at Olaf's house, but she wouldn't."

"Bazzu would have found someone to care for him if you had asked."

Beside them Olaf twisted in his saddle. "If they were going to stay anywhere it was with Fatima." He glanced at the sky. Clouds scudded from the south, but there were breaks here and there. "We'll need to stop soon for noon prayer. The Imam will let us know exactly when."

Thomas studied the path ahead. It led down to what would normally be a dry gulley, but now it tumbled with snow-melt. He glanced left and right but saw no bridge, and no easy crossing.

"You ought to call a halt before we reach there," Thomas said. "I could look for a safe place to get across."

"You will pray with the rest of us," said Olaf.

Thomas shook his head. He knew Olaf was no Muslim, and Jorge, like himself, had lost faith in all religion. But he knew the prayers and rituals and was able to recite them when needed, as were the others.

"I still think we'd be better to keep going," Thomas said. "The Quran allows it when necessary."

"You go tell the Imam that," said Olaf, raising his hand and wheeling about to halt the procession.

Thomas tied his horse to a cart beside a line of others, then found a place at the back of the gathering facing east. It took a while before everyone was ready, each helping others by pouring water over their hands before finding a place. Thomas knelt, bowing his head, making a pretence of piety. Ahead of him others did the same, except for most of them the belief was real, an integral part of their lives. There were times Thomas envied them, as he envied Lubna her faith. It brought her comfort, a solid core to her life he knew he lacked. Or had done. He was beginning to think she was becoming that core.

Glancing around he saw Eva half way toward the front, where the Imam was still standing gazing at the sky. Thomas wondered if she had converted or if, like him, this was a pretence.

Something must have told the Imam it was noon—exactly what remained a mystery to Thomas. Perhaps his God sent a message. Whatever it was, if anything at all, the Imam turned east and knelt, his voice calling out the prayers and the small gathering responding. The sound washed across Thomas, hypnotic, his lips moving without conscious thought. He had heard the words often enough, they had seeped into his being. Perhaps Lubna would consider that enough. He knew they would have to talk soon. Their relationship had experienced a sudden change and the sex would only be enough for so long.

Thomas stared across the bowed heads, looking beyond to the way they had come.

A group of men were outlined on the far ridge. A dozen, on good horses. Thomas looked around for Olaf, finally found him at the front where he was expected to be. He saw the general's head lift. He had seen them as well. The prayers went on, but now Thomas no longer heard, no longer gained the little comfort he had found in their repetition.

Were they soldiers sent by al-Zagal? If so, to what purpose? And why only a dozen? There were two score gathered around the carts and horses by the gully. Admittedly, most would be of little use if there was a confrontation, but numbers counted for something. Thomas scanned the bowed heads, trying to judge how many fighting men there were. He came up short. Not enough. Not nearly enough.

If it came to that.

He narrowed his eyes, trying to make out details, but they were too far away. Were they al-Zagal's men, or even a wandering group of Spanish soldiers? The land they were travelling through was close to the border, and the border itself was a fluid concept out here. Perhaps they had been sent to scout for their party, even to escort them in. Thomas wished he could stand, could mount his horse and ride toward them. He wanted to know who they were, but had to remain where he was. He was part of this charade now, not just the prayers, but the negotiations too. Whatever the outcome of the talks he was sure they were already decided. Had been decided months before, even while he and Jorge resided in Qurtuba.

When his attention returned from the ridge it was to find people rising, rolling prayer mats, making their way back to carts and horses. Eva detoured to come close but didn't stop. A smile, no more. A knowing smile. Thomas wondered what was going on. She acted as if she was attracted to him, but if Helena had been talking to her that was unlikely. He watched her make her way to the cart, pull herself up on the flat bed and sit. She glanced at him again. That same smile. Thomas shook his head and deliberately turned away. Did she think him a fool?

They came to the town as it was growing dark. The journey should have been less than a day, but it had taken over an hour for them all to cross the tricky waters racing down the gulley. Throughout it all the band of men had remained on the ridge.

"Are they the Sultan's?" Thomas had asked as he stood beside Olaf, waiting to offer assistance to those crossing.

"He's not Sultan yet." But Olaf knew who Thomas spoke of.

"He will be, unless we bring Muhammed back soon."

"It's too late already, I'd say. Power has shifted. It takes a while to change, but once it does it takes even longer to reverse."

"So what happens when they release him?"

Olaf shrugged, then reached out a broad fist to grab the reins of the Imam as his horse stumbled sideways in the current.

They both watched the man move away before Olaf spoke again. "I should have let the water take him. They're all sour faced, these priests. Sour-minded too."

He shook his head. "Muhammed will have to find somewhere else. There are towns to the east he could set himself up in. Al-Zagal's power base is Ronda and the west. There are enough places north of al-Mera that would benefit from a strong hand."

Thomas smiled at the judgement in Olaf's words, knowing he didn't believe Muhammed was the strong hand Gharnatah or any other city needed. As the last of the group crossed, the two of them stood and watched the soldiers come down from the ridge.

"They could catch us within the hour if they wanted," said Olaf.

"If they want. They waited patiently enough up there until we were all across. An attack while we were scattered would have made more sense."

Olaf glanced at him. "Tactics? Be careful, Thomas, or I'll think you're after my job."

"No chance of that."

Olaf rode to the front of the column, which was stretched out, some hurrying ahead, others still gathering themselves after crossing the gully. Thomas mounted his horse and found Jorge, fell into step beside him. They remained that way as the afternoon drifted into evening. Occasionally Thomas slowed and turned in his saddle. The followers reached the gully, but instead of crossing they turned north and climbed the hillside, eventually disappearing from sight.

"Do you think they've arranged accommodation?" asked Jorge as they entered under low walls still showing signs of the battle to take the town. The houses were built around a low, conical hill, topped by a small castle. The Spanish flag flew from the ramparts, other banners flapping and cracking in the southerly wind. The low cloud that had hung over them all day was finally clearing and the night would be cold.

"We'll all have a place," Thomas said. "Depending on our status."

"Ah. A barn then, if we're lucky."

Thomas smiled. "That castle, I reckon. This is a Spanish town now, and it's they who invited us."

Spanish the town might be, but it wasn't obvious. Street corners still held stone butts of clean water. Islamic script decorated the walls and doorways, and the inhabitants wore Moorish dress more suited to the landscape. Only the mosque was changed. Masons had chipped religious texts from the walls and erected a rough stone cross beside the entrance.

"Gods, I need a bath," said Jorge. "Do you think there's any chance?"

"There'll still be baths around somewhere. Whether they're allowed to open, or let us in, is another matter." He watched as Eva dropped from the side of her cart and came across to them. Two men arrived from another direction to take their horses.

"Do you want me to show you your lodgings?" said Eva. "The cart driver has a list with all the assignments."

"A cart driver who reads," said Jorge. "It is indeed a world of wonders we live in."

"Don't judge people by their station in life," said Eva. Her gaze returned to Thomas. "It seems we will get the chance to dine together after all."

"I expect someone will send for me," Thomas said. "If we are needed for the talks."

Eva smiled, as if humouring him. It was obvious she

considered their presence without purpose.

"Tell me where we are," said Jorge. "I will dine with you this evening, even if Thomas refuses." He reached to rap Thomas's skull with a knuckle. "Hear that? Empty of sense or logic."

Eva afforded Jorge a coy smile that was blatant enough to make Thomas laugh. He raised his hand, turning it into a cough. Eva lifted on her toes while Jorge bent down so she could whisper into his ear.

"She's trouble," Thomas said after she had moved away.

"Beautiful trouble," said Jorge. "Exactly how I like it."

Thomas cast him a glance, unsure whether to give credence to his words or not. He found Jorge watching Eva weaving between the suddenly crowded square and knew he wasn't joking. He shook his head in wonder at the man's infinite capacity for sensuality.

A sudden clatter made him spin around to find twelve horsemen entering the square, the same men who had watched from the ridge. Olaf stepped forward, his hand on the hilt of his sword, and Thomas matched him, his own arm falling to the blade at his side. But the men slowed, dismounted, shaking their legs to restore circulation. They led their mounts away, looking neither left nor right. Two of them handed their horses to others and climbed the long set of steps toward the castle. Both had hoods pulled over their heads, obscuring their faces, but Thomas watched one, a nagging familiarity teasing at the back of his mind. Whatever the memory was it wouldn't come and he turned away.

"Did Eva say where we were staying, or was she simply whispering words of lust in your ear?"

"That too. We're not in the castle, I'm afraid. There's an inn at the foot of the hill. We're there."

"Who else?"

"I didn't ask. Should I have?"

"It doesn't matter. We'll find out soon enough." Thomas started forward, knowing Jorge would catch up and show him the way.

CHAPTER 28

Thomas woke with a start. For a moment he had no idea where he was. The figures in front of him, the stone walled room, all were unfamiliar. Words washed over him without meaning until his mind caught that the voices spoke Spanish and it came back to him. The negotiations. The dullness of it. And his exhaustion.

He straightened as Jorge nudged him, leaning close to whisper in his ear. "You were starting to snore, so I thought it wise to wake you. It's dull, isn't it? Even I nodded off at one point. How many days does this go on for?"

Thomas shook his head, clearing the last traces of confusion. "Many days. Sometimes weeks."

"Then God help me. I can feel myself ageing already."

"You didn't look like you were ageing much last night."

Jorge smiled but said nothing. He was the cause of his lethargy. Thomas had stayed downstairs drinking wine, finally ascending the stairs on legs that ached from a day's riding. He had entered the room and closed the door behind him before the scene on the wide bed came into focus and he stopped dead.

Eva sat astride Jorge, her head thrown back. Her snow white body glowed in the candlelight. Long black hair cascading down her narrow back, for once both sides released from the gold clasp. She moved in rapid jerks. Jorge lay passive beneath, his eyes closed.

Thomas stood rooted to the spot, knowing he should turn away but unable to. Neither participant was aware of his presence, both fully immersed in their own pleasure. He knew he had to leave before they saw him. Still he stayed. The sight didn't shock him, nor even surprise him. He knew Jorge of old, a man who embraced rather than resisted temptation. Except Jorge didn't regard it as temptation, rather as a missed opportunity should he not submit. Sweat streaked their bodies. Thomas wondered how long they had been there, what pleasures they had anointed each other with. Then Jorge opened his eyes. He stared at Thomas without expression, as if he had known he was there all along. His hands rose to Eva's breasts. Only when his eyes closed once more was Thomas released. He snapped backward, fumbling at the door, sure they both knew what he had witnessed.

Thomas pushed his hair back, rubbed a hand across his face in an attempt to wash away the last traces of sleep. At the front of the hall men sat at a table, their words too soft to carry.

"It was you she wanted," whispered Jorge, leaning close.

"I'm spoken for."

Jorge chuckled. "Since when did that ever stop a man? Is it time for dinner yet? I missed breakfast. Where did you sleep in the end?"

"On a bench downstairs."

A man at the back of the group of observers turned and hushed them.

Jorge nudged Thomas, rose and slipped along the wall to the doorway. The man looked again, frowning. Giving him cause for even more annoyance, Thomas rose and followed Jorge. He retrieved his sword from the stack in the outer lobby and slid it into the scabbard at his waist.

The talks were taking place in a squat hall on the south side of the town square. Since they had entered that morning traders had set up stalls across the area. The local population moved between them, testing fruit, sampling nuts and slivers of cooked meat. Multi-coloured fruits sat beside root vegetables and cabbages. Other stalls sold dried herbs, cardamom seeds, and all nature of spices. On one stall someone had laid out salt cod and other dried fish.

Thomas wound his way through the crowd, his hand tight on his leather purse to discourage pick-pockets.

"Are we going to eat?" asked Jorge. "I missed break-fast, remember."

"Your own fault. We're going to find Pilar and question her."

A middle-aged man moved fast from one of the stalls and careened into Thomas, who pushed him away. The man turned to him, angry until he saw the sword strapped to his waist.

"You think we might end this today?"

"Everything points to Pilar being the killer. So yes, if she's holed up in her old family house, here in al-Khala, we will end it."

They moved out of the square and started up a narrow street which wound around the hill marking the centre of the town.

"What will you do? Hand her over to the authorities here?"

"We'll have to take her back. The Spanish don't care who gets murdered in Gharnatah."

"That could be difficult. All the signs are we'll be here a week at least."

"Longer, I judge. I don't need this, I should be at home with my son."

"We should all be at home," said Jorge. "I've no idea why they want us here. It's not as if we're doing anything."

"I'll wait another few days. If we're still sitting listening to those idiots then, I'm going back."

"Taking Pilar with you."

"If we find her. She could have run anywhere. We might find out now—that's her house at the end of the row."

It was a substantial dwelling, sitting high on the hillside with a view across the surrounding country. To the west that year's crops had been burned during the attack, the stain of their destruction still marking the land. Thomas wondered if it was the reason the market had been so busy, because the Spanish had destroyed the local food supply when they captured the town.

Jorge peered through a small window set beside the door. "I can't see anyone. Do you think she's expecting us to come looking for her?"

"I doubt it. The town's Spanish now, no doubt she believes herself safe here."

Jorge grinned. "Then she's going to get an unpleasant surprise." He put his face against the glass again. "I think I saw someone crossing the doorway."

Thomas pushed close, shading the glass with his hands. He found himself looking in on a narrow hallway that stretched deep into the house. Two doors marked the left side of the corridor. They were closed, but a third at the far end stood open. He stared at the section of room beyond but saw nothing, not even a shadow.

"Did it look like her?"

"I've never seen her," said Jorge.

"Neither have I, but you've heard her described. Short, slim, dark-haired."

"Whoever it was passed too quickly, but it might have been."

Thomas stepped back, reaching into an inner pocket. He pulled out a surgical instrument and handed it to Jorge. "You can pick this lock, I take it."

Jorge took the instrument, but before kneeling to make an attempt he first tried the latch. The door swung inward. Jorge glanced at Thomas, who nodded him aside so he could enter first. He reached to his waist but left his sword where it was, instead drawing a slim knife. If Pilar was what he believed, she would have no qualms about killing again.

He stood, listening.

Nothing.

Reaching out he rapped his knuckles on the wood of the door.

"Pilar? Are you home?"

Silence.

He stepped along the corridor. Stopped at the first

doorway and opened it. A sitting room, chairs and table and bookcase. He left the door open and moved on. The second door gave into a bedroom, a leaded window offering a view across the town. A wide bed filled most of the space. A set of shelves on one wall held bottles and creams, a second feminine clothing neatly folded. Dresses and robes hung from a wooden bar across one corner.

"It's a good house," said Jorge. "Something like this would suit me when I'm too old for the harem."

Thomas stepped back from the door. "You'll never leave."

"Sometimes I think it might not be such a bad idea. When the Spanish come there will be no more harem. Perhaps I should purchase a house for when that day comes. I have enough money with my share of Javier's gold."

"You could buy a castle with your share."

"I don't want a castle. Something like this would be sufficient. But not here. Somewhere where the women are prettier. Have you ever noticed how in some towns all the women are pretty, and in some they are not?"

Thomas started down the corridor, but Jorge pushed past, impatient perhaps to get the search finished so he could sit down to his meal. Perhaps impatient to return to Eva.

As they approached the door Thomas glimpsed a shadow crossing the stone floor and called out a warning. A short woman appeared in the doorway. Her arm was raised, one hand holding a weapon. Thomas darted forward, pushing at Jorge, trying to force him out of harm's way. He was too slow. The knife came down and embedded itself in Jorge's shoulder, then he fell onto his face with a cry.

Thomas leapt over him, grabbing for the woman, but she was fast, turning and running through the rear door which already stood open. Thomas hesitated, wanting to pursue her, but he knew he had to attend to Jorge first.

He knelt beside him and gripped the handle of the knife. Jorge cried out again.

"Be still. It's not deep. She hit your shoulder bone. It probably saved your life."

"Take it out," grunted Jorge.

"In a minute, once I'm sure I won't do more harm." Thomas took his own knife and slit Jorge's robe to expose the skin beneath. Blood flowed from the wound, but it emerged slowly. "It's nothing," Thomas said. "The blade is so narrow it won't have damaged anything."

"*This* is *nothing*? It hurts. Take it out, take it out."

Thomas pulled the purse from beneath his robe, emptied coins onto the floor before handing it to Jorge. "Here, bite on this."

Jorge looked at the purse, shook his head.

"Suit yourself, but don't say I didn't warn you. Are you sure you don't–" Without warning Thomas drew the knife out. He didn't jerk but drew the blade steadily free. Jorge tried to grip his arm, but Thomas used his side to block the move. Then the knife was free and he tossed it aside. He used his own blade again, this time cutting strips from Jorge's shirt to bind the wound.

"Is it bad?" asked Jorge, his face turned away, not wanting to see.

"You'll live." Already the flow of blood was easing.

The blade had penetrated hardly at all before hitting bone. "It might slow your love making down though."

"Don't joke," said Jorge, taking Thomas's hand to pull himself up. "Eva will just have to do a little more of the work." Jorge rolled his shoulder, already coming to terms with how close he had come to a more serious injury.

"From what I saw last night she was working pretty hard."

"She is nothing if not enthusiastic. But then, I am also a good lover, and she achieved her own satisfaction." Jorge drew his torn robe together to cover himself. "Several times." Obviously completely recovered.

Thomas went to the door Pilar had escaped through. It gave into a narrow yard devoid of any decoration, exactly as her house in Gharnatah. A gate to the side led to a path that descended the hillside in a series of steps, other alleyways running from it as it fell away.

"She'll be long gone," said Jorge, joining him. "We won't catch up with her again now."

Thomas turned to re-enter the house. "If she's who we're after there'll be some clue inside."

"I'm injured," complained Jorge, "and I need to eat and sleep."

"I know the kind of sleep you're after. Go if you want, I can search as well alone as with company. Your shoulder will bruise soon, and I expect it to hurt more for a while before it gets better. You're right, you should eat and rest. I can give you something for the pain."

Jorge looked uncertain.

"She won't be back," Thomas said. "I'll be perfectly safe without you."

"As long as you're sure."

"Go." Thomas pushed him away, careful to avoid the injured shoulder. He turned without waiting to see what Jorge's decision would be.

He started with the discarded blade. Thomas wiped the blood from it and took it to the courtyard to examine where there was more light. It was unlike anything he had ever seen. Short and very slim. It didn't look like much of a weapon, except he had seen the damage it could inflict. The wooden handle was wrapped with leather strips. The blade was honed sharp on both edges. He lifted it to his own chin and pressed the tip into the skin. He imagined the blade thrusting upward, too slim for much resistance to be offered. He tossed it onto the table as he returned through the kitchen.

In the small room at the front he found some papers, a book of recipes, but nothing that might incriminate Pilar. The bedroom yielded no more until Thomas found a narrow trunk pushed beneath the bed. It was small, tucked tight against the wall, and he almost missed it. He went on his belly, wriggled underneath and hooked a fingertip through a handle top to tug it out. Like the trunk under his own bed this one was devoid of dust and obviously frequently used. Three straps held it closed, each with a lock attached. But the straps were leather, and Thomas's knife sharp.

He raised the lid, nodding in satisfaction at what he saw. There were five velvet pouches, no doubt containing coin, but it was what else lay within that offered a final confirmation. He was familiar with the instruments, some almost identical to those he owned himself. Small blades with razor sharp edges. More than capable of piercing skin, muscle and sinew. Thomas opened one of the velvet pouches, its contents confirming what he had already guessed. Gold and silver coins. More than three years' wage for a cook, even one as skilled as Pilar was claimed to be. Five pouches. She had been stealing from Javier for a long time, salting money away inside the trunk together with the tools of her trade.

Thomas sat back, leaning against the side of the bed. A wave of tiredness washed through him. He considered climbing onto the bed and allowing himself to sleep, but there was too much yet to do. His eyes tracked across the contents of the trunk. Passed over a linen pouch. Came back. Wearily he reached for it.

The bundle was light. When he shook it he was rewarded with a soft rattle and excitement sparked in his chest. He tugged at the cord holding it closed, used his teeth when it didn't open. When it finally gave way he tipped the contents into his hand. Whatever was inside slithered like a snake, tumbling from the bag to drape across his fingers. A set of finger bones, each drilled and threaded onto a slim silver chain. There were at least a dozen, and when Thomas had gathered his wits he counted them. No, not a dozen, but fourteen. He leaned forward and dug through the contents of the trunk.

There were more. Another necklace with the same count of bones, then a third. A fourth bag contained nothing more than the finger ends, some already drilled, others waiting to be worked on. Fourteen and fourteen and fourteen, plus… Thomas pushed the bones to one side with his finger. Another six.

Forty-eight bones.

Twenty-four victims.

CHAPTER 29

Thomas led Jorge to a table tucked in the corner of the packed room. He checked those around him but they were all concerned with their own business. He reached into his robe, pulled out a single necklace and dropped it on the table top.

Jorge reached for it then stopped as he recognised the object for what it was.

"Bones?"

"Finger bones. The tips of little fingers. Remember the murder scenes."

"How could I forget?" Jorge's hand remained almost touching the gruesome object. His eyes rose to meet Thomas's. "How many? A dozen?"

Thomas shook his head. "I thought that at first. But there are fourteen. There were another two complete and a fourth being fashioned. Pilar has been doing this for years, and she'll continue if we don't stop her."

"Why fourteen? It's an odd number, isn't it? I could understand ten, twelve even, but fourteen?"

"Seven victims," Thomas said.

"Again—even stranger. Five, eight, ten. But seven? If

we ever catch this Pilar we'll have to ask her."

"I don't think she's left al-Khala yet. Her instruments are still in the house. I left everything but this one necklace, in case she comes back. These are her mementoes; she won't want to abandon them. The number must have significance to her."

"Fourteen or seven." Jorge shook his head. "Isn't seven meant to be some kind of magic number? Or the number of sins. Aren't there seven deadly sins? It's a while since I read a bible."

Thomas laughed. "When have you ever read a bible?"

"But I've heard of the seven sins. Do you believe she will return for these... what did you call them... her mementoes? Shouldn't we be waiting in her house to ambush the woman?"

"She won't come yet. If she returns it will be in the small hours. I intend to wait for her then." Thomas smiled. "It will give you a chance to entertain Eva again–without disturbance this time."

"I'm coming with you," said Jorge. "This Pilar is dangerous. My shoulder's testament to that."

"You know I can take care of myself."

"Two are better than one. We can take it in turns to rest." Jorge finally reached out and picked up the necklace, pouring it from hand to hand. "If you didn't know what went into the making of this its surprisingly beautiful."

Thomas watched Jorge's hands move. "I don't see any beauty."

"No, you're probably right." Jorge dropped the necklace and covered it with his hand as a girl approached to ask if they wanted food. Thomas ordered for them both. Broth—the safest option.

Thomas leaned forward and lowered his voice, although there was enough noise in the room to make it unnecessary. "I wish I knew where else she's been. There are too many victims for them all to be from Gharnatah."

"A good cook can move around with ease. I don't see how we'll ever know who these bones belong to."

"Still, I'd like to try." Thomas frowned. "The crumbs we found, traces of bread, are they significant or not? Are they because bread is one of the things she makes for her masters? Does she force them to eat it as some kind of penance? I wish I understood her reasons better."

"What difference does it make now? You can't bring them back. Better to capture her and put at end to it here."

"There may be wives or children, people who would welcome closure."

Jorge shook his head and rattled the bones together inside his cupped hands. "These could be ancient. Years old. Their families will have found their own closure by now. Unless the victims are all like Alvarez and Javier— men who won't be missed."

"Alvarez and Javier were punished," Thomas said. "They were punished for their sins. Is that what she's doing? Searching for those with sins and bringing retribution? That might be a reason behind the fourteen."

"You're trying to impose rationality on something irrational, as usual. Pilar's mad—it's as simple as that. The fingers, seven sins if that's what it is, mean something only in her own mind."

"It's a ritual," Thomas said, then sat back, staring at

Jorge but not seeing him. His mind had spun back years to a tale he had heard as a boy, when an old man passed through Leominster. It was market day, Thomas's father roaring drunk as usual. Thomas knew he would be expected to get him home safe, so sat quiet in the corner of the inn nursing a cup of weak ale. The man had been sitting at a table nearby, regaling anyone who would buy him a drink with his tales. The voice had been lyrical, the lilting accent of Wales full, unlike Eva's which had faded to almost nothing.

There had been stories of red devils who lived in the wild heights and came down to steal a man of his silver, perhaps his life too. Of headless horsemen, of silkies and fairies and trolls that haunted bridges. And then the man had told the tale of the sin eaters.

Women, the man said. It was always women. It was a thing of the south, a thing of the welsh borders and hinterland, but he had heard of such things in other places as well, in the north, in Ireland and across the sea among the Bretons. As a body began to fail the sin eater would be called. Bread would be laid around and atop the body, a pitcher of water or milk. Sometimes the subject still breathed, but not always. The soul takes time to leave the body, so the presence of life was not always necessary.

Thomas reached out and gripped Jorge's wrist, startling him.

"Pilar's a sin eater!"

"A what?"

"A sin eater. Pilar is a sin eater. She's…" He waved a hand, impatient, thoughts tumbling through his head too fast. Why couldn't Jorge see it as clearly as he did.

"It makes sense. And it will make perfect sense to her."

"I'm glad it makes sense to someone."

Thomas slapped his own face, the sound making those sitting nearby look around. "I'm stupid. I should have known it all along. The signs were there and I was too stupid to see them."

"Well I'm stupid too, then. Tell me what you're talking about."

The girl came with their food and Thomas ignored it as he told Jorge about the old man and his tale.

"These people believe they can literally eat the sins of the dead. Can release the soul into heaven untarnished by whatever they did in their lives."

"Why not? The church of Rome believes they eat the body of Christ and drink his blood. Is the idea of taking another's sins so absurd?"

Something else occurred to Thomas. "Alvarez was a sinner if anyone was. A dark soul. Javier too. What is it the church says about the seven deadly sins? What are they? I can't remember. Tell me, Jorge."

"Don't look for me to know. I've forgotten all the religion that was ever hammered into me."

"Gluttony, that's one, isn't it? And Javier was a glutton."

"But not Alvarez," said Jorge.

"No, of course not. But he was… he was evil. Lust is a sin. What are the others?"

A chair scraped beside him and Eva sat. How long she had been there Thomas had no idea. Long enough, it seemed.

"Lust," she said, counting off on her fingers. "Gluttony. Greed. Sloth. Wrath. Envy. Pride. I thought everyone knew them. Is the broth any good?"

Thomas looked down at his bowl. It had gone cold and he pushed it away.

"You're from Wales," he said. "You must have heard of sin eaters."

Eva frowned. "There was a crone in our village. She was called to every death."

"I don't understand," said Jorge. "What happens to these sins that are eaten? Do they accumulate in the eater? Do they fade? What happens?"

"They fade in time. Although... this woman scared us. There was something in her eyes, something dark. Maybe she ate too many sins and they settled inside her, blackening her soul in turn. What's this?" Eva reached out for the necklace that lay discarded in the middle of the table. She picked it up, turning it over, her eyes widening. "Are these what they look like?" Her face was set hard.

"I found it in Pilar's house," Thomas said.

"What was she doing with this?"

"She's a sin eater. Those are the finger bones of her victims."

Eva closed her slim fist around the necklace. "That's a jump, isn't it? From sin eating to the taking of finger bones? That doesn't fit at all."

"It does if she wants to keep a memento of her kill. A necklace she can wear out of sight, at all times if she wishes. Something meaningful only to her."

Eva ran the bones through her fingers. "Is this how many have been killed?"

"More," Thomas said. "Twenty-four, I judge."

"Over a score?" Eva's eyes glittered, and Thomas

wondered if she was about to weep. "This sin eater has killed *twenty-four* people?"

Thomas nodded and held his hand out for the necklace. Eva tightened her grip, as if unable to release what she held.

"I heard you and Jorge talking about the deaths in Gharnatah. It seems to me those men deserved to die."

"It's not for us to judge."

"No. God judges," said Eva. "But sometimes man must help him."

Eva's intensity unsettled Thomas. He knew hardly anything about her. Had she, like him, been raised a Christian, but unlike him retained her zeal? Thomas knew many who believed without question. He had assumed any youthful devotion was lost when she became a concubine. If not at first, then over the years. It would be impossible to live the life she did and still yearn for old certainties.

Except Eva wasn't the issue here. Thomas met her eyes and said, "We need to stop her before she kills again."

"Stop her..." said Eva, her voice soft. "Yes... You need to stop her, this woman..."

Thomas looked toward Jorge, interested in his reaction to Eva. He wondered if the killings had sparked some sense of justice within her. Or was it the necklace, the idea of a sin eater here in Spain, a dark memory following her across many lands. Except Jorge was staring across the room and Thomas didn't even know if he had heard any of the conversation.

Thomas turned, wondering what was so fascinating.

A tall soldier stared back at them. A familiar figure

Thomas couldn't believe was really there. A figure he had almost recognised as he climbed the steps to the castle on their arrival.

Fernando, King of Castile and Aragon, raised a hand, nodded and turned away.

Thomas rose so fast his stool toppled over. He pushed through the crowd, spilling the drink of one man who grabbed his arm.

"I apologise," Thomas said, scrabbling in his robe. He pulled out a coin without looking at its value and pressed it on the man. "I must see someone. Let me buy you another."

"Not good enough."

Thomas pulled away. "Yes, it is good enough." He moved on, the man calling after him. At the door Thomas turned. Jorge had also risen, but Eva was clutching his wrist and they appeared to be arguing. Thomas shook his head and followed Fernando outside.

CHAPTER 30

The king stood in the square, his back to the inn. He was talking to another man Thomas recognised as Martin de Alarcón, Muhammed's gaoler. Or host, if you believed some people. As Thomas approached, Martin looked up and said something. Fernando turned, a smile on his face.

"My wife's favourite Englishman." He embraced Thomas.

"I suspect that is an exceedingly a short list."

"Perhaps. But you are at the very top, all the same. Is your friend with you?"

"He's coming."

"Good. It is you we need, but he is always welcome. A man after my own heart, lacking only in a few essential elements."

"Jorge believes he is all the better for that lack."

"We should go, Your Grace," said Martin de Alarcón. "It wouldn't do for anyone to recognise you."

Fernando spread his arms wide and turned a circle. He appeared to be enjoying himself. "Who is going to recognise me, Martin? You have seen the court portraits that hang in the palace. If I looked anything like those I would throw myself off the parapets. We are in a Spanish town. I am their king. What harm can befall me?"

"A town only recently Spanish, Your Grace, with a population constantly grumbling over that change."

"Thomas will let no harm come to me. He is a fierce warrior. I told you that, didn't I?"

"Several times, Your Grace." Martin de Alarcón looked beyond Thomas. "Is that the other one?"

Thomas turned. Jorge stood outside the inn. Eva was still with him, their argument continuing.

"Who is the woman?" asked Fernando.

"A concubine," Thomas said. "She's from England too." He didn't bother trying to explain the subtle difference between England and Wales, knowing the king wouldn't understand.

"She is very beautiful," said Fernando. "Don't you think so, Martin? Ah, he comes. We can go."

Fernando turned away and started toward the wide set of steps that ascended the hillside, confident the others would follow. Thomas held back a moment, waiting for Jorge to join him. Eva remained outside the inn, her dark eyes watching them both, as well as the other men.

"What were you arguing about?"

"Nothing," said Jorge. "She wanted to know when I would be back and I said I didn't know." He shook his head. "She acts as if we have a relationship of some kind. It was fucking, nothing more. *She* should understand that better than most."

"Has she told you yet why she's here, or why al-Zagal

has allowed her to come?"

"She hasn't. But I know why, it's obvious."

"Not to me." Thomas started up the steps. When he glanced ahead Fernando and Martin were already half way up the slope.

"She's insurance, or a bribe, there's no real word for what she is. She is beautiful, you agree?"

"Of course. But she is also damaged."

"Sometimes that appeals to a man as much as the beauty. Her life is one of sensual duty, so of course that is why she is here. Some Spaniard may need additional persuasion to see our point of view."

Thomas stopped and looked back, but Eva was gone. "Al-Zagal would do that?"

Jorge laughed. "Of course he would."

Thomas started climbing again. "Did she give you the necklace back?"

Jorge slowed again. "Shit. It didn't occur to me. I'll go and get it." They had reached the half way mark. Fernando and Martin de Alarcón were already on the second tier.

Thomas stared up after them. "Don't go now. We can get it later. I'm sure she's not going to try to sell it."

"Who would buy such a gruesome trinket?"

"Oh, you'd be surprised."

Jorge nodded at the figures ahead. "What do they want of us?"

Fernando glanced back, saw they were following and continued.

"Muhammed, without doubt," Thomas said.

"But *what* about him—release or further imprisonment?"

Thomas smiled. "Not imprisonment. He is their honoured guest, with an entire castle at his disposal."

"A castle he isn't allowed to leave."

"Naturally. We'll find out what they want soon enough. I only hope they don't keep us too long. I want to be at Pilar's house before midnight. I'm convinced she'll return in the small hours."

At the head of the steps they encountered a heavy oak door which lay open for them. Inside four guards stood, their swords unsheathed. They made Thomas and Jorge stand beneath an arch where flickering torches would show their faces.

"Leave your weapons," one said, motioning to Thomas's sword.

"Let them come," called Fernando. "They are trusted."

The guard looked unsure, but his king had given an order and he reluctantly stood aside. The others busied themselves with closing the doorway and dropping a heavy iron bar across it.

Fernando led the way across a courtyard and through a second door, also guarded. They entered a wide room, fires burning in grates at either end. A long table was spread with food, far finer than the fare offered by the inn, and Thomas was glad he had allowed his broth to go cold. Sitting on the other side, picking flesh from the breast of a roast pigeon, sat Muhammed, dressed in Spanish clothing. Twenty years of age, his face had aged since Thomas last saw him. And it had lost some of the arrogance of privilege. Muhammed glanced up but offered no greeting.

Thomas hadn't seen him since they left Gharnatah for Qurtuba nine months earlier. During their stay, and after Muhammed's capture, he had been kept at a safe distance. Thomas knew that Martin de Alarcón had spent almost the entire time with him, and it was interesting to see that although Muhammed ignored them, he nodded his head toward the Spaniard.

"Sit," said Fernando. "Eat."

Jorge had already pulled out a chair and started to pick through the array of delicacies. Thomas sat toward the head of the table, expecting that to be where Fernando would go. Instead the king sat on the other side from Muhammed, while Martin de Alarcón went around the table. He deliberately sat tight against Muhammed, making him move along a place.

Fernando leaned toward Jorge. "Is that pale woman good in bed?"

"How would I know?" said Jorge.

Fernando laughed and slapped him on the back. Jorge winced, his wound still recent. "Don't pretend, my friend, I know you better than that. You'll have bedded her, or at least know how she performs when bedded."

"Would you like an introduction?" asked Jorge.

"Is such a thing possible?" Fernando glanced toward Thomas. "My wife knows how it is for a soldier on the road. She understands and forgives me. In turn, I understand her wishes and never make mention of what might have occurred. Isn't that right, Thomas? Soldiers live by their own rules."

"I wouldn't know, Your Grace."

"Don't pretend. Remember I've fought beside you. You've served somewhere. Where was it, in England? Or the war against France?"

"I was too young, Your Grace."

"Call me by my name, Thomas. We are all friends here." He glanced toward Muhammed, back to Thomas. "You and I must talk. If you're not going to eat we can do so now."

Thomas looked at the array of fine foods on the table. He picked up a pigeon breast and rose from the table. "Yes, let us talk."

Fernando led the way into another room. Smaller. The windows were draped with ornate tapestries to shut out the night. Fernando walked to a burning fire, knelt and tossed on another log. Sparks tumbled upward in the chimney draft.

"We don't want him," he said, looking back at Thomas. "He's demanding, annoying, and he insults the servants. Martin too. We send him women and he abuses them."

Thomas raised a shoulder. "None of that comes as news to me. You reap what you sow, Your Grace."

"God's teeth, Thomas, don't call me that! Not now, not here. I won't have it from you. We are friends, are we not?"

Thomas nodded. "It was you who captured him, Fernando. Your general, at least. And yes, he can be difficult. It's the way he was raised. Privileged." He didn't add *like you* but the implication was clear.

Fernando wasn't stupid, and it was obvious he had heard the unspoken words as well. "I too was raised to be a king, but as I recall it involved a great deal of being shouted at, hit with blunt swords, and months of trying to learn Latin and Greek when I would rather be playing or fucking."

"Not so different then. Muhammed enjoyed the

fucking and the fighting–but in his case nobody dared hit him, and no-one dared refuse him. As a result, he has an inflated opinion of his own skills, both as a soldier and lover." Thomas drew a chair to the fire and set it beside Fernando, drew a second for himself. "And now his mother has offered a fortune for his release. No doubt he sees this as a reflection of his true value."

"Has he one? I have my own people in Granada. They tell me of a new power, a new regime. Military. Disciplined."

"You forget I have only recently returned." Thomas had no intention of telling Fernando of events within Gharnatah, however much he might like the man.

Fernando leaned forward, his arms across his knees. "You are in a difficult position, Thomas, I understand that. But so am I. This Boabdil has been with us too long. The negotiations drag on and they are a distraction from my real work." Fernando used the Spanish bastardisation of Muhammed's common name, Abu Abdullah. Thomas wondered if that was what his capturers called him. If so, he knew it would anger the man.

"I know of your real work," Thomas said. "It is to destroy the land I love. I am sorry if my words annoy you, but they are the truth. And friends must always speak the truth to each other."

"Granada will remain after we triumph. The great cities of Spain were Moorish three centuries ago, but times change and now it is our turn to rule this land. All of this land. And when we achieve that victory you are welcome to remain in your home. You above all men, Thomas. My wife wishes it to be so, as do I."

"And my friends?"

"Those close to you too, of course."

"I am…" Thomas stopped. He had been about to say married. He shook his head. What did it matter. Fernando would understand that better. "I am married to a Moor."

"There are Moors living throughout Spain. We do not expel them, not if they convert."

"I'm not sure Lubna would want to do that."

Fernando stood, paced the room. "Damn it, Thomas, your wife is not the issue here! The issue is that… that strutting peacock next door, stuffing himself with our finest game, accosting the female servants and insulting the males. He is a pig of a man. You must know this."

"He is the Sultan of Gharnatah," Thomas said.

"No, he's not. Not unless I choose to release him into your care."

"My care?"

"And those with you. But yes—your care. The care of someone we trust."

Thomas sat back with a sigh. "How long must the talks go on to make this appear seemly?"

"A week at least. Better if it is two."

"And Muhammed remains here all that time?"

"Martin can control him. He does as Martin asks. They have come to an accommodation."

Thomas waited for Fernando to stop pacing, waited until he turned to him. "You talk to me as if I have influence. I am a physician, nothing more, and those in power barely know I exist."

Fernando shook his head. "You're wrong. Boabdil told me all about you. How you are accepted within the palace. How you were instrumental in overthrowing his father and raising him to be Sultan. And I say again, we trust you, my wife and I trust you completely. You cured our son. You fought alongside me and caught the killer in our own midst. We will release Boabdil into your care and you will return him to Granada." There was no softness to Fernando's voice now. This was the king, used to issuing commands, used to being obeyed.

Thomas looked away, staring into the fire. Fernando was demanding something he was unable to give, and the man was unwilling to listen.

He looked up. "Give me some time, Your Grace."

"How much time? I want rid of this louse who gives me an itch I cannot scratch."

"Until tomorrow," Thomas said.

Fernando stared at him. "No longer."

"I will give you an answer tomorrow." But Thomas wondered if it would be possible to give the answer Fernando wanted, and doubted it. The king wished only to hear the words he sought.

CHAPTER 31

"You're quiet," said Jorge as they reached the town square. Across from them a torch beside the inn door offered the promise of a soft bed and sleep.

Instead of accepting the promise Thomas turned left until he came to another roadway and began to ascend once more. "I'm always quiet," he said. "Unlike some people who love the sound of their own voice."

"Or have something important to say. So—what happened?"

"I'll tell you later, after I've made a decision."

They climbed for a while in silence. A quarter moon showed low in the sky, framed above jumbled rooftops. To either side the houses were dark. Below them the town lay still, only an occasional bark from a dog to disturb the silence. Midnight had come and gone, but it had been impossible to leave until Fernando dismissed them.

The roadway levelled out as they approached Pilar's house. A faint illumination showed on the cobbles and Thomas hurried forward. He peered in through the window. Candlelight flickered in the kitchen at the back.

Jorge tried the door but it was locked.

"Open it," Thomas whispered, and Jorge went to his knees and held out a hand. Thomas searched, passed across the blade he had used before. The lock gave easily, but when Jorge pushed against the door it remained stubbornly solid.

"It's barred inside."

"Around the back then. That's where she is, anyway, and if this door is barred she won't be able to flee."

Thomas led the way, trying to curb his desire to run. It was too dark to hurry in case they stumbled and alerted Pilar. The gate at the side was also bolted, but the wall wasn't high and Thomas pulled himself over, then unbolted the gate for Jorge to enter.

From the yard the candle-light in the kitchen was brighter. It showed a shape moving, more shadow than substance. Thomas approached closer, trying to keep away from the light that spilled out. He found he was breathing hard, breath pluming from his mouth in the cold air.

The shadow moved again and he approached even closer, trusting to the darkness to cloak him.

Pilar had her back to him, the hood of her robe pulled over her head. She was leaning across a table, and as Thomas watched a knife glinted sharp in her hand before descending.

"She's doing it again!"

"Quick, the blade," said Jorge.

"No time." Thomas ran at the door, crashing into it shoulder first. The lock smashed and he almost fell to his knees it gave so fast.

Pilar spun around, the deep hood cloaking her face. Blood dripped from the blade, more blood arcing high into the air from the figure tied to the table. Thomas took everything in within a second, but it was enough time for Pilar to turn and run deeper into the house.

Thomas started forward but Jorge's hand stopped him.

"Look after the woman, I'll find her."

"Watch yourself. She's insane."

Jorge nodded and disappeared into the hallway. Thomas turned to the figure on the table. She was short, dark haired, naked. She was also alive, but he could see it unlikely she would remain so for long. If he hadn't disturbed Pilar by bursting through the door her strike would no doubt have already taken the woman's life.

Thomas stripped from his robe, took a knife and cut a length from it. Bending over he wrapped the makeshift bandage as tight as he dared around her neck. It immediately grew soaked in blood. The thrust had missed its mark. Instead of piercing the base of her throat to enter the brain, it had severed an artery on one side. Despite knowing it was hopeless Thomas continued to work. He exposed the wound once more, hoping perhaps he could squeeze it shut to stem the flow. But it was already easing. Not from anything he had done, simply because there was less blood in the body.

He leaned closer, peering in the gloom. The woman lifted a hand and grabbed his collar. For a moment he felt a surge of fear that she too had a knife, but all she did was pull him close to her lips.

Her voice was no more than a whisper. "She told me … nobody else had … had to die."

"Tell me your name," Thomas said. He promised himself to contact her family, to make amends if he could.

"You know my…" Breath sighed from her and Thomas banged his fist on the table. But her eyes opened again, circles of black in a deathly pale face, and he saw her draw strength from somewhere deep inside. "You know my name. You came looking for me. I thought it was she who sent you—to kill me. It is why I fled here. But it wasn't you came after me, was it. It was her. She came into my house and … she has left things here, incriminating things… I know too much about…"

Thomas watched her eyes close. Her chest barely moved. He leaned closer. "You are Pilar," he said.

Her eyes fluttered, tried to open, but the effort was too much and she let the last of her breath loose in a long sigh that ended in a final rattle. Thomas swung around. He wanted to strike out, to hit something, but reined himself in. Jorge was somewhere in the house with a mad woman. He turned and ran into the hallway. There were only two rooms and the first, the bedroom, lay empty. He moved to the next, cautious.

The door to the front room was closed. Thomas pressed his ear to it but heard nothing. He took a breath, gripped the latch, lifted it and rushed into the room.

Jorge sat in a chair, clutching his side. "She cut me."

"Where is she?"

"Back in the hall. She must have passed you, unless she left through the front."

Thomas knelt, drawing Jorge's hand aside. More blood. It was turning into a night of blood. The wound was little deeper than the one to his shoulder. It would need cleaning and a salve to prevent infection, but no stitches.

"I had her," gasped Jorge as Thomas's fingers pressed the edges of the wound together.

"Did you see her face? Will you recognise her again?"

Jorge shook his head. "The hood covered her. But I felt her. I'll know her when we find her. I know her body now."

It was Thomas's turn to shake his head. "Trust you. A woman stabs you and all you remember is how big her tits are."

"At least you know I'm not dying." Jorge put his head back against the chair. "I'm not dying, am I?"

"Not right this moment." Thomas pressed a temporary bandage to the wound. "Here, hold this hard, I need to check on something."

"You're going to leave me?"

"If you were dying I would stay, but you're not."

"I'm bleeding!"

"It's already stopping. Stay here until I return."

Thomas ignored Jorge's protests and stepped into the hallway. The only light came from flickering candles in the kitchen, everything else was cloaked in darkness and shadow.

The killer hadn't passed him. That meant he must have missed her, and the only place she could be was the bedroom. Whoever she was had nerve—unless she truly believed herself invulnerable. That wasn't so unlikely, considering the number of deaths she was responsible for.

Thomas moved into the kitchen, picked up one of the candles and returned. He slipped into the bedroom, holding the candle high so the light filled as much of the room as possible. There was nowhere to hide. He had already searched beneath the bed earlier in the day and it was too low for someone to squeeze beneath. He moved around the room, tapping against wood panels, searching for a hidden space. Nothing.

Finally, he stood in the middle of the room, shaking his head. Where had she gone? It was impossible. He went out into the hallway and examined the ceiling, wondering if there was an entrance to the roof space. As he started back to check on Jorge there came a noise, the sound of wood on wood, and he darted back toward the bedroom. When he entered the dresser was teetering as someone behind tried to escape from it. Thomas rushed in, his timing wrong as the furniture crashed forward on top of him. He pushed it away, scrabbling from beneath as someone darted past. He reached out, grabbing the hem of her robe. There was a tearing sound and he glimpsed a length of pale leg, and then she was gone. When he finally got to his feet Jorge was standing in the doorway.

"Did you see her this time?" Thomas asked.

"Her back, no more."

Thomas held up the strip of robe. "I almost had her."

Jorge reached out and took the cloth from him. "This is good quality. Whoever it is can afford the best. There's silk in this as well as cotton."

"Whoever it is, she killed the richest man in Gharnatah. She can afford whatever she wants. How's your side?"

"It hurts, but at least it's on the opposite side to my shoulder, so they balance out."

"I'll clean and dress it back at the inn, I've got my satchel there." Thomas led the way into the kitchen. "We'll have to get someone here to take care of the body."

"Olaf can probably arrange that."

Thomas stopped, looking around. For the first time he noticed small chunks of bread laid on the table either side of Pilar's body. A jug sat between her ankles. Thomas went to it, sniffed. Ale.

"She was planning another killing, just like the others. She was going to consume Pilar's sins."

"If she had any."

"We all have sins. Pilar said something before she died. She knew her killer. Helped her in the past." Thomas stared at the naked figure before him. Her vulnerability disturbed him and he went to the bedroom, stripped off the sheet and brought it back. He covered her pale limbs, drew the cotton over her face.

"This is Pilar?" said Jorge. "So who was the other one?"

"Not Pilar, obviously. We've been pursuing the wrong woman and finding the right one anyway." Thomas glanced at Jorge. "I think from what she said at the end, Pilar was helping the true killer. Perhaps she introduced her to Javier. It's even likely Martinson would know Pilar and introduced the two of them." Thomas picked up a piece of bread and tore it in two. The food was fresh, of good quality. "Had we not disturbed her she would have consumed Pilar's sins, whatever they were."

"Nothing to compare with Alvarez, or Javier," said Jorge. "You said we all have sins, and you spoke the truth. But wouldn't this killer only want to take sins worthy of her?"

"The woman is mad, Jorge. For all we know, to her all sins are equal. What is it she thinks she's doing? What does she get out of eating her victims' sins?"

"Perhaps to increase her own. Perhaps she doesn't fear sin but worships it."

"Who would do such a thing?"

"You know who, Thomas. We were both in Qurtuba when we saw how the Inquisition works. Mandana embraced his own sin."

"Mandana was mad."

"And this woman is sane?"

Thomas leaned against the wall, suddenly weary. "We're back to the beginning, with no idea who this woman is or where she's gone."

Jorge grinned. "Except I will recognise her tits."

Thomas shook his head, not in the mood for Jorge's attempt at humour. Everything Thomas had believed true lay dead on the table in front of him. He didn't know if he had the strength to start over. He would go to Fernando in the morning and tell him to release Muhammed. Then they could return to Gharnatah and forget all about this sin eater.

CHAPTER 32

It was almost noon before Thomas rose. He checked on Jorge, who remained asleep, then dressed and descended the stairs. The sound of conversation grew as he approached the wide room filled with too many people, none of them whom he sought. The innkeeper, an older man with a grizzled beard that hid half his face, filled mugs from behind a table, together with his wife. A slim girl, most likely their daughter, carried food from the kitchen in the back. She weaved between men–for the occupants were mostly men–expertly avoiding their attempts to reach for various parts of her anatomy. Many of the customers were soldiers, a mix of Spanish and Moor that sat uneasily together. Both sides had declared a truce for the duration of the negotiations, but soldiers liked to fight, and there was a tension in the air thick enough to slow a man's passage across the room.

Thomas saw Olaf on the far side, his height making him stand out above the crowd even when he was sitting. Thomas glanced around for Eva but still couldn't find her. He wondered where she had slept, assuming she had a room at the inn or somewhere nearby. He wondered if Jorge was right about her reasons for being with them.

He pushed through the crowd toward Olaf, who stood when he saw him, waving a hand. Thomas pulled up a stool and sat, pushing aside a plate scraped clean. Thomas and Jorge had found Olaf nursing a flagon of ale on their return from Pilar's house, claiming he had been unable to sleep.

"How is he?"

"Resting," Thomas said. "Best thing he can do at the moment."

Olaf waved a hand at the passing girl and pointed at the table.

"Nothing for me," Thomas said.

"I was asking for me." Olaf leaned forward. "So—what happened?"

"Two wounds. One to the shoulder, which was nothing, it hit bone. The slice on his side is a little deeper, but I've dressed it. He'll be sore for a day or two but he'll live."

"The woman got clean away?"

Thomas nodded. "But Jorge said he'd recognise her again." He shook his head, smiled. "From her—ah, her figure."

"If any man could do such a thing it's surely Jorge," said Olaf. "Aren't you meant to be attending the talks? They started at dawn."

"And they'll go on until nightfall. The same tomorrow. The talks are a sham, we both know that. Any deal brokered will be done elsewhere."

A fresh plate was dropped on the table and Olaf reached out, started to chew at a chunk of unidentifiable meat. "It's always the same. All these men and women for show while the real business is done between a few individuals."

"You've been involved before, I assume," Thomas said.

"Not directly–all my negotiations are done with a sword. But I've been around others long enough to know how things work. So who's doing the real negotiation? Faris? The vizier's man?"

Thomas raised a shoulder as if he neither knew nor cared.

"Can I ask you to keep an eye out for Eva?"

Olaf smiled. "She's easy to keep an eye out for, isn't she."

"If you see her, try to keep her here. I want to talk with her when I get back."

"Where are you going now? The talks?"

"I need to see someone, that's all."

"The man you went with last night?"

Thomas watched Olaf, wondering whether he knew who he had climbed the hill to the castle with. If anyone was likely to recognise Fernando it would be Olaf. And if he did, what then? Would he be wondering if capturing the King of Spain might shorten or even end the war?

"Just look out for Eva. And don't allow her up to Jorge."

"I've work of my own. But if I see her I'll try to keep her here. What if she insists on seeing him, do I stop her?"

"He needs to sleep." Thomas knew Olaf had no work, his presence more ceremonial than practical.

Sending the Sultan's most feared general was a petty act of defiance.

Olaf offered a nod, but whether it was to indicate he would watch out for Eva or something else entirely, Thomas couldn't tell. Olaf's expression offered no clue.

"I expected you before now." Fernando stood in the inner courtyard, a blunted sword in one hand, a shield in the other. Two men faced him, circling, and Fernando kept moving to keep both in sight.

"I had things to do."

"You have something more important than discussing matters of state with the King of Castile?"

"Don't forget Aragon, Sicily and Naples, Your Grace."

Fernando grinned. "Fuck you, Thomas Berrington." The man on the left launched a fast attack, his sword a blur. Fernando barely moved, but all at once the sword flew through the air and the man lay on his back. Fernando laughed, spun around and launched himself at the remaining man.

Thomas crossed his arms and leaned against the wall. He had seen Fernando fight in anger and knew he was good. As good as himself? Possibly. He was younger and moved with grace, always aware of what lay around him. Thomas knew his own skills were instinctive and untutored other than through the fire of combat, but he trusted them well enough against any man.

As if reading his mind Fernando said, "Do you want to try your luck, Thomas? These two provide little sport."

"I have come with your answer."

"Then tell me while we see which of us is the better swordsman."

"I know it is you, Your Grace."

"Give him your weapon." Fernando snapped at the man he had sent tumbling. The soldier tossed a blunted sword toward Thomas with a grin, almost certainly expecting him to miss it. Instead Thomas snatched the twisting blade from the air, his fingers closing around the pommel. He swung it, judging the balance. It was heavier than a Moorish scimitar, but lighter than his own sword.

"A shield too," Fernando said. "And then leave us. We have matters of state to discuss in private."

"I need no shield."

Fernando circled, watching Thomas as the two soldiers left the courtyard. "When we fought together you used no shield then, I recall."

"A man can rely too much on protection and deflection, and not enough on his own wits and skill." What Thomas didn't say was he had never felt comfortable with a heavy shield. He had learned to fight as a boy, but his skills hadn't coalesced until he found himself alone in France after the battle of Castillon. There had been a shield at first but he had discarded it as too heavy for a fourteen-year-old boy.

"There is some truth in what you say." Fernando threw his own shield aside. He swung his sword in an elaborate circle, laughing. "So tell me what you have come to say." Without pause Fernando stepped close, his sword rising from beside his leg in a savage thrust.

Thomas twisted aside, using the tip of his own blade to deflect Fernando's. It was a subtle move and Fernando nodded his approval before immediately launching a rapid series of attacks. Thomas stepped back, stepped again as their swords clashed, the sound echoing from the stone walls.

Fernando stopped, barely out of breath.

"You're better than those two idiots. But it's never the same knowing the blades won't cut."

"I've seen men killed with blunter instruments," Thomas said.

"Of course. If a man knows where to strike." Fernando lifted his sword, pressed the point against Thomas's throat. "Here." He moved the tip to the centre of Thomas's chest. "Or here."

"And here," Thomas said, raising his own sword to point at Fernando's eye.

"It's lucky we are friends then, is it not?"

"Are we, Fernando? Are we truly friends?"

"I could be jealous, you know." Fernando began to circle Thomas slowly. His sword hung slack at his side as if forgotten, but Thomas knew better than to assume such.

"Jealous of me?"

"My wife likes you. I see this. It is only her great piety that prevents me considering you a rival. She wanted to accompany me so she could meet with you again and I told her she could not."

"I have a woman of my own."

Fernando put his head back and laughed. "Since when has that ever stopped a man bedding another one? God's teeth, man, do you think me a fool?"

"Never that. And the Queen admires my mind, not my body. You know that, I am sure." Thomas flicked his wrist, deflecting Fernando's blade as it darted in.

"Who was that woman with you last night? The dark haired one with the pale skin."

"She is a concubine. And dangerous."

"I've never bedded a concubine. Is it true they have skills no other women possess? Or are those only tales told to make men jealous?"

"Oh, they have skills, I assure you."

Fernando smiled. "Of course, I remember, you have your own concubine." He flicked his wrist and Thomas allowed the blade to slap against his arm.

"I have a new woman now. A Moor."

"You mentioned her. Is she beautiful? Dark skin is good too. I have bedded girls with skin as pale as your friend's and others whose skin was gold as honey, still others as dark as pitch. My wife understands the ways of a general in the field."

"Or you believe she does."

Fernando lifted a shoulder. "It amounts to much the same thing." He shook his head. "Are we going to fight or not? I grow bored with conversation. Next time bring your concubine. She will be flattered to meet a king. And it will amuse me to plow her."

Thomas skittered backward as Fernando came at him. He raised his sword to block a savage swing to his head—a killing blow if he had been less skilled. Did Fernando know he would block it? There was no time to consider the implications as a series of thrusts of equal power came at him. Thomas twisted, parried, replied, even as he did so working out how much to show the man. Fernando was the best he had ever fought. Better than Olaf. But better than himself...?

For a moment Thomas doubled his effort, putting together a series of thrusts that had Fernando retreating. The King of Castile's face showed a wild elation, his mouth a rictus grin. He fell back again as Thomas's blows grew wilder.

Sweat dripped from Thomas's chin, pooled beneath his robe. Perhaps, he thought, I have over-estimated the man. Even as he strung thrust after thrust he was looking ahead, searching for the blow to end their contest.

When the parry came he allowed it through, knowing Fernando had to win this contest. Fernando's sword pressed hard into the soft skin beneath his chin, and Thomas wondered if he had made a mistake. He stumbled back, crashed into the stone wall. Fernando followed, the pressure of his blade increasing.

Thomas dropped his sword to clatter on the cobbles, but still the pressure didn't ease.

"Are you enemy or friend, Thomas Berrington? You live among my enemies but you feel like a friend. It is confusing. Both for me and my wife."

"Do I have to be either?"

"Yes, I think you do. We have allowed you into our lives. Perhaps that was a mistake on our part, perhaps not." Fernando lifted a shoulder. Thomas felt the tip of the blunted sword break skin. Blood trickled along his throat.

"Kill me if you want," Thomas said. "But then you'll be stuck with Muhammed."

Fernando laughed and dropped his sword. "God forbid you would visit such a punishment on me." He flicked his fingers at Thomas's neck. "I apologise, I must not know my own strength."

Thomas supposed it was a lie but allowed the moment to pass.

"Your terms are acceptable, Your Grace," Thomas said. "The ransom will be paid, the agreed hostages released, and you can return Muhammed at your convenience."

"If only you could take him with you," Fernando said. He came close and put an arm around Thomas's shoulder. "Come inside and break bread with me. Tell him yourself." Fernando laughed. "I want to see his face when you tell him his freedom is in your hands. And I really am sorry for cutting you. I want us to be friends. Good friends. This land needs friends on both sides, does it not?"

CHAPTER 33

Light had faded from the sky by the time Thomas descended the wide steps into the market place. It stood empty, not even a stray dog in sight. On the far side the inn invited, yellow lamplight spilling through the windows and open door, the sound of raised voices coming across the square. Thomas was in a foul mood. Spending time in the company of Muhammed's had made it so.

He wasn't hungry or thirsty, but the sense of life spilling from the inn drew him. He stood inside the door and looked around, recognising faces but no names. Olaf wasn't in sight, neither was Eva. He had given more thought to the woman, and knew he needed to ask her questions. Her presence was too convenient, other things about her too much of a coincidence.

Thomas dragged a hand across his face and turned away from the offer a pretty young woman whispered in his ear. All he wanted was to lie down and sleep and let the world disappear for a while. He was tired of intrigue and false friendship. And he missed Lubna. He wanted her beside him, above him, below him. Wanted her with an ache he had never felt for Helena.

As he climbed the stairs he had to step back as the bulk of Olaf came in the opposite direction.

"Is it done?" said Olaf, once more surprising Thomas.

"How long have you known?"

"What other reason is there for you to be here?"

"Muhammed is to be freed. If you wait around long enough you might be able to accompany him back to Gharnatah. For myself I plan to leave in the morning. If Jorge's well enough he can come with me. Have you seen him?"

"He's still in bed as far as I know, although he sent down for food half an hour since. He's still not himself though—all he wanted was bread and ale."

"Eva?"

"No sign." Olaf stepped back, making space for Thomas to continue upward.

Thomas almost told the man of his suspicions, then simply eased past. He wanted to find Eva first. A wish granted him sooner than expected.

As he pushed open the door to the room he stopped dead.

"Gods, can't you two control your—" And then he saw there was something wrong with the scene before him. True, they were both naked, but Jorge's hands were tied to the bedstead, his ankles the same, and a silken gag closed his mouth. Food had been brought to the room and arranged across his body.

Eva looked up, a snarl on her face at the interruption. *Did she not expect me?*

Thomas saw her hand rise to her head and pull free the golden clasp. She flicked her wrist and the pin flashed in the light of the candles burning around the bed. The room was hot, a fire filling the grate. Thomas saw something else, taking the entire scene in within a moment. Eva wore three necklaces at her throat. Necklaces fashioned of finger bones.

For a moment the tableau remained frozen as if the pair were modelling for some artist. Then Eva's hand began to descend, aiming the sharp pin at Jorge's eye.

Thomas roared and launched himself across the room. He leapt the last six feet, careening over the top of Jorge to grasp Eva's wrist. She fell away, turning, tugging her hand free. She slashed at Thomas, a blow he was unable to avoid as momentum carried him onward and he felt a fire burn along his arm.

He hit the floor and rolled, rose to his feet as Eva came at him again. At least her madness was directed at him now, and he could better defend himself.

She slashed again and he darted back as the pin opened a rent in his robe. He reached for her wrist, but Eva was fast and agile. She cut the back of his hand, then grabbed at her discarded robe, darted beneath his arm and ran toward the door. Thomas rose to his feet and started after her. From the edge of his vision he saw Jorge had freed himself and was rising from the bed. The two of them clashed as both tried to pursue Eva.

By the time Thomas could untangle himself the sound of Eva's flight down the stairs had stilled. He ran down the twisting steps, but instead of going into the main room turned through the kitchen. A cook stood over a stained iron pot resting over the fire.

"Did a woman come this way?"

"Short? Dark hair?" She pointed to where another

door stood open, offering an exit to the rear yard.

Thomas ran outside, but it was too late. The yard was empty. She could be almost anywhere by now. He went out onto the square and turned a full circle, but saw nothing to offer a clue to which way she may have gone. He returned to the inn and climbed the stairs once more.

"It was her," said Jorge. He had started to dress, sat on the bed wearing no more than a shirt, but at least it covered his thighs. "All this time it was Eva. I didn't suspect a thing, not even when she brought the bread. Not even when she tied my hands. I thought it was a game."

Thomas glanced around, taking in the simplicity of the materials Eva had gathered. Some strips of silk, her brooch, and it was so easy to have bread and ale sent up to the room. He looked harder, because something was missing. There was nothing to cut the fingertips from a hand. He searched for a pincer, a heavier blade, but there was nothing. It was this lack that showed the attack had been unplanned. This was retribution for their interruption at Pilar's house.

"What I don't understand," said Jorge as he stood and went in search of some pants, "is why me? It's not as if I have enough sins to make it worthwhile."

Thomas laughed, releasing the tension wound tight within. "That's because you regard nothing as a sin, my friend. Eva no doubt views your life differently."

"But she's a courtesan. I know her kind, I work with them every day. How could she regard what I do as a sin, when she does exactly the same herself? Is this the end of it, do you think? Where will she run to now?"

"Where did she come from before?"

"Before Gharnatah? She arrived with al-Zagal, a member of his harem. So Ronda, I expect."

"Before that. How long has she been killing? You saw how many finger bones were on those necklaces. That many deaths aren't achieved quickly, not if she wants to go on killing as she has done."

"Will she run for home?" said Jorge. "Is that what you mean?"

"Wouldn't you?"

"I wouldn't kill in the first place."

"But if you did," Thomas said. "Would you have somewhere planned to escape to if suspicion fell on you? Some refuge?"

"I don't know. You're talking about a circumstance I can't comprehend."

Thomas shook his head, sure Jorge was being deliberately stubborn. "If it was me I would have one. I'd have a place of safety, somewhere prepared ready for me. Wherever I went it would be the first thing I did." He thought back to a cave in limestone cliffs in the south of France.

"How are we supposed to know where such a place is? It could be anywhere, not even in Spain. The best we can hope is she's scared and will run as far and fast as she can. At least then she won't be able to kill anyone we care for."

Thomas sat on the bed, his body suddenly weary. "Tell me what she said when you were tied up."

Jorge had found a pair of linen trousers and pulled them on. "She talked, but it was gibberish, of how it was her life's work to grow, to imbibe the evils of others in order to increase her own." Jorge tied the string at his waist. "It's her plan to become the most evil creature walking the earth."

"She told you that?"

"Most of it, but her words were crazed."

Thomas leaned forward. "Tell me everything she said."

"Why?"

"I want to understand why she's doing this."

"Why?" Jorge said again.

"Because if I understand it I can use it to find her again."

"She accused me of pride. Lust I could understand—but pride?"

"Yes," Thomas said, "she has to be mad. Tell me."

Jorge sat on the side of the bed. He reached out and let his fingers drift through the crumbs of bread ground into the sheets. "What do you want to know? I'm not sure trying to remember what she said, even if I could, will be any help."

"Why does she eat sin? Because she is evil, or because she sees herself as some kind of angel of mercy taking on the sins of others?"

"She said…" Jorge frowned as he tried to recall what words were spoken. "She said God gave up on her, abandoned her. If God had turned his back on her, who was left but the Devil?"

"So she consumes their sins to become ever more evil. To cloak herself in their darkness." Thomas scratched at his head as if he could stimulate his brain to think more clearly. "And yet she came to this country with her father on a Crusade. Doesn't that make you think her religion runs deep enough for her to hold onto even after her capture?"

"Don't look at me for answers here," Jorge said. "You know I worship no God."

"Nor me. But I remember what I was taught to believe. And I see belief in others. The lives of most are controlled by the presence of their God." He sat up. "I don't believe Eva has abandoned her God completely. Part of her might think she is taking on sins, but I believe she hasn't abandoned her true self. Through all of this she is seeking something else."

"What?" asked Jorge.

"She is seeking something to absolve herself of sin. She is seeking innocence." Thomas stood. "I have to go to Gharnatah."

"Now? It's dark. And she won't go there, anyway."

"I think she will. I couldn't understand why she would befriend Helena, but I see it now. She doesn't care about Helena, not even her sins. It's the child she wants. The innocence of my son."

CHAPTER 34

Lubna had wrapped William to keep him warm while she descended the steps of the Albayzin, ascended the slope of al-Hamra, and taken Thomas's son to meet her mother. Lubna loved her father dearly, but sometimes it was easier when he was away from home. Then they could simply sit and talk.

She watched now as Fatima cradled William, a smile of contentment on her face. William was awake but quiet–a blessed relief. After being such a placid baby to begin with he had taken to waking in the night, and Lubna lacked what he needed to quiet him. The wet nurse had expressed some milk which she fed him when necessary, but the interruption to her sleep was making Lubna irritable.

"He looks like his father," said Fatima, bouncing William against her own breasts. His head turned, seeking, and Fatima laughed in delight. "A little like Olaf too, don't you think?"

Lubna only smiled. She had yet to decide if William was actually Thomas's son, but knew whether he was or not he planned to raise him as his own. It was a decision she was more than happy to accept. Whether Thomas was the true father or not, her own sister was certainly the mother, and that was reason enough in itself.

She wondered why Helena had so taken against William. Was it the reminder of her own failing, or simply that a courtesan was not meant to bear children? Occasionally Lubna experienced a nagging sense of betrayal, but each time it rose she pushed it down hard. Thomas had been no more than her employer when he returned to Helena's bed. Lubna knew he owed her nothing, however much he might believe he did. Now things were different. If Thomas were to be unfaithful again she wouldn't be so accepting. Not that Thomas would be unfaithful to her, she knew, now the step had been taken. Lubna allowed her eyes to close, wrapping herself in warm memories of what they had already shared in so short a time. She smiled to herself at the thought she had harboured–that she would prove a disappointment to him. Particularly after the delights her sister would have introduced him to. Instead he seemed even more content, and she liked to believe it was because of love. She had loved Thomas from the outset, even before she truly knew she did, even before she knew the man himself. Lubna had worshiped him from a distance. And when Helena herself had insisted she should join their household there had been no hesitation. Not that at the time she held any expectation other than work. Thomas's willingness to teach her, to expect more of her than act as a simple maid, only added to her feelings for him.

William's cry startled her awake and she sat up, rubbing at her face.

"He's hungry," said Fatima. "You should take him to Helena. I know her breasts ache with unshed milk. It will do them both good if she puts him to the nipple."

"She refuses to accept him," Lubna said.

"Surely if she sees him that must change." Fatima held William out. "Here, take him. I defy any woman, any mother, not to let her baby suckle when he is crying."

"She will turn me away," Lubna said. But she accepted the baby, wrapping the blankets tight about him in preparation for going outside. The kitchen was warm, the fire burning in the stove radiating a scented heat.

"When do you expect Thomas home?" Fatima rose, coming close as Lubna got to her feet.

"You likely know better than me. When did father say he'd be back?"

"He never says. Claims he doesn't know. He always tells me such matters take time. Do you miss him?"

"Father?"

"No." Fatima smiled. "Thomas."

"I miss him now more than ever. When he was in Qurtuba it was different. Now he's back I want him never to leave again."

"He was not your man then."

"I will take William to Helena," Lubna said. "If nothing else she deserves the chance to see her son."

But as she crossed the practice yard toward the gate that led to the Alkazaba and Helena's house, she wondered if there was even a shred of truth in her parting words. Lubna had been the youngest, raised among beautiful sisters, all of whom resembled their mother, not hers. They were all tall, blonde, achingly beautiful.

Two had married well. Helena and the remaining sister had entered the harem. Lubna had few fond memories of any of them. Not because of their beauty but because of their natures. To them she had been an afterthought, a changeling among their ice-blonde perfection. They had treated her as little more than a slave. The harem hadn't been an option for her. Instead she had worked as a servant, moving from house to house in Gharnatah, staying only as long as it took the master to push her against a wall and try to lift her robe. Until she had moved into Thomas's house. Lubna was aware he had been reluctant to accept her. That time felt long ago. The emotions and hopes she experienced then had belonged to someone else. Now Thomas made her believe she was beautiful too.

There was a hand cart in front of the doorway of Helena's house as Lubna approached. She dragged it out of the way, awkward with William cradled to herself, wondering who could have left it in such a careless position, and why. She called out as she entered the house but received no reply. It wasn't unusual. Lubna knew that sometimes Helena remained silent in the hope she would leave. But she was more confident now. She believed in herself, in her intelligence and abilities. Thomas had given her that as well.

William squirmed against her breast and she knew he was hungry again. He was always hungry, and she had noticed how he had grown in just the week since his birth. She carried him through to the wide room that looked across the Vega. It was empty. Lubna turned, tired of Helena's games, determined to return home via the wet-nurse's house. She stopped at a sound from the bedroom.

Lubna paused, listening. William whimpered a tiny cry and she rubbed his back.

The noise came again, as if someone was in pain. Lubna walked quickly toward the door, which stood open. The sight that greeted her took a moment to coalesce in her mind. At first it was a scene from a vision of hell, and then she made out what was happening.

Helena sat on the edge of the bed, leaning forward. Her friend Eva knelt before her. Helena's robe was loose, pooled at her waist. Eva's hands were on Helena's breasts. Lubna shook her head and stepped backward, embarrassed and shocked.

Helena made another sound and Lubna stopped. The scene shifted once more. The noise Helena made was one of relief. Eva was kneading at her breasts, releasing jets of pale milk which she caught in a jug Helena held between her knees. Lubna's shock turned to anger.

"If you're going to do that at least feed your own son."

Helena's head spun around, fear on her face, and Lubna wondered who she thought had interrupted them. She strode across the room, untangling William and holding him out.

"Look—here he is. Your son!" As if he knew what was happening William opened his eyes and emitted a squall of sound. "See, he smells your milk. His *mother's* milk. Would you deny him?"

"He's not my son," Helena whispered, her eyes drifting away from the child. There was no emotion in her voice, and her body was slack. Lubna wondered if she had been smoking hashish against the pain in her breasts.

"He might not be Thomas's–yes, I hear the rumours–
but you can hardly deny you birthed him."

"He is a mistake. Take him from my sight. Eva, please
continue. My breasts ache so deeply."

"Your sister's right, you should put him to the nipple," Eva said. "His suckling will ease the pain far better
than my efforts."

"Never," snapped Helena. "And if you're not going to
help me I'll find someone who can." She pulled at her
robe, trying to cover herself.

Eva reached out and gripped Helena's wrist. She
glanced toward Lubna. "You had better leave. Go to
your mother. If I can I'll bring you a little milk."

"No, you won't," said Helena.

"Ignore your sister, it's her pride. She is ashamed."

Lubna watched for a moment, anger still bubbling
inside, but she knew she had to suppress it. At least the
scene made her resolve one thing. William would grow
up believing *she* was his mother. He was too young to
know the difference. In a few years he would know
nothing of his birth mother, and be all the better for
lack of that knowledge.

She started toward the barracks, her feet dragging.
She couldn't decide what to do. Return to her mother's house and send for the wet-nurse or descend the
hill and go home. The builders would be making noise,
and William was now snuffling constantly with hunger.
Why had Helena refused him? Lubna failed to understand such lack of emotion. She tried to imagine how a
mother could reject her child and failed. She knew she
couldn't do it. Within the few days William had been
with her she had grown to love him with a depth she

hadn't believed possible. How could Helena not feel the same way? It showed some deep lack within her that she couldn't love her own son.

The anger within turned from a simmer to a boil and Lubna turned. She would confront Helena. Convince her to take at least some responsibility for William. If she could talk to her, persuade her, she was sure Helena would come around.

When she reached the house the cart was once more blocking the doorway and she kicked at it until she could squeeze past. She was about to call out when she saw Eva backing toward her. She was bent over, dragging something. With a cold leap of her heart Lubna saw it was Helena.

"What are you doing?"

Eva released her hold and straightened up. "Oh, thank God you came back. She passed out. We have to get her to a doctor."

Lubna released William and held him out. "Take the boy and let me see her, I might be able to help."

"She needs a physician," said Eva. She smiled as she took William and Lubna knelt beside her sister. "And you have saved me an extra journey."

Lubna felt for a pulse in Helena's neck, found it slow and strong. She lifted the lid of one eye. The pupil was blown wide, almost covering the pale blue surrounding it.

"What happened?" Lubna asked, turning to Eva. She frowned. Where was William? She had only handed him to her a moment before. And why was Eva holding a hammer in one hand? Then the hammer came down and the world turned dark.

CHAPTER 35

The horses picked their way with painful slowness through the dark. The moon which had illuminated the night earlier had disappeared behind a bank of cloud that rolled across the sky from the south. A gusting wind brought the dry scent of the desert. Thomas had considered stopping more than once, but even slow progress was better than no progress so they went on, stumbling, skidding, taking false trails. At the stables, they discovered Eva had taken the fine Arabian Thomas had ridden to al-Khala. Their own mounts were pedestrian by comparison, and Thomas was constantly aware of her gaining a lead on them.

As soon as the pre-dawn light allowed they sped up, pushing the horses into a canter that brought sweat to their flanks. Thomas expected Jorge to complain about his wounds, such as they were, but his expression was set, eyes scanning the ground ahead. Looking for the same as Thomas. The valley that would lead them down to the rich plain and show them Gharnatah.

It was almost noon before they glimpsed the white city walls, beyond the jumble of houses climbing one hill, the palace on the other side, and looming over it all the bulk of the Sholayr, its peaks white with snow. Shacks dotted the Vega, with here and there more substantial dwellings. Glittering canals carried water from the mountains to irrigate the rich soil.

"Where will she have gone?" asked Jorge.

"Nowhere obvious. If she has even come this way. I'm beginning to wonder if she would take the risk. She's likely fled al-Andalus altogether."

"Eva thrives on risk. She's like you that way."

Thomas glanced at Jorge. "I avoid risk where I can. But there are times you have to face it if you want to call yourself a man."

"Then I'm happy not to be a man."

"Don't fool yourself, Jorge. You enjoy risk more than most, just risk of a different kind." Thomas jerked on the reins to direct his mount around a boulder which sat in the path. "I believe she's returned to Gharnatah. She has unfinished business."

"Killing business."

"Of course."

"Who?" said Jorge.

"I believe she has a list—seven victims to create the fourth necklace. One for each of the sins. She used Martinson, who knew everyone, to identify those victims. And then she killed him to hide the fact."

"We don't even know if Alvarez and Javier are the first two of this cycle. What if there were more before them?"

"When did she arrive in the palace?"

"We weren't here, remember. But four or five months ago, from what I've heard."

"It will have taken her time to befriend Martinson and draw up her list. So they could be the first victims. I'd like to know who else is on it. What age would you put on Eva?"

"She's not young," said Jorge. "Older than Helena, I'd say. Almost thirty."

"I'll take that as the word of a man who can tell such things. I expect if pushed you could tell me how many months' shy of thirty. It's the skin, I suppose, isn't it."

Jorge shook his head. "There speaks a physician. It's nothing to do with the skin, nothing to do with the body even. Oh, breasts start to sag, flesh loosens, but remember these women are different. It's why they were chosen in the first place. And they spend an inordinate amount of time caring for their bodies. No, it's her mind, her thought process, that gives the clue. Eva has experienced more than most."

"You told me you would know the killer from her breasts, remember? What happened to your expertise?"

"The woman shared my bed. It was a clever move, I admit. She knew I wouldn't suspect someone who had… well, never mind what we did. As I said, a clever move. How long have you suspected her? From the start, I expect."

"Only yesterday. But you're right, I should have suspected her before now. Perhaps if I'd worked out the sin eating sooner I would have. But it was only after she killed Pilar I saw the truth. How many pale, dark-haired women are there in this land?"

"She was clever in befriending Helena," said Jorge. "She got close to us so we didn't even consider her. A killer hides, they don't sit in plain view. We couldn't have known."

Thomas turned in his saddle to look at Jorge. "What does your expertise tell you about where she'll go now. The harem?"

"At first, perhaps. She has a start over us, but she knows we're coming after her. By the time we sourced the horses and told everyone where we were going she had at least two hours start."

"There was too much explanation. We should have just left."

"We couldn't. You can't destroy the kind of bridges you have built, Thomas. You'll need Fernando and his wife one day."

"Which is why I spoke with him. But it put us at a disadvantage. If we'd pursued Eva immediately we might have caught her before she reached Gharnatah. That would have put an end to it."

"In the dark? If she even came this way. And if we'd caught her, what would you have done? Killed her there and then?" Jorge glanced at him. "No, not you."

"You would have?"

"It would end things," said Jorge.

"So much for bedding her."

"We both know what she's done. So what will you do when you capture her?"

"Take her to the palace for judgement."

Jorge laughed hard. "Oh, of course, deposit her back in the bosom of those who have made her what she is. If she's al-Zagal's he's not going to punish her. From his reputation he might even reward her. And we both know the men she killed deserved their fate."

"And the others? Nobody deserves what she did to

them. Was Pilar a sinner too? No—she was used and discarded. Eva planted those tools and the necklaces in Pilar's house to make us believe she was the guilty party. And we did."

"If what you say is true," said Jorge, "why did Eva carry out the same ritual on her?"

"We all have sins. Pilar likely shared her master's bed. There might have been other sins too. Eva befriended the woman, she would have teased out her past. But I suspect Pilar's sins would have proven a sparse meal for one such as Eva."

Thomas rode on, staring ahead as the city walls grew. "So where might she go?" He trusted Jorge in this, trusted his knowledge of women, particularly those of the harem.

"Assuming she has come this way, and not fled never to be seen again? She'll go to the palace first. She'll have things there she won't want to leave behind. This list you claim she has."

"Eva knows she can't stay there. She'll have some-where else in mind." Thomas gripped the horse's flanks tight as it dropped into a water channel. Its hooves sank into soft mud which flew up in fine drops as it jumped the far bank. He glanced back to make sure Jorge wasn't about to tumble off, but saw he had grown confident in the saddle.

When they fell into step beside each other again Jorge said, "You said she has unfinished business. Personally I don't believe her so insane as to think she can complete her list."

"If she has a place of safety what's to stop her?"

They passed men and women at work, an occasional

soldier coming the other way, who nodded at them, both familiar faces.

"Because you will stop her," said Jorge. "She knows you will. She knows you won't abandon the search."

"There are many places to hide in Gharnatah."

"And many curious people. It's not her city. She doesn't know it like you and I do. We'll find her if she stays."

"And hand her over to the authorities," Thomas said.

"As you say."

Jorge knew where al-Zagal's concubines had rooms and led Thomas directly there. Jorge was a known presence, but Thomas following behind caused consternation. Even though he was familiar to almost everyone, he had never before invaded these inner chambers without invitation. Women clutched silks around their bodies. Others approached, angry, until Jorge glared at them and they shrank back. They had never seen this side of him before. As for Thomas, he had a reputation none of the inhabitants of the palace wanted to test.

"Where does Eva sleep?" demanded Jorge of a senior female. They were in a deep part of the harem now, a place Thomas had never seen before. This was where the concubines lived. The atmosphere was different here to the places where they worked. Less decoration marked the walls, and small rooms led off on either side of a wide corridor, scattered with cushions and low tables, some set with games, others with books.

"She has a room at the end. Shall I send for her?" The woman glanced at Thomas, and he saw she wanted to confront him but didn't dare.

Jorge started on and Thomas ran to catch him. "If she's there, we capture her. I'll do the work, but you might have to help. Watch out for brooches or blades. She's good with them."

"She won't cut me again." Jorge reached the end of the corridor and pushed open an unlocked door. None of the doors had locks. The room was unoccupied, but it was clear Eva had been here, and her scent still clung to the air.

"Go and ask that woman when Eva came, and when she left," Thomas said, examining the bed, shelves where papers had been disturbed. And a chest, the lid open. As Jorge left, Thomas rooted through the contents but found nothing of interest. Whatever it had contained was gone.

"She arrived three hours past," said Jorge, re-entering the room. "Left half an hour later."

"What was she carrying?"

"You didn't tell me to ask that."

"No." Thomas brushed past Jorge and strode along the corridor to the older woman. She was the only person left in sight. "What did she carry away?"

"A cloth bag."

"Did you see what was inside?"

She shook her head. "Eva was almost running. I saw nothing. But I heard."

"Heard?"

"A rattling, a jingling. Like metal on metal. Then she was gone. I tried to confront her but she pushed me aside. I never liked her."

"Where did she go?"

"How would I know that?"

"Not even rumour? I know how things work within these walls. Some word would have come back, would it not?"

"I heard something about her visiting Helena often." The woman's eyes met Thomas's. "She might have been going to that fine house you were given." Her expression made it clear she didn't understand why he deserved such a gift.

"Perhaps she's saying her goodbye's," said Jorge, jogging beside Thomas as they rushed through the corridors.

They turned a corner and skidded to a halt. Ahead of them stood Aixa, behind her Abu al-Hasan Ali and his brother. The sight of all three together showed how the balance of power had shifted while they were away.

"I didn't believe it when word came," said Aixa. "That you would invade the inner chambers of my palace."

Thomas strode toward them, a cold determination filling him, and he allowed it to spread to the tips of his fingers. He still had his father's sword strapped at his waist and he dropped his right hand to the pommel. Saw al-Zagal push his brother to one side and mirror the gesture.

"You are harbouring a killer against your bosom. Who does Eva belong to?" He glanced at Abu al-Hasan, then al-Zagal, and saw the man offer a tiny nod.

"She is a skilled concubine," said Aixa. "I hear nothing but good reports of her."

"She's a murdering bitch," Thomas said, watching Aixa's eyes widen, unused to being addressed in such a way. "And if you prevent us passing she will kill again."

He turned, meeting Abu al-Hasan's milky gaze full on. "She has gone to kill Helena, Malik. Do you want her death on your conscience, along with all the others?" He didn't know if the old Sultan could see the anger on his face, but knew he would hear it in his voice.

"Let them pass," said Abu al-Hasan Ali. "I trust Thomas's word in this matter." He glanced toward his brother, who stood with face set hard. "If he says Eva has killed then he speaks the truth. Let him bring her to us for judgement."

"I hear you are a wild-card, Thomas Berrington," said al-Zagal, still standing in the middle of the corridor, blocking the way. Thomas had already judged he could disarm him and get past if need be, but was willing to allow one last moment of diplomacy. "I don't know you, but my brother appears to put a great deal of trust in your abilities." Al-Zagal took a single step to the side. "Bring Eva to me. I am fond of the girl." As Thomas went to pass, al-Zagal put a hand on his chest. "Do not kill her. Do you understand me? Whatever she might have done, she is mine to judge."

Thomas offered a brief nod and leaned into al-Zagal's hand. For a moment the pressure remained, then the man stepped aside and Thomas broke into a run.

CHAPTER 36

Lubna was drowning. A weight pressed on her chest, squeezing the air from her lungs. She fought upward, knowing others depended on her. William. Her sister. And above all, Thomas. The darkness gave way to grey and she shook her head, ignoring the nausea that filled her. Sensation returned, driving away the lack of knowledge, and with it came memory and a realisation of her own stupidity. Why hadn't the cart alerted her? Why did she have to push it aside–not once but twice! Thomas would never have made the same mistake.

Still she couldn't breathe. Couldn't move. She pulled on her arms but her hands remained locked behind her. Something else too. A solid column pressing against her spine. She inhaled, scared when barely any air entered her lungs.

Finally, she opened her eyes. They darted from side to side, taking in what little she could see. Her head was locked in place. Her legs, her arms, her torso. However much she strained, movement was impossible.

Lubna stopped struggling. The strain only made her situation worse. She felt the bindings tighten as she fought them and chose a different strategy. She took the weight of her body on her legs and the terrible pressure around her chest eased a little. She drew in air, breathing in short, sharp gasps.

"Ah, you're awake at last. Good. I thought I might have to start without you."

Lubna's eyes ached with the pressure of trying to see where the voice came from. Then Eva moved into her field of vision. A pair of pincers hung from one hand, like those used by metal workers to snip through sheets of copper.

"You," said Lubna, her voice strained from the tightness of her bindings.

"Yes, me." Eva smiled. "And I'm sorry, Lubna. You were not meant to die. It is your sister and the boy I want." She raised her free hand. "But now, of course, I can't allow you to walk free." Eva sighed. "Such a shame that Thomas knows about me, too. I'll have to find a new place to continue my work."

"If Thomas knows you might as well let me go," said Lubna.

"Yes, I could. But you thwarted me, and that I can't forgive."

Eva disappeared from view again. When she returned the snips had been replaced by a knife. The razor sharp edge glinted in the light that fell from directly above. Lubna struggled, but all she achieved was to cut off her supply of air again.

"Oh, I'm not going to kill you yet. You have to watch first. Your sister is so beautiful. And so evil. A worthy subject, don't you think?" Eva came close, reached out with the knife, and all at once Lubna sagged as the ropes around her chest fell away. Eva knelt and sawed through those at her waist and around her knees. "I'm afraid I can't release your hands, or the bindings at your throat. But I do want you to see, so–" She reached close, for a moment the knife flashing a bright reflection against Lubna's vision, and then the bindings holding her head dropped away.

She tried to slide down the column, but as soon as her knees bent the rope tightened at her throat and she straightened quickly.

"I think you can turn if you shuffle your feet," Eva said. "Helena is over here, so if you want to see, you'll need to turn around."

"Where is–" Lubna broke off, her throat raw. She tried to swallow but her mouth was too dry. When she managed to find her voice it emerged as a croak. "What have you done with William?"

"William is safe. I allowed him to relieve some of the pressure in Helena's breasts while she slept. I'm sure it did them both good. It's so sweet to watch a baby suckle on a mother's teat. You would have enjoyed the sight." Eva smiled. "I might let him feed again if he wakes. But for now he's warm and sleeping. You'll see him too if you can only turn. Try for me, Lubna." Eva reached out and ran a finger down Lubna's cheek. "What a shame you don't share your sister's talent for sin. I have never taken on the sins of two at once. It would have been an interesting experiment." Eva's finger withdrew, leaving Lubna's cheek feeling violated.

As Eva moved away, Lubna shuffled her feet, able to take only tiny steps before the rope tightened around her throat. Slowly she began to turn, more of the chamber coming into view. She risked a glance upward, discovered a high domed ceiling studded with openings. It was from these the light spilled in. Lubna tried to judge how bright the sky was, how much time had passed while she was unconscious, but all she could discern was a vague grey cloud cover that offered little information.

More of the chamber came into view and Lubna saw it for what it was. They were in one of the food-stores that lay beneath al-Hamra. This one was almost empty, only a small pile of sacks holding grain leaning against a wall. She also saw her sister.

Helena lay naked on a wooden table. Her belly showed evidence of her pregnancy, but already she was recovering the almost mesmeric beauty that had marked her out as a palace concubine. Beyond the table Eva busied herself. Had Lubna not been aware of its purpose the scene would have been almost domestic. Eva opened a basket and from inside withdrew items of food and drink. There was a jug of wine and a silver goblet which she placed between Helena's ankles. Small pieces of bread were placed across Helena's body, between her breasts, on her belly.

Lubna searched the room until she found what she was looking for. William lay on a blanket set hard against the wall. Two of the sacks of grain had been used to form a crude crib to prevent him rolling free. He appeared unharmed. How long that might remain so, Lubna had no idea. She wondered how Eva had managed to trundle the pair of them through the streets without raising suspicion. Their bodies would have been light enough to manage in the cart, and she assumed they had been covered by something.

"She's hardly worth it," Lubna said.

"Oh, you don't know your sister at all, do you." Eva's voice was conversational, completely rational.

"Helena pretends she cares for nothing and no-one," Lubna said, "but it's only show."

Eva laughed. Her hand rose to her head and unclipped the brooch holding her hair in place. She opened it out, the pin long and sharp, and placed it on the table next to Helena.

"Your sister may be my crowning glory, you know. She isn't even aware of how evil she is, so self-centred everything is the fault of someone else. When I take on her sins, I expect to discover how putrid her soul truly is." She glanced toward Lubna. "I think we are ready, don't you?"

"Tell me why," Lubna said. She had to slow Eva down, distract her in some way—although to what purpose she didn't know. Nobody knew where they were. Nobody was coming to rescue them. "Is it because you want to increase the evil in the world or dilute it? Why take their sins?"

Eva looked up. A trace of rationality remained in her eyes, but for how much longer Lubna could not tell. Eva crossed the room, stood in front of Lubna.

"I could tell you, couldn't I. I could tell you the entire truth." She smiled. "Confess my sins and the world would never know, because of course I will have to kill you too when I am finished with your sister."

"Then tell me."

"Why? What good will it do you to know?"

"If not me then for yourself. You said you would

confess your sins to me. Lighten the burden you carry by telling me why."

Eva laughed, the sound less rational than it had been. She came close to Lubna, gripped her chin and held her face rigid while she put her mouth against hers. Lubna tried to twist away from the kiss but Eva held her fast. When the kiss broke, Lubna spat on the floor.

"Did you not enjoy that?" Eva dropped a hand to Lubna's breast and squeezed. "Or this? Oh, there have been many women who have writhed in pleasure at my touch. Many men as well. I am skilled, and I am wanton. But you want to know why, don't you." Eva's finger traced the side of Lubna's cheek. "Would it do me any good to tell you? Does confession truly ease the soul? Do I even possess such a thing as a soul anymore? Oh—such interesting questions. Such interesting, interesting questions."

Eva turned away and walked back to the table.

"Tell me about your father," Lubna cried.

Eva stopped, her shoulders tightening.

"Tell me why he brought you here. How old were you? A girl, no more. Why didn't he leave you at home?"

Eva spun around and came fast at Lubna. She had picked up the brooch and held it now as a weapon. The needle point flashed and Lubna felt a pain sear her brow.

"You want to know about my father? There is only one thing to know about him—he was the devil incarnate. He brought me to this land because he wanted me with him." Eva's voice rose. "Wanted me with him all the time! You are an innocent, you would not understand. My father, the great and good man admired by Lords and Ladies alike, he took me as his wanton before I was even a woman. But I had my revenge. It was not the Moors who killed my father but me. When I was old enough I used this brooch, the brooch he gave me as a gift to keep his secret safe, and I pushed it slowly into his chest to still his heart. And then I laid bread on his chest and took his sins unto me. Except they were already here." She punched her chest. "Already inside me. He had seen to that."

Eva turned and hurried to the table. There had been tears in her eyes during her confession.

"Take me instead," Lubna said.

Eva laughed, a harsh sound, half a sob. "You? What do you have I could possibly want? I know all about you. Helena and I have talked. She has told me how great an innocent you are." Eva gripped the edge of the table and pulled deep gasps of air into her lungs. Slowly she stilled, getting control of herself again. She lifted the brooch and cocked her head to one side as her eyes flickered across Helena's figure. "Now if it had been Thomas who made the offer I might have been tempted. He pretends to civilisation, but Helena has told me such interesting tales about him. He acquired the scars on his body from somewhere. He has a past. A dark past, I would say."

Lubna saw Eva shiver. She pulled at her bindings but they held firm and she only succeeded in almost choking herself.

"What will happen to William?"

Eva glanced at the sleeping child. "Oh, I think I may take him with me when I leave." She smiled. "He is so innocent. An empty vessel. And when he grows I will decide what to do with him." She glanced at Lubna. "What do you think–is he good or evil? Will he take after mother or father? Neither of them are innocent, but one at least fights his darker desires. Such an interesting experiment, don't you think?"

"You'll never find out. Thomas will come after you."

"He has tried to capture me already and failed. Next time I might kill him. But we are wasting time, and I have work to do. Afterward I might enjoy talking, to explain myself before I kill you. I can tell you anything I want, because you'll never be able to repeat it. Delicious." She picked up a piece of bread and nibbled at it. Then she leaned close and laid the needle point of the pin against Helena's throat.

She glanced at Lubna. "You have been with Thomas for some time now, so you must understand my predicament. Where should the thrust take place? Here?" She pressed the pin against the angle of Helena's neck and chin. A bead of blood bloomed. "Up into the brain through the gap beneath the skull? Or should I be more adventurous… an invasion through the nose or eye. I cannot use the back of the head again, not until the next time." Eva's breath came faster, a rare flush rising into her cheeks. She moved her hand. "Here, I think. Right here." She moved the brooch. "As punishment for her wickedness." Eva grinned. "I have heard it said Helena has no heart. Let us discover the truth of that claim." She pushed the needle into Helena's breast.

"Stop!" Lubna screamed. "In the name of all that's holy, stop what you are doing!"

Cradled among the sacks, Lubna's shout woke William and he began to wail loudly.

Eva glanced up, her eyes bright, insanity shining in them.

She reached for the wine and drank, red running down her chin and over her breasts. Then she took the tin snips and closed them around the tip of Helena's smallest finger on her left hand. She snapped the ends together and more blood ran.

CHAPTER 37

The house was empty. In the bedroom Thomas found the bed unmade. He leaned close and drew in air, inhaling the unmistakable scent of Helena, which could still trigger his body into betrayal. There were other scents mixed there, too. A slight sourness from the milk she refused William, but also the scent of another woman. The bed was wide, made for two, and he saw there were indentations on both pillows.

"Smell that," he said to Jorge, pointing.

Jorge frowned but did as asked. He sniffed at the first pillow, then the other, before returning.

"It could be Eva, but she changes her scent too often to be sure. The other is definitely Helena."

Thomas turned a circle, trying to work out what had happened. The room was a mess, clothing discarded in no discernible order. A cup sat beside the bed and Thomas picked it up, once more using his sense of smell.

He pulled a face. "Opium mixed with hashish in wine," he said. "She never could stand the slightest discomfort."

"Unless Eva gave it to her," said Jorge. "She must drug her victims to do what she does to them."

Thomas returned to the wide living room. It lay sterile, unlived in. Helena lacked the spirit to fill a house, to make it a home.

"What happened here, Jorge?" He put his back to one wall, began to move slowly across the room, his eyes scanning the marble tiled floor. "Has she taken Helena as victim or accomplice?"

"Accomplice? You know what I think of Helena, but she would never involve herself in murder."

The living room had shown Thomas all it could. He moved into the hallway. "I'm not so sure. She spent nine months growing my son. Pregnancy changes women. Some thrive. Others sink into a strange darkness. I've seen mothers blossom, others who try to kill their newborn."

"Then she's not strong enough to be part of this."

"You're right, I expect she isn't. Perhaps I don't want to consider the alternative." Thomas stopped abruptly as he approached the door to outside and went to one knee. He reached out, his hand hovering above a stain. "Look. Blood."

Jorge knelt beside him. "I'll take your word for it."

Thomas rubbed his finger across the faint stain. It came away tipped with a red smear.

"This is no more than an hour old. Eva must have hit Helena and then… I don't know, taken her somewhere."

"Why not kill her here, in her home, like the others."

"Because she knows we are coming—right behind her." Thomas banged his fist on the floor in frustration. "Where will she have gone? Where? There are too many places they could be, how can we possibly find them before she begins to eat?"

They climbed the steep alleyways of the Albayzin toward Thomas's house. It had been Jorge's idea, but Thomas was annoyed at himself it hadn't occurred to him.

"What if Eva has taken Helena to a place that meant something to her. Not to Eva, to Helena."

"Why?"

"All we know about are those she's killed already," said Jorge.

"In their homes. Are they special enough places?"

"Think about it. It was in his own house Alvarez abused his children. Javier never left his home–he was too enormous, the outside too dangerous for him."

"You think she chooses the place because it means something to those she kills?" Thomas asked.

"It's a possibility, don't you think?"

"An outside possibility. It might be as simple as she kills people in their own homes, and that was Helena's blood on the floor and we're already too late."

"She hasn't had time," said Jorge. "It's a ritual she undertakes. She could have killed me the instant she came to my room at the inn, but she didn't. She has to go through the steps, because each one means something to her, each layer builds on the next. And who knows what else she might throw in the mix for each victim." He was barely out of breath, while Thomas's lungs burned, but he knew it was fear that made him weak.

"Then let's hope Lubna knows where such a place might be." But Thomas was sceptical. Helena was six years older than her sister. By the time Lubna was old enough to be included in any games, Helena would already be training for the harem, picked at an early age for her beauty.

The house was empty when they arrived, the fire in the kitchen hearth barely warm. Thomas ran upstairs anyway, but both Lubna and William were gone. A sound of hammering reminded him the builders were still around. He was about to start back down the stairs to question them when he realised there was no need. He made his way across the walkway above his study that would soon become another corridor linking the old house to the new.

He found Britto applying lime plaster to a completed wall. The work had progressed remarkably in the time he had been away, and he could see how it would look, see how it would transform their lives.

"When did Lubna leave?" Thomas asked.

The builder put down his trowel, dropping it into a leather bucket filled with a thick white mixture. Beyond them other workers continued, some laying bricks, others nailing wooden boards down to form a floor.

"Early. Said she was going to visit her mother."

"Damnation—we've only just come from the hill."

Britto laughed. "What do you think of the work? Going well, no?"

"Yes, going well. I have to leave again."

"Let me show you your new bedroom—"

"I have to go." Thomas ignored Britto's calls, running through to the kitchen where Jorge sat waiting, nibbling at a chicken leg he had found from somewhere. "We have to go back. Lubna's at Olaf's house. I'm not convinced you're right, but I can't think of anything else to do."

Except, as they reached the foot of the Albayzin something did come to him. "What if Eva's taken her to a previous scene? She could have gone to Pilar's house, it's empty now. So are the houses of Alvarez and Javier."

"We're not climbing back again, are we?" said Jorge.

"It might be worth checking the other two houses first, they're not far out of our way. Then we'll go find Lubna and see if she knows anything."

Alvarez's house was a waste of time. Already it had been sold on to another family, his children no doubt glad to rid themselves of one more memory of his abuse. Javier's house lay silent, empty and locked. They went around the back and scaled the wall, and once more Jorge picked the lock in the rear door. As soon as they stepped inside Thomas knew they were wasting their time. The air was stale, the house devoid of any human presence. They left through the front door, turning left toward the palace. As they jogged, attracting stares from those they passed, the cry for midday prayer ululated across the city, and Thomas cursed.

"We could try Pilar's place first," said Jorge, knowing what Thomas was thinking. "Lubna will have finished her prayers by then."

"No—we'll only be wasting more time. I think you're right—Eva's taken Helena somewhere from her past. Pilar was killed in her family home, not her own house here."

"Helena's memories will be within the harem," said

Jorge. "Eva will never risk taking her there."

"She's more resourceful than we've given her credit for. I wouldn't be surprised if she finds a way. There are still a few tunnels that remain open."

"But she'd never be able to drag Helena through them. I think it's somewhere else."

A guard nodded them through the outer gate. They turned away from the inner gate and crossed the training yard. Thomas entered Olaf's house without knocking.

Fatima emerged from the kitchen, wiping her hands on a cloth. Her fingers were stained dark. "Oh, you've missed Lubna, if that's who you're looking for. She went to see Helena."

"When?"

"I'm not sure. It was before I started peeling the walnuts, so mid-morning, a little later perhaps. She was going to try one last time to get her to feed William."

Thomas sat down hard. Had Helena rejected Lubna and sent her away? Had they missed her, she returning to the Albayzin even as they rushed through the city?

But Thomas knew he was deluding himself. Eva had taken Lubna as well. And his son.

His body trembled with the need to act, but he knew it would be a mistake. He saw Jorge start for the door and held up a hand.

"Wait. We need to know where to look. Chasing shadows will only get more people killed."

"What people?" Fatima came to stand over Thomas. "Who's in danger? My daughter? My grandson?"

"Both of them," Thomas said.

Fatima reached back, searching for a chair. Jorge pushed one to meet her as her legs gave way and she sat hard.

"Who is threatening my family, Thomas?" Her eyes narrowed. "Is this something to do with you again? If you have invited yet more danger into your life, I–"

"What was Helena like as a child?" Thomas said, interrupting.

"What has that to do with anything? You should be out there finding my daughters." She clenched her fists, raising them as if she wanted to strike him. "If only Olaf was here."

"I will find them." Thomas leaned forward and gripped her fists, holding them inside his hands. He felt a tremble running through her. "I believe Eva has taken them somewhere that means something to Helena. Some place significant to her."

"Eva has taken her? Her new friend? What nonsense is this?"

"Please." Thomas squeezed Fatima's hands harder. "Answer me and I will find them, I promise. What places did Helena go to when she was younger?"

"The palace, of course. Living so close she was always in and out. Even as a child she was especially pretty, especially loved."

"Not the palace. She won't have been taken there. Somewhere else."

"I can't think. When she was little she played on the hill beyond the walls. But once she became a woman she stopped all play. She became serious and... different."

Thomas thought he knew what she meant. Helena had always possessed a self-serving cunning. Something Fatima said triggered a thought. "You said when she became a woman..."

"When she bled, of course. She was precocious even in that. And it wasn't long–" Fatima broke off, her eyes meeting Thomas's for a moment before skittering away.

"Wasn't long before she became a woman in another way."

Fatima's eyes refused to meet his.

"It's all right, Fatima, I know what she's like." Thomas leaned forward, trying to stem the panic flooding his mind, stifling rational thought. "Nothing you can say will shock me. She became a woman at a young age, I know that. I even think she told me once, about how…" He trailed off. Released Fatima's hands and sat upright. Closed his eyes.

"It's true," Fatima said. "But she never spoke to me of it. Why would she confess something like that to me? It's not as if I'm her mother."

Thomas waved a hand to silence her, sinking back into memory. Helena had not long come to his house. Had not yet come to his bed, but that would happen… in fact it happened on the night she told him. Of course, it was all part of her ploy to seduce him. A pretence at honesty accompanied by words of sensuality to draw him in, even then believing he was like other men she had been with.

Her scarred face had been savage then, but Thomas barely noticed it.

There had been a man. Her first. He remembered Helena smiling as she told the story, omitting no detail, elaborating even. Her scent had enfolded him. She sat so close the heat of her body touched his. And then she had risen and climbed the stairs, leaving him to follow.

"Where was it?" he muttered.

"Where was what?"

He opened his eyes to see Fatima and Jorge staring at him.

"Helena's first time. She told me about it. I know who, and I know when. She told me where but I can't remember…" He slammed his fist against the table top. "Somewhere they wouldn't be disturbed, somewhere close to the palace, but underground."

"The tunnels?" said Jorge.

Thomas shook his head. "A poor place for a tryst, even one as desperate as the first." Even so he recalled the sensuality of the tunnels, the serving girl Prea showing him concubines at their bath. Perhaps… yes, it was a possibility, he could see that. Except surely he would remember such a description, the scent of the soaps and oils, the heat of the steam. Instead the words that came to him were of the smell of barley and the roughness of hessian sacking.

"Food," he said, and stood. "They store food over-winter, somewhere underground beneath the palace."

"The stores," Fatima said. "Everyone knows about them. They'll be half empty at this time of year."

Thomas turned toward Jorge. "Do you know where they are?"

"Not me. I have a vague idea I heard about them, but why would I know where they are?"

"I know," said Fatima.

Thomas looked at her. Could he put another of Olaf's women in danger? But he knew he had no other option.

"Take me," he said. "Show me from a distance and then come back here."

Fatima nodded and rushed to fetch an outer robe.

CHAPTER 38

The storehouse was built into the south wall of the palace. Only those who knew of its existence would be aware it lay there, for it looked to be nothing more than a vertical wall standing above the drop to the river. Thomas remembered he and Jorge crawling along the base once searching for a secret entrance. They must have passed directly behind the storerooms when they followed a tunnel into the palace.

Fatima took them as far as a doorway, but when Thomas told her to leave she refused.

"I can't look out for both you and your daughters," he said.

"Lubna is my blood. William is not, but to me it feels as if he is. I stay."

"No." Thomas pushed her away and she swayed on her feet but didn't move. "I won't put anyone else in danger. Go to the barracks and bring soldiers. Tell them to guard the entrance and allow no-one to leave." He saw a change in the stubbornness locked on her face and fought impatience, knowing she would have to come to the conclusion herself.

Eventually Fatima nodded. "It makes sense, yes." She put her hand behind Thomas's head, pulled him down and kissed his cheek. "Take care. You are my son now." As she turned away she nodded toward Jorge. "You too, pretty one."

As soon as she had gone Thomas turned to Jorge. "This time, *stay* behind me. I don't want Eva cutting you again."

"It's a scratch, nothing more."

"Even so, remember what I say. She's far more resourceful than we've given her credit for."

A wide passageway ran directly against the outer wall. The floor was fashioned of smooth stone laid to make it easier to bring carts. At intervals doors to the right offered glimpses into store rooms. Most of the chambers they passed were still full, stacked with casks, sacks and crates. Each room was arranged by an expert hand with the least robust items at the front.

"I thought Fatima said these would be almost empty."

"I remember this place now," said Jorge. "Bazzu used to bring me here. But it was a long time ago, soon after I first met her. The distant chambers are emptied before these. Items that spoil first are stored further in. Eva will be there."

"She'll need space to work." Thomas shook his head. "Is this the fate she had planned for Helena from the beginning? Is it the reason she befriended her?"

"Who knows what goes on in a mind like hers. Let's hope we're not too late."

Jorge pushed past Thomas. "There are ramps leading to higher levels. If this place is truly half empty we need to go up, perhaps to the very top, then work our way down."

"We search the first rooms we come to," Thomas said. "Eva will be impatient and, I hope, afraid. She knows I'll come after her."

"Of course. But there are many rooms here. Enough to feed an entire city for half a year. These aren't just for winter. They're for when the Spanish come."

Thomas expected narrow, winding stairs, but when Jorge led them upward it was through a passageway that rose only gently, wide enough to allow a cart to pass. It made sense. There would have to be enough space to carry goods up and down.

At intervals windows were cut into the thick walls to splash daylight in. There were also torches burning, but widely spaced, and after they had fumbled along a particularly dark section, Thomas pulled one from its sconce and held it above his head to light the way. As they progressed his eyes tracked the stone blocks of the floor looking for some sign. But too many feet, too many carts, had passed this way.

They reached the second level and still the chambers were full, carved back into the rock underpinning the palace. They ran the length of the passage and climbed a third time. Finally, they came to a room that was stacked to the roof, but a small area had been cleared next to the doorway.

"How far does this go on?" Thomas asked.

"We're not quite half way," said Jorge. "There are eight levels, as I recall, with a walkway running above the topmost."

"You know this place well. Why did you pretend otherwise?"

"There is an entrance from within the palace," said Jorge. "Bazzu always brought me that way. Always on some pretext of fetching a delicacy for the Sultan."

"So why did you–" Thomas stopped, Jorge almost running into him. He had almost rushed past it. A strip of cloth, fashioned from loose cotton that might have been cut to form a blanket. Thomas knelt and picked it up, lifted it to his nose and inhaled. The scent was familiar, unique, that only a baby could produce, a heady mix of sweet and sour. The smell of life itself. Except when he turned it in his hands he found one edge soaked in blood. He sniffed again, but knew it was impossible to tell whose blood it was. Perhaps whoever had left the mark in Helena's house.

He showed the cloth to Jorge. "Eva was moving fast here. She can't have noticed this fall or she'd have picked it up. We have to go slow now and be quiet."

"It's not me asking all the questions," whispered Jorge.

Thomas started forward. As they approached each doorway he went ahead, ducking forward to look inside before pulling back. The first chamber contained bolts of cloth and a stack of boxes. From the smell they contained spices. He moved on, fighting an urge to run as fast as he could, wondering how much of a lead Eva had on them, and what she had managed to do in the time.

They reached the end of the set of rooms and came to the next ascent, which curved in a wide arc to deposit them on the next level.

"What if we missed her?" Thomas said, his voice barely a whisper. "She could have made a hiding place in one of the rooms below us."

"There'd have been a sign. Keep on, she's here somewhere."

But the next level was also devoid of what they sought. Here most of the chambers had been depleted of their stores. Thomas tried to remember how many levels they had climbed and couldn't. Was it five or six? No more than six, he was sure.

He went on, aware of moments passing, each of which might signal the end of another life. But in this case not just one. Eva had taken Lubna and William, too.

They came to chambers stacked with blocks of ice. They must have been carved from high on the Sholayr and carried down on carts. The air spilling from the rooms was cold, a faint mist clinging to the floor. Inside were stacks of delicate produce which needed to be kept cold. Also jars of frozen sweets. Not what they sought.

Thomas began to feel optimism drain from him. Too much time had been lost. They had been too slow during the night. Eva had taken more risks in the dark, buying herself precious hours.

"I think we've missed them," Thomas said when they reached the next curving ascent. "We have to go back."

"Not yet," Jorge said, pushing ahead. "If we get to the last room and it's empty we go down then, not before."

Thomas stayed where he was, watching Jorge ascend the shallow slope. Dread settled like a lead weight in his chest. His limbs were heavy, numb. And then there came a cry.

First Lubna's voice, screaming for something to stop. And then the cry of a baby, less strident, but an infant's wail always carries further than any other sound made by man.

Thomas broke into a sprint, leaving Jorge behind. He came out onto the next level and ran on, slowing only a little, listening hard for another sound. Nothing. He passed open arches showing chambers denuded of their contents. Still nothing. Then a second cry, louder than the first, closer, and he skidded to a halt at the next arch.

Too late!

Thomas saw Eva turn at the interruption. Her hands were coated in blood. Drops fell from the brooch onto Helena's naked breasts. More blood pooled between them, even more onto the floor where her left hand hung free of the table. The glitter in Eva's eyes showed nothing of rationality.

Thomas started toward her, his eyes locked on the blade she held.

"Any closer and I finish her now." Eva's hand moved so the blade lay against Helena's throat.

"And then what? I will still be here."

Eva laughed, a delighted sound at odds with the nightmare vision she presented. "You won't let her die, not if you think you can save her. Helena told me all about you, Thomas Berrington. Told me how much you love her even after she betrayed you, even after she lost her love for you. Told me too of your irrational sense of justice. No, you won't let her die."

"Kill her then. See if I care." Beyond the figure on the table, beyond the spread of food, he saw William cradled on the floor and Lubna tied to a stone column. She was staring at him wide-eyed, listening to his words.

"We appear to find ourselves at an impasse." Eva

waved the brooch. "Stay where you are, eunuch. Any closer and she dies. I will tell you what is going to happen." Her eyes returned to Thomas. "You will allow me to leave. Then you can see if Helena is beyond saving." She glanced down. "Almost certainly she is. I have pierced her heart. Her chest is even now filling with blood, but if you let me leave your new lover lives."

"What if I simply take the brooch from you?"

Eva lowered it once more, drew the needle sharp end across Helena's throat. A bloom of red rewarded the wound. Thomas could see the cut was too shallow to kill, the blood a distraction. He took a slow pace closer to the table.

"Stop there. I'll do it. You know I will. What do I have to lose?"

"Go ahead."

Eva lifted her hand. Thomas had been waiting for the moment, knowing she would want to end things with a flourish. She could have simply pressed on the vicious pin, so sharp no force was needed. But that wasn't her way. So she raised her hand to make a statement.

Thomas leapt at her, arms out. He flew across the table and crashed into Eva just as the blade came down. It cut deep into his arm but he ignored the pain as he crashed on top of her, flailing, reaching for the blade before it could inflict further damage. Beneath him Eva writhed. The blood streaking her made her slippery and she slid from under Thomas, rolling away, slashing backward as she went.

"Jorge, get her!" Thomas shouted as he struggled to his feet. He saw Jorge run at Eva and then stop. She had reached William and dragged him from the makeshift crib. She clutched the baby to her gory breasts and laid the brooch's pin against the soft fold beneath his chin.

"Now this one you *do* care for." Eva straightened up. She shuffled along the wall. Jorge remained where he was. Thomas backed against the table, his hand seeking Helena. He found her shoulder and traced his way to her neck. It was slick with blood, but when he searched a pulse remained. He bent to examine the wound beneath her breast. He saw it had been made in the right place to pierce her heart, but there wasn't enough blood. Not nearly enough. Eva's skill had, for once, failed her.

"Let her go," Thomas said to Jorge. "She can't run far."

Eva kissed William's cheek. "At last you see sense. He is too delicious to kill, but if you follow me I promise I will."

"I won't follow."

Eva smiled. "You think you're so clever, don't you. Helena said it is one of your failings. You possess too great a belief in your own abilities. Though I judge you are more able than she told me, I give you that." Eva reached the doorway. Thomas tried to judge if he could reach her before she killed his son. He believed he might, but wasn't going to risk the chance of failure.

Eva ducked through the doorway and was gone. Thomas listened to the slap of her feet on the stone floor until it faded to nothing. Then he turned to Helena.

"Free me!" demanded Lubna, and he glanced up.

"Jorge, cut Lubna free. I'm busy here." He lifted the weight of Helena's breast and pulled the skin to stretch the wound Eva had made. Blood continued to flow from it, but as he had already guessed her heart had not been punctured. Helena's lung might be damaged, but there was no blood on her lips. There were other organs too, available for someone who knew what they were doing. He glanced toward Lubna and saw Jorge had almost released her.

"Come here," he ordered as soon as she could move.

Lubna came across the room, rubbing at her wrists.

"I want to see if Eva's blade has gone right through or not. I need you to hold Helena's weight when I lift her." He waited until Lubna nodded, ignoring the expression on her face. "Are you ready?"

Lubna nodded again, and Thomas heaved Helena into a sitting position. He waited until Lubna took the weight, then lifted Helena's blonde hair and examined the base of her skull. It was unmarked. He ran his fingers along her back, but the skin showed no blemish. Helena groaned, pain beginning to seep through her drugged state.

Finally Thomas turned to her hand. The end of her finger had bled almost as much as the wound to her chest. The tip of her finger still lay on the stone floor where it had fallen, ignored by Eva.

"Jorge, I need your shirt," Thomas said. "I need strips of cloth to bind the wounds."

Jorge stripped his shirt over his head and ripped it down the back, then tore each side into smaller lengths. He brought them to Thomas who wound them around Helena while Lubna continued to hold her. Jorge pressed in, replacing Lubna's hands with his and she moved away and stood with her back to the wall.

"Lubna, run down and fetch the soldiers I hope are outside by now. Bring them up and have them carry

Helena out of here."

Lubna only shook her head, and Thomas saw she was in shock, unable to respond.

"Jorge, you go, as soon as I'm sure she's safe." Thomas took Helena's weight, laid her onto her side. She was beginning to move, her hands moving, although her eyes remained closed.

"Where do we take her?" asked Jorge.

"The infirmary. Lubna, go with them, do what you can for her until I find you." Thomas hoped activity would pull her out of her fugue. He imagined what was happening to her, the events spinning through her head, a vicious cycle she couldn't break. He checked Helena wasn't going to roll off the table and went to Lubna, taking her shoulders.

"I want you to go with Jorge. He needs you. Your sister needs you."

Finally, her eyes appeared to focus. "What are you going to be doing?" Her voice remained cold, totally lacking emotion.

"Saving my son."

As he started for the door Jorge put a hand out to stop him. "She'll have gone up."

Thomas gave a curt nod. "I know."

"Be careful. The last set of steps are narrow and lead to a walkway, but there's no way off it."

Thomas gave a grin, cold fire filling his chest. "The only way she's coming down is as a captive."

Fatima had sent men into the store to cut off escape in all directions. At the foot of the narrow stairs Thomas found one of them. He lay on his side, eyes wide and staring, the floor slick with his blood.

Thomas ignored the man and started up the steps. They twisted around within the thick walls, rising steeply. When he came out wind gusted at him and he saw the afternoon was fading fast. He also saw Eva.

She had lain William on the ground and now kneeled over him. Her head snapped up as Thomas appeared.

"Damn you, man, why can't you give up?"

"You know why." He waited on the ramparts, trying to judge how insane she truly was. The walkway wasn't as long as the chambers beneath, and narrower than Thomas had expected. Barely a foot and a half, then a low stone wall. Beyond it the palace walls fell over a hundred feet to the banks of the Hadarro. The steps had brought Thomas up at one end of the ledge. Eva crouched at the farthest point, more than fifty feet between them.

Thomas began to walk slowly toward her.

Eva reached out and grabbed at William, clutching him to her chest. The brooch glinted in her right hand. "I keep my promises, Thomas Berrington."

"I imagine you do. And I keep mine."

"Not to Helena you didn't. She told me."

"I gave her everything she ever wanted."

"Men are blind. You more than most. You never saw what she truly wanted."

"I'm not the only blinkered one on this ledge." Thomas continued to walk, the distance between them closing. Twenty feet now. "Put William down. Throw the brooch over the edge. I will help you."

Eva barked a harsh laugh. "Help me? I am beyond

help. I have done things that should never have been done."

"So why do them?"

"Because man is carved by sin. Without me the sin festers. I have cleansed the world by taking its evil into myself."

"And it's made you mad."

"No, not mad." Eva rose to her feet, clutching William against her. She glanced over the wall, back toward Thomas. Her grip on William was loose and he was afraid the boy might simply tumble from her arms. "I am the most sane person in the world, because I see how it really is. I am the only one who can cleanse it." She smiled, and this time it was she who took a pace forward. "Let me go, Thomas, so I can continue my work. You saw those men I took the sins from. Can you tell me they didn't deserve to die? Here, you can have your son." She held William out. Still not far enough to reach. And still too loosely held. The wind funnelled along the cliff face, lifting Eva's black hair until it rose high like a cloak above her head. Her robe fluttered, clinging to the perfect body beneath. "Let me walk away. Allow me to disappear and you can return to your cozy little life."

"You know I can't do that."

Eva shook her head, disappointed. "Then you leave me no choice."

"There is always a choice." Thomas took another pace. If he leapt now he might be able to snatch William from her grasp. He might not, but it was a chance. The only one he had.

As Eva raised her hand gripping the brooch, its

wicked spike flashing, Thomas moved. But instead of thrusting at William or him, she put it beneath her own chin and pressed it home.

Blood gushed in a great arc directly against his face and chest, its iron heat coating him. Thomas wiped at his eyes to find Eva trying to smile at him, but her mouth worked only on one side.

"Here," she said, gasping, her words slurred, "accept my final gift. I anoint you with my gathered sins."

She stepped onto the low wall. Swayed.

Thomas came close, grabbing for her, but she fell backward away from him. He grasped, almost following her over, his fingers catching in blood-soaked cloth as he closed his fist.

Eva fell away, silent, her robe fluttering until she hit the rocks beside the river.

Thomas gave a cry. He drew back as the drop called to him. He looked down at his left hand as William cried from the indignity of hanging inside a scrap of filthy cloth. When Thomas sat back he saw Eva's golden brooch abandoned on the walkway. He stared at it a long time, wondering how many people such a perfect object had killed. Then he reached for it, tucked William against his chest and rose to his feet.

CHAPTER 39

It was six months before Lubna came again to Thomas in the night. Six months in which he tried to decipher the mind of a woman. Six months in which he sought for what he had done wrong. Jorge had tried to help, but it was as if he spoke a different language, one Thomas failed to understand. A language of trust and love and loyalty.

"But I do love her," Thomas said, as he and Jorge sat in the warmth of an early summer evening, swallows chirping their cries above. "And I trust her. Nobody can doubt my loyalty."

"But your loyalty to what?" said Jorge. "What Lubna saw was your loyalty to Helena, not her. You sent me to free her while you saved the mother of your child."

Thomas made a snorting sound. "Helena still refuses William. And she blames me for the loss of her finger-tip, too."

"Of course she does. But that's not the point. You still don't understand, do you?"

"Can't you talk to Lubna?" Thomas asked.

Jorge sat up, rose to his feet. "I have work to do. I'm

an important man these days. And the harem is busy since al-Zagal returned his brother to the throne. Much has changed."

Thomas knew there was no point in pleading. "I hear Helena has entered the harem again."

"She is al-Zagal's new favourite. Although he still hasn't forgiven you for killing the last one. You should think of moving to the hill now you're a family man. Your house there has stood empty for three months."

"Some family," Thomas mumbled. "One that sleeps in separate rooms."

Jorge laughed and walked away, the soft night swallowing him.

The builders had long finished, but Britto still called on occasion. He and Thomas would sit in the courtyard, a little smaller than it once was, to drink wine and talk. Britto proved a carrier of every piece of news and gossip in the city, on both sides of the river, and he told Thomas there was a growing tension among the citizens of the Albayzin. The Sultan was reinforcing his reign with new rules. The relaxed lifestyle of Gharnatah had become little more than a memory.

Another visitor had called at noon. Lubna had gone to the mosque in answer to the call to prayer. She rarely prayed in the courtyard anymore, and Thomas missed the sight. Her devotion used to calm him.

When Thomas opened the door he stepped back in surprise to find a Spaniard standing there. A Spaniard dressed as a Moor, but he recognised Martin de Alarcón and dragged him inside.

"He's going to have to come home," Martin said over a meagre meal which was the best Thomas could put together.

Muhammed had remained a guest of the Spanish for too long. His ransom had been paid, prisoners released. There was only one issue preventing his return. He had nowhere to go. Abu al-Hasan Ali was Sultan once more on the hill and there was no place for a second.

"He'll have to go elsewhere," Thomas said. He glanced up as Lubna returned. He saw Martin look at her, but offered no explanation.

"He wants to return to Granada."

"Gharnatah doesn't want him."

Martin shook his head. "That doesn't matter. Fernando has agreed to come as close as ten miles. He will hand Boabdil over to you and no-one else."

Thomas slapped his hand on the table. "Damn it, I'm a physician, not a diplomat. I don't want him. I don't want anything to do with him or any of this."

"Be that as it may, Fernando will not allow him into the care of anyone else. You must find some way of spiriting the man away. The further the better as far as we're concerned."

Thomas found wine and they took it into the courtyard.

"Is that it?" Martin sat on the bench beneath the balcony and nodded at the glittering bulk of the palace atop al-Hamra.

"It's the palace, if that's what you mean."

"Fernando wants it," said Martin, his voice low. "It is the jewel of Spain. There is nothing like it in all the land, and he wants it as his. The Queen, too. You have seen them. They dress as Moors when their citizens cannot see them." He looked away from the palace.

"You will be safe when they come. You know that."

"What about her?" Thomas nodded toward the kitchen door.

"Your wife? Of course. All who are with you will be safe. Isabel keeps her promises. They both do."

Later, when Martin had gone, Thomas climbed to the new part of the house where he slept. William lay in a small alcove half way between his room and Lubna's. The child slept fitfully, his thumb in his mouth. He was teething and Thomas kneeled to rub oil of cloves on his gums to ease the pain.

He glanced up as Lubna came upstairs. She leaned against the door.

"If he wakes tonight I'll see to him," Thomas said.

"I should think so."

"I was busy last night, you know–" He stopped when he caught her smile. She seemed to grow more beautiful each day. Or perhaps that was simply her unavailability.

Lubna knelt beside him, her arm pressing against his. She reached in and pulled at the covers around William.

"He looks more like you every day."

"Hmm."

"You're still not convinced, are you."

"It doesn't matter. He's mine whether I'm his father or not."

"No–he's ours," said Lubna. She looked up at him, let her breath out in a sigh. "This is stupid, Thomas. Why are we punishing ourselves this way?"

"It's not me doing the punishing."

He saw her expression stiffen and cursed himself for being unable to keep his mouth shut. But for once it appeared not to matter.

"*I'm* being stupid then." Lubna rose and held out her hand. "I think it's beyond time I found out what this new bedroom of yours is like."

HISTORICAL NOTE

The period at the end of 1483 and into 1484 was pivotal in the fate of the Moors in Spain. Abu Abdullah, Muhammed XII, who took power from his father at the end of the events recounted in *The Red Hill*, was captured in a stupid and unnecessary raid into Spanish held territory, and was kept a captive for over a year. Muhammed was indeed a supposed guest of Martin de Alarcón, and it has been suggested that during this period of captivity psychological pressure made him buckle until he was completely under the control of his captors.

As *The Sin Eater* states, power abhors a vacuum, and the old Sultan, Abu al-Hasan Ali, and his brother known as al-Zagal, returned to Granada after Muhammed was captured. Initially Abu al-Hasan resumed his position as Sultan, but he was ageing, losing his sight, and possibly suffering from a degenerative disease. I have not stated what this is but his symptoms might indicate Parkinson's Disease, which was obviously not recognised at that time. But not recognising a disease does not mean it may still not have severe effects.

Martin de Alarcón is known to have been Muhammed's gaoler for much of the time he was held in captivity. Several sources cite that during that time Muhammed fell in thrall to the man. However, although much of this is speculation, I have based the relationship of the two men on such hints.

The food stores are taken from a passage in *The History of the Mahometan Empire in Spain p. 198*:

> *Several matamoros, or subterranean galleries, still exist in the eastern and highest part of the fortress beyond the palace. For the use of the palace inhabitants such a number and size of store would not be required–they seem large enough to hold grain for the entire city.*

There were indeed negotiations to free Muhammed, and he was released late in 1484. He was unable to return to the Alhambra, which was now the residence of his father and uncle. Instead he set up an alternative court on the Albayzin, where his mother Aixa already had a substantial house, in turn creating a conflict that would rage for several years, sparking civil war in Granada and presaging the end of Moorish rule in al-Andalus.

I based the medical passages here on information from *Medieval Islamic Medicine* by Peter E. Pormann and Emilie Savage-Smith (publ. 2007).

Another text that proved useful in the writing of *The Sin Eater* was *Sexuality in Islam* by Abdelwahab Bouhdiba (publ. 1975).

And as always I returned again and again to *The History of the Mahometan Empire in Spain* by James

Cavanagh Murphy (publ. 1816). This book was the very first reference material I obtained when I began looking into the history of the Moors in Spain. Originally I took notes from a manuscript copy in the John Ryland Library in Manchester. Only subsequently did I discover that a facsimile of this book was available for purchase through Amazon and other sources, and I obtained my own copy, now extensively thumbed and highlighted.

In book 4 of the Thomas Berrington series, *The Incubus*, Thomas, the two women in his life, and Jorge, are taken to Ronda where al-Zagal needs to restore his power base after being away from his stronghold for an extended period of time.

CPSIA information can be obtained
at www.ICGtesting.com
Printed in the USA
LVHW011143120519
617538LV00003B/459/P

9 780993 076152